THE FAMILY

MICHAEL MANLEY

Harmon House
Copyright © 2014 Kenneth M. Sheldon
All rights reserved.
ISBN: 0990939413
ISBN-13: 978-0-9909394-1-2

There was a time before the Internet was omnipresent, before everyone had a computer or cell phone with instant access to a vast storehouse of knowledge and foolishness, a time before a single organization extended its reach into the lives of millions of people in every country on every continent.

This is the story of the early days of that organization, which remains to this day privately owned, the identity of its principals and inner workings still a closely guarded secret.

MICHAEL MANLEY

Prologue

1990 - The dawn of the social media era

They were parked on Mallorca Boulevard, two men in a black van with smoked glass windows. The driver, a tall man with white-blonde hair swept back over his head, looked into the rear-view mirror as a pewter-colored Mazda 626 came around the corner. "Heads up."

The other man—stocky, balding—glanced into the side mirror and spoke into a microphone headset. "Unit two, engage."

On the other side of the street, a tan Lexus pulled out of a parking spot near a small Victorian apartment building.

Normally, Peter Jacobson had to circle the Marina twice before finding a parking space anywhere near his apartment. Tonight, on the first pass, a car pulled out of a spot just steps away from his apartment. In San Francisco, this borders on a supernatural event.

He eased into the spot, still listening to the cassette in the deck. He pulled a hand-held computer from a briefcase on the seat next to him and began to scribble notes across its opaque surface. The tape ended, and he hit the rewind button.

He glanced up at the apartment's windows. They were empty. Allison hadn't arrived yet. He picked up the cell phone and dialed a number.

"Thank you for calling the Peabody Herald. Our normal business hours are..."

Jacobson punched an extension number, left a message, and hung up.

1

Randall McLagan walked out of the Peabody News Shop, stuffing change into his wallet, the latest copy of PC Monthly tucked under his arm. He wasn't watching where he was going and almost walked into a young man who stood just outside the door.

"Excuse me, sir?"

Randall looked up and eyed him warily. The kid wore dark pants, a white shirt and a plain, pencil-thin tie. He looked like a contestant on a high school quiz show. Amway, Randall thought. Maybe Mormon. But then he remembered that Mormons generally come in pairs, and he didn't think Amway sold on the street. He lowered an eyebrow. "Yes?"

The kid held out a colorful package. "Would you like to try out a new online service? It's free."

Randall snickered. Over the years, people on street corners had tried to sell him everything from television sets to "solid gold" watches. Nobody had ever tried to sell him software, especially not in Peabody, New Hampshire. Times were definitely changing. All right, he'd play along. "What's it called?"

"The Family, sir?" he said, his voice rising slightly as if he weren't sure himself.

"The Family." It had the sound of something a bunch of teenagers had cooked up in their garage. Randall took the package from the kid and looked it over. It was a bright, colorful design, emblazoned with promises of free access to the Internet, e-mail, and a host of other services. "What's the catch?"

"No catch, sir. We're just trying to introduce people to our service."

"How much?"

"It's free, sir. The introductory disk comes with all the software you need to connect to the Family. Even the phone call is free."

"You're kidding. How do you make any money at that rate?"

The boy shrugged. "You can make a donation if you'd like."

Randall nodded and pulled a dollar from his wallet, remembering P.T. Barnum's comment about the birth rate of suckers. "OK, I'll give it a shot."

As he handed the bill to the kid, the door to the news shop flew open. The owner, an old man with thinning white hair, emerged like an angry bear from a cave, waving his arms and yelling at the kid. "I thought I tol' you to get the hell outta here."

The kid mumbled a quick thanks to Randall and headed off down the street. The shop owner dismissed him with a wave of a liver-spotted hand. "Bunch a' nuts. Hanging around, bothering my customers."

"What's the problem?" Randall asked. "He was just..."

A telephone rang in the shop. The old man cast a suspicious eye at him and disappeared back inside.

Randall turned, shaking his head. Apparently, that kid "wasn't from around here," as the old joke went. In Peabody, you weren't considered a local until you had lived in town for twenty years. Randall had lived in the area for four years. It only felt like twenty years.

He had come to Peabody straight out of college, taking

an entry-level job with the Peabody Herald—not the type of job a Dartmouth graduate dreamed about, but it was a job. He had planned to spend a couple of years at the Herald before moving up to a larger, daily paper like the Boston Globe or the Chicago Sun.

Four years later, Randall was still at the Herald, still writing about controversies over school budgets, the disturbing problem of teen loitering at the town park, and an endless stream of births, deaths, and basketball games.

Recently, the monotony had been broken somewhat by a new assignment, a weekly column of local news and gossip called "Around Town." He had been asked to write the column when its previous author passed away at the age of eighty-five.

"Dear God," Randall whispered as he leaned against the huge wooden door of the Peabody Herald building. "Don't let me be here till I'm eighty-five."

The door creaked open into a wooden-floored lobby where a chunky woman with hair like a blonde Brillo pad looked up from the reception desk. "Good morning, Randall."

"Morning, Linda."

As he passed the desk, the switchboard buzzed and the receptionist punched a button. "Good morning, Peabody Herald." She paused, punched another button and called after him. "Randall?"

"Yes?"

"It's Mrs. Torelli," she said, clearly sorry to be the bearer of bad tidings.

He winced. Just what he needed first thing on a Monday morning.

Rita Torelli owned a piece of property that the old grange building sat on and was trying to sell the property to the Medi-Aid drugstore chain. She was the scourge of town fathers, zoning boards, and anyone else who dared criticize her plans, which Randall had done in his last column.

He lowered an eyebrow in Linda's direction. "Technically, I'm not in my office yet, am I?"

"That's right, you're not." She punched a button. "I'm sorry, Mrs. Torelli..."

Randall retreated to his office, a converted storage closet with a single small window. He opened the window, which faced the newspaper's parking lot, allowing a faint breath of fresh air to flow into the office. He would have to close it before the end of the day, or the exhaust fumes from the cars leaving the lot would asphyxiate him.

The message light on his phone blinked insistently. He tossed his jacket over a chair and punched the button to retrieve his messages.

"You have eight messages," the system informed him. The first message had arrived at 5:10 PM on Friday afternoon.

"Mr. McLagan?" it began. "This is Rita Torelli. I just read your column and I'm..."

Rita hadn't wasted any time. The paper didn't even hit the stands until five o'clock. He jumped ahead to the next message.

"It's Rita Torelli again. I'd like you to call me as soon..."

He sighed and skipped ahead.

"Mr. McLagan, how is an honest woman supposed to..."

And the next message.

"Yes, I've already called several times..."

He hung up the phone. Knowing Rita Torelli, all eight messages were from her. She was a firm believer in the squeaky wheel theory, and would never rest until she had given him a piece of her mind. Maybe several pieces.

Right now, Randall had a more pressing problem than Rita Torelli. His column was due, and he hadn't started it yet. In fact, he didn't even know what he was going to write about. He had already covered all the latest controversies, and the old chestnuts—New Hampshire's arcane tax structure, problems with schools, the lack of parking in downtown Peabody—had all been done to death.

It wasn't exactly what he'd had in mind while studying journalism at Dartmouth. He had pictured a career at a large city newspaper or a national magazine, where he would expose government corruption, ferret out the truth about corporate scandals, and write poignant commentaries about modern society. Instead, his days were filled with annual budgets, track meets, and Rita Torelli.

He turned to his computer and flipped it on. If not for the computer, he was sure he'd have gone insane long ago. The computer was his link to the world outside Peabody, a world where real issues were debated, real work was done. He turned it on each day with the expectant desperation of a man on a desert island scanning the horizon for a rescue ship.

As the computer booted, his eye fell on the disk from the kid outside the news shop, and he had a thought. Maybe that was his column: the computer revolution was everywhere these days, even on the sidewalk outside the Peabody news shop.

He zipped open the package and stuck the disk in the computer. He knew his editor wouldn't like this. Harold Dodge, the crusty owner and editor of the Peabody Herald, already thought Randall spent too much time on the computer.

A peaceful, classical theme emanated from the computer and an icon appeared on the screen: a spinning globe, superimposed with the image of a large Colonial house. He clicked on the icon and the image enlarged to fill the screen.

"Welcome to the Family," a silken female voice said. "You are about to enter a world of entertainment, activity, and friendship. You are about to enter the Family."

The door to the house swung open, revealing a large foyer.

"Here in the Family, you'll find free access to the Internet, free e-mail, and a teleconferencing system with ongoing discussions on hundreds of topics, from Art to the Zodiac." Graphic images representing the topic areas drifted across the screen.

"You'll also have access to the world's largest collection of free software, as well as an incredible library of online sources for personal and business growth." Well-known magazines, journals, and references appeared, glinting as if illuminated by a spotlight, then faded.

"Health, personal finance, travel...it's all available in the Family. And it's all absolutely free."

So far, Randall had heard the word "free" three or four times. He was beginning to pick up a theme. So what was the catch? They promised a lot, considering they were giving it away. So how did they pay for it? Advertising?

"You can become a member of the Family in the comfort of your own home," the voice said. "To join the Family free of charge—including the phone call to connect to the Family—please enter your area code, and the first three digits of your local telephone exchange."

Randall entered the digits. A moment later, the voice said, "We're sorry, it appears there is no direct local access number for the Family in your area."

He sighed and leaned back in his chair. That figured. Peabody was so far off the information superhighway there wasn't even a sign for it, let alone an on-ramp. So much for signing up for the free service.

"However," the voice continued, "we have provided a toll-free number which you may use to connect to the Family."

Randall's eyebrows rose. Without asking him, the program dialed the number.

Now logging on to the Family via toll-free number.

There was a series of beeps, followed by a high-pitched whine indicating the connection had been established. A message appeared on the screen.

Congratulations! You are only minutes away from entering the exciting world of the Family. To complete the setup process, we'll need to copy some files to your computer. Hit Enter to begin.

The installation took less than a minute. When it was complete, the image of the house appeared again, and the front door swung open. A narrow box appeared across the bottom of the screen. On the left side of the box was a photograph of an attractive young woman. A message appeared in the space next to the image.

Hello. My name's Carolyn. What's yours?

The image shifted slightly, and he realized it was a video image, one that was being updated periodically. He hesitated, then typed

I'm Randall. Who are you?

I'm a greeter. We welcome new people who sign on to the Family for the first time.

He shook his head. Greeters at the door. These people had thought of everything.

Welcome to the Family, Randall. Would you like me to

show you around?

In for a dime, in for a dollar, he thought.

Sure, why not.

Great! Let's go.

She led him to the Library, which contained virtual shelves loaded with free books, as well as software programs—graphics, word processing, finance, games. Another section contained online reference works: dictionaries, encyclopedias, atlases, also free for member's use. Next to the Library was a Meeting Hall, a large room with dozens of doors leading off to other rooms, labeled by topic: Computers, Current Events, Environment, Hobbies, Sports, and so on.

This is the Chat area, Randall. There are hundreds of discussions going on right now. You name it, there's a Chat for it, with people from all around the world taking part.

The tour continued with visits to the Mailroom, the Newsroom, the Home Office, and the Game room—all stuffed with state-of-the-art features, and all free. And as far as he could tell, there were no advertisements anywhere.

Randall noticed a Member's Area and asked Carolyn about it.

That's an area containing special features available only to members. If you'd like to join the Family, I can sign you up today, Randall.

What kind of special features?

I'd be happy to tell you about all the member benefits once you sign up. Would you like to do that today, Randall? There's no cost to join.

She hadn't answered the question. But before he could repeat it, she broke in.

Are there any other questions I can answer for you, Randall?

Just one. If this is all free, how do you pay for it? Where does the money come from?

The Family is a non-profit organization, Randall. We receive support from our members and from a variety of private institutions.

That sounded like a canned answer if he'd ever heard one.

Would you like to sign up today, Randall?

He was tempted, but he was also skeptical. The Family sounded too good to be true, and if Dodge found out he had signed up for something that cost money, he'd never hear the end of it.

Thanks. I'll need to think about it for a bit.

There's no obligation, Randall, and no fee. If you like, I can sign you up for a free membership right now.

This lady sure knew the hard sell.

Let me think about it. I'll get back to you.

OK. It was great to meet you, Randall. Come back soon!

He leaned back in his chair. He had plenty of material for a column, but he needed a local angle, something more than meeting the kid outside the news shop. Then it came to him: the town grange, once home to a vibrant social structure, now stood empty, facing destruction and replacement by a discount drugstore. Where had the people gone who once frequented that building? These days, they were meeting electronically, via computer.

He began writing, and the words flowed. In half an hour, he had a good chunk of the column done. But he still had a few questions. How did the Family give away so much for free? Was there some catch?

He glanced at his watch. There wasn't time to do a lot of research on this. If he was going to get this column in on time, he needed the inside scoop, and needed it fast.

Then he remembered. Of course: Peter. If anyone

would know about the Family, it would be Peter.

Peter Jacobson had been his best friend in college. After graduation, Peter had landed a job with PC Monthly magazine, a West Coast startup that had since become one of the most successful publications in the business.

Randall reached for the phone, then hesitated.

He hadn't spoken to Peter in months. They had drifted apart in recent months. After the move to San Francisco, Peter's career had soared while Randall's floundered. It seemed San Francisco and Peabody were far apart in more ways than just geography.

He had visited Peter once, but they argued most of the time, Peter trying to convince him to move to the West Coast. Randall had found himself defending a job he hated, his pride keeping him from admitting that Peter had chosen the better path.

His ego bruised, he had only spoken to Peter a few times after that. The last time he'd called, Peter had been with a woman—Angie, or Andrea, a new girlfriend apparently—and he seemed distracted. He said he'd call back, but never did. Randall had meant to call again, but hadn't gotten around to it.

He hesitated a moment longer, then decided it had been long enough. If nothing else, this was a good excuse to reconnect. He needed some information on the Family, and Peter was the person to supply it.

He pulled a phone list out of the desk, found Peter's work number, and dialed.

A receptionist answered. "PC Monthly magazine. How may I direct your call?"

"I'd like to speak to Peter Jacobson."

The receptionist hesitated. "Just a moment, please."

Canned music drifted over on the line for a few seconds, then a woman's voice spoke. "Human resources. Can I help you?"

Human resources? Why couldn't companies hire receptionists who knew what they were doing? "There's been a mistake," Randall said. "I'm trying to get through to Peter Jacobson."

"Can I ask who's calling, please?"

"My name is Randall McLagan," he said, beginning to be irritated.

"And your company, Mr. McLagan?"

What was this? Was Peter so important now that he had everybody in the company screening his calls for him?

"I'm a personal friend."

She hesitated. "Mr. McLagan, my name is Joanne Reed." Her tone had changed slightly. It was softer now, less guarded. "I'm the director of human resources for PC Monthly."

Nice to meet you, Randall thought. Now put me through to Peter.

"This is very difficult...I guess you haven't heard yet."

"Heard what?"

"It's...I'm afraid I have some difficult news for you."

He felt something sink inside. Her tone, her manner told him this was not good. "What?"

"Peter...died this weekend."

"What?"

"I'm sorry. It came as a shock to all of us here, too."

His mind raced. "What happened?"

"We don't have all the details yet. Apparently he...fell from the Golden Gate Bridge."

A chill passed through him, dragging a hundred questions behind it. Fell? How did he fall? What was he doing? Wasn't there anyone with him? Don't they have guardrails on the bridge?

He wanted to ask if she was sure but stopped himself. Of course she was sure. His mind seized, not knowing what to say next.

She spoke into his silence. "The funeral service is tomorrow. I can fax you the information if there's any possibility you can attend."

The words landed in his ear like stones skipped over dark water...a funeral...for Peter...Could he go?...Of course he would go...but could he get the time off...for a funeral...for Peter...

She spoke again. "Would you like me to fax that to you?"

The words penetrated the fog that had settled around him. "Yes, yes, please."

She waited. "If you'll just give me your fax number."

"Sure." He tried to recall the office fax number, a number he normally knew by heart. He stared blankly at the telephone list. A moment later, he remembered that he was looking for the fax number. When he found the number, it didn't seem right somehow. Nothing seemed right now. He had not seen Peter in months. He'd been meaning to call, but hadn't gotten around to it. Now it was too late. He was angry, frustrated.

How could Peter die before he'd a chance to talk to him?

At the front desk of the Peabody Herald, Linda put a caller through to the advertising department and went back to daydreaming about Randall McLagan. Like most of the single women in Peabody—and more than a few of the married ones—she lusted after Randall. He looked like a young Paul McCartney, his eyes dark brown, his hair thick and worn a bit longer than most of the guys in Peabody. It was the kind of hair a woman wanted to stick her fingers in and mess up—a fantasy she entertained herself with periodically.

A door opened in the hallway behind her and she

glanced over her shoulder. Randall appeared in the doorway to Harold Dodge's office.

"All right," came Dodge's gravelly voice. "I'll run a repeat or something. Just make sure you're back here by Wednesday. We can't afford to be late to the printer again."

Randall nodded, as if he'd barely heard the words. "OK."

He closed the door but remained standing outside it for a moment, staring blankly down the hall as if he was having a hard time deciding what to do. He looked like a child playing a game for the first time, not knowing what the rules called for next.

He went to his office, and minutes later walked to the front desk, pulling on his jacket. "Linda, I have to go away for a couple of days. Would you go through my voice mail and take care of whatever's on there?"

"Sure, Randall. Have a good trip."

He said nothing, and left. She pulled out a message pad and punched in the access code to retrieve his voice mail. There were eight messages, seven from Mrs. Torelli, and one that seemed to be personal. She thought about calling Randall at home to pass that one along, but decided not to. He didn't look as if he needed to be bothered right now. Besides, he'd be back in a couple of days. She would leave the message on the system and he could return the call when he came back.

"Randall," the message began. "This is Peter."

Somewhere in the Midwest, a high-speed computer noted the exact time Randall McLagan had logged onto the Family. It knew how long McLagan had been on the system and what he had done while there. It knew how much memory was in the computer he used to log on, the size of the hard disk drive, and the peripheral equipment attached to it. It knew what programs were installed on the computer and the last time each of them had been used.

The computer transferred McLagan's name, along with the area code from which he had called, to an automated program that cross-referenced the information with a database of addresses. Within seconds, the program had located McLagan's home address and telephone number. In two days, Randall McLagan would receive a colorful mailing encouraging him to join the Family. The mailing would not mention his recent tour of the system, making it appear as if the timing of the solicitation was purely coincidental. If McLagan did not respond within 14 days, a telemarketer would call his home to offer him a free membership in the world's fastest growing online computer group.

2

The flight was uneventful, hardly registering in Randall's consciousness. A movie flickered on the tiny screen wedged over his head. Sounds drifted up from earphones that hung limply around his neck, as if coming from another room. This did not seem odd to Randall. It was what life felt like now, action going on around him, but little or no sound, as if he were emotionally deaf, hearing everything through a cottony filter of pain and sadness.

The flight arrived in San Francisco at 5:46 p.m. He had reserved a room at the Best Western on the corner of Grant and North Point near Fisherman's Wharf—not a four-star hotel, but he was used to that. The few times that he traveled for the Peabody Herald, Dodge insisted he find the cheapest room available. When more than one person went on a trip, they doubled up. It had been different for Peter, he knew. When Peter traveled, PC Monthly had booked him into the best hotels. He had eaten at expensive restaurants, often courtesy of the computer companies he was writing about. His expense account was generous, and not closely monitored.

At the hotel, Randall checked into his room, a Spartan cubicle that smelled of disinfectant and old cigarette smoke. Among the few amenities was a copy of the San

Francisco Chronicle, which lay folded on top of the television set. He opened it aimlessly and an item at the bottom of the front page caught his eye.

Popular Columnist Dies

SAN FRANCISCO - The body of journalist and San Francisco resident Peter Jacobson was discovered by police in the shallows near the base of the Golden Gate Bridge on Sunday morning. Jacobson, author of a popular column for PC Monthly magazine, was last seen by his coworkers late Friday afternoon. He is believed to have fallen from the bridge that evening. The cause of the fall is under investigation. "At present, we're classifying it as an accidental drowning," said SFPD detective William Latimer, who could give no explanation for the accident.

He sat, staring at the paper. No explanation for the accident. A wave of anger passed over him. His best friend was dead, and San Francisco's finest couldn't even offer an explanation.

He tossed the paper on the bed. Now what? The funeral wasn't until tomorrow, and he had nothing to do until then. He could not eat. He didn't know anyone in San Francisco, and it was pointless to try watching television or a movie.

Finally, his body acted when his brain could not. He left the hotel and headed toward Fisherman's Wharf, following the crowd. He could still walk. He could still place one foot in front of the other. It wasn't much, but he could still do that.

He drifted past the wharf and Ghiradelli's chocolate factory, then skirted the bottom of Russian Hill, continuing along Fort Mason. He passed landmarks that were familiar from his previous visit, but they had an unreal quality about them now, like scenery from a play after the final performance was over, pointless somehow.

He came to a corner and looked up at the street sign. It was Laguna Street, only a few blocks from the Marina. Without thinking, he had walked in the exact direction of Peter's apartment.

Now the walk became a pilgrimage. He turned on Alhambra Street and then to Mallorca. He recognized Peter's apartment building instantly, a yellow Victorian with white trim set in the middle of the block.

Peter's car sat on the street in front of the building. Another wave of sadness passed over him—it hadn't occurred to him that the car would still be there. He approached it slowly, as if it were a shrine. The car was empty, except for a Peet's coffee cup sitting in the cup holder.

He glanced up toward Peter's apartment. The living room window was open and a curtain fluttered slightly, a light shining behind it.

Someone was in the apartment.

In an instant, he realized what had happened. There had been some kind of mistake. It was some other Peter Jacobson who had died. It had all been a ridiculous misunderstanding. In a minute, he and Peter would be laughing about it, tears streaming down their faces.

He trotted to the door and pressed the button marked "Jacobson." A buzzer sounded inside, the door clicked open, and he climbed the steps two at a time, his heart pounding.

At the top of the stairs he heard music coming from the apartment: a Peter Gabriel CD, one that Peter had purchased when they'd been in college. It was his favorite album, and he'd listened to it almost continuously throughout their college years. Randall had grown so tired of it that he'd had threatened to break the CD over Peter's head. Now, it sounded like the Hallelujah Chorus to him.

The door to the apartment stood open, revealing a hallway and the kitchen beyond it. He walked in.

"Peter?"

He walked to the kitchen. Dirty dishes filled the sink, a cereal box on the table. A large stack of mail overflowed next to it. The place looked like a museum exhibit entitled, "Habitat of West Coast Man, Late 20th Century."

"Peter?"

Still no answer. Following the music, he came to the living room, where disorder had erupted. Papers lay strewn about, books open, empty boxes piled haphazardly, clothes thrown on the backs of chairs. The CD played unattended. Below the music, from another room, came a different sound, like papers shuffling. Or someone crying.

"Hello?"

The crying stopped. A woman appeared in the hallway. She was blonde, her hair pulled back in a ponytail. Her eyes were blue, but red from crying. She wore a Dartmouth sweatshirt that was several sizes too large— Peter's, he was sure. She seemed startled to see him, as if she'd been expecting someone else. They stared at each other for a second, and in that moment he realized the truth.

Peter was not here. Peter was gone.

She took a half step back. "Can I help you?"

"I'm a friend of Peter's," he said. "Randall McLagan."

Her eyes relaxed, and she exhaled slowly. "I'm Allison. Allison Hughes."

Allison. The girlfriend. Now he knew now why Peter hadn't had time for old friends. "Peter mentioned your name," he said.

"Yours too. A lot."

The thought pleased him. He wondered what Peter had said about him.

She pushed the sleeves of the sweatshirt up her arms and sniffed away tears. "You caught me at a bad time. I was trying to sort through some...stuff."

"I'm sorry. I just got into town. I was out for a walk and saw the light. I didn't mean to interrupt you."

"That's OK. I wasn't getting much done."

She offered him a seat on an old green sofa in front of a window that looked out onto the street. Lowering herself onto the seat, she closed her eyes for a moment and shook her head gently. "Sorry. They've got me on some kind of medication. It makes me a little dizzy. I don't really like taking drugs."

"I understand."

They talked about how they'd met Peter. Allison worked at a travel agency that PC Monthly used to schedule its business trips. As a rule, the agency delivered travel tickets to the magazine office by mail. "But one time, Peter scheduled a last-minute trip and came to pick up the tickets himself. After that, he always came in to pick up his tickets."

Randall smiled. For any woman who was paying attention, that would be a dead giveaway. "How long have you lived in San Francisco?"

"Not long." She had come from Arizona only a few months before meeting Peter. Before that she had lived with an aunt and uncle who had taken her in when her parents died. "They were pretty old, and I was a handful," she said. "I think they were just as glad to see me move out."

He could see why Peter had been attracted to her. She was beautiful, vulnerable, and alone. An irresistible combination for most men.

They were silent for a moment. He hesitated, took a deep breath and said, "Can I ask you something?"

Her eyes pinched together slightly. "What?"

"Do you have any idea what happened?"

She pulled her knees up and hugged them, as if steeling herself for the words. "I was supposed to meet him here that night but I was late. When I got here, his car was out front and he wasn't around."

She had waited for him, and when he didn't show up after several hours, she called the police. "They said they couldn't do anything until more time passed, so I went home." She still did not hear from Peter, and the police finally called her on Sunday. She put her hands over her face and wept. "If only I'd been here on time."

He knew what she was saying, blaming herself for Peter's death. He had done it himself—what if he had been in touch with Peter, had made contact with him sooner?

He put a hand out to touch her shoulder, but couldn't reach her without moving closer, and that felt too familiar. His hand hung aimless in the air for a moment, then returned to his lap. "It's not your fault..."

"Yes it is," she said quickly. She hesitated, then took a deep breath. "I broke up with him up the night before. He called me that day and said he had to talk to me. I should have been here," she said, her voice cracking.

He blinked, registering what she was saying: she and Peter had broken up, and Peter was so upset that he killed himself.

He was silent for a moment, thinking. Would Peter have killed himself over a woman, even a woman as attractive as this one? The answer was no. Not the Peter that he had known. But then, maybe he hadn't known Peter as well as he thought he did.

He wanted to ask her more questions. Why did they break up? Had anyone seen Peter that night? What did the police know? But this wasn't the time for questions. He sat until she regained her composure and then stood. "I should let you get back to your work."

She nodded, not speaking.

"Is there anything I can do?"

After a moment she said, "The funeral is tomorrow. I didn't really know the people from his office that well. And I never even met his stepfather."

That didn't surprise him. Robert Gebhardt was a banker. Peter once described him as a gold-digger who had married his mother for her money. The two had never gotten along, and when Peter's mother died, there had been some disagreement about her estate. As far as Randall knew, Peter hadn't spoken to Gebhardt since then, so it was no surprise that Allison hadn't met him.

"I just don't know if I can handle going to the funeral by myself," she said.

"I'd be happy to take you."

For the first time, a faint smile creased the corners of her mouth. "Would that be OK?"

"Sure," he said, and looking into her eyes he could not help thinking, that would be very OK.

3

Alan Reingold checked his notes one more time before closing the computer file on his new neighbors, the Millers. They had moved to San Francisco three months ago. Sam Miller, a programmer with Digitopia, was busy adjusting to his new job. Julie Miller was a nurse, but not working now. She was at home, setting up house, and lonely. The Miller's son Josh was in school, and not doing that well according to the school's computer.

They were the perfect candidates.

The doorbell rang. Alan fixed a broad smile to his previously impassive face and opened the door wide. "Come on in, neighbors. We've been waiting for you."

Sam and Julie Miller edged past Alan into the entryway, their son Josh trailing behind. Sam, who wore a decidedly un-San Francisco sweater, raised his eyebrows in the direction of his son, a sullen teenager in an untucked flannel shirt and baseball cap. Josh removed the cap with a slow scowl and tucked it into a rear pocket.

Margaret Reingold appeared from the kitchen bearing a tray of cheese and crackers and greeted them in a voice that swung like a back-porch settee. "Well, hel-lo. It's about time we had you folks over here."

Julie, thin and blonde with an anxious smile, handed Margaret a plate with a cake on it. "It's German chocolate. Just something I threw together."

"Oh, it looks wonderful," Margaret said. "I'll just take it into the kitchen."

The sound of a clicking keyboard drifted down from upstairs. Alan called up the stairs. "Scott? Come down and meet the Millers."

Scott Reingold appeared at the foot of the stairs, looking more like a West Point cadet than a high school student. He greeted the Millers with stiff, formal handshakes.

Margaret reappeared and said, "Dinner will be ready in a minute. Why don't we go into the living room?"

They ate crackers and cheese, the Reingolds expressing interest and delight in everything Sam or Julie said. Then came dinner: chicken Marengo with wild rice, fresh steamed vegetables, home-made bread, an expensive bottle of wine—Margaret had checked beforehand to make sure Sam and Julie drank and what kind of wine they preferred. After dinner came gourmet coffee and Julie's German chocolate cake.

Margaret held a forkful of the dark-brown cake over her plate. "This is so moist," she said. "You have to give me the recipe."

Julie beamed, squeezing Sam's hand under the table, and he grinned back at her. This evening was just what Julie needed. They had hardly been out of the house since moving from Minneapolis to San Francisco. What with work and a new home, they'd had little time to make new friends, and hadn't met a single neighbor until the Reingolds came over to introduce themselves. And the Reingolds were the friendliest people they'd ever met: Alan, with his thinning, swept-back hair, looking like a young Jack Nicholson; Margaret, a homebody with short, curly hair and a persistent motherly smile; and Scott, who seemed too neat and polite to actually be a teenager. In a city where people passed every day without even acknowledging each other's existence, meeting the Reingolds had been like coming out of a dark tunnel.

Alan finished the last bite of his cake. "This really is delicious."

"Too bad she doesn't make it at home," Josh muttered.

Sam shot a stern look at Josh, and a moment of awkward silence followed.

Alan turned to his son. "Scott?"

"Yes, sir?"

"Didn't you just get a new video game? Why don't you take Josh up to your room and give him a shot at it?"

"Yes, sir."

The boys left as Sam tried to remember if Josh had ever said, "Yes, sir," in his entire life. He didn't think so.

Julie watched them leave, a wistful expression on her face. "Your son is so well behaved."

"Thank you," Margaret said, smiling and pouring more coffee. "He has his moments. But overall, we're pretty proud of him."

"I can see why," Sam said. At the moment, he felt like strangling his own son.

Julie glanced at Sam, then smiled sheepishly. "We're going through a rough stage with Josh. He just doesn't want to do anything we tell him. And he's so rude." She shrugged helplessly. "Maybe it has something to do with adjusting to a new school."

Alan and Margaret smiled sympathetically. They had a confident air about them, as if they had discovered some secret drug that transforms teenagers into reasonable human beings. "How do you folks do it?" Julie asked.

Alan nodded at Margaret; apparently, this was her territory.

"Well, to begin with, we home-school Scott," Margaret said. "That gives us more control over his environment."

"Really?" Julie asked. "Isn't that a lot of work?"

"Not really. We do most of it by computer. And we belong to a group that helps us."

"A home-schooling group?"

"No, it's a computer group called the Family. We use it to shop, talk to friends, plan our travel. I don't know what we'd do without it."

Julie looked at Margaret blankly, as if she'd just attributed their successful family life to membership on a bowling team or a steady diet of rutabaga. "Well, that sounds like...fun."

The Millers retrieved their son, thanked the Reingolds for a lovely evening, and left. Alan and Margaret stood in the door and waved, their broad smiles disappearing as soon as the Millers were out of sight.

"What do you think?" Margaret asked.

Alan nodded, the corners of his mouth tucked in pensively. "I think it went well."

He returned to his study, where the computer was still on—he rarely logged off these days, having installed a separate phone line for the Family. He opened the Millers' file, and the system automatically added the date to the entry as he typed.

Subjects successfully initialized.

In the kitchen, Margaret fed the remainder of the German chocolate cake into the garbage disposal.

4

Allison lived in the Sunset, that perpetually fogbound section of San Francisco on the west side of the city, where moist Pacific air passes over warm land to produce a damp haze, draping the tiny houses and turning even the brightest colors into muted pastels.

Randall rang the bell at the address Allison had given him. He heard an upstairs door open and close, then footsteps descending the stairs. He looked through the beveled glass of the door. A pair of legs descended the stairs, black pumps and dark stockings, and he realized he was staring.

He turned away as Allison came to the landing and opened the door. Her lips almost formed a smile. "Thanks for doing this. I really appreciate it."

"No problem," he said, aware that his heart was beating faster than normal, hoping Peter would forgive him for that.

They drove north, toward Tiburon. The funeral was at an Episcopal church that Randall doubted Peter had ever attended in his life. He would be buried next to his mother, at an equally indifferent cemetery.

They rode in silence, the tires hissing over damp pavement. As they crossed the Golden Gate Bridge, Allison turned to look out the window, squinting against the morning sun. With a chill, he realized that at some point they would pass the place where Peter had spent his last moments alive, and wondered if she was thinking the same thing. She rested her temple against the glass, her eyes closed. She was.

The funeral was short, riddled with phrases that Randall had heard at funerals for elderly relatives and grandparents, but had never paid much attention to.

"Yea, though I walk through the valley of the shadow of death, I will fear no evil."

"I am the resurrection, and the life: he that believeth in me, though he were dead, yet shall he live."

"And God shall wipe away all tears from their eyes; and there shall be no more death, neither sorrow, nor crying..."

For once, he listened closely, hoping the words might help him make sense of Peter's death. But they remained hidden, like coded messages that he did not have the key to decipher.

The minister didn't appear to have known Peter personally; the few words he spoke about him were generic platitudes about the difficulty of losing someone in the prime of their life. Nothing was said about the circumstances of Peter's death.

After the service, the mourners retreated to their cars and followed a slow-moving hearse to the cemetery. They emerged from their cars, a mist gathering around the small circle of people that ringed the hole into which the mortal remains of Peter Jacobson would be lowered.

Randall and Allison stood at the foot of the casket, as far away as they could get from Peter's stepfather, who had positioned himself at the head of the casket with his new wife Barbara—or, as Peter had called her, Bunny. Gebhardt was stone-faced, his head lowered, frowning at the ground as if it were an intractable business problem. His wife gripped his arm as she would a pole in a subway car in which she was afraid of losing her balance. Neither of them had spoken to Randall or Allison.

To one side of the casket stood a knot of people that Randall assumed were Peter's coworkers. A bulky middle-aged man in a dark topcoat stood at the head of the group, towering over the others. His eyes peered across the casket and over the heads of the mourners on the other side, examining memorial stones in the distance, like a person at a cocktail party looking for the right people to talk to. Occasionally, he whispered something to a top-coated young man beside him, whose ready nods and efficient manner betrayed the role of a lackey. The others in the group deferred to the large man as well, with the exception of one woman who stood slightly apart from the group. She wore a dark gray dress suit, her arms crossed over her chest, staring at the casket almost angrily. She looked up as Randall's eyes passed over her. Her eyes met his for an instant, flicked to Allison, then looked back at the casket.

The committal ceremony was brief. Allison held up well until the final prayer, when she put her hand over her eyes and leaned against Randall's shoulder. He put his arm around her and thought, the story of my life—the shoulder that Peter's girlfriends cry on.

The minister pronounced the benediction and an awkward moment followed, the time when mourners were expected to tell those closest to the departed how sorry they were. But no one seemed to know to whom they should offer condolences. Gebhardt and his wife turned to leave. The others stood awkwardly, staring at the casket for a few moments. The tall man asked a question of his assistant, who gestured toward Gebhardt. The tall man moved purposefully to intercept him.

"Mr. Gebhardt," he said, his voice booming over the mist-shrouded grounds. "I'm Jack Bragdon, editor and publisher of PC Monthly." He shook Gebhardt's hand firmly and lowered his voice somewhat, but snatches of the conversation drifted over the open grave: "...a great asset to the company...damn shame...great career ahead of him...real loss..."

Gebhardt nodded, saying little. The ritual concluded, Gebhardt and his wife left, while Bragdon scanned the mourners for anyone else he should address. His eyes passed over Randall and Allison without any sign of acknowledgment. He turned and left.

The woman in the gray suit trailed behind, pausing as she passed Randall and Allison. Her hair was reddish-brown, cut to a business-like shoulder length, her eyes gray-blue, high cheekbones flushed slightly. A tiny scar ran across the bridge of her nose.

"Are you a friend of Peter's?" she asked.

"Yes. We went to college together. I'm Randall McLagan." He considered holding out a hand, but her arms were still crossed tightly, hands stuffed under the armpits of her suit.

"Erica Steiner, from PC Monthly," she said. "Peter and I worked together."

Randall nodded and gestured toward Allison. "This is..."

"Right," she said, barely looking at Allison. "We've met." She put her hands into her jacket pockets and took a deep breath, as if she were an actress about to deliver a line she didn't like. "I'm sorry...we all are. Peter was a wonderful guy."

He nodded. "Yes, he was."

"If there's anything I can do, please let me know."

He thanked her, though the offer seemed odd. He had been close to Peter, but he wasn't immediate family, and he had no responsibilities in Peter's affairs. Still, the offer seemed sincere.

She pulled a hand from her pocket and held it out to Randall. "I mean that," she said.

He shook the hand. "All right. Thank you."

She left, and Randall turned to Allison. "Are you ready to go?"

Allison nodded silently. As they returned to the car, Randall glanced back at the grave site, where three men in work clothes loosened the straps on the casket and lowered it slowly into the ground.

Randall opened the door for Allison, then walked behind the car to the driver's side. As he did, he glanced at the business card Erica Steiner had pressed into his hand and the message scrawled on the back.

Call me.

5

Cindy Conners punched another button on the LifeCycle. It responded by beeping loudly enough for everyone in the club to hear.

"Damn," she muttered, hoping she didn't look as stupid as she felt. She had spent several hundred dollars on a membership in this club, more money on a new body suit with matching leggings and headband, and now she couldn't get the stupid exercise bicycle to work.

A woman with long chestnut hair tied in a ponytail stepped off a treadmill and walked over to her. "Can I help you with that?"

Cindy grimaced. "Oh, um..."

The woman grinned. "Don't worry about it. I had the same problem when I started using these things." She held out her hand. "My name's Jennifer."

"Hi. I'm Cindy." She winced at the bicycle. "I've never been very good at electronic things."

"Let me show you how to work this." She walked Cindy through the programming procedure, setting the machine for a 20-minute ride with alternate periods of warming up, coasting, uphill climb, and cool down.

Cindy shook her head. "I don't know why I have problems with these things. I don't even know how to use all the buttons on my microwave."

Jennifer smiled. "I used to be that way."

"Really? You sure seem as if you know what you're doing."

"It's not really that hard. Mostly a matter of confidence. Once you realize that you can work with machines, they're pretty easy to understand."

"I wish I felt that way."

"Well, as I said, I didn't used to. Till I joined the Family."

Cindy wasn't sure she'd heard her correctly. "The what?"

"The Family. It's a computer group. One of the things we do is to help people overcome their fear of computers."

"Wow. I'd like that. I'm terrified of computers."

"So was I. But you know what? It's not our fault. Men always treat women as if they can't handles things like computers. But really, the nice thing about computers is that they don't know what sex you are. Everyone's the same when you're sitting behind a keyboard."

Cindy looked doubtful. "You think so?"

"I know so. You should check out the group. You'd love it. The people in it are really friendly, and we have a lot of fun."

Cindy hesitated. For her, joining a computer group was on a par with attending a lecture on nuclear physics. But Jennifer seemed nice, and her enthusiasm was contagious. "Well, I guess I could give it a try," she said. "When does the group meet?"

"Actually, it's mostly an online organization. I'll give you my address and you can come over to my place for a demonstration."

Randall parked in the financial district and checked the address he had scrawled on a scrap of paper. He had called Erica Steiner as soon as he'd returned to the hotel.

"Can you meet me downtown?" she had asked. "I'd like to talk to you."

He had barely an hour to spare before his flight back, and he had just dropped off Allison, the most attractive woman he'd met in a long time—a woman who had indicated she wished there was time to get to know him better—and instead of doing that, he was going to meet an old coworker of Peter's. His luck was running true to form.

He passed a street-level health club with smoked-glass windows and a row of exercise machines pointed out to the street. Two young women stood at the end of the row. As he passed, one handed a piece of paper to the other.

He looked up and saw the building Erica Steiner had described to him. PC Monthly's offices were located in a gleaming monolith that towered over the street, mirrored sides reflecting images of the city around it. It was a building that reminded him of silvered aviator glasses; you could never tell what was going on behind them.

Erica Steiner stood waiting by the front door to the building. She acknowledged Randall's approach with a quick nod and, without a word, turned to walk away. He fell into step beside her, wondering if she were always so cordial.

"There's a coffee shop over on Stockton," she said. "It's a bit of a walk."

"Fine with me," he said, though he wasn't sure why they had to walk all the way to Stockton. They had just passed one coffee shop and were coming up on another; San Francisco has more coffee shops than fire hydrants. He pegged Erica Steiner as a woman who would go out of her way to get what she wanted, even down to a favorite kind of coffee.

They dodged traffic, Randall making feeble attempts at small talk. Erica responded to his questions concisely, if at all.

They arrived at the coffee shop, which seemed no different than a half-dozen others they'd passed along the way. A glass counter ran down one side of the shop, a menu on the wall behind it listing exotic coffees, cappuccinos and espressos. Randall studied the list, not used to having so many choices. In Peabody, asking for anything but regular coffee was putting on airs.

"I'll have a latté," he said to the lip-ringed young man behind the counter, then turned to Erica. "You?"

"Doesn't matter," she said, scanning the shop distractedly. "I don't like the stuff anyway."

Randall ordered another latté as Erica staked out an empty table at the rear of the shop. He carried the drinks to the table and sat opposite her. He decided to be blunt. "Let me ask you something. Is there a reason we came all this way if you don't even like coffee?"

She studied his face for a moment, then reached into her purse, pulled out a piece of paper, unfolded it, and placed it on the table before him.

Interoffice memo
To: all staff
From: Jack Bragdon, Editor and Publisher

We are all greatly saddened by the loss of Peter Jacobson. Out of respect for Peter and his family, please refrain from discussing the details of his passing. It is sufficient to say that we will miss him and that his passing is a great loss to the magazine.

"Bragdon," Randall said. "Is that your boss?"

She nodded. "The tall guy at the funeral."

"'The details of his passing,'" he read. "I wish I had some details."

"You and me both."

He handed the memo back to her. "I take it you're as confused by this as I am?"

"I was hoping you could help me figure it out."

He hesitated. "Allison thinks he took his own life."

She shook her head, a slight dismissive movement. "Allison still thinks the earth is flat."

Randall looked down at the table, pondering the remark. Beautiful girlfriend. Less beautiful but still attractive coworker. What had the relationship between Erica and Peter been?

"Why do you say that?" he asked.

She began to say something, then stopped. "Never mind."

"Did you know they had just broken up?"

She snickered. "Is that why she thinks Peter killed himself?"

"Apparently, yes."

She leaned toward him. "There are all kinds of attractive, available single women in this business. Most of them would have loved to date Peter. So who did he fall for? Someone who works in a travel agency." She said the words as if she were saying "laundromat."

Clearly, she had no use for Allison. But that part of the conversation didn't interest him. "So you don't think he killed himself?"

She cocked her head. "What do you think? You knew Peter as well as I did."

He didn't have to consider the question for long. Of course not. No matter what he'd been facing, no matter what the issues were, he would never have taken that way out. "So what did happen?"

"I don't know," she said, irritated. "No one knows, and that's what bothers me. No one seems to be trying to find out what happened."

He nodded, certain that she was wrong and simply speaking out of frustration. "I'm sure the police..."

She shook her head. "The police don't give a damn. They're up to their necks with criminal cases. They're not going to spend a lot of time figuring out why some guy fell off the bridge."

He considered Peter's family, which consisted of his stepfather, Robert Gebhardt, with whom he had been arguing about his mother's estate. Now that Peter was gone, Gebhardt would probably get the whole thing. That didn't leave a lot of motivation for him to press for an explanation of Peter's death.

"What about the magazine?"

Erica shook her head. "Jack Bragdon isn't going to do anything about it."

"Why not?"

"You don't know Jack. The last thing he wants is any kind of negative publicity that might hurt the magazine. Trust me, he isn't going to dig too deeply into this. Besides, he and Peter didn't get along."

"Why is that?"

She shrugged. "They'd been fighting ever since Jack became editor of the magazine."

"About what?"

"The column, the way Peter handled it. If a new program was garbage, he said so, whether it came from Fly-By-Night Software or from one of the big players like CompuSys or Dulterra International. The problem is, those big players are the ones with the big advertising budgets. Essentially, that lets them buy good editorial coverage. Didn't you ever wonder why new products from the big computer companies get splashed all over the covers of every single computer magazine as soon as they're released?"

He shrugged. "I guess I thought they were

newsworthy."

"Guess again. If you look inside the magazines, you'll find big ads for the same products that are on the covers. And if a magazine tells the truth about those products, the ads go away."

"And Peter had a bad habit of telling the truth."

"You've got it. So Jack was in a bind. He had one of the most popular columnists in the industry, writing negative reviews about companies that were threatening to pull their advertising."

"And Bragdon didn't have the guts to stand up to them."

She cocked her head. "Jack Bragdon is an empty suit."

"A what?"

"Empty suit. A manager whose primary task is to occupy space. Bragdon started out as a salesman, became head of sales, and then publisher of the magazine. Peter hit the roof when that happened."

"How come?"

"Well, to begin with, if you're running a computer magazine, you might like to have someone in charge who knows something about computers."

"And Bragdon doesn't?"

She frowned contemptuously. "Jack Bragdon doesn't know a computer from a toaster oven."

He was beginning to see why Bragdon and Peter hadn't gotten along. Peter did not suffer fools easily.

She said, "The day Jack took over, he called Peter into his office for a little talk about the column."

"I'll bet that went over well."

"Like a lead balloon. From there, things only got worse. They argued constantly, Jack trying to tell Peter what do to, Peter refusing to go along."

Randall took this all in, but there was a connection he was missing. "What does this have to do with Peter's death?"

She hesitated. "Peter and Jack had a big fight on Friday afternoon."

"About what?"

"I don't know. Probably something to do with the column. I could hear Jack shouting all the way down the hall. 'The advertisers pay the bills around here' and 'This is PC Monthly, not the goddamn Washington Post.' I thought Peter was going to quit right then."

"But he didn't?"

"No. He just took off."

"What time was that?"

She shrugged. "About four, I guess."

He remembered the newspaper article about Peter's death. It had said Peter fell from the bridge in the early evening. That left a couple of hours unaccounted for. "Where did he go after he left the office?"

"I don't know." She blinked, looked away for a moment, then looked back at him, her eyes filling. "He didn't even say good night."

Randall nodded. Apparently he wasn't the only one who hadn't had a chance to resolve things with Peter. He looked down, giving her a chance to recover. "Do you know what that column was about?"

"No. Peter had been playing his cards pretty close to his chest lately. I don't blame him, the way things were going with Jack."

"Is there any way to find out?"

"No," she repeated, sounding irritated. She sighed, and seemed to soften. "Even if I could find out, I couldn't tell you. The magazine has to sign all kinds of confidentially agreements to get advance information about new products, and Jack is paranoid about information leaking out before the release date. I'm already sticking my neck out just talking to you." She glanced at her watch. "I have to get back."

They walked back to her office, saying little. Erica stopped at the corner opposite the building and said, "Thanks for taking the time to talk to me. I don't know what I expected you to do about this. I just needed to talk to someone."

"That's OK. I understand."

They shook hands quickly and parted. She crossed the street and disappeared into the building, not looking back.

Randall stood for a moment, staring at the door through which she had disappeared. Three days earlier, Peter had argued with his boss and walked out those same doors. From there, no one seemed to know what had happened to him. His only remaining family member was his step-father, who wasn't inclined to care. His boss wouldn't press the issue because he didn't want a scandal that might hurt the magazine. Peter's coworkers were afraid for their jobs. And his girlfriend was certain she was to blame. None of them was going to press for an answer about what happened to Peter. So who did that leave?

The answer was immediate, obvious, and disturbing.

It left him.

6

Detective Bill Latimer ran through the file on the death of Peter Jacobson one more time: a white male, twenty-seven years old, body found in the shallows on the San Francisco side of the Golden Gate. No witnesses. No evidence of foul play. A wallet with credit cards and a little over a hundred dollars in cash.

Latimer sighed and passed a hand over his balding head. It was just his luck. If Jacobson's body had drifted to shore a few yards closer to the bridge, it would have landed on Golden Gate Park property and it would have been the park police's responsibility. Instead, it landed on city property, which made it the city's problem. And since Latimer was the homicide inspector on call when Jacobson's body was found, that made it his problem.

It was Latimer's job to determine whether Peter Jacobson's death had been an accident, a suicide, or a murder. That wasn't going to be easy. There were no witnesses—or none that were willing to come forward. Jacobson's family, friends and coworkers didn't have any idea what had happened to him. To listen to them, Jacobson was a model citizen, with no enemies and no apparent reason for taking his own life aside from a fairly stressful workload.

Latimer spun his chair to the computer beside his desk and called up the "triple-eye"— the Interstate

Identification Index, a computerized database of criminal records maintained by the FBI. When all else failed, the triple-eye sometimes turned up a lead.

Jack O'Neill appeared in the doorway holding two cardboard cups of San Francisco's finest police department coffee. "You ready for a nice hot cup of chemicals?"

Latimer didn't look up at his partner. "Don't make it sound so appealing. I'm trying to cut down."

O'Neill handed a cup to Latimer. "What's up?"

"Jacobson," he said, turning in his chair and gesturing to the open folder on his desk.

"The floater?"

"Yeah. The mystery man."

O'Neill clucked sympathetically and sunk into the chair opposite the desk. At any given time, a homicide detective might have as many as a dozen open cases. Some cases were resolved fairly quickly, others dragged on for months or even years. Of all the cases homicide detectives dealt with, drownings were among the most difficult to resolve. "What have you got?"

"Not much. A jogger finds the body in the water. No signs of foul play. No strangulation marks. No wounds. Water in the lungs."

O'Neill nodded. When there wasn't water in the lungs, it meant the person wasn't breathing when he hit the water—a telltale sign that someone had committed murder and then dumped in the water to get rid of the body. But water in the lungs was more ambiguous. "So you think he's a jumper?"

Latimer sipped the coffee. "What else? No signs of foul play, no struggle..."

O'Neill cocked his head doubtfully. "No suicide note..."

47

"Hey, how's he going to leave a suicide note on the Golden Gate Bridge? Nail it there?"

O'Neill grinned, enjoying his partner's dilemma. He picked up the folder and glanced through it. "Maybe a stickup gone bad?"

"Right. Some punk's going to mug the guy and leave him with a wallet full of cash and credit cards."

O'Neill skimmed the rest of the folder and tossed it back on the desk. "Looks like you're stuck with accidental drowning, then."

Latimer leaned back in his chair and crossed his arms over his chest. "Nobody accidentally falls off the Golden Gate Bridge unless they're very stupid or very drunk. According to the autopsy this guy wasn't drunk, and judging from his background, he wasn't stupid."

O'Neill sipped coffee. "What's his girlfriend think?"

"Who knows? She's a mess. They've got her on medication."

"Coworkers?"

"His boss thinks it was some kind of personal problem. Says Jacobson seemed upset toward the end."

"The triple-eye turn up anything?"

"I was just getting ready to check it."

O'Neill finished his coffee in one gulp. "Tell you what." He crumpled the cup and tossed it into the wastebasket by the door. "You check the triple-eye, and I'll to talk to Antonelli. He owes me."

Paul Antonelli was a private investigator who had once been a detective with the department. As a PI, he could get away with things that were out of bounds for the police, such as running computer checks of financial reports and medical records. He and the detectives on the force had an unofficial favor-exchange program.

"Good idea," Latimer said. "Remind me to recommend you for a raise."

O'Neill snorted and headed for his own office as Latimer turned back to the computer. Hunting and pecking with two fingers, he entered Jacobson's name, date of birth, and social security number into the appropriate spaces on the screen. He had barely learned to use this system, and now the department geeks wanted to replace it with a new system. He wasn't thrilled about the prospect.

As Latimer waited for the system to respond, O'Neill walked back into the office, waving a piece of paper. "That didn't take long."

"You got something already?"

"Jacobson's financial report," O'Neill snickered. "Antonelli knows how to use his computer."

Latimer scanned the fax. There was no indication where it had come from. Antonelli was no fool.

Latimer whistled low. "Well, that explains a lot. This guy was leaking money like a sieve."

"I'll say. If I were him, I'd have thought about killing myself, too."

Latimer handed the fax back to O'Neill. "Of course, we don't know anything about that stuff."

"Right," O'Neill said, folding the fax and tucking into his shirt pocket. "No idea whatsoever."

"Which leaves us with an accidental drowning," Latimer said. He opened Jacobson's folder and began filling in the section on cause of death. As far as he was concerned, the investigation into the death of Peter Jacobson was closed. Technically, of course, the case would remain open. But there would be no new action taken, and after a few months, he would move the case to the inactive file, where it would be as good as dead.

Sometimes, for the sake of those left behind, a painful untruth was better than an even more painful truth.

The Reingolds' parenting group began at seven. In the dining room a lace-covered table overflowed with chocolate chip cookies, mini-cheesecakes, multi-layered brownies, and Julie's German chocolate cake—Margaret had called her for the recipe that morning.

Alan supervised Sam and Julie as they loaded their plates, then steered them toward a young couple named Giordano. Phil Giordano was ruddy-cheeked, dark eyebrowed, and prematurely balding. His wife Olivia— Livvy, to her friends—was tall and immaculately manicured, with short-cropped dark hair that framed an oval face.

"Phil's in public relations," Alan said, introducing them. "And Livvy's an intensive care nurse."

Julie bonded to Livvy instantly, sharing tales of nursing. As they talked, Sam gazed around the room, picking up snatches of the other discussions: mortgages, job interviews, childhood illnesses, auto repairs.

Eventually, Alan called the meeting to order. He introduced Sam and Julie to warm applause from the others, then began the meeting with a report on a new piece of legislation being considered by Congress. "HR-3099 would provide a tax credit for families that buy a computer for educational purposes."

Phil Giordano leaned toward Sam and said with a grin, "Alan's our political watchdog."

Alan encouraged them to contact their representatives to support the bill, and passed around sheets with the phone numbers and e-mail addresses of their representatives.

Next came Elizabeth, a slight woman with curly hair who read capsule reviews of current movies, noting which ones contained language or subjects that might not be appropriate for children. A discussion on children and chores followed, and the group was in general agreement that assigning children regular duties would help them become more responsible citizens, prepare them for the working world, and generally make life easier.

The meeting ended, and there was more dessert and socializing. Gradually, the group members left, each telling the Millers how wonderful it was to meet them. Julie and Sam were the last ones to leave.

"That was wonderful," Julie said, taking her coat from Margaret.

"Sure was," Sam said. "It's nice to be in a group where you don't have to feel like a Nazi for telling your kids to make their beds."

"And everyone's so friendly," Julie said.

The Reingolds smiled, saying little. Scott Reingold—invisible during the entire evening—came downstairs, said good night, and went back up to bed.

Julie paused at the doorway and sighed. "Your life seems so...together. How do you do it?"

"Well, it's just a matter of being organized," Margaret said. "The computer helps a lot."

"That's for sure," Alan added. "We use our computers for everything."

"Computers?" Sam asked, emphasizing the plural.

"We each have our own. I think someday, everyone will have their own computer."

Sam nodded, doubting that but saying nothing.

"And of course, we get a lot of help from the Family," Margaret said.

"The Family?" Sam asked.

"It's a computer group," Julie said.

Alan added, "A lot of the other folks who were here tonight belong to the Family as well."

Margaret touched his shoulder. "Honey, don't you have a free disk that lets people sign on and try it out?"

"I think so. Hang on." He went to his study and

returned with a brightly packaged disk, which he handed to Sam. "Check this out. I think you'll really enjoy it."

The Millers left, and Alan returned to his study. The drawer to his desk was still open, revealing a large stack of sign-on disks for the Family. He closed the drawer, sat at his computer, and opened the Millers' progress report.

Configuration begun.

Dorothy Toomey dragged herself up the wooden banister by a wiry hand, gasping between sentences. "It was a terrible thing," she said. "Thirty-seven years, I've been a landlady. Nothing like this ever happened to any of my tenants before."

"I really appreciate your letting me in," Randall said, following her up the stairs and hoping she didn't have a stroke before she made it to the top. It had taken him some time to convince her that he wasn't a burglar, a con man, or a drug addict, just a friend of Peter's who needed to get into the apartment.

"He was such a nice person," Mrs. Toomey wheezed. "A good tenant. Very quiet. Never gave me any trouble." She stopped at the head of the stairs to catch her breath, then opened the door. "Will you be cleaning out the apartment?"

"No, I hadn't planned to."

She waved a hand as if it weren't any of her business. "Well, the rent is paid up until the end of the month. After that, I'll have to get someone else in here. His young lady..." She closed her eyes and clenched her fist, trying to remember the name. "Amy...Andrea..."

"Allison."

"Yes, Allison. She was here for a few things. I don't know if she's coming back. If no one comes for the rest, I'll have to call the Salvation Army." She turned and began the long trek down the stairs, directing Randall several times to be sure and lock up when he left.

The apartment didn't look very different from the time he'd been there before. Whatever Allison had done didn't show. The pile of mail still sat on the kitchen table. He picked up the top piece, an open envelope marked "Urgent Attention"– a notice from the telephone company, warning that if the enclosed bill was not paid promptly, the service would be disconnected.

That seemed odd. Peter wasn't the type to neglect his bills, and he was certainly making enough money to pay them. He glanced at the balance due: $3,427.18.

He flipped to the list of long-distance calls. Johannesburg. Perth. Bucharest. What was Peter doing calling those places?

He looked around the kitchen. In the corner lay a crumbled ball of blue paper. He flattened it out—another disconnect notice, this one from Pacific Gas and Electric. According to the power company, Peter hadn't paid his electric bill in months. The amount due was over a thousand dollars. If they didn't receive payment within a week, they were going to turn off the power.

He flipped through the rest of the mail, a mix of bills and junk mail, from every conceivable type of outfit, including several that he found it hard to believe Peter ever patronized: Pleasure Seekers, which purported to have the "World's Largest Selection of Sex Enhancers!" The Adults Only Video Club. And even one that promised photos of "Hot Teenage Girls." Randall handled the stuff guiltily, ashamed for Peter, not wanting anyone else to see it.

There were bills from companies he'd never heard of, for products that he couldn't imagine Peter ever purchasing: full-length fur coats, Rolex watches, kangaroo-leather boots.

It didn't make sense. Even back in college, Peter had always paid his bills on time. He wasn't the type to spend money on luxuries before paying his utility bills. And if he had bought a lot of fancy clothes, watches, and boots, where were they? He checked Peter's closets, and found only the ordinary shirts, jackets and ties that Peter might wear.

Across the hall was a smaller bedroom, which Peter had set up as an office. Randall stood in the doorway and surveyed the room. A plain desk dominated the room, with a computer enthroned in the center of it. Around the computer were the paraphernalia of a computer journalist: fax machine, telephone, answering machine, and piles of papers. The papers had been tossed carelessly about. That wasn't like Peter either.

He checked the closet. A laser printer sat in the gloom, its red power light glowing silently. On the floor of the closet and on the shelves above were empty boxes, software packages, loose pages from manuals. But no fur jackets, no leather boots.

He sat at the desk, opening its drawers, poking through the hanging files. Other than the mess, nothing seemed unusual about the contents. He glanced at the shelves above the computer and saw a large black book lying open atop other books. It was a Bible, which surprised him. Peter had never been, as far as he knew, a person who read the Bible.

It was a plain black Bible with red edging on the pages, a name stamped in gold along the lower right of the cover: Gloria Jacobson. Peter's mother. He thumbed through the pages. Here and there, someone had highlighted verses with a yellow marker. He was fairly sure those were Peter's marks; his mother came from a generation that would never have written in a Bible. For Peter, it was simply another book, a resource to be studied, marked up.

He put the Bible back on the shelf. Next to it was a photograph that showed Peter and Allison sitting on the green sofa. Allison had squeezed in next to Peter, and had that silly, posed look of someone who is taking a self-timed photo. Peter's feet were up on the coffee table, his open briefcase stretched out in front of him, a look of controlled amusement on his face.

Randall examined the photograph closely. Along the front edge of the briefcase were the initials "PAJ." He recognized it instantly. It was the briefcase he'd given Peter as a graduation gift, an expensive leather model he'd strapped himself to buy. Peter had still been using it when he died.

He scanned the room but didn't see the briefcase anywhere. A check of the bedroom, the living room, and closets didn't turn it up either.

He went back to the study and sat at the desk. On impulse, he turned on Peter's computer. It clicked and whirred for a few moments, then presented a message:

DataSure Protection
Enter password:

He had no idea what Peter's password was. He hit the Enter key a couple of times.

Incorrect password. Please try again.

Incorrect password. Please try again.

He turned the system off. He wasn't going to find out anything there.

He gazed around the room. Next to the desk was a wastebasket, overflowing with crumpled papers. He dug through them and came upon press releases, an interoffice memo about photocopier use, random notes from articles. Beside the wastebasket lay a crumpled piece of note paper. He picked it up and smoothed it out. It was a list of names, in Peter's tight, forceful scrawl.

His own name was on the list:

Ed Truman
Laurie Donoway, Martin A Marks
Randall M.
Harry Arnofsky

A line had been drawn through the first name, and there was a check mark next to the second one. He stared at the list. Who were these people, and why was his name listed with theirs?

A business card file sat next to the telephone. He flipped through it, but found no cards for Ed Truman, Laurie Donoway, or Martin Marks. Then, under "A" he found "Harry Arnofsky, Dalek Consulting."

He picked up the phone and was relieved to hear a dial tone. Apparently the phone company hadn't cut Peter off yet. He punched out the number on the card.

The phone rang four times, then clicked. Odd noises, like the beeps and squawks from an old science fiction movie, drifted across the line, then a voice. "This is Harry. I'm tied up in an alternate universe right now. Leave your coordinates. I'll contact you later." A loud beep followed.

Randall hesitated, not sure what to say. "Hello...I'm a friend of Peter Jacobson's. I found your name in his apartment–"

The answering machine clicked, as if it had stopped recording, and a distinctly live voice said, "This is Harry."

7

The New World Café was located on Belvedere Street in Haight-Ashbury. A carved wooden sign hung over the entrance to the café, chips of bright green and orange paint flaking off onto a narrow flight of steps that led down to a dark door. Randall descended the steps, past posters for film festivals, political action groups and meditation societies. A bell jingled as he opened the door.

Caribbean music percolated beneath the conversations that filled the room. One or two heads lifted to note Randall's arrival, then returned to their coffee and newspapers.

He took in the room, his eyes adjusting slowly to the dim light. Despite its name, the New World had a distinctly old-world atmosphere, lit only by lamps and candles on small, mismatched tables. The clientele consisted largely of students and other academic types dressed in blue jeans and tweed jackets, gigantic sweaters and floppy scarves, long hair and copies of the latest New York Times bestseller.

In a far corner, a man with wild, curly black hair looked up from beneath heavy eyebrows and squinted through thick-rimmed glasses. He lifted a hand to signal to Randall, a gesture that seemed uncomfortable to him. He stood as Randall approached. "Randall?"

"Right."

"Coffee?"

"Sure."

At the back of the café, a serving window opened into the kitchen. Beside the window, urns of coffee on a narrow table wafted the smells of French roast and hazelnut throughout the room.

"How did you meet Peter?" Randall asked as he pumped coffee into a mug.

"He was working on an article about Houdini," Harry said.

"The magician?"

"No. The virus. Ever hear of Mark Roberts?"

Randall searched his memory. "Was he the kid that broke into all those computers?"

"Close. He created a virus called Houdini and put it on the Internet. It infected three-quarters of the systems connected to the net."

Randall remembered now. The virus had caused a logjam that tied up computers around the country for days. Roberts had claimed it was just an innocent experiment that went awry, but he'd gone to jail anyway.

"Peter was looking for background on the virus and somebody gave him my name. I helped him out, and after that, he'd call me when he needed technical background on a story. Like the DoorWay virus." DoorWay, he explained, was a much-hyped new product that had been years in development. Shortly before its release, word got out that it had been infected with a particularly nasty virus during the disk manufacturing process.

Randall winced. "That must have hurt sales."

"Stopped 'em dead. The developer spent millions recalling the packages and checking them out."

"Did they catch it?"

Harry smirked. "Turns out it was all a false rumor.

There never was a virus."

"You're kidding. Did they find out who started the rumors?"

"No. Peter was keeping a file on it. Said he was going to follow up when he could." He swirled the coffee in his cup thoughtfully. "We used to get together every once in a while to play racquetball or go to movies. Then he disappeared."

"Disappeared?"

"Got busy, I guess. Didn't have time to get together."

Disappeared, Randall thought. Became unavailable. Yet another person Peter seemed to have written off.

He hesitated. "How did you hear...about Peter?"

Harry shook his head. "I was in here, reading the paper. Pretty weird, sitting at a table where you had coffee with someone and reading about his death in the paper."

With a chill, Randall realized that he was probably sitting in the same chair Peter had occupied when he and Harry met. He reached into his pocket and pulled out the paper he'd found in Peter's wastebasket. "This is the list I told you about. Do you know these people?"

Harry looked it over and shook his head. "Did you check with the magazine?"

"No." He told Harry about his conversation with Erica Steiner. "She was taking a risk just talking to me. Couldn't even tell me what Peter was working on when he died."

Harry cocked his head. "Oh, yeah?"

"Some kind of internal policy."

"Right," Harry said, looking doubtful. He was quiet for a moment, then stood up. "I'll be right back."

He crossed to the opposite corner of the café, where an army-jacketed youth sat peering into a laptop computer, its display casting a dim blue glow over his face. The young man glanced over the top of his computer as Harry spoke, his hands never leaving the keyboard. A thin smile spread over his face.

A few minutes later, Harry returned to the table and slid a scrap of paper to Randall. A telephone number was written on it.

"What's this?" Randall asked.

"The phone number to dial into PC Monthly's computer system."

Randall glanced at the kid with the laptop. "How'd he do that?"

Harry shook his head. "Rule number one. Don't ask."

OK, Randall thought. "What am I supposed to do with this?"

Harry took the paper back and pocketed it. He gulped the remainder of his coffee and plunked the mug on the table. "Come on. We'll go to my place."

Jack O'Neill was headed to the men's room when Latimer called to him. "Hey, check this out."

O'Neill stuck his head into the office. "What?"

"Just came in," Latimer said, waving a piece of paper. "The triple-eye report on Jacobson."

O'Neill scanned the report. "My, my."

"Yeah. Looks like Mr. Clean wasn't so clean after all." He pointed to the offense section, which listed two numbers. "Nailed a couple of times on 3530 and 3532." The numbers were codes from the Justice Department's Uniform Offense Classifications.

O'Neill handed the paper back to Latimer. "Doesn't look as if he did any time, though."

Lawrence gave him a skeptical look. "Are you kidding?"

It was an old problem. Very few people who were ever arrested actually went to jail for their crimes. Unless a suspect was found with a bloody knife or a wheelbarrow full of cocaine, he usually got off on a plea-bargain—especially if he had a good attorney. "That kid probably had the best lawyer in the business," Latimer said.

O'Neill handed the paper back to him. "Says he was in New Hampshire at the time."

"College," Latimer said, shaking his head. "Dartmouth. These rich kids think they can get away with anything."

"Kind of odd that he hasn't had any contact with the law since then."

It seemed odd to Latimer too. A person with that kind of record was unlikely to reform overnight. He shrugged. "Maybe he cleaned up his act. Or got lucky."

O'Neill chuckled. "Until last week."

"Right. Until last week. Then his luck ran out."

Harry Arnofsky's apartment looked like a library after an earthquake. Books and papers littered every flat surface, spilling onto the floor. Electronic devices—computers, test equipment, monitors—occupied tables, chairs, and floor space. A bookcase lined the longest wall of the room, the central section of it dominated by an immense television and stereo system, with books, videotapes and software packages wedged into every nook and cranny around it. A coffee table in front of the television held a collection of remote control devices. A nearly-empty bag of Doritos completed the decor.

"Sorry about the mess," Harry said. "Maid's year off."

He pulled a swivel chair up to a computer with the largest monitor and pointed to a straight-backed chair with a pile of clothes on it. "Toss that stuff on the floor."

Randall searched the floor for a clear space, but soon abandoned the effort and dropped the clothes onto a stack of papers. By the time he sat down, Harry had already fired up a telecommunications program and dialed into PC Monthly's network.

This system is intended for the use of staff members of PC Monthly magazine, Hildebrande Publishing, and assigned authors only. Use by other parties is prohibited.

The system asked for a user name and password. Harry tried a couple of entries without luck. "Make yourself comfortable," he said. "This may take me a few minutes."

As Harry tapped away, Randall surveyed the room. On the floor nearby was a stack of mail and magazines. A copy of PC Monthly stuck out of the pile. He pulled it out—it was the most recent issue. He flipped to Peter's column.

TrendWatch
Peter Jacobson

A Brave New User Group

A new online service meets needs once filled by civic and religious groups.

Sandra Lopinski was standing in her kitchen when she first heard a far-off rumble, like a freight train approaching from a distance. She recalls thinking it was odd; she didn't know there were any trains in the area.

Sandra hadn't lived in Silicon Valley very long, or she would have known better. The freight train she heard was an earthquake, measuring 6.9 on the Richter scale, and it rumbled through her tiny house, bound not for glory but for destruction.

Sandra Lopinski survived the earthquake, but her house did not, nor did any of her possessions. By some miracle, though, the house next door to Sandra was spared. Its owner, Thom Shepard, couldn't help Sandra very much by himself. But Thom belongs to a unique organization called the Family, whose members rallied to Sandra's aid.

Randall scanned the column. The whole thing was about the Family. Once again, Peter had been one step ahead of him. "Figures."

Harry glanced over. "What?"

It was too much effort to explain the coincidence. He held the magazine up. "Do you know anything about the Family?"

He snickered. "Zomblies."

"What?"

"That's what we call them: Family zombies. A strange bunch."

"Strange, how?"

Harry shrugged. "It started out as a bunch of hackers on the net. Then they went commercial. Added a glitzy interface, started attracting a lot of new members."

Randall pointed to Peter's column. "Says here they've got over 500,000 members."

"I believe it. They're everywhere these days. All over the net, at computer shows. A lot 'em are novices, people who never used computers before, the kind who think they're going to blow something up if they hit the wrong key. Then they join this group and suddenly they're infatuated with computers, like someone who just fell in love or found religion."

He was typing as he spoke. He entered a command and watched as a message appeared on the screen. "All right. We're in."

"Really? How did you—"

Harry shook his head. "Rule number one."

"Right. Don't ask."

On the screen was a list of the system's file areas. Harry pointed to one called PCMSTAFF. "That's where we want to go."

He entered the appropriate command, but the system refused to let him enter. Alternate commands failed as well. "Looks as if this is for editorial staffers only. Guess they don't want the janitor rummaging around here. We'll have to see if we can find a back door."

He continued the search, and Randall turned back to the column.

Family members aren't just glued-to-the-tube nerds. They are community-oriented, helping each other out in times of need and getting involved in civic projects such as providing computer training in schools, low-income areas, and prisons.

Harry stopped typing and chuckled. "Son of a gun." He pointed to the screen. "See that?" His finger indicated the word "HDFIX.DAT" on the screen.

"What is it?"

"Remember the Houdini virus I told you about? There's a program called HDFIX that removes the bug. When it does, it creates HDFIX.DAT, a data file that keeps a record of the infection, when it was removed, and any problems that popped up. That file is a sure sign that a system has been infected by Houdini. Kind of like an appendix scar."

"Seems odd that a major computer magazine couldn't keep its own system from being infected by a virus."

Harry smirked. "Sure does." He entered a few more commands. "Here we go." The screen displayed a long form with highlighted fill-in-the-blank sections. "An online personnel form," Harry said, grinning. "We're about to be hired by PC Monthly."

"What?"

"Don't worry. We'll fire ourselves after we're done."

Moments later, Harry had completed the screen and obtained access to the magazine's entire system.

He did a quick survey. "Looks as if everybody has their own place on the server to store their files." He switched to Peter's section and asked for a list of the files in it.

File area is empty.

Randall frowned at the screen. "I don't get it."

"Someone cleared out the files," Harry said. He thought for a moment, then began searching the other areas. "Here we are: UPCOMING. Let's see if there's anything in here about Peter's column."

He entered the search phrase "peter AND column," and a message appeared on the screen.

==========

pcmstaff #143, from esteiner
Comment(s).

I'm trying to pull together my first TrendWatch column on short notice. Has anyone seen the rough draft of the last column Peter was working on? I can't find it.

==========

They scanned the responses. No one had seen anything.

"No wonder she wouldn't tell you what Pete was working on," Harry said. "She doesn't know herself."

"Strange."

"Very strange." He entered a series of commands. The

screen cleared and a single line appeared along the top.

```
D:\NET\COMNET\MAIN>
```

"What's that?"

"The basement."

"I don't follow you."

"These systems usually have a trap door. It lets the guy who wrote it get at the guts if he needs to make repairs. If you know the programmers, you know where the trap doors are."

He found a directory called TOOLS and asked for a list of the files there. "Great. They've got Rescue."

"What's that?"

"Lets you recover files after they've been erased."

"You can do that?"

"Sometimes. It's like that list you found in Pete's wastebasket. The files aren't really gone until you empty the trash."

He directed the program to list the files that had been deleted from Peter's area. One of them was a subdirectory labeled AUGUST. "Let's see what was in there."

Name	Created	R.I.
NEWS.TMP	5-7-90	-3
DIANE.BAK	5-9-90	-3
COMDEX.BOB	5-9-90	-3
AWARDS.TMP	5-11-90	-3
COLUMN.AUG	5-12-90	-3
LOGIN.EXE	5-19-90	-3

"Interesting," Harry said, and pointed to the last line on the screen.

"What?"

"That's a log-in program. Lets you create your own trap door in a system."

"Did Peter do that?"

"Not too likely. He already had access to the system."

"So who–"

"Somebody else must have gotten in—probably the same way we did. But they wanted to make sure they could get back on any time they liked. So they installed their own trap door to the system, then erased the program that made it. Covering their tracks."

Randall pointed to the screen. "What does 'R.I.' mean?"

"Rescue Index. Tells you the chances of recovering a particular file. Minus three means 'fat chance.' Let's try this. If you know how to ask, it'll tell you when a file was erased."

He entered a command and the list of files appeared again.

```
Rescue analysis: D:\NET\PETERJ \AUG

Name          Created Erased
-------------------------
NEWS.TMP      5-7-90   5-19-90
DIANE.BAK     5-9-90   5-19-90
COMDEX.BOB    5-9-90   5-19-90
AWARDS.TMP    5-11-90  5-19-90
COLUMN.AUG    5-12-90  5-19-90
LOGIN.EXE     5-19-90  5-19-90
```

Harry stared at the screen. "They were all erased on May 19."

"May 19," Randall said. "The day Peter died."

8

Phil Giordano pulled the Saab into the carport and saw that Livvy's car was already there. He smiled, his pulse quickening. Normally, he arrived home before she did. She must have left work early today. He was pretty sure he knew why.

They had not had sex in two weeks. This "fasting period" was important, they were told, as it helped clear the mind of the bad programming they'd received about sex.

Phil didn't know anything about bad programming, but he was sure of one thing. They had never gone this long without sex. In the early days, they had made love several times a day—sexaerobics, they called it. And even after a few years, they were still doing it at least three times a week. They had never gone more than a few days without making love. After two weeks, Phil was more than ready.

Livvy heard Phil's car pull up and rubbed her bare legs together under the sheets. At the thought of his arrival, a warm, liquid rush went through her. She was ready.

She heard his footsteps bounding up the stairs, and Phil appeared in the doorway, breathing hard. She threw the covers back, revealing the new black negligee she'd bought that day. "Hey, you."

Phil undressed in about ten seconds and leapt on the bed. Their foreplay took another fifteen seconds. Normally, Phil was a sensitive, careful lover, attentive to his wife's needs, timing his own excitement to hers. Today, they were two wild animals. He lifted her, covered her body with his, rode her like a wild pony, and she loved it.

She shuddered, and he came, his warmth hitting her higher up and stronger than it ever had before. She groaned with pleasure, and a broad smile creased her face. She knew instinctively that this time was different from all the others. This time they would conceive. They had a guarantee of that. Their Shepherd had said so.

Randall returned to the hotel, his mind replaying what he'd learned. On the day Peter died, someone had deleted his files from the computer at his office. Was that just routine housekeeping, something the company did when a person left the company? If that was the case, why didn't anyone at the office know about it?

He fell onto the bed and leaned against the headboard. He was tired, but his mind was going too fast to allow sleep, and he was tired of thinking. He grabbed the remote control from the bedside stand and flicked the television on.

Upbeat music blared from the set as images of computers and electronics crossed and faded into one another. The music tapered off, the images dissolving to show a dark-haired woman in a green suit behind a news desk.

"Hello, and welcome to the PC Show. I'm Virginia Jones. Today we'll be looking at new accounting software from ZyTech, and an exciting new multimedia presentation of Shakespeare's works. Then we'll talk with Fordham Graves, Executive Director of the fastest growing–"

The phone rang. Randall hit the mute button on the remote control, silencing the television.

"Hello?"

"Yeah. It's Harry." Harry's voice was flat, and although Randall had just met him, he could tell something was wrong.

"What's up?"

"I was thinking about the police and wondering what they knew. So I decided to do some checking."

He was beginning to realize that Harry's idea of "checking" wasn't the same as other people's. "Yes?"

"I got a copy of the police record on Peter."

He considered asking how he'd done that, but decided against it. "Do they know what happened to him?"

"No. The report doesn't say anything about his death."

"Then what–"

"This was from before," Harry said.

"Before what? What do you mean?"

"I mean," Harry said slowly, "Peter had a police record."

Randall felt disbelief, sadness, and disappointment all at once, like a kid being told the truth about Santa Claus. "What kind of record?"

"If I'm reading these codes right, he was arrested on drug charges. Several times."

"What?"

"That's what it says here. Possession. Intent to sell."

"That's crazy. Peter?"

"Yeah," Harry said gloomily. "Peter."

Randall sank back against the headboard of the bed. With a sickening sensation, he realized that drugs explained a lot: the financial problems, the stress, the distancing from old friends. Still, it seemed impossible, so totally unlike the Peter he'd known. "Are you sure you've got the right person?"

"Peter Alan Jacobson," Harry said. "Born August 17, 1963. Five feet 11 inches. Brown hair. Brown eyes."

It was Peter.

Neither one spoke for a moment. "Well, I thought you'd want to know," Harry said.

"Yeah. Thanks." He hung up the phone.

On the silent television, the host sat with a pin-striped young man in front of a flickering computer screen. She turned from the computer and mouthed words to the camera. The screen dissolved to a commercial.

Virginia Jones readjusted her lapel mike to make sure the cord was still hidden in the folds of her moss green suit. She glanced at the monitor between the two cameras, satisfied that the suit highlighted her dark hair and eyes.

A voice came through the earphone in her left ear. "Virginia, we're coming out of the commercial in five."

The red light on camera one blinked on. A young woman in blue jeans held up five splayed fingers, then four, three, two, and one. She pointed to Virginia.

"Hello, and welcome back to the PC Show." As she spoke, the words scrolled down a see-through teleprompter attached to the front of the camera. "With me now is Fordham Graves, executive director of the fastest growing online computer organization in the country, the Family."

Camera one pulled back to include Virginia and her guest in the shot. Fordham Graves was a broad, middle-aged man with thick white hair that swept back from his forehead, a neatly-trimmed white mustache framing his square jaw. A bright white dress shirt—practically glowing against his florid, craggy face—pinched his neck muscles into tiny pleats. His suit was impeccable, from the double-stitched lapels to the perfect quarter-inch of sleeve at the cuff. As they chatted during the break, Jones had noted the suit. Clearly, this was no off-the-rack garment. If Fordham Graves had not been a corporate

CEO, he would have made a good United States senator.

"Welcome to our show," she said. "Can you tell us a little about the Family?"

A confident smile creased Graves' ruddy face. "Certainly. The Family is a unique combination of online service, user group, and volunteer organization."

"Would that be something like America Online or CompuServe?" The question was a "toss," a comment that gave her something to say and kept the conversation from becoming a monologue.

"Exactly, although we consider those systems to be first-generation technology. The Family is a much more advanced system."

She let him ramble about the Family's features for a minute, then said, "I understand the Family is different in other ways, isn't it? Your members are active in public service projects, teaching others about computers, that kind of thing."

"That's correct. We're not ashamed of the fact that service to others is a key principle behind our organization. We want to help people use computers to make the world a better place to live in. We're not out to make money."

Right, Jones thought, although she nodded thoughtfully—she had long ago learned not to let her face show what she was really thinking, regardless of how silly or self-serving a guest's comments might be. "Is it true that membership in the Family is free?"

"That's right. The group is entirely supported by donations from individuals who believe in what we're trying to do. Also, it's important to note that the Family is a non-commercial organization run by its members."

"When you say the Family is run by its members, how does that work?"

Graves spread his hands wide. "We're really a grass-roots organization. This allows us to function without a huge organizational structure. Each of the members takes part in activities, community service outreach, training—"

"But you're the head of the organization, is that right?"

Graves smiled patiently. "Not exactly. I'm merely the executive director. The senior member, if you will."

"So how does the group operate?"

"It really runs itself. The entire point of the operation is to put computing power into the hands of people, not to invest it in some large organization or company. We really feel that the large computer companies like CompuSys and Megasoft have had far too much power—"

A groan came through Jones' earphone. It was her producer. CompuSys and Megasoft were both large advertisers on the PC Show. It was time to change the subject.

"Can you give us a demonstration of the system?" she said quickly.

Graves' smile dimmed just slightly. "Certainly."

On the counter behind them, a computer displayed the colorful opening screen of the Family. They turned to the computer and Graves reached for the mouse next to it. The sleeve of his jacket slid back to reveal a large gold Rolex watch. Like the suit, it bespoke money and power—not the kind of accouterments Jones associated with a "volunteer organization." She had worked with grass-roots political and cultural groups when she was younger. In her experience, volunteer organizations usually went hand-in-hand with crummy offices, lunches from McDonald's, and a dress-code just a few notches above that of the average street person. Graves certainly didn't fit the mold.

Graves led Jones and her viewers on a tour of the Family's house. Despite her skepticism about Graves, she was impressed by the technology behind the Family.

A studio assistant held up a card indicating there was one minute left in the segment. It was time to wrap up.

"How can our viewers find out more about the Family?"

"We welcome people to call our 800 number and try out the Family free of charge," Graves said. "There's no obligation to join."

"But you do have to join before you have access to all the services of the Family."

"That's right. There are various features and privileges that are available only to members, and these features require a commitment to the organization in terms of time and effort. This allows us to keep our expenses down. As I said, we're not in this for the money, like most large computer companies–"

The producer's voice came through Jones' earphone again. "Oh, for cryin' out loud."

Jones knew she'd need to sidetrack Graves before he got too far into dangerous territory. "And again, there's no cost to–"

Graves seemed not to hear her. "Our goal is to use computers to make the world a better place in which to live, not to make the heads of corporations rich or famous."

Her gentle nudge hadn't moved Graves off his soapbox. She would have to give him a more forceful shove. "I've heard that members of the Family can be a little fanatical. Is that true?"

Graves paused, smiling indulgently. "The group does inspire a certain loyalty. That's because our members understand how important our mission is to–"

"But you don't do anything to foster that sense of zealousness?"

"No, not at all."

"No secret handshakes or initiation rites?"

Graves' manufactured smile became tense. A hard cast appeared in his eyes. "No. No secret handshakes. This is an organization of computer enthusiasts, not the Masonic Lodge.

"Well, thanks so much for taking the time to be with us tonight."

"You're welcome," Graves said.

She turned to camera one. "We'll be right back with a look at a new word processing software from Dulterra International. Don't go away."

The light on the camera went out as Jones turned back to Graves. "Thanks for–"

Graves was already standing, the smile gone from his face. He stripped the lapel mike from his tie, deposited it on the desktop, and strolled off the set without speaking or looking back at Jones.

9

Randall stepped from his room into the hallway of the hotel. A copy of the morning paper lay in front of the door. He picked it up, tossed it back into the room, and closed the door.

At Allison's apartment, he buzzed several times before she answered in a sleepy voice. "Yes?"

"It's Randall," he said, and she buzzed him in. She opened her door looking sleepy and puzzled. "Hi. I thought you were leaving."

"I was. But I...had something to do first."

She nodded uncertainly. "Do you want some coffee?"

"Sure. Thanks."

He followed her in. She wore a man's dress shirt—Peter's, he was sure—and as far as he could tell, little or nothing underneath it. He tried not to stare at her legs.

He took a seat at the kitchen table. "How are you doing?"

She shrugged, a gesture that said "not great." She reached into a high cabinet for a mug, exposing even more of her legs. He tried very hard not to look at them.

"I was planning to go back to work today," she said. "But I couldn't do it."

She poured coffee for him and sat. "I try not to think about it," she said. "But it's not easy." She rested her forehead on her hands and began to cry. "If only I'd been there..."

He reached for her and this time did not hesitate, taking her hand in his. "Allison, it wasn't your fault."

"Yes it was. If I hadn't–"

"No," he said firmly, gripping her hand. "It wasn't."

She looked at him doubtfully and withdrew her hand from his. "What do you mean?"

"I don't know exactly. But there are odd things going on, things I don't understand."

"Like what?"

He hesitated. The last thing he wanted was to upset her more than she already was. But she had been closer to Peter than anyone else.

Start with the easy questions, he told himself. He pulled out the list of names he'd found in Peter's wastebasket and slid it across the table. "Do any of those names mean anything to you? Other than mine?"

She stared at the list without touching it. "No." Then she added, "Maybe the last one. He talked about someone named Harry. But I never met him."

"The first two names don't mean anything to you?"

"No."

He took the list back. Now for the hard part. If Peter had been using drugs, did that mean she was too? Would she answer him honestly if she was? He took a deep breath. "Allison, did Peter have a drug problem?"

She blinked, and frowned. "No," she said, as if annoyed by the question.

"He never used illegal drugs as far as you know?"

"Never."

He stared into his coffee cup. Either she was lying, or Erica Steiner was right about her. Maybe Allison was just naive and had totally missed—or fooled herself into ignoring—Peter's involvement with drugs.

"The police have records," he said finally, and now that

he had begun, there was no stopping. "According to their files, Peter was arrested on drug charges. Several times."

Allison shook her head, as if confused, unable to get her bearings. "The police told you that?"

He decided not to tell her how he'd found out. No point getting her involved, or upsetting her about things she didn't need to know. "Yes."

"It's not true," she said, crossing her arms tightly over her chest. "Peter wasn't like that."

"I know," he said. Peter hadn't been like that, at least not the Peter he had known. Apparently neither of them had known Peter as well as they thought.

"Peter was upset," Allison said, as if trying to convince herself. "He was...stressed out from work. But he didn't use drugs."

Randall nodded, but said nothing. If it was easier for her to think that Peter had killed himself because he was stressed out and upset over their breakup, so be it.

"You don't believe me," she said.

He looked up at her. He wanted to believe her, for her sake as well as his own. But the police had records. He said nothing.

She stood and walked quickly from the room, wiping tears from her cheeks. Moments later, a door slammed down the hallway.

He sat for a minute. The coffee maker dripped, hissing on its metal warmer. Allison didn't return, and he thought about checking on her, but decided against it. She had to deal with this in her own way. He left, closing the apartment door quietly, a deep furrow creasing his brow.

Bill Latimer read the article on the front page of the morning paper, his mood darkening as he did.

Feds Report Credit Break-In

PHOENIX, AZ - The FBI revealed today that computer hackers recently broke into the computer system of the American Credit Bureau, one of the nation's three largest credit reporting institutions. Apparently, no damage was done to ACB's computers during the break-in, which occurred last month. The break-in was not immediately reported, according to FBI spokesperson Margaret Bradford, because the agency hoped to catch the criminals in the act. When the break-in was not repeated, ACB programmers decided to close the loophole that had allowed the computer criminals to crack the system.

The incident marks the second time the bureau's computers have been broken into. Earlier this year, the system was the victim of a computer virus called Houdini that spread via the Internet.

"Bastards," Latimer muttered. Though he would never have admitted it, computers made him nervous. When he started out as a detective, crime was dirty, mean, and ugly, but at least you could see it. In the computer era, crime had become neat, clean, and practically invisible.

Latimer was not in a good mood, had not been in a good mood for days, and it was Peter Jacobson's fault. Although he had filed the Jacobson case away, his mind refused to let it rest. It came back to him as he watched television at night, as he lay in bed, as he drove to work in the morning. The case was like a dog barking in the backyard, complaining until you let it back in.

The bark went like this: a rich kid has an expensive drug habit, one that even his closest friends don't know about. He runs through his own money, as well as the money his mother left him. He's estranged from his stepfather, so there's no more cash there. He borrows money, but can't pay it back. He's strung out, and now he can't buy his way out of trouble. Eventually, things get so bad, he decides to end it all.

It was neat, it was clean–and something about it bothered him. He just couldn't figure out what. He opened the paper to the second page and spread it out on his desk.

Possible Drug Connection in Journalist's Death

SAN FRANCISCO - A source close to the investigation into the death of Peter Jacobson has indicated that drugs may have been a factor. Jacobson, a popular columnist for PC Monthly magazine, fell to his death from the Golden Gate Bridge on May 19. The circumstances of the fall are still under investigation. However, a source close to the case has revealed that Jacobson had previously been arrested on charges of cocaine possession as well as possession with intent to sell.

Latimer pounded a fist on the paper. "Son of a bitch." He scanned the story for a byline, but found none.

He picked up the phone, called the Chronicle and asked for the news desk.

"City desk," came a man's voice. "Wayne Stoller."

"Mr. Stoller, this is Detective Latimer at San Francisco Police Department."

There was a pause. "Good morning, Detective. What can I do for you?"

"This item in today's paper about Peter Jacobson. Did you write that?"

"Jacobson? Hold on a minute."

Latimer waiting, steaming. As if a reporter couldn't remember every word he'd written for the last ten years.

"Yes, I guess I did write that."

"This bit about drugs being a factor. Where'd you get that?"

"He did have an arrest record, didn't he, detective?"

"That's confidential information. Obtaining that kind of information for anything other than investigative purposes constitutes a serious criminal offense."

"I suppose that depends on where one obtains the information, doesn't it?"

Latimer's ears burned. Stoller was right. Anything a person found out on their own was perfectly legal. It was only illegal to obtain information using the NCIC system. And even with the NCIC, there was no uniform code of law regarding the use and abuse of the system. "So where did you obtain the information?"

"That's confidential information, detective. I'm afraid I can't reveal my sources without jeopardizing their privacy."

I'll jeopardize your privacy, Latimer thought. I'll wring your friggin' neck.

"Is there anything else I can do for you?" Stoller asked.

Latimer wanted to tell the weasel where to shove it, but restrained himself. It never helped to piss off members of the press, even if they were weasels.

"No," he said, and hung up quickly.

Wayne Stoller put the phone down, grinning. As a rule, it didn't pay to piss off members of the law enforcement community, even if they were self-important bastards. You never knew when you might need their help. But Latimer had pushed him too far with that "serious criminal offense" business.

Stoller reached for his in-basket and thumbed through the papers until he found the fax on Peter Jacobson and pulled it out. There was no originating number on the fax, no indication where it had come from. Some anonymous benefactor had simply taken it upon himself to fax Peter Jacobson's criminal record to him. Latimer's warning about the illegality of accessing the criminal records system might have worried Stoller if he had used the system himself. But he hadn't been anywhere near it. He'd simply received a fax.

He stuck the fax back in bottom of the pile, chuckling to himself. "That's confidential information, detective."

10

The receptionist at the Hildebrande Building, a middle-aged black woman with dark-rimmed glasses, asked Randall his name, then punched a button on the console. She listened through her headset and looked up at him. "Ms. Steiner is out of the office today."

"Do you know when she'll be back?"

"Not till tomorrow. She's at PC CON."

"Where's that?"

"PC CON," the woman said patiently. "Big computer show. Over at Moscone." She gave him directions to Moscone Center and said, "She'll be there all day."

He decided to try finding her there. The disappearance of Peter's files still bothered him, and he wanted to know if that was just routine maintenance, or worse. But there was something else he had to check first.

He found a phone booth and pulled out the list of names from Peter's wastebasket. The phone book had no listing for Ed Truman, Laurie Donoway or Martin Marks. There was, however, a listing for a company on Washington Street called Martin & Marks. He looked at the paper again. He had misread Peter's handwriting. "Martin A. Marks" was actually "Martin & Marks," apparently the company Laurie Donoway worked for.

He called the number.

"Good afternoon, Martin & Marks. How may I direct

your call?"

"Can I speak to Laurie Donoway, please?"

"She's at PC CON today. Is there anyone else who can help you?"

Everybody in the city, it seemed, was at PC CON. But now he knew Martin & Marks had something to do with computers. "I was planning on heading over there. Can you tell me where I might catch up with her?"

"Your best bet is to check with the folks at the CompuSys booth."

"CompuSys?"

"That's right. CompuSys is her account."

"Thanks. Hey, can you give me Laurie's exact title? For my records?"

"Sure. She's a public relations associate."

He hung up the phone. Martin & Marks was a public relations firm, representing CompuSys. Now he was getting somewhere.

Moscone Hall is located in the SoMa district, "south of Market," the broad thoroughfare that cuts across the center of San Francisco and separates the older, gentrified districts in the northern half of the city from the apartments, warehouses, condominiums, and warehouse-condominiums in the southern half. Moscone is large, gray, and not particularly attractive, like a giant parking garage on steroids.

Randall parked at an off-street lot and found his way to the front entrance of the building. Outside, a carnival atmosphere reigned: vendors peddled gourmet ice-cream bars at twice the normal price. Men in white styrofoam straw hats and women with banners across their chests pressed fliers into the hands of attendees that streamed into and out of the show. A line of taxies discharged and picked up passengers, all of whom were dressed in business attire.

A group of people paraded on the sidewalk in front of the building, shouting slogans and carrying signs that read, "CompuSys: Just Say NO!" and "PC Power to the People."

Randall passed two young men in dark suits and overheard one of them say, as he gestured to the protesters. "What's that about?"

"Zomblies," his companion said. "They've got something against CompuSys."

The first man nodded, as if that were explanation enough. "I made the mistake of criticizing the Family when I was online once. Won't do that again."

"They harass you?"

"You wouldn't believe it. I got all this e-mail telling me what a great organization it was, how I should give it another chance, yada yada. They were nice enough, but who wants to bother with all that?"

"Nuts."

Randall passed through the entrance into the lobby, where a line of booths stretched along the wall, and large signs overhead stated "General Admission" and "Exhibitors." To one side was a booth marked "Press." He presented his business card to the woman behind the desk, hoping the Peabody Times would pass muster as a legitimate publication. She scanned the card over the top of her half glasses, like an inspector at Ellis Island. With a quick glance at him, she copied his name on a list and handed him a fat convention guidebook and a badge with a bright green ribbon attached to it.

He joined the stream of people passing under a large archway into the main show floor. If the atmosphere outside the hall had seemed like a carnival, the inside was Mardi Gras, Las Vegas, and Disneyland all rolled into one. Huge, colorful banners hung from the ceiling proclaiming the names of the hardware and software companies occupying the booths below—although "booths" hardly described the giant, store-like displays that had been erected there. Music blared from speakers, punctuated by the sound of voices like barkers hawking their wares. In the aisles outside the exhibits, handsome young men and women in matching polo shirts pressed literature into the already-stuffed arms and plastic bags of people walking the aisles.

The hall had been divided into rows, with hundreds of exhibit booths lining the aisles, like a giant supermarket of computer technology. The largest booths, located in the high-traffic area just inside the entrance to the hall, had been claimed by the major computer companies.

Randall scanned the hall and saw a towering sign that jutted up from a nearby booth: CompuSys. He edged his way toward the booth, where four large-screen projection televisions hung suspended from the ceiling above the heads of the conventioneers, one at each corner of the booth. All the screens showed the same image: Gerald Barr, standing at a podium, delivering an address. The camera had been positioned slightly below the podium, at an angle that accentuated Barr's pointed chin and large forehead topped off by the characteristic curly hair. The unfortunate choice of angle reinforced an image that more than one journalist had suggested: Gerry Barr was a chicken, or—as some had more cynically ventured—a vulture.

Barr's words echoed over the buzz and chatter of the show: "The coming information revolution will call for new approaches to software design."

Randall took a position next to a young woman who stood, arms crossed, staring up at the screen. "What's this?" he asked.

"Keynote address," the woman said. "They're

broadcasting it from the main hall." She shook her head disdainfully. "His royal highness addresses the masses."

Barr continued, "These new approaches will open a world of interactive computing, with a free flow of information across all types of computers..."

The woman rolled her eyes. "What a joke. The only free flow Gerry's interested in is the flow of money into his own bank account. This is like Rockefeller talking about the evils of monopolies."

Randall nodded. From what he'd heard, Barr was a shrewd businessman in nerd's clothing. More than one competitor had underestimated his abilities.

"Well, with any luck, the government will fix his boat," the woman said.

"How so?"

She glanced at him as if wondering what boat he had just stepped off of. "They're under investigation? By the government?"

"Oh, right," he said. "I heard about that." He hadn't.

"Special Senate committee," she said. "There are all kinds of allegations–unethical practices, squeezing small companies out of business. They're even making noises about breaking the company up, like Ma Bell. Which would serve Barr right."

"You're not a fan," Randall said.

"I almost took a job with them once. You wouldn't believe the baloney they tried to hand me. All this stuff about the 'culture of CompuSys'. No smoking, mandatory health program, required carpooling." She shook her head. "I told them to forget it. I've already got a nagging mother." She laughed and headed off down the aisle.

Randall waded into the CompuSys booth. It had been designed like a mini-mall, with separate areas and salespeople for each of the company's many products. He roamed for a while, scanning name tags for that of Laurie

Donoway. After several minutes of fruitless searching, he stopped at the front desk, where two perky young women—"booth bunnies" he had heard them called—handed out CompuSys pens to passing conventioneers.

One of the bunnies handed Randall a pen. "Thanks," he said. "Can you tell me where Laurie Donoway is?"

She glanced at Randall's green ribbon and cranked up her smile another notch. "Sure. She's right over there, talking to someone from PC Computing."

He followed her gesture. Laurie Donoway was model-thin, with sandy-blonde hair cut very short—the assertive female executive look. She wore heels, a dark skirt and matching jacket over a silky white blouse. She was talking to a short bearded man in an ill-fitting suit, who seemed to be held in rapt attention, either by what she was saying or by the blouse.

Randall walked toward them and heard her say, "Thanks so much, Russell. I'll be in touch with you." She shook his hand, indicating clearly that her business with him was finished.

The man left reluctantly, and Donoway turned to Randall, a bright smile on her face. "Hi, how are you?" She shook his hand firmly.

"Fine. My name is Randall McLagan."

"Nice to meet you, Randall. I'm Laurie Donoway. How can I help you?"

"I'm a friend of Peter Jacobson's."

She nodded, still smiling. "Uh-huh?"

He waited for her to make the connection. Finally, light dawned. "Oh, yes. My gosh." She took Randall's hand again and held it warmly. "I was so sorry to hear."

"Thanks. I was wondering if you could help me out with something?"

She cocked her head slightly. "Of course. What is it?"

"I was going through Peter's stuff and I found this

piece of paper." He pulled the list of names from his pocket. "I was wondering if you had any idea why Peter might have written your name on this list?"

She smiled quizzically. "Well...I work with an awful lot of writers. That's what I do."

"Had you talked to Peter recently?"

"No. I gave him some information for a column a few months back." She looked down, tapping her foot, then back up at him. "I was so sorry to hear...well, you know..."

"So you hadn't spoken?"

She glanced at her watch. "Oh, my gosh, I've got a two o'clock and I'm late. Can we talk later?"

"Sure, I guess so."

She picked up a purse from behind a nearby counter and pulled a formal-looking card from it. "CompuSys is having a reception at the Meridien Hotel downtown. Why don't you come? We can talk more there."

He took the card and slipped it into his coat pocket. "OK. Thanks."

"Great. Any time after six. I'll see you there." With that, she was gone.

All right, he thought. Next task–find Erica Steiner.

But if Steiner was at PC CON, she was not being highly visible. He began at the first aisle of the show and traversed the hall, looking for the tell-tale green press ribbon and scanning faces. Finally, he saw a short young woman whose badge read, "Marilyn Hillson, PC Monthly."

"Excuse me. Do you know where Erica Steiner is?"

She glanced at his badge. "You could try the press room."

He found his way to the press room, a long rectangular space with four rows of tables placed end to end running most of the length of the room. Each table was laden with stacks of press kits, arranged in alphabetical order by company. Men and women with green badges, cameras, and notepads wandered up and down the rows, picking at the materials as if they were entrées at a buffet table. A few took one of everything, stuffing the colorful folders into plastic bags. Others strolled casually, sampling a press release here and there, scanning and replacing those that didn't appeal to them

At the far end of the room were a dozen round tables where members of the press sat eating, drinking, and scanning the press kits. Against the wall was another long table that held bowls of ice and soda, trays of cold cuts, cheese and crackers. People who looked as if they hadn't eaten in days hovered around the table like flies around a carcass.

Randall circled the room, but there was no sight of Erica Steiner. At a table near the buffet, a man and a woman sat eating sandwiches. As he passed, the man said, "You heard about Peter Jacobson?"

Randall glanced at them quickly—a chubby middle-aged man in a bulging gray suit and a small woman with curly brown hair. He turned to the buffet table, picked up a plastic cup from the table and filled it with punch, listening intently.

"Yeah," the woman said. "What happened to him?"

"Flipped out, I guess. Too much pressure."

"Sheesh. We're all in trouble, then."

"Right. But apparently there was more to it." Randall watched from the corner of his eye. The man leaned toward the woman, held a finger aside one nostril and whispered something Randall couldn't hear.

"Really?"

"That's what I heard."

"Well, it's too bad," the woman said. "He was a good writer."

"Yeah."

Heat rose from Randall's collar. He wanted to confront them, to defend Peter's reputation, but he held back. He didn't know these people, and their conversation was none of his business. He was angry, and he realized that he was angry in part because he wasn't positive they were wrong.

A beep and a message at the bottom of the screen alerted Sam Miller that he had mail. He went to the Mail Room and clicked the Read button.

TO: Miller, Sam
FROM: Bob Dunbar
SUBJECT: Welcome aboard!

Hi, Sam,
You probably don't know me. I work in Digitopia's tech support department. I came across your name in the Family's new member list and thought I'd send a note.
Glad to see that you guys have joined the Family. Joanne and I have been members for a couple of months, and we love it. It's a great organization. If you need help with anything, send me a note or give me a call.

Bob

Sam was amazed. He and Julie had only been members of the Family for a day, and they had already connected with more people than they'd met in their first month in San Francisco. They had received e-mail messages from dozens of members welcoming them to the group, and others they didn't know at all but who shared their interests. It really was like a big family, or an extended tribe.

Julie brought in tea and sat beside him. "Has the meeting started?"

"Not yet."

As new members, they had agreed to attend a series of "onlines," lectures about the goals and philosophy of the Family. It seemed like a small price to pay, given all the services they were getting for free.

Sam entered the password for the special meeting room where the online would be held. A moment later, a slow, melodic theme flowed from the computer, like something by Mendelssohn or Schubert. Then, words and phrases began scrolling down the screen like a colorful waterfall—cities and towns from around the world, screen after screen of them. Eventually, the names dissolved, and a voice spoke, accompanied by text on the screen.

Welcome, children.

You have just seen a visible demonstration that you are not alone in this world. Each of the cities displayed represents someone who, like you, is online at this very moment. As you sit at your computer, you are part of a network that stretches around the world. If you have ever felt alone before, you know now that's not true. We are joined to others, though separated by thousands of miles. We are joined by our desire for peace, for a world without war, hatred, fear, or hunger.

That world is coming, but it will not come unless we are willing to work for it. The power to make that kind of world is at your fingertips right now. It is in your hands, this very moment, in the form of the keyboard in front of you.

You may wonder what you can do to bring about a world of peace and justice. By yourself, you cannot do much. But united with millions of others, you can change the world. We stand on the threshold of a future than can hold either peace and hope, or destruction for all of us. We will decide which one comes to pass.

To that end, each member of the Family must commit to abide by a basic principle known as the First Protocol:

The First Protocol is Love.

Strive at all times to treat others as you would like them to treat you, with respect, courtesy, and kindness. When in doubt, give the other person the benefit of the doubt. Do not judge your fellow members. In all your dealing with other members of the Family, consider love to be the first priority. If each of us adheres to this simple rule, we can lay the foundation for a better world, beginning with our own organization.

The Father

11

By the time PC CON closed for the day, Randall had covered every square inch of the exhibit hall looking for Erica Steiner. He hadn't found her, but he had passed up numerous offers for free software packages, T-shirts emblazoned with company slogans, coffee mugs, pens, key chains, pocket protectors and lapel pins—not to mention exuberant demonstrations of "revolutionary new products" that vendors were sure he, as a member of the press, would be very interested in. He decided that one computer show was probably going to last him a lifetime.

He joined the crowd leaving the hall and pulled out the invitation Laurie Donoway had given him. A map on the back of the card indicated that the Meridien Hotel was a short walk from Moscone.

The weather was cool, as it had been ever since he'd landed. He wondered when the warm, sunny days happened, the days when all those movies and TV commercials set in San Francisco were shot.

A sign in the lobby of the Meridien indicated that the CompuSys reception was in the Baytower Suite. He boarded an elevator with two men and a woman, each of whom wore PC CON press badges.

"You going to the Novell party?" one man asked the other.

"I don't know. AstroTech is having some kind of reception at the Museum of Modern Art."

"Oh, that'll be a real blow-out."

"What do you mean?"

"They're all Mormons," the woman said. "No booze."

"Oh. Well, the food's always good."

"Hey, food you can get anywhere."

They laughed, and the elevator doors slid open to the sounds of a large party already in progress. In the foyer outside the room, a young woman sat at a table taking invitations and business cards. Beyond her, a large door opened into a room crowded with people.

Randall handed her his invitation and business card. "I'm looking for Laurie Donoway."

She checked a list. "She's here, but I'm not sure where. You'll just have to go in and look around." She wrote his name in large round letters on a self-adhesive name tag and handed it to him. He thanked her, stuck the tag on his jacket and headed into the party.

A long buffet table ran down the center of the room, parallel to an immense picture window that looked out toward the bay. In each of the four corners of the room, bartenders tended fully-stocked bars—no one would have to walk far to get another drink at this party. Randall made his way to the nearest bar, asked for a Newcastle, and took up a position at the picture window.

It was dusk, and the Golden Gate Bridge sparkled against the night sky like a giant necklace. He stared at it, focusing on the center of the bridge. In his mind's eye, he saw Peter standing there, staring down at the water.

He closed his eyes to dispel the image and turned back to the party. Two modes of attire dominated the room: one group wore the standard-issue dark suit, dress shirt and fancy tie for men, suit dress, blouse, and matching shoes for women. Those, undoubtedly, were the CompuSys executives and their clients. Others were dressed less formally: short sleeves, tweed jackets, shoes that didn't match the pants. Those were the press folks. Many of them seemed to have come directly from the show floor, their shoulders burdened with bags of press materials, shirts untucked, loud buttons proclaiming their allegiance to a particular operating system or software package. He recognized some of the same people he'd seen in the press room. Now they were loading tiny dishes with as many shrimp as the plates could hold. To one side, a group of grinning subjects gathered around some important personage who was holding court.

Bits of conversation drifted past him, the standard schmooze mix: 1 part business, 1 part pleasure, three parts ego:

"I told them there was no way they could go from beta software to final product in two months."

"She said that? She actually said that?"

"They've always been bottom-line oriented, that's their problem. No vision."

"All right, let's do it. I'll call you next week."

A flash of green caught Randall's eye: a brilliant emerald dress, fitted tightly to the wearer's slim body, with a hem several inches higher than the knee and a cutaway back that exposed smooth shoulder blades. The woman wearing the dress turned slightly, laughing. It was Laurie Donoway.

Randall elbowed his way over and tapped her on the shoulder. "Laurie?"

She turned, glanced quickly at his name tag, and smiled broadly. "Oh, hi." She acted as if they were best friends who hadn't seen each other in months. "I'm so glad you made it."

"Thanks."

She slid an arm under his, the soft curve of her breast

rubbing against his arm. A jolt of testosterone-induced adrenaline surged into his bloodstream. She leaned toward him. "Would you like to meet Gerry?"

"Gerry?"

She grinned. "Gerald Barr."

"Oh." He flushed. Apparently, one was supposed to know who "Gerry" was without asking. "Maybe later," he said, trying to get a grip on himself. "I really wanted to talk about Peter."

"Peter?"

"Peter Jacobson?"

Once again, the light dawned. "Oh, that's right. I was so sorry to hear the news."

She had said the exact same words earlier, and he wondered if that her standard line when acquaintances plunged to their deaths from the Golden Gate Bridge?

He glanced around. "Is there someplace a little quieter where we could talk?"

"Sure. There's a private suite next door. We can talk in there."

She led him across the room, arm still in his, followed by several pair of envious male eyes. They passed through the heavy mahogany door to the suite and she closed it behind them. The muffled sounds of the party filtered through the walls. A despoiled buffet table occupied the middle of the room.

"We had dinner in here before the party," she said. "Would you like anything to eat or drink?"

He hoisted his beer. "I'll just finish this."

Laurie poured herself some white wine and nodded toward a huge white leather sofa by the window. "Let's sit over there."

She sat, leaned back and crossed her legs, the dress riding up even higher on her obviously Stairmastered thighs. Randall sat beside her, leaning forward so as not to sink into the enveloping sofa.

"I really was sorry to hear about Peter," she said. "I didn't know him very well, but he seemed like a nice guy."

Randall nodded, gripping his beer with both hands. "You mentioned that you had helped him out with him a column?"

She took a sip of wine and rolled it around on her tongue. "Uh-huh."

"What was that about?"

"CompuCalc. It's the new spreadsheet program from CompuSys. Have you seen it?"

"No," he said slowly, wondering if his tone betrayed how little he cared about CompuCalc. "Peter contacted you about that?"

"Right. He was looking for background information, technical details, that kind of thing."

"How did he seem? When you talked to him?"

She shrugged. "Fine."

"Did he seem upset, or stressed out?"

She thought for a moment. "Well, he did seem as if he were under a lot of stress. But I think that's normal for this business."

"And that was the last time you talked to him?"

"Right." She put her wine glass down and moved closer to him. "This has been really hard for you, hasn't it?"

He glanced at her, then away. "How do you mean?"

"I mean, losing your friend and all."

Randall sipped his beer. "Losing him is hard enough. Not knowing what happened to him is harder."

"What happened? But didn't he..." She hesitated, unwilling or unable to complete the sentence.

"Kill himself?" He shrugged. "I don't know. He wasn't the kind to do that. And there are other things..."

"What kinds of things?"

He turned to face her. She stared into his eyes, open, willing to hear him out. He decided not to mention the drug question or the police record. "Well, there was the column he was working on when he died. No one seems to know what it was about."

She took a large drink from her wine glass. "Not even the people at the magazine?"

"Not as far as I can tell."

"Does it really matter?"

He shrugged. "I'm just looking for answers. Anything that will help me figure this out."

She moved still closer to him. "Randall? Can I say something?"

Her side was pressed against his now. The smell of her perfume was strong. It occurred to him that this was the kind of woman Peter hung out with, the kind Erica Steiner said would have been glad to be with him—strong, intelligent, beautiful. And she had something she wanted to tell him.

"I think you need to let go of this," she said.

"How do you mean?"

She squeezed his hand. "Peter's gone. Nothing you can do will bring him back. I think you're just torturing yourself with this."

He looked at her closely. They had barely met. What made her think she knew him well enough to make that kind of judgment? Her eyes were liquid; she'd probably had too much to drink. Maybe that accounted for her forwardness.

"I've got an idea," she said, leaning forward.

"What's that?"

"Not many people know this, but CompuSys has a cabin in the mountains. It's for the senior staff and guests, when they need to get away or have meetings. I happen to know it's not being used this weekend. How would you like to go up there?"

He looked at her, surprised, unsure of what was really being offered.

"It's a beautiful spot," she said. "There's a stream nearby, and–."

He shook his head. "I don't think–"

"I think it would be good for you to get away. It's not like you'd have to schmooze with anyone. We'd be the only ones there."

Now, at least, he knew what was being offered. And he couldn't believe it. He'd just met this woman, and she was inviting him to the mountains for a weekend. Alone.

He stared at the empty beer bottle in his hands. The offer was more than tempting. And maybe she was right. Maybe he was inventing difficulties where none existed. Maybe he just needed to give it a rest, to let go of Peter.

She took his arm and stood. "Don't make up your mind right now. Let's go back to the party. We can visit a bit more, and then you can decide. Besides..." She took the bottle from him. "You need another beer."

Randall looked in her eyes. They played back and forth on his, calculating, analyzing.

It was the eyes that made him realize what was happening: Laurie Donoway had no interest in him. He wasn't sure why she wanted him to go to the mountains. Maybe she was trying to get him to forget about Peter, or maybe she just wanted to get some PR for CompuSys. But something in her eyes told him clearly there was an ulterior motive to this offer.

"Is there a restroom around here?" he asked.

"Sure. Back through the door to the other room and to the left down the hall."

"OK. I'll catch up with you."

"Don't get lost."

They went through the mahogany door. Laurie went to the right, back into the fray of the party. Randall turned left, where a small group of people stood in the hallway chatting. Past them was the bathroom, and beyond that a door with an exit sign over it. As soon as Laurie was out of sight, Randall slipped past the group in the hall and through the door.

The door opened to the foyer. By now, the party had spilled out there as well. He made his way through the partygoers to the elevators.

An elevator opened and a load of guests erupted into the foyer. The last person off the elevator was Erica Steiner.

She saw Randall and cocked her head. "Well, look who's here."

"I was going to say the same thing." He nodded toward the empty elevator. "Ride down to the lobby with me."

They entered, and the doors closed behind them. "Peter's files aren't on the system at the office, are they?" he said.

Her face went blank. "What makes you say that?"

"I found out."

She looked away for a second, hesitating, as if coming to a decision. "I've checked with everyone. No one knows where Peter's files went. Somebody must have erased them, but no one will admit to it."

"Did you ask Bragdon?"

"Jack? Are you kidding? He wouldn't tell me."

"Maybe he can't."

"What?"

"Maybe it wasn't someone at the office."

She frowned. "What do you mean?"

"Someone broke into your system the day Peter died."

She looked doubtful. "Who told you that?"

"Nobody. I found out. And I think whoever broke into

your system erased Peter's files."

"Why would they do that?"

The elevator came to the bottom floor. Randall held the Close Door button and pressed the button for the Baytower Suite again. The elevator began to climb. "I don't know. That's what I'm trying to find out." He pulled the list of names from his pocket. "Do these names mean anything to you?"

She scanned the list. "Only one. Laurie Donoway. She's a flack for Martin & Marks. Stay away from her."

He shook his head. "Too late."

"Oh, yeah? Well, be careful. She's dangerous."

"In what way?"

"Well, to begin with, she's in bed with half the columnists in the industry."

"She feeds them information?"

"No, she's in bed with them."

"Oh." He felt foolish. Then a thought occurred to him. "Including Peter?"

Erica shook her head firmly. "No. He didn't have very good judgment when it came to women, but he was on to her."

"In what way?"

Erica lowered her eyebrows. "Just stay away from Laurie Donoway."

He decided not to tell her about Laurie's offer of a weekend getaway. "She thinks I should drop this, that I'm making something out of nothing."

"If she thinks you should drop it, there's a damn good reason not to."

They rode in silence for a while. "Was Peter having financial problems?" he asked.

"Not that I knew of. Why?"

"I found some unpaid bills at his apartment. Big ones."

She rolled her eyes. "I hope you don't come to my

apartment."

"That wasn't like Peter. These were huge bills, months overdue."

"OK, that's hard to believe." She agreed that Peter wasn't the type to let bill slide.

The elevator arrived at the top floor.

"I've got to get off of this thing," she said. "The ride is starting to get to me."

"OK." The door slid open and he held it with his arm.

A woman appeared out of the crowd and yelled to her. "Errr-ica?" She had clearly been drinking for some time. "Where have you been, girl?"

Erica saw her and turned quickly to Randall. "I'm going to keep looking for those files. Let me know if there's anything else I can do."

"OK. Thanks."

She turned to leave, then turned back. "I'm on your side."

"Thanks."

The elevator door closed. He leaned against the back wall. In the absence of other instructions, the microprocessor operating the elevator consulted its memory banks, which contained information on all the trips the elevator had made in the past hour. Based on that information, it determined where the next passengers were most likely to call from.

It wasn't until the elevator door opened on the first floor that Randall realized he hadn't pressed a button, and that the elevator had decided for him where he would go.

12

As she and Margaret Reingold carried dishes to the kitchen, Livvy Giordano said, "That was a wonderful meal."

"It was nothing."

"Nothing? Margaret, you must have spent hours preparing the veal piccata. Where did you get the recipe from?"

Margaret raised her eyebrows, like a school teacher who expected her to know the answer. "Where do you think?"

"Of course," Livvy said, laughing. "The Family."

As Livvy placed a stack of dishes on the counter, Margaret put a motherly hand on her shoulder. "So how are you folks doing?"

"Oh, we're fine. Phil's been a little stressed out at work. They're getting ready for some big sales meeting. And of course, things are always hopping at the hospital. But we're doing fine."

"I mean...you know. In terms of..." She nodded toward Livvy's tummy.

"Oh." Her smile faded. "Not so good in that department, I'm afraid."

"No news?"

"Not yet. We've got another appointment at the clinic. Thank God for the health plan." Livvy and Phil had signed up for the Family's health program shortly after becoming members. Phil had researched every option available to them and found that FamilyHealth provided the best coverage at the lowest cost. "The fertility treatments would have cost us a mint without it."

Margaret nodded sympathetically. "Well, don't give up hope. Sometimes these things just take time."

"I know," Livvy sighed. "At least we're getting a chance to save some money. That should help when the baby comes."

"Of course."

They carried dessert and coffee into the dining room, where Alan and Phil were discussing finances.

"I'll tell you," Phil said, "I've looked at every personal finance program on the market, and FamilyBank beats them all."

"It must be good," Livvy said, placing a plate with chocolate truffle in front of her husband. "This guy couldn't even balance the checkbook before he started using it."

"You laugh," he said. "But it's sure made life easier. It used to drive me nuts trying to keep track of our banking and checking accounts. Now it takes a couple of minutes a day. I think I'd belong to the Family just for that, if nothing else."

"Same here," Alan said. "And I like that the updates happen automatically. If there's one thing I hate, it's having to buy new software every six months, load it up, and transfer files."

Margaret poured coffee as the others sampled the truffle. Appreciative murmurs rose from around the table.

"Speaking of updates," Alan said, "are you folks ready to upgrade your membership?"

Phil looked bewildered. "Upgrade?"

"In the group."

"I guess I'm not following you."

Alan leaned toward him. "There's an opportunity that's just come up, for a few people to become more actively involved in the Family. We've been thinking that you folks might be good candidates."

"What kind of opportunity?" Livvy asked.

"How would you folks like to be Guides?"

"You mean, like the online Guides?"

"That's part of it, being online and helping newcomers. But there's more to it. Guides are on a level just above that of ordinary members. There are special privileges for Guides, and some responsibilities that go with those privileges."

He had directed all this to Phil, but Livvy didn't want to be left out of the conversation. "What kind of privileges?" she asked.

"Well, to begin with, there's the financial management program," Alan said. "It's tied in with FamilyBank, but there are additional services: online banking, bill payment, investment tracking. That's all free, if you become a Guide."

Margaret pushed her dessert plate aside and leaned toward Livvy. "There's an online co-op that's only available for Guides," she said. "You wouldn't believe the deals they have."

Now Livvy was interested. "Really? What kind of stuff?"

"You name it. Food, clothes, toys, electronics. The Family has arrangements with every major catalog sales company, and you can get incredible discounts on just about everything they sell. Better than you can get anywhere else."

"As a Guide, you can actually invest in the Family," Alan said. "And the way it's growing lately, the return on investment is double what other investments are bringing in."

"I don't know," Livvy said, looking to Phil.

"Let me run a few statistics by you," Alan said. "We've found that people who upgrade their membership in the Family have fewer divorces. Their children do better on standardized tests. They have no drug or alcohol problems."

"And you'd need to upgrade before your children could sign up for the Teleducational Institute, anyway," Margaret said.

"Oh," Livvy said. "I didn't realize that."

"It's no big deal. That's how we avoid people who just want to take advantage of the services without being committed to the group."

"So what do we have to do?" Phil asked. "To...what did you call it?"

"Upgrade. To begin with, there's a small financial commitment. This varies, depending on your income. Basically, it's a contribution to help advance the work of the Family."

"How much does–"

Alan didn't let him finish the question. "And part of that contribution is offset by missionary activity."

"Missionary activity?" Livvy asked.

Alan laughed. "Don't worry, it's nothing spooky. It just means spending a little time each week recruiting new members."

"It's really fun," Margaret said. "There are all kinds of ways to do it. Some folks just hand out sign-on disks, or go to meetings of computer clubs and talk about the group. Others meet their commitment by helping newcomers online."

"There are all kinds of ways to do it," Alan said. "And for every new member you initialize–"

"Sign up," Margaret said quickly.

"Right," Alan said, without missing a beat. "For every new member you sign up, you get credits that offset your required contributions. A lot of people end up not having to make any contributions at all."

"But doesn't that take a lot of time?" Livvy asked.

"Not really," Margaret said. "Besides, the more you use the Family, the more time you have anyway."

Alan leaned back in his chair. "Think about it: for a small contribution of money and time, you get advanced privileges, access to the co-op, electronic banking, the Teleducational Institute—not to mention a chance to actually invest in the Family."

"I'd like to hear more about this investing business," Phil said.

Alan waved the question off, as if it wouldn't interest the women. "You and I can talk about that later."

Margaret said to Livvy, "Do you think you'll do it?"

"Well, it sounds pretty good. But we'll need to talk about it."

"Of course," Alan said. "I'll be honest, this isn't for everyone. This is for people who are willing to take a bit of risk, to be committed to something bigger than themselves. That's the Second Protocol."

"I didn't realize there was a second protocol," Phil said.

"That's because not everyone's ready for it," Alan said intently. "We think you folks are."

Margaret nodded. "The Second Protocol is commitment."

Phil and Livvy glanced at each other, assessing the other's reaction. Finally, Livvy grinned and said, "I wonder what kind of deal we could get on a Fiske-Wells baby stroller through the co-op?"

When the Giordanos left, Margaret loaded dishes into

the washer mechanically, her eyes half closed with fatigue. Lately, it seemed as if they'd had people at the house every evening for one Family-related meeting or another. On the few nights when they didn't have meetings, there were online sessions, and during the day, she'd been busy sending notes to new members, making meals for folks who were sick or needed help, and coordinating the local outreach to elementary schools.

On top of all that, she was supposed to be keeping track of Scott's educational program—making sure he was doing his assignments, checking his work—but there just wasn't enough time. These days, an aching heaviness settled on her each time she passed his room and saw him huddled in front of his computer, no longer even expecting her help. She consoled herself, knowing that his grades were excellent and the reports from his online instructors were always positive.

It was all part of the work, she knew. The sheep had to be cared for. She and Alan had understood the responsibilities when they'd agreed to become Shepherds. It was important work they were doing, work that required personal sacrifice.

"The Third Protocol is discipline," she reminded herself quietly, placing the last of the coffee cups into the rack. "A Shepherd is always working, always on the alert, always keeping an eye on the sheep."

She felt a little guilty about the sales pitch they'd given the Giordanos about becoming Guides. But it wouldn't do to explain everything too soon, especially how their commitment of "a little bit of time" could mushroom to take up all of their time, how a "small financial commitment" generally turned out to be a significant sum of money. And as for those people who "ended up not having to make any contributions at all," she'd never met them. Like the Giordanos, she had simply been told about them, and took their existence as a matter of faith. There could be such people.

The money didn't bother Margaret as much as some of the other requirements of being a Guide. Before joining the group, she had been an avid reader, but their Shepherd suggested strongly that members avoid reading any material not provided by the Family—a suggestion that became a requirement when they upgraded to Shepherd status.

She knew it was all necessary to advance the cause. But at times like this, when she was tired, doubts crept in. Did they have to be so busy all the time? Why couldn't life be as simple as it had been before?

She thought of the other women she knew who were Shepherds. Could she really call them her friends? Would she have had anything to do with them if they hadn't been fellow members? Did they ever feel the way she did? It was a question she could never ask, of course, one that would have been met with mild astonishment if she had. But she could see the signs—the weariness in their eyes, the tell-tale blankness behind the constant cheery smiles.

She saw the signs in Alan, too, and it worried her. He would never admit to being over-stressed, of course—he seemed to enjoy the responsibilities of being a Shepherd—but she was afraid it was wearing him down. True, he didn't have to spend as much time with their personal finances since they'd handed all that over to the group. But any time he might have gained was now taken up with missionary work, filing reports, keeping watch over the sheep. They no longer took part in any social activity that didn't advance the Family in some way. They hardly spent any time alone together. And they had not, she thought sadly, made love in months.

She had tried, once or twice, to talk to him about her fears, but he refused to acknowledge them. The Family was his life. His work at the telephone company was now like a mere afterthought to his real work, the Family. The Family had become his reason for living.

She finished loading the dishwasher and pressed the start button. For several minutes, she leaned against the counter, comforted somehow by the steady hum of the machine, the water pouring into it, the warmth radiating through its false mahogany front panel.

In the study, Alan completed the report on the Millers, noting that their configuration had been successfully completed, and opened the file on Phil and Livvy Giordano.

> *Subjects have been contacted regarding upgrade to Guide level. Initial response was positive. Expect to commence formatting soon.*

"Formatting" was the foundational teaching upon which all advanced membership in the Family was based. Without it, a person could not be expected to understand the importance of commitment to the group and the sacrifices necessary to achieve the goals of the Family.

Alan remembered the hunger with which he'd approached his own formatting. Against the dreariness of his job at PacBell, the goals of the Family were a brightly-lit signpost to the future, providing purpose and direction to his days. Once formatted, he had become an ardent champion of the Family.

For some members, the approval of those above them was a prime motivation—no one wanted to get e-mail from an Overseer reprimanding them for failing to meet a quota. For Alan, however, the most powerful motivation was his own intense appetite to achieve. Long before anyone else noticed he might be slipping in his missionary activities, Alan would become aware of the deficiency and work overtime to correct it.

Margaret had been a big help in the work, though lately she didn't seem to feel the same urgency about it as he did. He couldn't understand her slackening enthusiasm. It wasn't as if their mission wasn't clear. It was a simple calculation. If each person in the Family convinced just one other person to join the group, the membership would double in a year. In two years, there would be two million members. In ten years, every person on earth would be a member of the Family.

A beep alerted him that he had mail. He clicked quickly to the Mail Room and read the message. A look of astonishment spread across his face.

Margaret appeared in the doorway. "Honey?" He seemed not to hear her. "Alan?"

He turned toward her, his face a combination of excitement and disbelief, and pointed to the screen. "It's from Overseer Blackburn. He wants to nominate us to become Overseers."

Margaret exhaled slightly and put a hand down to steady herself against the doorjamb. "Oh, Alan..."

He frowned slightly. "What?"

"It's just that...the group already takes up so much of our time."

"Can you think of anything more important we should be doing?"

"No, but...I'm worried."

"About what?"

"About you. About us."

"Us? What is that supposed to mean?"

"We're...doing so much."

"That's because there's a lot to be done. Do you realize what an honor it is to be asked to be an Overseer?"

"Of course...but it's also a great responsibility," she said, as if searching for some firm ground to stand on.

"We shouldn't rush into it before weighing the decision carefully. We should consider all the...implications, before deciding whether or not to accept."

He looked at her as if she were crazy. "Margaret, this isn't the kind of thing that you can turn down."

"Well, can't we just think about it? Talk it over for a while?"

"What is there to talk over?"

"I don't know. I just have a lot of questions."

"Like what?"

"Well...what the requirements might be. Would we have to go through debugging again?" The process of debugging—mandatory for those who became Shepherds—had been long and painful for Margaret. Candidates were required to examine every aspect of their lives, analyzing every motivation to make sure their commitment to the group was real and total.

"Why would we have to go through debugging again?" Alan said, with mild annoyance. "Have you done something you shouldn't?"

"No. I just..." She sighed heavily. "Oh, I don't know."

"You know as well as I do that a person only needs to be debugged once. After the old programming is corrected, the only reason for debugging is if you've committed some kind of error."

"I know..." She turned away as if to leave the room.

He couldn't leave it this way. "Margaret, wait a minute."

She turned back, a dim hope appearing on her face.

He would have to handle this carefully. He could, of course, insist that she go along with the upgrade. But that wouldn't be best. Couples were required to upgrade together, and if both parties did not agree to it, neither one could upgrade. The purpose, according to the Overseers, was to bind marriages together. In practice, it also had the effect of playing on one person's enthusiasm to convince a somewhat reluctant spouse. Alan had used the principle himself when upgrading his sheep.

"Of course we have to talk about it," he said. "It's just that...this is the most important thing in the world to me. And I need for it to be important to you too."

The computer beeped again. He turned to the screen and scanned the message, his eyes widening.

"What is it?" Margaret asked.

"It's from the Father," he said in a reverent whisper.

Shepherd Reingold,

I know that you have been nominated for upgrade to the level of Overseer. I have checked the archives, and find that you and Margaret would be excellent candidates. I offer my approval of the nomination. The eye of the Father is upon you.

13

The message light on the telephone was blinking when Randall walked into his room. The first message began with a hacking cough, like chains being dragged over gravel—the sound of two packs a day for thirty years.

"Yeah," Harold Dodge wheezed. "I thought you were supposed to be back today. What's going on? Call me."

Randall looked at his watch. It was too late to call Dodge now. Besides, what was he supposed to tell him? It's like this, Harold. My best friend is dead, and no one knows what happened. His girlfriend thinks he killed himself, and according to the police, he was doing drugs. The day he died, someone erased all the files from his office computer. You don't mind if I stay out here until I sort it all out, do you?

The machine beeped for the next message.

"Hi. It's Allison." She paused, then said. "Thanks for coming over this morning." Another pause. "I guess I'll talk to you later."

He put the phone down, his heart beating faster than it had been. Calm down, he told himself. She's just being polite.

The maid had placed the morning paper on the dresser. He sat and scanned it distractedly. An item on the second page jumped out at him.

Possible Drug Connection in Journalist's Death.

He read the piece quickly, his eye jumping to the last sentence.

> *...a source close to the case has revealed that Jacobson had previously been arrested on charges of cocaine possession and possession with intent to sell.*

He dug through his pockets and found Harry's card. Harry answered on the first ring.

"Yeah?"

"It's Randall. Listen, Peter's police record—did it say he was arrested for selling cocaine?"

"Hang on." There was a sound of papers shuffling. "Yeah. That's what it says."

"It specifically mentions cocaine?"

"Yeah. Why?"

"Because it's wrong. There's no way Peter could have done that."

He drove to Allison's apartment. It was late, but he wanted to talk to her in person. He pulled up in front of the apartment, glad to see the lights still on.

He rang the buzzer twice before she answered. "Who is it?" She sounded sleepy, far away.

"It's Randall. Can I talk to you?"

The door buzzed, and he climbed the stairs. She met him at the door wearing a nightshirt, a puzzled look on her face. "Hi."

"I'm sorry to be coming by so late. But I wanted to tell you something...and apologize."

She smiled sleepily. "You want to apologize? I'm the one who should apologize. I was a real mess this morning." She gestured toward the living room, where quiet jazz played. "Do you want to come in?"

He wanted very much to come in. But something stopped him. "That's OK. I just wanted to tell you that you were right."

"About what?"

"About Peter. The police are wrong...about the drugs."

She leaned against the door and closed her eyes for a moment. "How–"

"It doesn't matter. But I'm sorry. I shouldn't have said anything."

"Thanks." She looked as if she were going to fall asleep standing there. "I'm sorry. It's the medication."

"That's OK. I should go. I just wanted to apologize."

"Well...thanks for coming by." She reached out to hug him, and he put his arms around her. They stood that way for a few seconds, her body soft beneath the nightshirt, his pulse quickening.

She looked up at him through half-open eyes, smiled, and kissed him. He kissed her back, and she responded, pressing her body into his. He held her more tightly. She caressed his lips with kisses, pressing, sucking gently, her breath escaping in short gasps.

His mind raced. This was wrong. She was Peter's girlfriend. Peter had only been dead for a few days. And she was on medication; she probably didn't even know what she was doing.

He pressed her head to his chest, breathing heavily. She pulled away and looked up at him, her eyes questioning. "What?"

He didn't meet her eyes. "I should go."

She moved out of his embrace, crossed her arms over her chest, and looked down. "OK."

He wanted to explain. "It's just–"

"I know," she said, her eyes moist. "Too soon."

Yes. Too soon. How did women always know what men were thinking, when men rarely knew what women were thinking? "I'll talk to you later."

"OK. Goodnight." She closed the door, looking away as she did.

He drove back to the hotel, still feeling the warmth of her body in his arms, her lips on his. And he argued with himself:

It's not right. She's Peter's girlfriend.

But Peter is dead.

He's only been gone a few days. What kind of guy would come on to his best friend's girlfriend three days after he died?

It wasn't all your doing. She seemed attracted to you, too.

She's still in shock. She probably didn't know what she was doing.

She knew what she was doing. And so did you.

14

The intercom buzzed on Latimer's desk. "Someone named Randall McLagan here to see you," desk sergeant said. "Says he's a friend of Peter Jacobson's."

Latimer didn't recall anyone named McLagan connected to the Jacobson case. "All right. Send him in."

His first thought was that the guy looked tired. "Bill Latimer," he said, holding out his hand. "What can I do for you?"

McLagan introduced himself and took the seat Latimer pointed him to. He hesitated, as if not knowing where to start. "I have some questions about Peter's death."

"Of course. How can I help?"

McLagan pulled a clipping from his jacket and placed it the desk. "I wanted to ask you about this item in yesterday's newspaper."

Latimer glanced at the article but left it sitting between them. He didn't have to read it. "Yes?"

"The information there is wrong. Peter didn't do cocaine."

"I have no idea where the paper got that information," Latimer said, shrugging.

McLagan looked away, and Latimer's intuition told him he was hiding something. "But you do have a criminal record on Peter?"

"Afraid I can't answer that question. That's restricted

information."

"I understand. But I happen to know it's wrong information."

Latimer crossed his arms and leaned back in his chair. "What makes you say that?"

"Because Peter was allergic to cocaine."

"He was," Latimer said, not quite a question.

"Yes. I was with him the one time he took cocaine. It almost killed him. Believe me, I'm absolutely positive that was the last time he ever did cocaine."

Latimer nodded slowly. "You realize that a person doesn't have to be using a drug in order to sell it?"

McLagan thought about that for a moment. "How likely is that?"

Latimer shrugged, sipping his coffee. "People sell drugs for all kinds of reasons. Some do it just for the thrill. They like living dangerously."

"Peter wasn't like that."

"Maybe. Maybe not. I wasn't thinking of anyone in particular."

McLagan frowned. "Peter was my best friend. When we were in college, we spent all of our time together. If he had ever been involved with something like that, I would have known about it."

"Were you with him twenty-four hours a day? Every day? People who deal drugs are smart. They don't do the nasty stuff in their home town. They find some city nearby."

McLagan tapped on the newspaper article. "But it says he was arrested. I would have known if he'd ever gone to jail."

"Arrests don't necessarily mean convictions. People get arrested all the time without going to jail."

McLagan fell silent. Latimer had met all his objections, but he clearly wasn't convinced. "Could the record be wrong? Could someone have messed with it?"

"No. Absolutely not."

That was a lie. Latimer knew that triple-eye reports were sometimes wrong. The system was only as good as the information entered into it, and mistakes did happen. Innocent people had had their identification stolen and later found themselves linked to crimes in places they'd never been. People whose names were spelled the same as some criminal's—or even sounded the same—were arrested. Others had been wrongly accused because they were born on the same day as a known felon.

But those were just mistakes. Latimer was sure there was no way anyone could have changed Peter Jacobson's record.

At Harry's apartment, Randall filled him in on the meeting with Detective Latimer.

Harry snorted derisively. "He's either lying, or he doesn't know what he's talking about."

"He's the detective in charge of the case," Randall said, dropping into the only empty chair he could find. "Who else would know about it?"

"I'm not talking about Peter. I'm talking about the NCIC."

"What's that?"

"The National Crime Information Center—the FBI's criminal database. It's not as bulletproof as he thinks." He pulled a handful of pages from a pile and handed them to Randall. "Check this out. It's a report I found on the net. Basically, every law enforcement agency in the country is tied into the NCIC. But each state makes up its own rules regarding access. A lot of places have no rules at all. The terminal sits out in the open, and anyone can get at it. A janitor working the night shift can check your criminal record if he wants to."

Randall flipped through the report. "Don't they have passwords?"

"Sometimes—but not always. And often they have one password for the entire department. A person signs on, uses someone else's name, and no one ever finds out." He gestured to the report. "There's a story in there about an ex-cop who used the system to track down an old girlfriend."

That didn't seem like a big deal to Randall. "So what?"

"He murdered her."

"Oh."

"Then there was a terminal operator in a police department. Her boyfriend was dealing drugs, so she used the system to check all of his customers and see if any of them were undercover cops."

"You're kidding."

"Nope. Politicians have used the system to dig up dirt on opponents. Businessmen have paid cops to run reports on prospective employees."

"So why doesn't the FBI crack down on this stuff?"

"They'd like to. But the system is a cooperative effort between the FBI and the states. The FBI doesn't have any jurisdiction over the local agencies. If they tried to insist on stricter controls, the states would have a fit. States' sovereignty and all that."

Randall tossed the report on the table. "Do you think someone screwed with Peter's record?"

"There's no way to tell from the file. All it tells you is when the last changes were made."

He dug through the pile again till he found the printout of Peter's record. "See, right here–" He stopped. "Damn."

"What?"

"I can't believe I didn't see this before."

"What?"

Harry pointed out a line on the bottom of the report.

*Most recent modification to records:
5/19/90*

"So?" Randall said. "That's the day he died. They had to enter that in the system."

Harry shook his head. "There's nothing in the report about his death—they hadn't gotten around to that yet."

"So what would they be doing–" The thought exploded in his mind like a firecracker. "Someone changed the record."

"Yep," Harry said. "Probably the same person who erased his files at PC Monthly."

"And if we knew what was in those files, we might have a clue about who did it."

They were silent for a moment, then Harry said, "Did Peter have a computer at home?"

"Yes. But I already tried that. You need a password to boot it up."

Harry lowered one eyebrow. "Maybe you need a password."

Mrs. Toomey was only too happy to let them into Peter's apartment. "Don't bother coming up," Randall said. "We just need to sort through Peter's things and begin packing them up."

As they passed through the kitchen, Randall pointed to the unpaid bills on the table. "There's another thing that doesn't make sense. Unpaid bills. A lot of unpaid bills, for some very strange items."

Harry flipped through the pile. "Weird."

"Sure is. And not like Peter."

Harry checked a light switch. "It's a good thing they haven't shut the power off yet. Hard to compute without electricity."

In the office, Harry pulled a laptop computer from his knapsack and plopped in on Peter's desk. He unplugged the keyboard from Peter's computer, inserted a cable into the empty socket, and plugged the other end into the laptop.

"What's that for?"

"We may have to try a lot of passwords before we find the right one. The laptop can do that faster than I can."

Peter's computer responded as it had before.

DataSure Protection - Enter password:

"Good," Harry said.

"What?"

"This password program didn't come with the machine. That should make things easier."

"Why?"

"Pre-installed programs are smart. They use made-up phrases—things like blarzap and panforz—words you won't find in a dictionary. When end-users install password protection, they use family names, birthdays—things that are easy to remember."

Harry tried several generic passwords. Each time, the computer responded.

Incorrect password. Please try again.

He shrugged. "It was worth a try." He entered a command on the laptop. It began feeding passwords to Peter's computer at lightning speed.

aardvark

Incorrect password. Please try again.

abacus

Incorrect password. Please try again.

abalone

Incorrect password. Please try again.

abandon

Incorrect password. Please try again.

As the words scrolled across the screen, Harry said, "Did Pete have any pet phrases? In-jokes? Sayings you guys shared?"

Randall searched his memory. "We used to say 'bummer' all the time, when we were in college."

Harry interrupted the laptop and typed 'bummer'.

Incorrect password. Please try again.

"Nope. Anything else? Old stories, private jokes?"

"Monsanto?"

Harry looked up from the laptop. "Huh?"

"We went on a road trip during a college break. It was the middle of the night, and I was driving. We passed a factory with a huge neon sign on the roof. It was like a beacon—you could see it for miles. Peter opened his eyes just as we passed it, then went back to sleep. When he woke up he told me he'd had a weird dream about seeing a huge sign that said 'Monsanto.' After that, any time we saw something unreal or bizarre, one of us would say, 'Monsanto.'"

Harry nodded, stopped the laptop, and typed 'MONSANTO.'

DataSure Protection - User identified.

The computer clicked, whirred, and began to boot up. Harry grinned. "You, sir, are a hacker."

On the basement floor of an apartment on Avila Street, two blocks away from Peter's apartment, an alarm went off. A thin young man with a dark ponytail and sparse goatee turned from a table full of computer equipment and clicked an icon on the computer behind him. A line appeared at the bottom of the screen.

Recording: PAJ0529.DOC

Text began scrolling up from the bottom of the screen.

DataSure Protection - User identified.

The text appeared courtesy of a microtransmitter located in Peter Jacobson's computer between the microprocessor and the video display. The transmitter intercepted anything being sent to the screen and sent it via low-frequency radio wave to the apartment on Avila Street.

The technology was no more complex than listening in on a cellular phone conversation, and just as illegal. It was also nearly impossible to detect, unless you were in the habit of taking your computer apart periodically.

Peter Jacobson's computer had not been taken apart since the previous year, when he'd brought it to a local computer repair shop to have a faulty memory chip replaced. The young man at the shop had promised to have the new chip installed within 24 hours, and he'd done the work himself. In the course of replacing the memory chip, he had installed an additional part, one that Jacobson did not know about.

The transmitter had sat in the computer for months, unused and unmonitored, until the young man received instructions to begin monitoring Jacobson's activities. He had passed the records of those activities to his Overseer, along with those of the dozen or so other systems that he had been assigned to monitor.

At first, there had been a great deal of activity on Jacobson's system. Then, for the past week, the system had been quiet. He assumed that Jacobson had been away on vacation or business. That morning, however, he had received e-mail alerting him to pass any new activity on to his Overseer immediately.

He entered a command on the keyboard. The system responded by connecting to the Family and forwarding the information from Peter Jacobson's computer even as it was being received.

15

Harry entered a command and a list of the directories on Peter's computer scrolled down the screen.

```
DOS       <DIR>   3-26-90  4:55p
WP        <DIR>   9-08-88  6:25p
LETTERS   <DIR>   6-29-90  5:17p
MAIL      <DIR>   4-13-88  7:14p
INTERNET  <DIR>  11-18-88  2:35p
NU        <DIR>   4-29-88  1:56p
UTIL      <DIR>   5-24-90  1:59p
DOLLAR    <DIR>   5-24-90  8:56p
FONELINE  <DIR>   3-18-88  2:35p
```

Randall pointed to the DOLLAR directory. "What's that?"

"Looks like DollarWise," Harry said. "It's a checkbook program. Keeps track of your bills."

"Let's take a look at it."

A facsimile of a checkbook register appeared on the screen, with entries for each of Peter's checks.

Randall instructed Harry to search for payments made to Pacific Gas and Electric. The program presented a list of checks and dates. "One for every month, right up till last month," Harry said.

"OK. Now look for PacBell."

He entered a command. "The same. He was right up to

date." He pointed to the screen's bottom line. "And it says here he had a couple thousand dollars in his account."

Randall shook his head. "Let's see if we can find that column."

Harry poked around the directory list. "Here we go."

```
JUN     <DIR>   2-16-90    9:05p
JUL     <DIR>   3-22-90   11:43p
AUG     <DIR>   4-27-90   12:38p
```

"The magazine works on a three-month lead time," Harry said. "So we want the August directory." He switched to that directory.

```
.       <DIR>   4-27-90   12:38p
..      <DIR>   4-27-90   12:38p
```

```
2 Files 0 Char.   4274176 Free
```

"Damn."

"What?"

"It's empty. If there were any files here, someone erased them. Time to go spelunking again." He pulled out the Rescue disk from his knapsack and ran it.

```
Rescue analysis: C:\COMPWEEK\AUG

Name          Created Erased  RI
----------------------------------
?OTES.UPL   4-28-90  5-21-90  -3
?OLUMN.AUG  5-1-90   5-21-90  -3
?MAIL       5-21-90  5-21-90  -3
```

"There it is," Harry said. "But the chances of recovering it aren't good."

Unable to recover ?OLUMN.AUG. Try another?

Randall sighed. "So we're sunk."

"Not necessarily. Knowing Peter, he would have been smart enough to make a backup. Look around and see if you can find any other disks."

Randall searched the room, opened drawers, pulled out books, and dug through boxes. In the closet, the red power light of the laser printer still glowed. Taped to the top was a note in Peter's handwriting.

This printer is connected to a separate power source from the computer. DO NOT TURN IT OFF. It takes more power to keep turning it on and off than it does to leave it on.

"I didn't know that," Randall mused.

Harry looked up from the computer. "What?"

"It takes more power to turn a printer on and off than it does to leave it on."

"Who told you that?"

"It says so right here."

Harry read the note, his eyebrows furrowing. "That's nonsense. Computer equipment is just like everything else. You turn it on, it uses power. You turn it off, it doesn't. Peter would have known that."

"Then why would he write the note?"

Harry's eyes narrowed slightly. "Because he didn't want anyone to turn the printer off."

"Why?"

"I'm not sure. But I've got a hunch."

He went back to the computer and began entering commands. "Printers have brains of their own—memory that lets them store information about fonts, graphics, and so on. With some printers, when you turn it off, it forgets what was stored in it, and the computer has to reload it each time you boot up."

"So what's this got to do with Peter's files?"

"Until you go to use it, a printer doesn't care what's stored in its memory. Technically, you could put anything you wanted in there—including files you were trying to hide. You'd just have to download them to the computer, then stick them back in the printer when you were done."

"Can we find out what's in the printer's memory?"

The computer beeped.

"Done," Harry said, grinning, and typed a command.

```
Directory of C:\COMPWEEK\AUG

NOTES  UPL  9206  4-28-90   3:15p
AUG    001  1500  5-1-90    9:43a
EMAIL       8912  5-21-90   9:27a
```

"Bingo." He entered another command, and the contents of AUG.001 began scrolling across the screen.

August column - rough draft

Give Me That Online Religion

Intro: I got a lot of mail after the last column about the Family; mostly from members of the group thanking me, telling me what a wonderful article it was, etc. But there were a couple of interesting letters, like this one from a guy in New York:

Dear Mr. Jacobson,

In view of your largely positive write-up about the Family, I thought you should know about an experience I had with the group. I recently received a sample disk that lets you check out the group's online system for free. The installation takes quite a while, which seemed odd. While it was installing itself on my system, my two-year old son, who was crawling around at my feet, accidentally hit the button on the power strip, turning it off.

I turned the system back on, and ScoutMaster told me there was a corrupted file.

"What's ScoutMaster?" Randall asked.

"A program that checks the system when you boot up," Harry said. "If a problem cropped up since the last time you used the system, ScoutMaster alerts you."

The corrupted file didn't look familiar to me, so I checked it out. It was full of information about my system: every piece of hardware and software I had installed, the names of files, how much memory I had, and so on.

I couldn't believe it. I saved a copy of the file on a floppy, then went back and completed installing the Family software, including signing on to the system. After I signed off, I went back and looked for the file. It was gone. The software had deleted it. It seems pretty clear that the program transferred the file to the group's computer, then erased it.

They may be just using the information for marketing purposes. On the other hand, a lot of people have sensitive information on their computers—private

132

data, projects they're working on for their companies—and most people would never even know they've been spied on.

Thought you might find this interesting. Maybe worth another column?

Roger Sprague
Internet: rsprague@english.suny.edu

"Can they do that?" Randall asked. "Capture information from people's machines?"

"Legally? Who knows? When it comes to electronic information, there are a whole lot of areas that haven't been nailed down yet. Ethically, of course, it's outrageous. But they aren't the first ones to do it." He hit Page Down and more of the column appeared.

I recently made contact with a former member of the group. He explained that basic membership in the group is free, but you don't have access to all of the Family's benefits until you make a commitment to it— which includes pledging up to 10% of your income to the group. Those are the "voluntary contributions" that provide all those "free" services.

My source told me the Family's news service filters out anything that's unfavorable to the Family. Most members don't know that.

He also told me about a number of "shadow" organizations associated with the Family. One of them is a political action wing that helped scuttle the Lawler-Adams Bill...

"What's the Lawler-Adams Bill?" Randall asked.

Harry looked disgusted. "Another lousy idea from Congress—a new way to tax telecommunications. The phone companies dreamed it up. Everyone was up in arms about it when it was introduced. But I haven't heard anything about it recently."

The Family orchestrated a massive campaign that swamped the e-mail, phones and fax-machines of Congress. Eventually, the bill was dropped. And no one in Congress wanted to blame the Family for fear they'd be targeted during their next re-election campaign.

"Now you know why you haven't heard more about it," Randall said.

Harry shook his head. "Strength in numbers."

Here's another little secret most people don't know: Mark Roberts, who created the Houdini virus, is a member of the Family. Most people also don't know he plea-bargained his sentence, and part of the plea-bargain was that he wouldn't talk about what he did— which is convenient for any groups that he belongs to. And he was able to trade the larger part of his sentence for "community service." He was recently released from prison after serving only 2 months of his sentence. According to my source, that took some high-level string-pulling with a few congress-critters. And guess who he's doing his community service for? You guessed it: the Family.

"Did you know Roberts was out of jail?" Randall asked.

"No."

[Still working on this: the Family may have been responsible for the Doorway virus rumors—cost Megasoft millions.]

"Ah," Harry said. "The plot thickens."
"Why would the Family attack Megasoft?"
"I don't know. I told you, they don't like big computer companies."

[Wilton insists I don't use his real name. People who leave the group tend to have problems with their finances. False information about them gets into personal records. They can't get loans, insurance, new jobs. Most folks keep quiet, don't speak out against the group. He says to be careful, it's dangerous to cross them.]

Randall pointed to the name Wilton. "Who's that?"
"Got me. Must be his source." He closed the file. "That's all in there. Let's look at the EMAIL file."

Memo #40123
From: jbragdon@COMNET.com
Date: Mon, 15 May 00 09:23:45 EST
To: peterj@COMNET.com
Subject: next column

I read the rough draft of the column. I think you're being a little rough on this group. Have you got any proof about the Doorway virus? I don't want to print a bunch of allegations that leave us open to legal action, especially if these people are as ornery as you say. As far as the Lawler-Adams Bill, there's nothing illegal about speaking your mind. That's just electronic democracy in action.

Skip this topic, or make it more generic. Maybe you can talk about computers and politics without pointing fingers at anyone.

Show me what you've got ASAP.

Jack

The file contained several messages from members of the Family, praising his previous column. Another was from a guy whose girlfriend broke up with him because he wouldn't become a member of the Family. He claimed she had been ordered to do so by her "Shepherd."

Harry typed a command to view the file called NOTES.UPL.

UPLOAD May 17, 2000 - 2 p.m.
Truman
look for insular attitude
siege mentality
effect of peer pressure
attempt to maintain distinctiveness while integrating into society
charismatic leader

"Truman," Harry said. "That was the other name on the list."

Randall pointed to the first line. "What does 'Upload' mean?"

"It probably means he took these notes on a hand-held computer and transferred them to this system."

They scrolled through the rest of the file.

talk to Donoway again
check CompuSys stock, ads - check with Sylvia
Matt 24:27
Who is the Father?
Talk to Wilton on Friday.

"Laurie Donoway told me she hadn't spoken to Peter in months," Randall said, shaking his head.

"Maybe he meant to but didn't get around to it."

"Maybe," he said doubtfully.

The other names meant nothing to either of them. "Maybe Matt's in the service," Randall said. He pointed to the numbers 24:27. "Isn't that military time?"

"Military time ends at twenty-four hundred," Harry said, shaking his head. "But it looks like he was planning to talk to this Wilton person again."

"On Friday," Randall said. "I wonder if he made it."

"If he did, there aren't any notes here. Could be on the hand-held, though. Have you seen that around anywhere?"

"No. And if it's at the office, we're out of luck."

"All right," Harry said. "Let's see if he has a phone number for any of these folks." He went back to the directory called FONELINE. "This is a phone dialer. Keeps log of who you called and how long you talked."

He searched for anyone with "Father" in the name.

No record(s) found for Father.

Neither "Sylvia" nor "Matt" were listed either. "Cross your fingers," Harry said, and typed "Truman."

1 record(s) found for Truman, Ed. Stanford, CA.

Press Enter to see record(s).

"There's our man," Harry said. "Ed Truman." He hit Enter.

A faint click came from the computer, and the monitor went dark.

Randall leaned forward. "What happened?"

"I don't know. It just died." He clicked the computer's power switch several times. Nothing.

Randall reached for the desk lamp and clicked it, to no effect. "The power's out."

"Great. Now they discontinue service." He picked up the telephone. "Let's see if directory information has this Truman guy in Stanford."

He put the phone to his ear, punched the button several times, then stared at Randall. "Dead."

16

Bill Latimer turned on his computer and requested the arrest records on Peter Jacobson. The request was passed to the originating police department through NLETS, the National Law Enforcement Telecommunications System.

Two minutes later, the response scrolled across Latimer's screen.

JACOBSON, PETER
B.D. 10/17/63
NO RECORD FOUND.

"What?" He checked the spelling of the name and the birth date and tried again, this time using Jacobson's middle name as well.

JACOBSON, PETER ALAN
B.D. 10/17/63
NO RECORD FOUND.

He tried once more, using Jacobson's social security number. Still no record. "Damn, damn, damn."

Jack O'Neill appeared in the doorway. "Having a good day?"

Latimer nodded toward the computer. "Stupid thing

can't find Jacobson's record. He's listed on the index, but when I ask for the actual record, it keeps saying there's nothing there."

"You double-check the name?"

"Yes, I checked the name, and the birth date, and the social security number."

O'Neill shrugged. "To err is human, but to really screw up, you need a computer."

"Hilarious."

Latimer found a phone number for the law enforcement agency closest to Dartmouth College: Lebanon, New Hampshire.

A young woman answered the phone. "Lebanon police."

Latimer identified himself and said, "I'm looking for the arrest records on a Peter Jacobson."

"I'll transfer you."

An older woman came on the line. "Criminal records." She took Jacobson's birth date and social security number. "Just a moment please."

She returned a moment later. "Sorry," she said perfunctorily. "We don't have any records for a Peter Jacobson."

"What?"

"I said we don't have any records for him."

"That's crazy. The triple-eye says your people picked him up half a dozen times for possession of cocaine with intent to sell."

"Well, I don't care what triple-eye says, our records don't have him."

Idiot, Latimer thought. She had probably just missed it. A lot of these smaller cities and towns were still on paper systems, and it was entirely possible to miss a file. He tried to be diplomatic. "Look, if the triple-eye has it, then someone had to enter the information from somewhere.

Maybe you should go back and check again."

"I don't need to go back. I just looked it up and there's nothing there."

Now his patience was gone. "What the hell kind of system have you got there?"

"Don't swear at me, buster. I've spent every evening for the last two months entering the old records into this damn computer, so I don't want to hear it. If it isn't on there, we don't have it."

"Well maybe you're not using it right."

"Yeah? Well then maybe you better talk to someone who knows how to use it."

The database operator slammed the phone down. "Asshole."

Peg Pillsbury, the evening dispatcher, looked up from her magazine. "Who was that?"

"Some jerk from San Francisco looking for records on a guy we never heard of. Just because his system is screwed up, he yells at me."

Peg nodded, but said nothing. She looked back at her magazine, hoping the operator wouldn't notice her hands shaking as she turned the pages.

No one will ever know, she thought. The NCIC terminal is in the other room. Anyone in the office could have used it. There's no reason for them to suspect you. No one in the office even knows you know how to use it.

She stared blankly at the magazine, pretending to read, repeating the Fourth Protocol to herself: The Fourth Protocol is obedience. I will do whatever is required of me.

Randall and Harry called the telephone company from Harry's apartment. There was no listing for an Ed Truman in Stanford.

"Let's try the power company," Harry said.

Randall made the call. He told the representative there had been some mix-up. "The bills have been paid right along, but for some reason, my friend received a disconnect notice. I was just over there and the power was shut off."

The representative went away for a long time. "Thank you for waiting. I've put in an order for the power to be connected immediately."

"It's going to be reconnected?"

"Yes, sir."

"Why was it disconnected in the first place?"

The woman seemed to hesitate. "I'm afraid I can't answer that. All the payments are listed here, but for some reason, those payments were not applied to Mr. Jacobson's account."

"So he wasn't ever really behind in his payments?"

"Not as far as I can see. It must have been some kind of computer error."

Randall hung up. "The power's back on."

"Computer error?"

"Right."

"How convenient."

Randall began making another call. "I'm calling Erica Steiner. Maybe she can make sense of those notes on Peter's computer."

The receptionist put him through to Erica. "Can you meet me at Peter's apartment?" he asked. "I want to show you something."

She did not answer immediately. "Lunch? Sure." She paused again.

Randall said nothing.

"OK, great," Erica said. "I'll meet you there in about half an hour."

Randall hung up. "She must have had someone in her

office. She didn't want them to know where she was going." He stood. "Do you want to come along?"

"You go. I'm going to search the net for Ed Truman's number. And there's something else I want to check out." He opened the bottom drawer of his desk, revealing dozens of disks that had been thrown haphazardly on top of one another.

"What's that?"

"The software graveyard. Samples, stuff people have given me." He dug through the disks until a colorful label caught his eye. "A-ha. I knew I had one of these." He pulled the disk out and held it up.

It was a sign-on disk for the Family.

Harry grinned. "I'm going to do a little exploring of my own."

The hunter tracked his quarry in what might have looked, to an observer, like a meandering, roundabout fashion—following trails, picking up bits of information, noticing the habits and behavior of his prey.

The hunt was not so different from the adventure games he had played when he was younger—exploring underground mazes inhabited by trolls and monsters, searching for clues and treasures, solving puzzles. There were always barriers along the way: locked doors, solid walls to get through, or over, or around. After a while, though, there was no challenge left in the games. He had seen every variation of every puzzle, encountered all the possible obstacles.

Now, he played the ultimate game: reality. This game involved real barriers and real dangers. The maze was the vast network of computerized databases and off-limits sites. The barriers were security controls and access restrictions. And now, instead of solving an obscure mystery, the objective was to track living game.

It hadn't taken long for the hunter to get a clear picture of his prey's actions over the past few days. He had traveled to San Francisco on May 22 on United Airlines flight #61. He had rented a Chevrolet Corsica with license plate BMR-242, and checked into the Best Western hotel on Columbus and North Point. He had made only a few phone calls, but the hunter knew exactly where each of them had been made to and how long they had lasted.

The hunt was picking up speed. With a little more work, the hunter would know everything there was to know about Randall McLagan.

17

Alan Reingold looked up from his desk as Phil Giordano appeared in the doorway to his office. "Phil! Great to see you. Come on in." He pulled a chair beside his in front of his computer. "Hope you're hungry. I've got Chinese food coming in a few minutes." He pointed to the screen. "Check this out."

The screen showed a video image with control buttons. He clicked the Play button.

The video showed what appeared to be an indoor movie set. Klieg lights hung from the ceiling, cameras stood at various angles. In the center of the set, a young man in an Armani suit threw a soundless punch that flew past the chin of a larger, mustached man. The larger man fell to the floor, hitting a well-padded mat that waited out of camera range.

A voice called out, "OK, Mitchell. That's a wrap."

Someone tossed the young man a towel. He wiped his face, turned, and spoke to the camera. It was a face that would be instantly recognizable to anyone who had watched television, been to the movies, or scanned the cover of a gossip magazine in the last five years.

"Hello, I'm Mitchell Fairchild. As an actor, I've played a lot of roles: doctors, lawyers, detectives. But among the hardest roles I've ever played was that of a computer consultant. You see, before making Crackdown, I didn't know a thing about computers. I was always afraid I'd break them if I did something wrong. And no matter how the salesmen talked about computers being "user-friendly," they sure didn't seem friendly to me."

He strolled to the side of the set, where a computer sat on a table, bearing the Family logo.

"That's where the Family came in." He sat at the table, and the screen zoomed in through the Family's front doors. "The Family helped me get comfortable with computers. They introduced me to people from around the world, beginners just like you and me. Now, when I use a computer, I don't have to act as if I know what I'm doing."

The camera returned to Fairchild's smiling face. "If you'd like to find out more about the Family, and how you can become a member free of charge, just call 1-800-YES-CODE. There are thousands of people waiting to welcome you to the group. Call now. Computers could play a big part in your life." The trademark grin spread across Fairchild's face as the phone number flashed across the bottom of the screen.

"Is he really a member?" Phil asked as the clip ended.

"Sure," Alan said, dismissing the question with a wave of his hand. "But that's not the point. The Internet is getting ready to take off in a big way. It's going to be a daily part of everyone's life. It won't be just computer nerds and lonely guys online anymore. Everyone will be online. And the Family is going to be the cornerstone of that growth."

He pointed to the screen. "This commercial is about to be played on every major television network, cable channel, and even in movie theaters. Once it hits, people will be signing up by the millions. The Family is about to experience a period of phenomenal growth. That means there's a chance for a few smart investors to make some really big money."

He clicked an icon on the screen and a colorful growth chart filled it. "This program calculates the rate of return you can expect based on a given investment in the Family. Go ahead, type in a figure."

Phil shrugged and entered $1000. A bright line zoomed up toward the upper right side of the screen.

"See? In ten years, you'd have $15,430."

Phil's eyebrows rose. He entered a larger figure, one closer to what he and Livvy could actually invest. The line leaped higher and further. A lot further.

Alan studied Phil's face. "That would take care of college tuition for a couple of kids pretty easily, don't you think? Tell me any other investment that will give you that kind of growth."

"It sounds great. Of course, I'll have to check it out with Livvy first."

"Oh," Alan said, mild disappointment registering on his face. "Does she know a lot about investments?"

Phil chuckled. "No. Not at all. But I generally like to run big decisions past her before I make them."

"I see. Well, that's fine," Alan said, clicking a button and closing down the program. "Ultimately, it's your decision. I just wouldn't wait too long. They haven't told me how long this opportunity is going to stay open, and it could be closed at any time."

"Really?"

"With returns like these, they aren't going to have any trouble finding investors."

Alan was probably right. Opportunities like this didn't come along every day. And ultimately, it was his decision. Although he generally liked to discuss things with Livvy, he was the one responsible for their financial well-being.

"I tell you what," Alan said. "Try it. If you're not happy with the rate of return after six months, let me know, and I'll buy the shares from you."

That sealed it. "All right. What do I do?"

"We can do it right from here," Alan said. He logged on and began filling out the electronic paperwork that would make Phil and Livvy Giordano investors in the Family.

Randall turned the car onto Mallorca Boulevard and saw a black van parked in front of Peter's apartment, its rear doors open. A man in a dark suit emerged from the front door carrying a computer. Randall was pretty sure Mrs. Toomey didn't own a computer.

He parked quickly and jumped out. "Hey, what's going on?"

The man looked briefly at Randall but ignored him and deposited the computer in the back of the van. Beside it was Peter's printer, the handwritten note still taped to the top.

The man headed up the stairs and Peter followed him. "Excuse me? Would you mind telling me what you're doing?"

At the top of the stairs, they edged past Mrs. Toomey, who stood frozen in the hallway, her hands kneading the top of a broom handle. "Oh, my Lord. Nothing like this ever happened before. Oh, my Lord."

Randall put a hand on her shoulder. "What's going on?"

She pointed a trembling hand into the apartment. "They say he was...some kind of criminal or something."

The stranger had disappeared into Peter's office. Randall followed him, and came upon two other men. The first was tossing disks, manuals, and computer paraphernalia into boxes. The third man stood writing on a clipboard. He looked up as Randall appeared in the doorway.

"What's going on?" Randall asked.

The man eyed Randall darkly. He flipped his jacket open, revealing a badge attached to his belt, and a holstered gun under his arm. "Stephen Rose, Secret Service. Who are you?"

"I'm Randall McLagan. A friend of Peter Jacobson's. What are you doing?"

Rose looked back at his clipboard. "We have reason to believe that your friend..." he said the word as if it were a slur, "was involved with the theft of proprietary information from several major computer corporations."

"What? That's ridiculous. Peter wasn't–"

Rose interrupted him. "What are you doing here?"

"I told you, we were friends."

Rose wrote something on the clipboard. "How long did you know Mr. Jacobson?"

"For years. We went to college together."

"When was the last time you saw him?"

Randall wondered what this was all about. "Why do you ask?"

Rose stared at him. "Mr. McLagan, are you involved with computers?"

"What do you mean, involved?"

"Do you use a personal computer?"

Suddenly, it didn't seem healthy to be too enthusiastic about computers. "At work. That's all."

"Did Mr. Jacobson ever pass on any software or other computer information to you?"

"No. Why?"

"How long are you planning to be in the area?"

"I don't know. I–"

"And where are you staying?"

"The Best Western hotel," he said through clenched teeth. "On Columbus."

Rose wrote the information on his clipboard as the

other men lifted the cartons they'd been loading and headed out the door with them.

"Wait a minute," Randall said. "You can't just come in here and start hauling things away."

"Yes we can," Rose said. He pulled out a sheaf of folded papers and held them up. "We have a seizure warrant."

Randall was dumbfounded. Rose surveyed the room, slapped the clipboard shut, and turned to leave.

"Where are you taking the stuff?" Randall asked.

"It will be held in storage until the case is resolved."

"How long will that be?"

"That's hard to say. A couple of months, maybe longer."

"A couple of months? But there are things on there that I need."

Rose gave him an appraising look. "What kind of things?"

"Just...personal things."

Rose opened the clipboard again. He signed the bottom of the top sheet, tore it off, and handed it to Randall. "Here's a receipt for the equipment. If you have any questions, you can call the phone number at the top of the page. Be sure to use the identification number for this lot."

"But—"

Rose turned and left, not waiting for Randall's final question.

He wandered back to the kitchen and sat at the kitchen table. The idea that Peter had contraband software on his system seemed ridiculous. He remembered Peter complaining about how much unsolicited software the companies sent him—free demos, advance copies of new products. How was the government supposed to know what was legit and what wasn't?

Mrs. Toomey shuffled in from the hallway and stood in

the door to the kitchen, still kneading the broom handle. "I can't have this," she said as if it had somehow been Randall's fault. "I just can't have this kind of thing going on."

"Mrs. Toomey–"

"He always seemed like such a nice person. But if I had known this was going to happen–"

"Mrs. Toomey, I'm sure Peter didn't do anything wrong."

"Then why did those men–"

"I don't know. There are a lot of strange things going on."

Mrs. Toomey's face went blank as she tried to absorb that information. After a few seconds, she gave up the effort. "I don't know," she said, shaking her head slowly. "All I know is, this apartment has to be cleaned out by the end of the month. This isn't a warehouse, I can't store things here forever." She turned and shuffled toward the stairs, murmuring, "This is a nice place. Nothing like this ever happened here before."

She left, and Erica Steiner appeared in the doorway. "What was that all about?"

"You just missed the action. I was going to show you some stuff I found on Peter's computer. It's a little late, now." He told her about the visit from the Secret Service.

"That's typical," Erica said. "These guys all think they're Elliot Ness. They probably found Peter's name attached to an e-mail message on someone else's system. In their minds, that's enough to implicate him."

"They can confiscate your computer because of something like that?"

"All they have to do is convince a judge there's enough evidence to write a warrant. These days, say the word 'computer' and people think 'national defense secrets' or something."

"The only secret on Peter's system was about his next column. And he went to a lot of trouble to hide that."

He explained about the files on the printer and what they found in them. Most of the names meant nothing to her. "But," she said, "Sylvia is the ad coordinator for PC Monthly. She decides which ads go where. I'll check with her to see what Peter wanted."

Randall searched his memory for anything else that was in the files. "Oh, it looked as if the notes came from a hand-held computer."

"That could be. Peter had a new unit he was testing out."

"Where is it now?"

"Good question. There's a person at the magazine who keeps track of the products companies send us for review. Apparently, the company that made the hand-held wants it back, but no one knows where it is. I thought Peter still had it."

Randall scanned the receipt Rose had given him. "At least the government doesn't have it. There's nothing about it on this list."

"That may be a lucky break. Maybe it'll still turn up." She looked at her watch. "I've got to get back. I'll let you know what I find out from the ad coordinator."

He recalled her earlier concern about Jack Bragdon. "What about your boss?"

"What he doesn't know won't hurt him."

"Thanks. Maybe you can finish Peter's column when we get to the bottom of this. There's got to be a story here."

She shook her head. "If there is, I don't want to write it. I just want to find out what happened to Peter. I'll let you write the big story."

He smiled faintly. The Big Story. When he and Peter

were in college, they had joked about the Big Story, the one that would make their careers. It would be what Watergate was to Woodward and Bernstein, a tale of corporate evil or corruption in high places. But he had always pictured them writing it together, chasing down leads, digging through research, brainstorming over countless cups of coffee. He never imagined that the big story would revolve around Peter's death, and that he would be writing it alone.

He returned to Harry's and found him hunched over the computer. "Where have you been?" Harry asked.

"I had a little run-in with the government." He explained about the visit from the Secret Service.

"Someone probably planted a rumor," Harry said. "Given the government's paranoia about computer crime, that would be a pretty easy way to harass a person."

"And prevent someone else from finding stuff you didn't want them to find."

"Right." Harry nodded to the computer. "I've been looking for this Ed Truman guy." On the screen, lines of information rolled by. Randall caught glimpses of names, cities and long strings of digits. "This is the phone company's database. They've got a record of every phone call Peter ever made."

Randall started to ask how he'd done that, but stopped himself. "I know. Don't ask."

A wry smile twisted Harry's mouth. "I worked as a telephone operator one summer when I was in college. Makes access pretty easy." He gestured to the screen. "Check this out."

Randall scanned the list of calls. Among the last phone calls Peter had made was one to a Stanford number. "You think that's Truman?"

"We'll find out."

A moment later, the system reported the name connected with the phone number.

Truman, Edward D.
Department of Sociology
University of California
Stanford, CA 94305

"He's with the university," Harry said. "No wonder it wasn't listed under his own name." He called the number and handed it to Randall.

A woman's voice said, "Sociology Department."

"Can I speak to Ed Truman?"

"May I tell him who's calling, please?"

"It's a personal matter."

There was a click, followed by a pause. The voice that spoke next was deep and musical, like a bass instrument. "Hello?"

"Dr. Truman?"

"That's right."

"Dr. Truman, my name is Randall McLagan. I need to talk to you."

18

*Travel in ancient times was slow, difficult, and dangerous.
The advent of Roman roads—designed for transporting
troops, supplies and weapons—also made travel safe for
business people, pilgrims, and evangelists. On a purely
practical level, the spread of the gospel was largely made
possible by the existence of Roman roads.*

*Raymond Tobias
A History of Christianity*

*The information super-highway provides a level of
interconnection and a body of knowledge previously
unknown in human history. The effect of this technology
on human social structures will be enormous.*

*Dr. Edward Truman
The Social Science Review*

Truman's office was at the end of a rabbit warren of
hallways that smelled of floor polish and academia.
The door to the office stood open.

Randall peered in. It was a small room, lined with
overflowing bookshelves and overhung with the pungent
smell of pipe tobacco. A single window looked out onto
the campus and spilled cool spring light over an ancient

wooden desk.

Truman sat in an equally ancient wooden office chair, reading what appeared to be a term paper. He was middle-aged, paunchy, with thick glasses and a profuse mustache topping a generous smile.

He read, chuckling, unaware of Randall's presence in the doorway. Randall waited another moment, then knocked. "Dr. Truman?"

"Oh, hi," Truman said, looking up and grinning. "Come on in. Didn't see you standing there." He gestured Randall toward a vacant chair and held up the paper he'd been reading. "Freshman term papers. Absolutely delightful. The funniest things I've read in years. How are you doing?"

The greeting seemed too familiar. He suspected Truman took him for a grad student. "I'm Randall McLagan," he said, sitting. "We spoke on the phone?"

Truman nodded, still grinning, but with a trace of bewilderment now. "Right. Of course."

"I'm a friend of Peter Jacobson's. I believe you spoke to him last week? It may have had something to do with an organization called the Family?"

Truman's eyebrows knit together for a moment, then erupted in comprehension. "Oh. Oh, oh, oh. Yes, of course." He held out a hand to Randall. "Sorry. How did your friend's story come out?"

"I'm afraid he wasn't able to finish it. He died last week."

Truman's grin disappeared, replaced by a look of genuine concern. "Good Lord. What happened?"

Randall told him what he knew, and what he didn't know.

Truman listened carefully, pulling on the pipe. "Well, whatever I can do to help. I really only spoke to him that one time."

"How did he come to contact you?"

"I wrote an article for the Social Science Review and happened to mention the Family. Apparently, your friend came across the article while doing his research." He pulled a magazine from a nearby stack, folded it open and handed it to Randall.

"The Rise of Secular Religions," Randall read. "Seeking Transcendency Through Affiliation with Non-Sectarian Associations."

"Catchy, huh? The original title was, None Dare Call It Church." He shook his head. "I think sociologists are afraid our influence will diminish if the average person has any idea what we're talking about."

Randall glanced over the article. "Can you summarize it for me?"

Truman leaned back in his chair and clasped his hands over his stomach. "It's about the decline of traditional religious institutions and how secular institutions are filling that gap. Membership in mainline churches is on the decline. Most people have no particular religious affiliation these days. But nature abhors a vacuum. People still feel a need to belong to something. So we revert to tribalism."

"Tribalism?" Randall said. "I don't follow."

"Groups. Self-identity by virtue of belonging. At the lowest level, it means putting a bumper sticker on your car that says you listen to a particular radio station, or that you like dogs, or cats, or whatever. It's a way of signifying who you are, what you like, what your values are."

"What your tribe is."

"Exactly. Then there are social groups. Bowling leagues, flower societies, gangs."

"Computer clubs."

"Yes. Now, most of the time, those groups simply

provide friendship, entertainment, and a sense of belonging. Occasionally, however, they take on a greater significance."

Truman opened a desk drawer and pulled out a pipe and pouch of tobacco. "Take the Family. Lonely people, isolated, lacking in social skills. They join this group and suddenly they're connected to people from all over the world. They belong. And they can do this from the comfort of their own homes. They don't have to go out in the world, they don't have to fight traffic, they don't even have to rub elbows with real people."

He lit the pipe and drew on it till a curl of smoke escaped from the corner of his mouth. "It's much easier to deal with other humans behind the facade of a computer screen than it is in person."

Randall noticed there was no computer in Truman's office. In fact, the most high-tech contraption appeared to be a pencil sharpener. "How did you first hear about the Family?"

"A former student of mine became involved with the group. A brilliant young man, computer science major. The kind of person that operates entirely out of the left hemisphere of his brain. We used to have long discussions about human behavior: how much of it was determined mechanistically, the existence of free will, that kind of thing. I don't think he had many friends. In fact, I may have been the only friend he had."

"What happened to him?"

"He graduated, got a job as a programmer. Did very well—became one of the top programmers in his company. But he was even lonelier than he'd been in college. I'm afraid his education hadn't prepared him for life in the real world."

He took a slow puff on the pipe. "Then he met a young woman and fell in love. It was the first time for him, I think. She was a member of the Family, and she got him involved with the group. He became totally wrapped up in the organization. Spent all his time online, doing projects for the group. He even tried to get me to join."

"He sounds like a convert."

"Exactly," Truman said, as if Randall were a student who had just grasped an important concept. "The group provided him with an identity. That's why religious cults are so successful. They offer a pre-packaged identity to people who are lost at sea. And a lot of people are at sea these days."

"What happened to him?"

Truman shook his head grimly. "He became so involved with the group that his work began to suffer. By that time, it didn't seem to matter to him. The group had become everything to him. He ate, breathed and slept the Family."

He leaned back in the chair, smoke curling around his face. "Eventually, he lost his job. Then the girlfriend dumped him, and his life fell apart. Eventually, his mother called me. She knew we'd been friendly in the past and asked me if I could help him. The poor woman was desperate. She wanted me to get him to leave the group."

"You mean, deprogram him?"

A pained looked flitted across Truman's face. "I'd rather not use that word. I'm not a therapist. And I'm definitely not a deprogrammer. I simply spent time with him, talking with him. I was trying to help him see what was happening to him, how the group was manipulating him."

"Was he able to see that?"

"Eventually. It wasn't easy for him. Belonging to the Family had become a kind of addiction for him. He had no social life apart from the organization. When he was out of contact with the group for too long he became nervous, agitated, as if he were going through withdrawal."

"Or getting out of a cult."

"Exactly."

Truman pulled an ashtray from the drawer and set it on the edge of the desk. Randall scanned the bookshelf behind him and noticed titles: The Kingdom of the Cults, Brainwash, Holy Deception. "Would you describe the Family as a cult?" he asked.

"That's an interesting question. It certainly exhibits many of the characteristics of a cult. The demand for unquestioning loyalty and commitment. Relinquishing personal control. An 'us versus the rest of the world' mentality. When a group really gets off base, it develops an ends-justifies-the-means attitude. The group is the only outfit that has the truth, so any behavior that furthers its goals is justified. Lying, deception—"

"Murder?"

Truman squinted at him through the smoke rising from the pipe. "Yes, in extreme cases, I suppose that could happen." He set the pipe on the edge of the ashtray. "Of course, for people to be driven to that kind of extreme, there would almost certainly have to be a religious component to the group."

"Such as?"

"Think Islamic terrorists," Truman said. "People who think they're acting on God's orders sometimes take God's law into their own hands." He took a draw on the pipe. "All you'd need to turn a computer group into a cult would be a messiah."

"Some charismatic leader," Randall said.

"Correct. The authoritative voice that takes care of the sheep, answers all their questions. A father figure. Ultimately, that's what James was looking for."

"James?"

"James Wilton. My student."

Randall leaned forward quickly. "Wilton was your student?"

"Yes. Your friend wanted to find out more about what went on inside the group, so I referred him to James."

"Can you give me his telephone number?"

"Of course."

He thanked Truman and left quickly, anxious to track down Wilton. The nearest phone was just outside the sociology building. He called the number and heard two loud rings.

"I'm sorry," a recorded voice said. "That number has been disconnected, or is no longer in service."

James Wilton stood in the farthest corner of the dingy room, trembling. The telephone in the hallway rang a dozen times, until heavy footsteps thudded down the hall, a surly voice echoing along with them. "Whyn't ya answer the goddam phone for Chrissakes?"

The voice belonged to the fat man from down the hall. He didn't know the man's name. He didn't know the names of any of the others who lived in the building. He didn't want to know them, and he didn't want them to know him.

"Yeah?" the fat man said into the phone. "Bartelewski!," he hollered. "Telephone," and dropped the receiver to thump rhythmically against the wall.

Wilton exhaled slowly and lowered himself into a plastic kitchen chair next to the window. The call had not been for him. They had not found him.

He pulled back the thin yellow curtain that hid the room from the street. Scanning the street, he assured himself for the thousandth time that no one was watching the apartment from outside.

He let the curtain fall back. Maybe he really was safe.

161

Maybe they wouldn't be able to find him. Still, he couldn't take any chances. Not after what happened to that writer.

He felt bad about the writer, but it wasn't his fault. He hadn't wanted to talk to him in the first place. But he had been so persistent. And he had a way of making you feel comfortable, getting you to say more than you'd meant to.

It was only after the writer had left that Wilton began to worry. Had he told him too much? Would they find out? He had promised never to use Wilton's name. But now he was dead, and Wilton worried. Had the writer spoken to anyone about him? Had he left anything behind that could help them trace him?

He put his head in his hands. He should have known better. He never should have let down his guard. They would never stop trying to find him, no matter how long it took. It was the Fifth Protocol—perseverance. Whoever had been assigned the task of locating him would not stop until their task was completed.

And when they found him...he knew he was beyond the point of error correction now. He was "asynch," totally out of compliance with the protocols. They would not try to reprogram him.

So they must not find him, no matter how many times he had to move or how many identities he had to take on. He could not allow anyone to find him.

19

Randall drove back to the city on Route 280, which meanders up the middle of the San Francisco peninsula, along the green-brown ridge of the Santa Cruz hills. It is a route that traces the path of the San Andreas fault almost exactly, a fact that Peter had pointed out to him with ironic delight.

And that, Randall thought, was a perfect metaphor for life. You went along, blissfully unaware that at any moment the ground could open up and swallow you completely, as it had Peter. And who would ever know what had happened to you?

He had made plans to meet Erica Steiner for dinner, but arrived in the city with an hour to kill. It was just enough time to stop at Allison's to ask if she'd seen the hand-held computer Peter had been using. He almost believed that was the only reason he wanted to see her.

She met him at the door and put her arms around him. "I was afraid you wouldn't come back."

"Why?" His heart was pounding.

"I thought you might be mad at me."

"No," he said, sighing heavily. "I'm not mad at you." Mad at myself, he thought, but not you.

"Good." She snuggled closer. "I've got coffee on. Do you want some?"

"OK. I can't stay long. I've got to meet someone." He

decided not to mention Erica's name.

She poured the coffee. "What have you been up to?"

"I went back to the apartment," he said, then tried to find a good excuse for having done that. "I was looking for a briefcase I gave Peter when we graduated. It wasn't there, though."

Allison looked into her coffee and nodded, but said nothing.

"Speaking of missing things," he began awkwardly. "When you were at Peter's, did you happen to see a hand-held computer?"

"No," she said, not looking up. "Why?"

He shrugged. "The people at his office were wondering about it."

Her brow wrinkled. "Why did they ask you?"

He was not a good liar. "I mentioned that I was going to the apartment."

"When did you talk to them?"

He had painted himself into a corner. He hesitated, finally deciding he couldn't hide things from her. "I wanted to talk to them about Peter. To see if they knew anything about...what happened."

She stared at him, her eyes filling. "Why? It doesn't matter. Peter is gone. Nothing's going to change that."

He took her hand. "It's not just Peter, now. There's something going on. Something big. And I think it has to do with a story Peter was working on when he died."

She pulled her hand back and turned away from him. "Oh."

"I'm sorry–"

"No you're not," she said, glaring. "You're just like him."

"What?"

"He didn't care about me," she said, tears streaming down her cheeks now. "All he cared about was the stupid story."

"What story?"

"I don't know. The one he was working on. He wouldn't tell me what it was about. I don't think he wanted me to worry. But how could I not worry? It was driving him crazy. And he wouldn't leave it alone."

"Maybe he couldn't."

"He could have," she insisted. "And so can you."

No, he couldn't. Maybe it was journalistic arrogance. Maybe it was some commitment to Peter. Maybe it was just his own ego. But he couldn't let it go.

"I'm sorry," he said. "I didn't ask to get drawn into this, but I have. And I'm going to follow it until I get to the bottom of it. I've got to, for Peter's sake."

She glared at him, her eyes red, smoldering. "You don't give a damn about Peter. You're just trying to prove you're better than he was. He never got to write the big story, so now you're going to."

He didn't know how to answer that. Maybe she was right. It had been Peter's story, and Peter's life. And here he was, scavenging through Peter's belongings, falling in love with Peter's girlfriend.

"I'm sorry," he said. "I know this is hard for you."

She shook her head. "You don't care about me."

In a moment of clarity, he realized she wasn't thinking about Peter now. She was thinking about him.

It was time to lay his cards on the table. "Yes, I do care about you."

She took his hands in hers. "Then leave it alone. Peter is dead. Isn't that awful enough? Why do you have to make it worse? Don't go digging around trying to find things that don't matter. It's not going to change anything."

It was clear that he had a decision to make. A choice between the beautiful, needy woman in front of him, and the search for the truth about what happened to Peter.

He looked down, then back at her. "I'm sorry. I—"

She stood up, not letting him finish. "Please...just leave."

Allison watched through the bedroom window as Randall left. Turning from the window, she opened the bedroom closet, moving mechanically, as if in shock. In the darkness at the bottom of the closet was a pile of laundry. She pushed it aside, exposing a leather handle, and pulled the briefcase out of the closet. A stray sock that had been draped across the top fell off, revealing the initials "PAJ" along the top.

She sat back on the bed and stared at the unopened case for a moment. She had found it in Peter's car that morning, when the police called her with the news. No one had asked her about it—there was no reason they should have—and she hadn't mentioned it to anyone. She had not opened it, not wanting to know what was inside. Until now.

She pressed a thumb to the latch button. The lock snapped open, and she raised the top of the case.

Roy Lincoln drove his rumbling, rust-riddled Chevy Nova past the sign that read "Employee Parking" and felt a surge of pride. Only a few months ago, he had been without work, without hope, and without any prospect of things ever getting better. Now he was an employee of the San Francisco Medical Center.

Lincoln parked the car and checked his tie in the rear-view mirror. The mirror hung at an odd angle, but the tie was arrow straight, dark brown against the olive-tan of his uniform. One of the things he'd learned in recent months was the importance of making a good impression. His Shepherd had taught him that.

The employee entrance was a steel door, entered by an identification code. He smiled as he entered his code, remembering a time when even an electronic device as simple as this would have terrified him. He had never been good with electronic devices. That was before he'd joined the Family, of course.

If Roy Lincoln was pleased by his new-found confidence, his family was amazed.

"Computer group?" his mother had said. "Why you wanna go join a computer group? Damn fool, you never gonna get no job with a computer."

But joining the group hadn't cost him anything, and he'd had plenty of time to learn about computers in prison. Besides, they had promised they'd get him a job when he got out. Sure enough, a member of the group had put in a good word for him when the opening came up at the hospital. He'd been worried, of course. Every other time he'd applied for a job, he had been told he "lacked the necessary qualifications." Prison wasn't exactly the best reference to have on your resumé. But the hospital didn't seem to know or care about his record. Someone in the group had put in a good word for him, and that was good enough.

It was a fine job too, with decent pay and good benefits. He worked with nice people. The nurses were friendly, and even the doctors said hello to him. All he had to do was walk the floors, check doors, and make sure everything was where it was supposed to be.

He owed it all to the Family. And he was grateful. The Family knew how to take care of its own. In return, everyone in the group did what they could to help out, including Roy Lincoln.

He began his rounds in the intensive care unit. In the report room, the evening shift nurses sat giving reports to the incoming night nurses on the status of their patients.

Around the corner from the report room was the nursing station, an island between the two long hallways of the unit. Sally, the evening receptionist, sat behind the counter of the station, entering data into a computer.

"How's it going this evening?" Lincoln asked.

Sally looked up and smiled. "Hi, Roy. Everything's fine here."

"Thas' good. Don't want no commotion tonight."

Sally laughed. From the console next to her came a single quiet tone. A light on the console blinked. She reached over and pressed a button next to the light. "Yes, Mrs. Horton?"

A tinny voice came from the speaker. "I dropped my water glass. Can you get it for me?"

"The nurses are all in report right now. I'll send someone as soon as they get out."

"But I'm dying of thirst. I can't wait."

Sally rolled her eyes at Roy. "All right. I'm coming."

She disappeared around the corner of the station in the direction of Mrs. Horton's room.

He waited until Sally was gone, then walked around to the computer. Attached to the left side of the monitor was a yellow sticky tag, with two words written on it:

Password - yertstor

He pulled a notepad from his vest pocket and jotted the word down, checking twice to make sure he'd spelled it right.

Sally returned from Mrs. Horton's room and shook her head. "That woman."

"Kinda fussy, eh?"

"The worst."

"Well, don't let her bother you, now." He straightened, hitching his pants up slightly. "I'll see you later."

"OK. Have a good night, Roy."
"You too."

20

Erica had told Randall to meet her at Khan Toke, a Thai restaurant on Geary Boulevard. A ragged line of couples and groups filled the tiny entryway, but he didn't see Erica. At the front of the line, a red-jacketed maître d' called the name MacGregor, but no one responded. He tried again, and Randall realized it was McLagan, filtered through a Thai accent.

He waved a hand and edged to the front of the line. "I take your shoes, please," the maître d' said, handing him a small round coat-check.

Randall looked down, confused, and then remembered: it was the oriental thing, no shoes in the house. He removed his shoes and handed them to the maître d'.

The room was dark, the ceilings and walls lined in mahogany, red and gold wall coverings alternating with bamboo designs. Erica sat in a sunken area that was almost completely filled by the table, her legs tucked underneath her.

He lowered himself into the space opposite her.

"You OK?" she asked, scanning his face.

"Yeah," he said. "OK. Given the circumstances."

The waiter arrived with menus. Randall scanned it, totally lost. In Peabody, New Hampshire, ethnic food consisted of pizza. "Why don't you order?" he suggested.

"Sure."

When the waiter returned she ordered beef satay, pad Thai, and curried chicken. "And two Tsingha." She saw Randall's puzzled look and said, "Thai beer. I don't know about you, but I need one."

When the waiter left, Randall he asked what she'd found out at the office.

"I spoke to Sylvia. Apparently, Peter talked to her just before he died. He was asking about CompuSys. Seems they had just canceled their advertising contract with the magazine."

"Why?"

"She didn't know. It was totally unexpected. They'd been with us a long time, and they hadn't had any complaints. And here's the odd part. They renewed the contract right after Peter died."

"Why?"

"You tell me."

The waiter arrived with the beers and began to pour Erica's into a glass. She waved him off and picked up the bottle, sipping from it.

"Any sign of the hand-held?" Randall asked.

"No. And the company that lent it to us is pressing harder to get it back. Which seems odd. A lot of times they just write that stuff off."

Randall related his conversation with Ed Truman and his failed attempt to contact James Wilton.

"The Family again," she said. "I did some more digging about them. But it isn't easy to find unbiased information."

"How come?"

She pulled a couple of press releases from her bag. "Check the tag line on the bottom of those pieces."

"The Computer Information Bureau provides items of computer-related news to print, radio, and television journalists," he read.

Erica tapped the paper. "Guess who's behind the Computer Information Bureau?"

"The Family?"

"You've got it. And every press release they put out has some slant that promotes the group or one of its affiliates." She pulled out a notepad and read from it. "The Association of Programming Professionals, an organization called Computers in Schools, Up and Out–that's a work-skills program for prisoners–they're all offshoots of the Family, designed to funnel people into the group."

The waiter arrived with their food, laid out the dishes, and left.

"If you weed through the press releases and cross-reference what you find, you begin to uncover some interesting things," Erica said.

"Such as?

"Does the name Fordham Graves mean anything to you?"

The name was vaguely familiar, but he couldn't recall where he'd heard it. "Not sure."

"He's the executive director of the Family. Before that, he was president of a small but innovative software company called Magnicom Software. A few years ago, Magnicom was approached by a company that wanted to buy its technology. The buyer offered Graves a ridiculously low price. But it was a much larger company, and they threatened to develop competing technology and put Magnicom out of business if Graves didn't go along with the deal." She took a sip from her beer. "Guess who the larger company was."

"CompuSys?"

"Right again. Graves realized he couldn't win, and sold out. CompuSys swallowed Magnicom and spit out the seeds. Fordham Graves was one of the seeds."

"So he founded a group that hates CompuSys."

"Actually, the group was already in existence before Graves came along, but it was a much smaller group. Graves was hired in an effort to make the organization more successful."

"Looks as if he's doing a good job."

She nodded. "I'd say a half-million members in two years is pretty good."

"And in the meantime, he managed to turn the group against CompuSys."

"Right. Now if we could only figure out what the group had against Peter."

Randall stopped eating, put down his fork and looked at her squarely. "Do you think the Family was behind Peter's death?"

"Don't you?"

"I don't know."

"Look," Erica said, holding up fingers and counting off the facts. "Someone broke into a government computer system and changed things to make it look as if Peter had a criminal record. Someone also broke into PC Monthly's system and erased his files. His finances were messed up, and his phone and lights were shut off because of a 'computer error.' All that sounds like someone who knows a lot about computers."

"There are plenty of people who know a lot about computers."

"Peter wasn't writing investigative articles about plenty of people."

She was right, of course. "But that doesn't get us any closer to knowing what they had against him," he said.

She stared at her plate for a moment. "You said Peter talked to this guy Wilton. Any idea what it was about?"

"No. But I'm willing to bet any notes from that meeting are still on the hand-held."

She pointed a satay skewer at him. "We've got to find that damned hand-held."

"I asked Allison. She hadn't seen it."

"And you believe her?"

"Why not?"

She shrugged. "I just wouldn't put much stock in anything she says."

Against his better judgment, he said, "Would you mind telling me what you've got against Allison?"

She blinked, as if she'd been caught at something. "Nothing." She toyed with her food, cheeks flushed crimson. "She just never seemed like...Peter's type."

"Well, obviously Peter thought..." He stopped. She had turned, her eyes hard but liquid. The straight line of her chin dropped slightly, as if she were trying to control her facial muscles. It was a brief moment of vulnerability, a soft edge to her personality that he had not seen before. He had not realized before what an attractive woman she was, and wondered if Peter had thought so.

And suddenly it was clear to him. How could he have missed it before? Erica Steiner had been in love with Peter. Whether he had reciprocated those feelings or not, the relationship had been thwarted by the arrival of Allison. Erica had been left out in the cold.

She turned back to him, blinking, frowning slightly. "I'm sorry. I shouldn't have said anything. This whole thing has just–"

"That's OK," he said, releasing her from having to say more.

The waiter arrived to take their dishes, which had barely been touched. He asked if everything had been all right with the meal.

James Wilton stared at the door as if it were an explosive device about to go off. The knock came again.

He stiffened in his chair and tried to breathe slowly. If he did not acknowledge the knock, maybe whoever it was would go away. Maybe it was just a salesman.

There was another knock, then a voice.

"James? Are you there?"

He gasped involuntarily. It was a man's voice, the tone flat, impersonal. He did not recognize the voice.

"James? Are you OK? Let us in."

Us. There was more than one of them.

He looked around the apartment, his eyes wild. There was no way out other than through the door. Somehow, the San Francisco housing authority had overlooked this tiny apartment in the Mission district, overlooked the absence of a fire escape, a way out for someone in danger.

There was another sound: metal scratching against metal. It was a key being fitted into the lock, jiggling and scratching. They were picking the lock.

He crouched behind the chair, horrified, his mind racing, his breath coming in short gasps. They had found him. In spite of all his precautions they had found him.

The door burst open. Two men filled the door to the apartment. They were large, dressed in dark clothing. They moved toward him.

He screamed—a loud, piercing wail, like that of an animal caught in a trap—then turned, running full force toward the room's only window. The window's aging sash gave way before him as if it were made of popsicle sticks. He crashed through the window and fell to the lamplit street below.

The message light was blinking when Randall returned to the hotel. He called for the messages, hoping it might be Allison. It was not.

"What the hell's going on?" came the voice of Harold Dodge. "Do you still work here?"

Randall groaned. In the midst of everything else, he had forgotten to call Dodge. And Dodge was not happy about it. "You better be back here tomorrow, that's all I can say."

He looked at the clock. Once again, it was the middle of the night on the east coast. There was nothing else to do; he would have to call Dodge first thing in the morning.

He sank onto the bed, replaying the visit with Allison, the conversation with Erica Steiner. Why had CompuSys canceled its contract with PC Monthly just before Peter died, only to renew it later? Where was Peter's hand-held computer? Had there been a romantic relationship between Erica and Peter? Her comment about Allison came back now: "I wouldn't put much stock in anything she says."

Stock. Stock.

Then he remembered. There had been something in Peter's notes about CompuSys' stock. What about it? Was there some connection between the company's stock and its advertising?

He tried to think of someone he could talk to, someone who would know about the stock market. The only name that came to mind was that of a college friend, Tom Landulfson. An old drinking buddy, Tom had made a phenomenal amount of money on Wall Street in a very short time. Then, to the surprise of no one who knew him, he had retired to an isolated area outside of Reno, Nevada and become a high-tech hermit. He lived alone, providing investment services to far-flung customers by phone, fax, and e-mail.

He called Landulfson, who was pleased to hear from him, and seemed stoic about Peter's death. "Damn. That sucks," was his curt assessment.

He explained about the mystery of Peter's final

column. "There was something in his notes about CompuSys stock. I was wondering if you'd heard anything about them lately."

"That's funny. I was just talking to someone at Our Lady of the Desert about CompuSys."

"Our Lady of the what?"

"Desert. It's a monastery just outside of town. Pretty well-endowed. Seems the trust officers handling their endowment funds have been talking up CompuSys, so they asked me to check it out. And there are some funny things happening. The fundamentals don't seem to account for the chart activity."

"I have absolutely no idea what you're talking about," Randall said.

"That's OK. I'll explain it when I figure it out. Right now I'm hip-deep in annual reports, appointments, investment patterns, that kind of thing. It takes a while to weed through it all. Now that I know you're interested, I'll turn up the heat."

Frannie Jackson looked up from her word processor as a folder landed in her in-basket. She pulled the headphones from her ears and let them fall around her neck. "What's up?"

Maria, the night secretary for the emergency room, said, "Another leaper."

"From where?"

"Second story, over on San Paulo."

Frannie glanced at the name on the folder. "Is he OK?"

"Touch and go. He's pretty banged up."

"They taking him to ICU?"

"Yeah, soon as he's stabilized."

"OK. I'll call his file up."

Maria spun on her heels. "Good. Then get outta here."

"Really." It was past midnight, and Frannie's work day

had supposedly ended over an hour ago. She had stayed late to finish some transcriptions, knowing that if they weren't done tonight, they wouldn't be completed until the next day, and the department would hear about it from the doctors. That meant Frannie would hear about it.

She called up the file for the new patient and moved it into the file area for the intensive care unit. The file gave the doctors and nurses in the unit immediate access to the patient's medical history, allergies, current condition, medications—everything there was to know about him.

Her work completed, she put the system into standby mode. This allowed physicians to call in from outside the hospital and check on patients' progress, change prescriptions, and make new orders.

Frannie put her coat on, gathered her belongings, and took a last look over the office. Everything seemed in order. She turned off the light.

As the door closed, she heard the phone ring on the outside line to the system–probably a doctor who was just going to bed and remembered something he wanted to add to a patient's record.

Frannie held the door and considered picking up the line to help the caller out. Most of the doctors hadn't bothered to learn their way around the system. She had watched them—without their knowing it— stumble around, wasting time, unable to even locate their patient's file, let alone make changes.

She glanced at her watch. No. Whoever it was could do it themselves. If worse came to worse, they'd leave a message and someone would take care of it tomorrow. She was going home to bed.

The telephone continued to ring in the darkened office. On the sixth ring, the system answered the phone and requested the caller's name. The name appeared on the screen.

NBYAM

Dr. Nicholas Byam, renowned heart surgeon, had performed countless multiple-bypass operations during his years at the Los Angeles Medical Center. He had once flown to the Bay area to lead the surgical team operating on a stricken ambassador. As a result of that assignment, he had been granted professional privileges at San Francisco Medical, including access to the hospital's computerized record system for physicians.

Byam had never had occasion to use the system, and had himself died of a massive myocardial infarction three months earlier. Unaware of his death, the administrators at San Francisco Medical had not removed his name from the system.

The system requested a password, and the caller entered

LAKERS

Dr. Byam had been a basketball fan, though he had never learned the first thing about computers. That kind of task belonged to support staff, who had more time for such things.

The caller navigated the system with the expertise of an advanced user. The "Patient Search" feature revealed that a patient named James Wilton was being transferred from the emergency room to the intensive care unit.

The caller requested Wilton's file. Normally, only the doctor assigned to a patient could make changes to records. However, because the patient had been admitted through the emergency room, he had no private physician yet.

The caller entered "Edit Mode" and scrolled through

the patient's medical history. The cursor stopped at a line, then moved to the beginning of it. One by one, the words in the line disappeared.

With the line deleted, the caller closed the file and placed it back in the queue for the intensive care unit. To the casual user, there was no indication that any changes had been made to the file. A more sophisticated operator might check the date-stamp at the operating system level and notice that a change had been made. The caller could have fixed that, but chose not to, and instead made another change, one that was certain to be noticed should anyone investigate the records carefully. Selecting the "User Options" feature, the caller chose "Change Password." The system requested the old password, then presented a box for the entry of a new password. Character by character, the new password appeared in the blanks.

MONSANTO

21

By now, the hunter knew more about Randall McLagan than anyone else alive, perhaps including McLagan himself.

He knew where and when McLagan had been born, where he had lived, and every telephone number he had ever used. He knew what kind of car McLagan drove, and when his license would expire. He knew that little Randy McLagan had suffered an inner ear infection when he was 6, and that Randall P. McLagan had received a C in Biology when he was a sophomore at Dartmouth. He knew that McLagan drank Newcastle Brown Ale and that he had recently purchased a six-pack of it from the Shop & Save in Lebanon, New Hampshire. At 6:15 p.m.

Until now, the hunter had merely been collecting information. Now he was ready to use it. He began, working with the skill of a digital sniper, slipping into private and governmental databases, completing his task and leaving without a trace. No one would ever be able to trace his activities, nor would anyone realize that the actions, spread as they were over a wide range of systems and domains, had been undertaken by a single individual.

Staring at his screen, with the vital statistics of Randall McLagan's life spread out before him, the hunter saw an image in his mind's eye: a person at ease, unaware he is being observed under the cross hairs of a gun.

The phone rang at 9 o'clock the next morning. "Hello," Randall said groggily.

"Mr. McLagan? This is the front desk."

He hadn't requested a wake-up call. "Yes?"

"We need to speak to you. Could you come down, please?"

At the desk, two clerks hovered in front of the reservation system. One saw him coming and whispered to the other, who looked up.

"Ah, Mr. McLagan." He lowered his voice slightly. "We're having a little trouble confirming your charges with the credit card you gave us. Apparently, you've reached your limit on that card. Do you have another card you could use?"

"Sure." As far as he knew, he had plenty of available credit on that card. But he wasn't in any mood to argue with them. He slapped another card on the counter.

"Very good, sir. That will be just a moment." He took the card, ran it through the card reader, and handed it back to Randall.

A moment later he said, "I'm sorry, sir. That card seems to be at its limit also. Do you have another?"

"What? I hardly ever use that card."

The clerk shrugged. "It's showing that you have a five hundred dollar limit, and that you're well over that amount."

"Five hundred?" The limit on that card was supposed to be five thousand.

Randall was fully awake now. He pulled his remaining card from the wallet and placed it on the counter. It was a card he never used, one that he kept purely for emergency purposes.

The clerk took the card, said nothing, and ran it

through the reader. A moment later, he looked up, his face blank. "I'm sorry, sir." He placed the card back on the counter, unsmiling. "That card has been deactivated."

"That's ridiculous. I never use–"

"Do you have another card, Mr. McLagan?"

"No."

"I'm sorry, sir. We really can't extend your stay with us without some kind of deposit. That's for your own protection."

Right. My protection. He flipped through his cards and came upon the ATM card from his bank. "Is there an ATM machine around here?"

"Yes, sir. There's one next door, just outside the bank."

"All right. I'll be right back."

Fuming, Randall thrust himself through the revolving doors and strode to a row of ATMs carved into the solid marble face of the Express Bank next to the hotel. He stuck his card in and requested two hundred and fifty dollars, the most he could withdraw on any given day. The system responded.

Insufficient funds to complete this transaction.
Do you care to make another transaction?

Insufficient funds? There was over a thousand dollars in that account. He pushed the buttons to repeat the transaction, this time for one hundred and fifty dollars.

Insufficient funds to complete this transaction.
Do you care to make another transaction?

He tried smaller amounts. The machine was unmoved.

The credit cards, the ATM card. This was more than just coincidence. This was just what had happened to Peter.

Someone was out to get him.

He checked his wallet and found 45 dollars. Fortunately, he'd already paid for his return flight home, so that was taken care of. If all else failed, he could just get on the plane.

No, he thought. That was just what they wanted. He wasn't leaving until he'd settled things. But where could he stay until then? Neither Erica nor Allison was happy with him now. And Harry's apartment didn't have room to turn around in, let alone put up a guest.

Then it came to him: Mrs. Toomey had said the rent on Peter's apartment was paid up through the end of the month. She wouldn't have new tenants moving in till the beginning of the next month. He could stay there.

And do what?

He recalled an assignment he'd had a couple of years earlier, an investigative piece about a company that had been dumping pollutants into the local water supply. He had been stymied, stonewalled by the company's officers, and not sure how to proceed.

He had discussed the issue with Peter. "Here's the secret of investigative reporting," Peter had said. "Don't ever be satisfied with the first answer you get. Most of the time, reporters let people off the hook. They don't dig deep enough. The secret is to ask the next question."

Now, contemplating what to do next, he heard Peter's voice as clearly as if he were standing on the sidewalk beside him.

Ask the next question.

Mrs. Toomey eyed him skeptically. "How long will it take?"

"I'm not sure. It just seems as if the only way to really clean the place out is to stay here until it's done." He tried not to sound too anxious. Really, he was doing her a favor.

Mrs. Toomey's face fluctuated between suspicion and relief. "All right. But you'll have to be done by the end of the month."

He assured her he'd be out in a week. Two at the most. She gave him the key, along with a few more admonitions and warnings.

In the apartment, he flipped the switch in the entryway and was relieved when the light came on. It wouldn't be any fun camping out without electricity.

He checked the telephone. There was a dial tone. Apparently, the problem with the phone company had been a "computer error" too. He considered who to call. If Harry or Erica were looking for him, they'd try the hotel. And if anyone from the newspaper...

The newspaper. He'd forgotten to call Harold Dodge.

He looked at his watch. Eleven a.m., which made it two p.m. on the east coast. Dodge would probably just be getting back from lunch. He called Dodge's direct number. No use putting it off.

Dodge answered on the first ring. "Peabody Herald. Dodge here." He was the only person Randall knew who could make his own name sound like an accusation.

"Harold. It's Randall McLagan."

There was a pause. In the silence, Randall imagined he heard a shotgun being cocked.

"Well, it's nice to hear from you. Did you have a good trip?"

He could tell Dodge thought he was back on the east coast. He would clear that up later. Groveling first. "I'm sorry I haven't gotten back to you–"

"Sorry? Hell, don't worry about it. I'm just trying to put this goddamn paper out by myself here. Why should I need a staff, for God's sake?"

"I know. But the situation here has gotten a lot more

complicated than I thought."

"Complicated?" Dodge roared, then flew into a spell of coughing. When he recovered, he said, "I'll tell you about complicated. Complicated is trying to explain to people why no one has returned their calls for a week. Complicated is finding enough material to fill a weekly paper."

"I know. But I'm working on a piece. A big piece."

"About what?"

"About my friend's death. I haven't chased it all down yet, but it has something to do with a computer group–"

"Computer group? What's this got to do with Peabody?"

He scrambled. "This is a big organization. They operate nationwide–"

"Great. Too bad we're not a nationwide newspaper."

He could have argued for the local connection. After all, he'd first heard about the Family while walking to work in Peabody. And he was sure he could find local people involved in the group.

But he was tired. He didn't feel like arguing. And Dodge was right. The article didn't have anything to do with Peabody. It was more important than anything in Peabody, New Hampshire.

He considered explaining about the circumstances surrounding Peter's death, about his credit cards being messed up, and about being thrown out of the hotel. But he knew none of that would carry any weight with Harold Dodge. All Dodge wanted to know was when he would be back at work.

So he said, "I'm not sure when I'll be back. I've got a few things to finish up out here."

"You're still out there?" Dodge growled. "Oh, for...you've got till tomorrow. If I don't see you at your desk first thing in the morning, you can look for another job."

Randall paused. The smart thing would be to pacify Dodge, forget about this whole mess, and go home. But he was sick of doing the right thing. He was sick of playing by the rules, obeying orders, and keeping his nose clean. And he was sick of Harold Dodge.

"Harold?" he said politely.

"What?"

"Go to hell."

He hung up. Now he'd done it. For better or worse, he was into this with both feet. He had no money, no credit, and no job. By the end of the month, he wouldn't have a place to stay. Maybe he'd write an article: "From Hometown to Homeless in One Week."

The phone rang. He picked it up cautiously. "Hello?"

"Hey. It's Harry."

"Hey." It was good to hear a friendly voice. "How'd you find me?"

"I called the hotel. They said you checked out, but they didn't know where you went. I figured you hadn't just split, so I put two and two together. What happened?"

He gave Harry the rundown on what had happened. "The good news is, I just quit my job."

"Damn. The bees don't start stinging till you get near the nest."

"What?"

"Something my grandfather used to say: When you start running into opposition, you're probably getting close to where you want to be."

"I must be getting real close, then."

"Did you talk to Truman?"

"Yes." He related the conversation, including the part about Truman's former student.

"Ah," Harry said. "The mysterious Wilton. I'll see if I can track him down. In the meantime, I've got something else I think you'll find interesting."

"What's that?"

"How fast can you get over here?"

Harry held up the Family disk he'd pulled from his salvage drawer. "Remember this?"

"Yeah. What about it?"

"I started out by checking it for viruses. It came up clean for all the standard viruses. Then I ran Bug-Off."

"I never heard of it," Randall said.

"Of course not. I wrote it myself," Harry said, in a tone indicating that real programmers wrote their own software. "Guess what it found?"

"Infected?"

"Not just infected. This thing is the AIDS of computer viruses. It's about the nastiest thing I've ever seen. And most people will never know they've been hit. It inserts its own code into the program it's infecting, in a way that's almost impossible to detect."

He began keying in commands. "To figure out what the virus does, I had to take it apart."

As he scrolled through the source code, Randall recognized words and phrases from the Family's setup program. "It took me awhile to find where the virus was hidden," Harry said. "Even then, I couldn't figure out exactly what it did. At first glance, it doesn't have any obvious function."

"Why go to the trouble of designing a nearly invisible virus if it doesn't do anything?" Randall asked

"That's what I wondered–until I stumbled on a piece of code that looked familiar." He pointed to a section of code on the screen. To Randall, it was computer gibberish.

"What's that?"

"A timer. A little program that repeats a task periodically. In this case, the timer was designed to flash messages on the screen."

"I don't remember any messages flashing on the screen when I signed on."

"That's because the messages only last for about 1/40 of a second—too fast to read consciously, but plenty of time to register with the unconscious mind."

"You mean subliminal messages?"

"You've got it."

"What kind of messages?"

Harry hit the Page Down key several times. A new section of gibberish appeared on the left side of the screen. On the right side, however, in the middle of various computer commands, an English phrase stood out clearly:

I will join the Family.

"Subtle, huh? And that's not the strangest one. Check this out."

The Father loves me.

"The Father," Randall said. "That was in Peter's notes."

"Right."

"Some kind of joke?"

"I don't think so."

Randall thought for a moment. "Ed Truman said cults need an authority figure, someone for the troops to rally around. A prophet or messiah."

"Well, if this guy is the messiah, he's managed to keep himself well hidden. Makes you wonder why."

"Maybe that's what Peter found out."

Harry stared at the screen for a moment. "This is serious stuff, man."

Randall nodded. "Yeah."

Harry picked up the phone and punched out a number. "I've got a friend. Someone who should be able to help us." As the phone rang at the other end he added, "If they want a fight, we'll give it to them."

22

They drove north over the Golden Gate, turning west at Marin City and passing through the Tamalpais Valley. The road turned abruptly, dramatically, skirting the shore in long, sweeping vistas. Passing the Muir Woods, they turned east, away from the ocean. Here the land rolled like a green-brown ocean, sparse trees dotting the tops of arroyos, dry creek beds occasionally crossing under the road. There were no houses or buildings of any kind to be seen.

"This guy likes his privacy," Randall said.

"Occupational bias," Harry replied. "He's an information broker."

"What's does that mean? He sells information?"

"More like a private eye with a computer. You need information, he finds it–for a price."

Sam Spade with a keyboard, Randall thought. "How does one get into that line of work?"

"Ferret got into it by being arrested."

"Ferret?"

"Ferris Tomzak. He was a tax consultant. Got mad about how the government was wasting money, so he set up a web site on how to fight the IRS. It was pretty popular for a while."

"I'm sure the government loved that."

"Right. He went away one weekend and someone

uploaded a stolen IRS document to his system. The Secret Service found it and arrested him."

"Sounds familiar."

Harry shook his head with disgust. "There wasn't anything in the file you couldn't find out by calling the local library. But it was stolen. That's all the government needed."

"Did he ever find out who planted it?"

"Nope. Probably some government drone who didn't like him telling people how to pay less taxes. They probably just wanted to scare him off."

"I take it that didn't work."

"Just the opposite. While he was putting together his defense, he found out just how much the government knew about him. He became an expert on computer databases—how to find information about people, how to protect yourself. So now he's a consultant, and makes about ten times as much as he used to."

"How much does he charge?"

"Don't worry about it. He owes me a favor. And I think this will appeal to his sense of injustice."

They turned on an unmarked dirt road. The road climbed, and became a rutted path that wound upward through thickening trees. The car churned up a cloud of dust, climbing till they came to a clearing. A concrete building stuck out of a hillside, tall evergreens standing sentry on either side.

Harry pulled up opposite the building. "One thing," he said as they got out. "Let him do the talking. He gets defensive if people ask him too many questions."

"Got it."

The building had no windows on the front, just a thick metal door that opened as they walked up to it. In the doorway stood a tall, middle-aged man with long gray hair tied in a ponytail, a matching grizzly beard. The stub of a cigarette jutted from the corner of his mouth.

"Hey, Harry," he said, not smiling and not removing the cigarette. "How you doing?"

"Good. This is the friend I told you about. Randall McLagan."

Randall held out a hand. "It's Ferret, right?"

Ferret ignored the hand. "Yeah. Ferret. A weasel-like mammal that hunts rats."

"Right," Randall said, his hand slinking back to his pocket.

He led them down a hallway to the back of the house, where a long room ran the length of the building. It looked like a computer flea market, rows of tables and desks bearing equipment of every size, type and description. A bank of television monitors displayed a long stretch of highway passing over rolling hills, the dirt driveway that led up to the house, Harry's car parked outside the front door.

Ferret gestured to a nubby sofa along one wall. As Harry and Randall lowered themselves into it, it gave off the smell of stale cigarette smoke.

Ferret fell into a large leather office chair on rollers, tossed the cigarette stub into a can on the floor, and lit a new cigarette. "Harry says you're in trouble."

Randall told him about the problem with his credit cards and the ATM machine. "But I know I've got all kinds of money in that account."

Ferret blew a stream of smoke from the side of his mouth. "Don't bet on it."

He rolled his chair to a nearby desk and swiveled the monitor it so Randall and Harry could see it. Resting the cigarette in an ashtray that blossomed with dead butts, he began typing. "What's your full name?"

"Randall Patrick McLagan."

"Birth date?"

"December 17, 1963."

"Social Security Number?"

Randall hesitated, not sure he should trust this guy with his social security number.

"Never mind," Ferret said. He typed a few commands into the system. A moment later, a number appeared on the screen. Randall peered at it. It was his social security number.

"Just trying to save time," Ferret said. "It'll go faster if you help me."

Randall swallowed once. "All right."

"Peabody Savings Bank?" he asked.

"That's right."

"You're overdrawn. Way overdrawn."

Randall leaned toward the screen. "How did you do that?"

Ferret snorted. "What do you want to know? You want to know the names of tall thin people who live Seattle? You want to cross-tab that with people who flew to Boston last month? And bought a new suit while they were there? I can tell you."

"That's OK. I believe you."

"OK. Let's check your credit cards."

His fingers flew on the keyboard. The screen filled with data and he paged down, a low whistle escaping from the shaggy beard. "Man. Somebody's been on a spending spree. You didn't happen to buy a new car in Dallas in the last couple of days?"

"What? I've never even been to Dallas."

Ferret nodded. "And you probably didn't use your calling card to make a whole bunch of overseas calls."

Randall fell back against the sofa. "No."

"Airline tickets to Germany?"

He sank lower and closed his eyes. "No."

"OK. We'll straighten all that out later. Let's check

your personal records."

Randall sighed heavily. "I thought all this stuff was supposed to be private."

"It is," Ferret said without taking his eyes off the screen. "Blame in on the Privacy Act of 1974. Before that, all your personal information was stuck away in filing cabinets in a hundred different agencies. The inefficiency of the system actually protected you. Along came the Privacy Act, and they started putting all this stuff on computers so folks could have access to their records." He shook his head. "Once it's on one computer, it's everywhere."

A new screen appeared on the monitor. "Do you have leukemia?" Ferret asked.

"What?"

"All right. We'll take care of that later." He flipped to another screen, his eyes flickering over it. "Don't be surprised if you get audited by the infernal revenue service." Another screen. "Let's see...your apartment may be dark when you get home. You'll probably have to reset the clock on the VCR."

Black humor, Randall thought. Just what I need.

"And don't be surprised if you have a lot of strange junk mail when you get home. Hard-core porno, S&M, that kind of thing."

It was all sounding too familiar.

"Any idea who's doing this to you?" Ferret asked.

Randall glanced at Harry, who said, "It may have something to do with the Family."

"Shit," Ferret said, sounding as if he'd rather have heard any other name. He stopped typing. "They're ornery bastards. True believers. The kind you don't want to cross."

"I'm finding that out," Randall said.

Ferret thought for a moment, then turned back to the

computer and began typing again. "OK, first you're going to need a new social security number." He entered some information into the system. "How much money did you have in your bank account before all this started?"

"A little over a thousand dollars."

"Good." A moment later, a number appeared on the screen. He wrote it on a piece of paper. "This is your new social security number. If anyone at the bank asks, give them this number."

"What bank?"

"BayWest. On the corner of Geary and Post in San Francisco. They're about to receive a wire transfer for a thousand dollars in the name of Bernard Salzman."

"Who's he?"

"A guy about your age who looked a little like you...except that he died about two weeks ago."

"And where's this money going to come from?"

Ferret grinned, revealing a large gap in his front teeth. "From your bank, back in New Hampshire." Before Randall could object, he said, "If you're worrying about the law, don't. The scary part about this isn't getting caught. The scary part is how easy it is."

He hit a key, printing out the information on the bank account, and handed it to Randall. "Get the money in small bills. All of it. That's going to be your operating capital for a while."

"Wouldn't it be easier to leave the money in the account and use an ATM?"

"No more ATM cards for you. You're going to pay cash for everything. No credit cards. No calling cards. As far as the system is concerned, you're going to disappear." He pulled out another cigarette and lit it. "Now tell me how you got mixed up with the Family. And don't leave anything out."

Randall told him about Peter's death, the missing files,

the police report, the unfinished column with the cryptic notes. "We're still trying to track down James Wilton. And we have no idea who the Father is."

Ferret glanced at Harry, who shrugged. "I tried. Nothing."

"Amateurs," Ferret said, shaking his head. "OK. Let's see what we can find out." He turned back to the computer and entered a string of commands. With a nod of his head, he gestured to a stove in one corner of the room. "Get yourself some coffee. This may take a while."

They poured coffee and wandered back to the sofa. On the wall over it hung a photograph of a contraption that looked like a cross between a weaver's loom and a player piano. The caption read, "Hollerith Machine - Forerunner of the Modern Computer."

"That was designed by a guy who worked for the census bureau," Harry told Randall. "Later founded the Tabulating Machine Company." Randall looked at him blankly, and he added, "IBM."

"Oh."

Overhearing, still typing, Ferret said, "They sold a lot of those machines. The Nazis even bought one to keep track of the Jewish population of Germany and the occupied countries. It was very good at keeping track of a rapidly decreasing number. I keep the picture to remind me."

Randall nodded. With a name like Tomzak, he probably had a good reason for not wanting to forget.

"Damn," Ferret said, shaking his head.

"What's up?" Harry asked.

"This guy Wilton has disappeared. I've got all his old records up until a few weeks ago, but then everything stops cold. It's as if he was trying to cover his tracks—the electronic equivalent of brushing the trail behind him, crossing streams, that kind of thing. Whoever he is, this guy knows what he's doing."

The system beeped, indicating that another search was complete. Ferret flipped to that window and scanned the contents of the screen. "Strange. Very strange."

He pressed a key, printed out the screen and handed it to Randall. "You were asking about someone called the Father. This was posted on the net a couple of years ago."

I have arrived. The culmination of the ages is upon you. You have struggled in darkness, but now the light has dawned. The medium has been prepared. Now, my message shall go forth to the ends of the world. The questions that have plagued all mankind for all time are about to be answered. The time predicted by the sages and prophets of all time has come. The hope of every nation, the essence of all true faith, the end point of history is here.

The Father

23

Getting the money from the bank was as easy as Ferret had said it would be. "There you go, sir," the teller said, sliding the freshly-counted pile of twenties toward him.

Randall stuffed the bills into an envelope and walked out, glancing up at the security camera by the door, wondering if it were connected to a computer.

Next move. Check in with Erica. He found a phone booth and looked up her home phone number. Pulling change from his pocket, he searched for the slot to insert it.

There was none. The phone accepted only calling cards or credit cards. Suddenly, he felt helpless. This was the electronic frontier, and he was homeless.

He found Erica's address in the book: 45 Cornwall, only a few blocks away. All right, he would do it the old-fashioned way. He would drop in on her.

45 Cornwall was a blue-gray colonial that had been split into apartments. Parked in front was a bright red Toyota with a bumper sticker that read, "God is coming...and is She ever pissed." That, he was fairly sure, was Erica Steiner's car.

He rang the bell, and Erica appeared behind the beveled-glass door. "Where the heck have you been? I called the hotel and they told me you left."

"It's been an interesting day," he said, relieved that she seemed to have put the previous night behind her.

She made tea while he filled her in on the day's events, including the incident with the pay phone. "You don't realize how dependent you are on the system until you're outside of it. I'm the invisible man."

She nodded thoughtfully. "Hang on. I've got something that should help."

She left and returned a minute later carrying a laptop computer. "This thing has a built-in cell phone. It's an evaluation unit the magazine gave me to review. You can use it until you get things straightened out."

He shook his head. "Thanks. But I don't have a cell phone account."

"Not a problem. The manufacturer set up a temporary phone account in my name. You don't think I'm going to pay for the calls while I review this thing? And they don't need to know who's using it."

"Are you sure you want to get mixed up in this?"

She shrugged. "If PC Monthly is involved—and it looks as if it may be—then I'm already involved."

She turned the unit on and slid it toward him. "Try it out. Call someone."

To Randall, it looked like a typical keyboard layout. "Where's the phone?"

"It uses the computer's microphone and keypad. Go on, call someone."

He called Harry. "I'm at Erica's," he said, and told him about the loaner.

"Good. The less you use the regular channels, the better."

There was a burst of static. "Hang on." Harry was gone for a minute, then came back. "That was Ferret. He found Wilton."

Randall pulled out a notepad, wrote down the address,

and hung up.

"You know," Erica said, eyebrows raised, "you can use the computer to take notes."

"I know." He closed the unit. "Right now, I trust pen and paper more."

"I hear you."

San Paulo Avenue was a tight row of run-down buildings in the Mission district. The house at #145 San Paulo had survived years of major and minor earthquakes, but the stresses showed in its sagging window sills, cracked foundation and lopsided clapboards.

"Nice place to hide in," Erica mumbled.

Randall pushed the doorbell again. From within came the sound of heavy, shuffling footsteps and a deep, whining voice. "I'm comin', I'm comin'."

The door opened, revealing a huge, bulging T-shirt that hung out over drooping pants. In the shadows atop the T-shirt was a round, balding head, shaggy patches of dark hair on either side, eyes ringed with red lines. From somewhere in the background came the sound of an auto race on a television. The man eyed Randall and Erica suspiciously. "Yeah?"

"We're looking for James Wilton," Randall said.

"You with the police?"

"No. We're just...friends. We've been trying to get in touch with him."

"Yeah? Well you're a little late. He's not here."

"Where is he?" Erica asked.

"Last time I saw him, he was lying out there," the man said, pointing to the street. He hooked a thumb upward, over their heads, where the center window of the second floor was covered with cardboard and duct tape. "Sonovabitch owes me about two hunerd dollars for that."

"What happened?"

"You tell me. About 10 o'clock last night, I hear this gawdawful scream, then a crash. I come out in the hallway just in time to see these two guys bookin' it outta here. Then I see him, lying out in the street."

"Did you recognize the men?"

"Nah. What am I, the doorman?"

"So you'd never seen them before?" Erica asked.

He glared at her. "Look, the people who stay here ain't exactly looking for attention. Most of 'em pay me in cash. Sometimes they stay a week, sometimes a coupla months. I don't ask a lot of questions, and they don't give me a lot of grief." He shook his head. "I shoulda known this guy was gonna be trouble."

"Why?"

"He was a nut case. Made me promise never to tell anyone he lived here. He hardly ever left the place, and when he did, it was at night. I mean, he was a real weenie."

"Do you know where they took him?"

He yawned, scratching his great belly. "Got me. Probably the City Medical Center. That's where they take all the wackos."

They turned to leave, and the man yelled after them. "Hey, you see him, tell him he owes me for the window. And he owes me for this week, too."

At the Division of Motor Vehicles office in Keene, New Hampshire, Toni Erickson pointed to the stool in front of the camera. "All right, Mrs. Thompson, if you'll just have a seat." She was trying to be pleasant, despite her annoyance. The whole point of evening hours was to allow people who worked during the day to get their licenses renewed. Edith Thompson, 83 years old, could have come at any other time of day. But no, she had to come right at closing time.

The old woman lowered herself onto the stool primly, trying to arrange herself as she sat.

"Look right up into the camera and smile," Toni said.

A minute later, Mrs. Thompson's new driver's license popped out of the machine. "There you go, Mrs. Thompson."

She winced at the photograph. "Oh, my goodness. How hideous."

"It's the new system," Toni said, trying to maintain her patience. "It's a lot faster, but the photos aren't as flattering as the old ones." She thought about explaining—the old cameras used regular film, while the new system was digital, and the images tended to be washed-out, the subjects looking as if they were in a police lineup. Minor wrinkles and blemishes became disfiguring scars. But she knew the technology would be lost on Mrs. Thompson. "Nobody looks good in them," she said.

Mrs. Thompson left, still fretting over her new license. Toni closed the office, in a rush to get to her sister's house so they could go shopping.

A half hour later, the outside line to the computer rang. The system had been set up so the department supervisor could check its status from home.

The system asked for the caller's password. A word appeared on the screen in the darkened office.

GUEST

Password incorrect. Please enter correct password:

The caller tried another password, and received the same message. Then this:

SUPER

Password approved.

A menu appeared on the screen. The caller chose option 4, "Search licensees."

Please enter licensee's last name: MCLAGAN

First name: RANDALL

Middle initial: P

Within seconds, the system located the file containing the digitized image of Randall McLagan. The caller downloaded the file, a transfer that took only seconds.

The caller logged off and the transmission was disconnected. No record was maintained of the call.

In the darkness of the alley, a huge 18-wheeler was backing up, its safety alarm beeping. Wilton had run until there was no place left to run. He was up against a brick wall, the truck growing closer, bearing down upon him. He tried to scream, but no words came out, because a long, thin snake had crawled down his nose, preventing him from making a sound. The truck grew closer, closer, and Wilton's eyes flew open in horror.

He was in a bed, staring up at a white ceiling. The beeping sound came from some mechanical device nearby. He turned his head slowly to the left; dull light filtered in through a curtained window. He looked right, and a sharp pain shot through his skull. He winced and tried to cry out, but as in the dream he could not make a sound.

Later—he had no idea how long—the pain subsided and he opened his eyes. He tried looking to his right again, and saw an interior window, behind which a woman in a white uniform sat writing at a desk.

He closed his eyes. When he reopened them, the room was dark. Now, vaguely aware that time had passed, he remembered what happened. The men...the fall through the window...and then, as he lay in the street, losing consciousness, the sensation that something was being torn from his wrist.

With every bit of concentration available to him, Wilton raised his right arm slightly and stared at his wrist.

His Med-alert bracelet was missing.

The arm fell back to the bed. He had to let someone know. But he was so tired, and every bone and muscle in his body ached.

He closed his eyes and reopened them a moment later. The light in the room had changed again. How long had it been?

Out of the corner of his eye, without moving his head, he saw a white cord hanging over the left guardrail of the bed, a button attached to the end. He raised his arm toward it.

Pain shot like a knife through his elbow, sending a spasm through his entire body, and pain echoed back from every imaginable joint. The device over his head beeped wildly, followed by the sound of a scraping chair and footsteps outside the room. A white uniform entered the room, but before he could acknowledge it, darkness washed over him again.

Time passed. He seemed to be under water now, but he heard a voice.

"Mr. Wilton. Can you hear me?"

He opened his eyes slowly. The blurry image of a woman hovered over his face. "James? Your sister's here."

He closed his eyes. His sister. It took him a moment, but then he decided. In spite of the pain and confusion, he was fairly sure. He didn't have a sister.

He opened his eyes again. The nurse moved aside, making room for another woman. This one had reddish hair and was dressed in street clothes. He felt the slight pressure of her hand on his. "James? Can you hear me?"

The nurse whispered to the woman, words that made no sense to him: "The nasogastric tube...difficult to talk." She said something else, then left the room.

Another person appeared behind the woman, a man. Wilton didn't recognize either of them, and he didn't want to be left alone with them. Panicking, he looked for the call button.

The woman patted his hand. "It's OK," she said quietly. "We're friends. We're not with them."

Wilton looked into her eyes. He tried to form the words, "Who are you?" but his lips were dry and cracked and he could not make enough air pass his lips to form the words. What breath he had smelled sickly sweet to him.

The man leaned towards him. "Can you tell us who did this to you?"

Wilton shook his head slowly, as best he could. He could not trust these people. For all he knew, they were disciples, testing to see if he was still configured to the group.

The man went around to the other side of the bed. "We're friends of Peter Jacobson," he said. "We have reason to believe that he was killed, and that the Family is somehow involved."

Wilton turned his head away.

"Do you remember talking to Peter Jacobson?" the man asked.

Wilton shook his head slowly, almost imperceptibly.

"Please," the woman said. "You've got to help us.

The man glanced out the window toward the nursing station, then leaned over the railing close to Wilton. "We know what happened to you. The police think it was a burglary. But I'm willing to bet there was more to it than that. And I think you know that."

Wilton forced himself to speak. The words came thin and rasping. "Leave...me...alone..."

"Mr. Wilton, you're in danger," the woman said. "We know that. We want to help you. But you have to help us."

He shook his head again.

"Please. We need–"

The nurse came back into the room, and the visitors stopped talking. All three stared at the bed, and the nurse said, "I'm afraid that's all the time we can give you. He really needs to rest."

The woman leaned close and took Wilton's hand. He felt a piece of paper being pressed into it. "We can help you," she whispered. "Call me when you're feeling better." They left, glancing back at him as they did.

The nurse lowered the side of the guard rail and fiddled with the IV connection on the back of his hand. "Wasn't that nice, your sister coming to visit you? I'm glad you were able to be awake while they were here."

Wilton glanced down at the paper in his other hand. It was a business card. He cupped his hand over the card, closed his eyes, and felt a bead of sweat drip down the side of his temple.

"Are you still warm, Mr. Wilton? You're sweating so much. Would you like me to turn up the air conditioner?"

He managed to shake his head slightly. He wasn't hot, in fact, he was cold. He remembered there was something he'd wanted to tell them, but he couldn't remember what.

The nurse busied herself with the IV bag. Wilton looked up and watched the process anxiously.

She saw his glance. "I'm going to have to get a new bag of IV fluid for you," she said. "We don't want you to get dehydrated."

As she left, Wilton looked up at the IV bag. It was almost empty. The final drops of fluid dripped into the chamber, down the tube and into his arm.

His eyes were becoming blurry. He forced them to focus so that he could read the label on the bag: D5W. An aqueous solution of 5% dextrose in purified water.

Dextrose. Sugar.

Then he remembered. His Med-alert bracelet. They did not know.

He turned, looking for the nurse, but she was gone. He searched for the call button, but it was attached to the lowered guard rail, and out of his reach. He tried to yell, but all that came out of his mouth was a hoarse groan.

Something was drastically, horribly wrong. He didn't know how they had done it, but he was sure it was them. This was blood atonement. He had sinned, turned against the Family, and they had made sure he would pay for it.

His head felt light, the room unsteady. He turned his head to the nightstand, where the nurse had left a pencil. With excruciating effort he raised his arm and grasped the pencil. He held it to the back of the business card the woman had given him. With all the strength remaining in him, he pushed the tip of the pencil across the card.

"He's scared," Randall said.

Erica turned the key in the ignition. "Wouldn't you be? It looks as if whatever he told Peter was important enough to get him killed."

"And unless he talks to us, we're not going to have any idea what that was."

"Not unless we find that hand-held with his notes."

Randall pulled out the laptop. "Will this thing work in the car?"

"It should."

He found the receipt the Secret Service had given him, opened the laptop, and called the number on the receipt.

A female voice answered. "Secret Service, Western Division. How may I direct your call?"

He glanced at the sheet. "I'd like to speak to Agent Rose, please."

"Thank you."

She returned a moment later. "I'm sorry, sir, I don't see any listing by that name."

"Stephen Rose?"

A pause. "No sir, there's no agent by that name here."

Randall frowned. "Maybe he's in a different division?"

He heard the sound of a keyboard clacking. "I'm sorry, sir, but I've checked the directory for the entire organization. There's no one by that name employed by the Secret Service."

He closed the laptop. "Damn."

24

Agent Karin Baker sat with her elbows on the ancient wooden desk, hands clasped together. She wore dark-rimmed glasses pushed up over a small nose, her face framed by short-clipped brown hair. No makeup. She looked like a woman who tried not to be too attractive out of fear she wouldn't be taken seriously. "What made you think he was with the Secret Service?" she asked.

"Because he told me he was with the Secret Service," Randall said, wishing Erica had come along so he wouldn't be the only one feeling foolish. "He gave me this," he said, handing Baker the receipt.

She scanned it. "Do you mind if I keep this?"

"It's not going to do me much good, is it?"

Baker said nothing, handing the paper to her partner, Bill Polk. Polk was a bulky Aryan who reminded Randall of a gym teacher he'd had in the seventh grade. He read the receipt with a blank expression that indicated either indifference or boredom. "So you let them take the equipment?"

"They had a warrant. What was I supposed to do?"

"Did you obtain a copy of the warrant?"

He sighed. "No."

"And what exactly did they say they were looking for?"

They had been through all this before. He wondered if

there was some government policy dictating that everything had to be repeated three times. "They said he stole some software. But I think they were really looking for some notes about an organization called the Family."

Baker scribbled on a notepad. "Was Mr. Jacobson a member of this organization?"

"No. But he was writing about it, and he'd found out some damaging things."

"What kind of things?"

Randall hesitated, and felt Polk's eyes boring through him. Maybe he was just getting paranoid, but right now he didn't trust anyone. "I'm not sure. Probably some things that the group wouldn't want the public to know."

"And you think it was this group that stole his system?"

His patience was wearing thin. "I think they killed him," he said sharply. "And now they're trying to cover it up."

The accusation didn't seem to faze either of them. "Were there things on the system that might implicate the group?" Baker asked.

"Maybe. I didn't have time to examine everything. That's why I wanted to get it back."

Baker shook her head. "I'm afraid the chances of that are pretty slim right now."

"So what will you do?"

"I'm afraid it's not really our jurisdiction."

Polk explained. "What you have here is a highly sophisticated ring of thieves. It's a clever scam, but it's basically a case of fraud. That's a matter for the police."

"But they were impersonating agents of the Secret Service."

Baker shrugged. "If they had been impersonating firemen, would that make it the fire department's responsibility?"

"But—"

"We'll file a report about the incident and let you know if we obtain any information," Baker said, standing. "In the meantime, you should contact the local police."

Randall stood. "Right," he said. "Thanks."

Polk closed the door as McLagan left. Baker shook her head and shot him a scornful glance. "A sophisticated ring of thieves?"

"Impersonating Secret Service agents, obtaining false warrants. I'd call that sophisticated."

"Too sophisticated. Do you have any idea what it would cost to pull off an operation like that?" She didn't wait for a response. "A van, forged papers, decent suits, someone who can impersonate an agent."

"What's so hard about that?"

"In your case, not much."

"Hey—"

"And what for? A computer system that anyone could walk into a store and buy for under two thousand dollars. Why bother? It's not worth it."

Polk sank into the chair that McLagan had vacated. "Not for a single job. But maybe it's a computer-theft ring, and they're pulling a string of these things."

"Right. Have you heard reports of anything else like this going on?"

He had to admit he hadn't. "So what do you make of it?"

"I don't know. But somebody went to a lot of trouble to get that computer. They must have wanted something on it pretty bad."

"Maybe he did have stolen software on it. Maybe the company hired someone to get it back."

She shook her head. "What legitimate company would take that kind of risk?"

"You don't really think it was this computer group he was talking about?"

She glanced at her notepad. "The Family? I don't know. What do you know about it?"

"It's one of these online things. Like CompuServe or America Online." Polk fancied himself a computer expert, having taken an introductory class in computers at San Francisco State as part of his continuing education requirement for the agency. He occasionally picked up computer magazines to see what was new, and watched the PC Show when there wasn't a football game on. "From what I hear, it's a pretty tame group."

"It's not exactly the Lions Club, according to McLagan."

Polk sneered. "He probably thinks the government is listening to his brain waves, too."

"This guy's not a nut. You can tell that by looking at him."

"Why, because his shirt was tucked in and he wasn't drooling? Anyway, it doesn't matter. It's not our problem."

"It is our problem. Haven't we had enough public relations fiascoes? Wait till our friends at the bureau hear about this."

The Secret Service and the FBI shared responsibility for enforcing laws against computer crime. Both agencies had endured their share of botched operations—raids that violated civil liberties and raised the ire of watchdog groups, convictions that were thrown out of court for lack of solid evidence. Each considered their own agency to be staffed by seasoned professionals, while the other was full of trigger-happy idiots. Both feared the passage of legislation that would limit the scope of future investigations. The last thing either agency needed was accusations—even false ones—of heavy-handed search and seizures. And either one would be sure to make hay out of any investigatory screw-ups that might involve the other.

"I'm telling you, it was just some clever crooks," Polk said.

"Right," Baker said, waving the receipt McLagan had given her. "Clever enough to produce a perfect forgery of one of our evidence receipts."

Polk shrugged. "Yeah."

Walter Borden had worked for BayWest banks for 19 years. In that time he had advanced from teller to assistant comptroller for the entire northwest region. His income was in the high six figures, and he owned a house on Telegraph Hill, the center of Walter's universe. From the townhouse, he could walk to the financial district, the restaurants in North Beach and Chinatown, Fisherman's wharf. There were a half dozen movie theaters within a 10-minute walk of his home, and the library was a short bus ride away. For years, that circuit had marked the perimeter of Walter's world.

In recent months, however, Walter's world had grown even smaller. Trips to the movie theater had been replaced by hours online. Now, he shopped without ever leaving his home. If the bank had been more reasonable, he could even have worked from his home, full-time. His world had contracted to the size of his computer monitor, online activities substituting for a failed social life in the real world.

Then he joined the Family. Suddenly, he had friends, many friends. He belonged to something larger than himself. He had a mission.

For a man like Walter—whose name most people never seemed to remember—joining the Family was like a conversion experience, like falling in love. He quickly became one of the Family's most devoted members, accumulating responsibilities and rising within the ranks. He was proud to have been recruited for special services for which his occupation uniquely suited him.

On this evening, Walter began by signing on to the bank's computer system, going through a series of connections that would be impossible to trace. Once connected, he used a password known only to himself and the two most senior executives of the bank.

He then initiated a program he had written himself, one that no one else knew about. The program opened random accounts in each of the bank's offices—never the same account on the same day—and subtracted exactly four cents from each one. He knew the system rounded off discrepancies of less than 5 cents in the customer's favor. The time spent tracking down such discrepancies, it was felt, was not worth the minuscule amounts involved. It was a technique that had been perfected by butchers a century earlier. By cutting a thin slice of salami from each roll—an amount that would never be missed by any individual customer—the butcher soon had an extra pound of salami to sell.

Over the past six months, Walter Borden had perfected the salami technique. He had skimmed more than $300,000 from the bank's coffers and transferred the money—through a series of complex wire transactions—to a numbered account in the Free Bank of St. Thomas.

He kept no money for himself. If a discrepancy were ever to be discovered, it would be impossible to trace the loss to him. And he doubted that the money would ever be missed. Since no individual customer was ever shortchanged, no one complained. And in the vast billion-dollar holdings of BayWest Banks, the amount he had taken was trivial. Even if the theft were to be discovered, the bank would probably sweep it under the rug.

Admitting that the money had been stolen would cause more embarrassment than it was worth. Embezzlement makes bad public relations.

Walter watched as his program gleaned the selected accounts, and felt no remorse. The bank's investment was a modest one, especially given the importance of the Family's mission. If he could explain that mission to the bank's board of directors, he felt sure they would understand. They would probably make a voluntary contribution, perhaps an even larger one.

He was merely saving them the inconvenience of having to deal with the paperwork.

25

Randall drove carefully, remembering what Ferret had told him. "Once you turn that rental car in, there's no way you're going to get another one. Just keep driving it until you don't need it any longer, or until they catch up with you. If they do, just claim ignorance and give it back. And don't get caught speeding."

So he drove as if he were back in driver's ed class, obeying speed limits, using his turn signal and following every road sign scrupulously.

He arrived at the apartment and remembered Tom Landulfson. If Tom had found out anything about CompuSys and its stock, he'd have no way of getting in touch with him.

Landulfson answered on the first ring. "Where the hell have you been?"

He filled him in. "Did you find out anything about CompuSys?"

"Sure did. It looks as if some of the larger institutions like universities are moving to divest themselves of CompuSys stock."

"Why?"

"I'm not sure. It may just be the Senate investigation and the talk about splitting up the company. Academics are notorious for taking stock positions based on social platforms. But that's not the worst problem for CompuSys right now. It looks as if some folks are shorting them."

"What does that mean?"

"Short selling. That's when you borrow stock that you think is heading downward. You sell the stock at today's price. Tomorrow, when the stock is lower, you buy stock to replace the stock you borrowed. Since the stock you're replacing costs less than the stock you sold, you make money."

"Nice trick."

"Nice if you guess correctly...or if you've got inside information. In this case, somebody's taking advantage of the bad vibes coming from Washington to sell CompuSys short. Add in the fact that the company's been expanding rapidly, buying up smaller companies, investing in new technology. The word on the street is that Gerry Barr may be overextending his reach, which always tends to weaken a company."

"But you said before that someone has been buying CompuSys stock."

"Right," Landulfson said. "I just can't figure out who. There are lots of good-sized purchases being made, but they're all in blocks of less than five percent."

"Does that mean something?"

"Sure does. If you purchase less than five percent of a company's stock, you don't have to report it to the Securities and Exchange Commission."

"Handy."

"Oh, yeah. There are all kinds of rules about public disclosure, but there are also all kinds of ways to get around them. So if you want to find out what's really going on, you have to dig–read research reports from financial institutions, annual reports, client lists. For example, right now I'm picking up a buzz about a new mutual fund called the Cortez Fund. The smart money really likes this fund. And according to its quarterly reports, Cortez has been gradually increasing its position in CompuSys."

"Any idea why?"

"I'm not sure yet. I'm still reading up on Cortez's fund manager, some wunderkind named Ronald Eden. He's a principal with a law firm called Miller, Eden and Schank. They do big-league SEC work for the financial community. In his spare time, he manages the Cortez fund, and he has a knack for getting in and out of stocks at just the right time. Right now, he's getting into CompuSys."

"I don't get it. Why would he be buying up CompuSys stock if the price is falling?"

"That's the sixty-four million dollar question. They must think something is happening with CompuSys. I'll let you know if I figure out what."

The doorbell rang as Randall hung up the phone.

Erica Steiner stood in the darkened hallway. She was trembling, hands clutched at her side. "James Wilton is dead."

He led her to the kitchen and made her sit down. "When I got home, there was message on the machine from the hospital," she said. "They wouldn't say what it was about, but they wanted me to come right over. I couldn't get you, so I went by myself."

"What happened?"

"There was some kind of mistake with his records. He was diabetic, but they had him on an IV with sugar in it." She shivered and crossed her arms over her chest. "He went into a coma and died about an hour after we left."

"Idiots," Randall said. "How could they–"

She shook her head. "I overheard the nurses talking. They didn't know I was listening. One of them said it was a computer error."

"What?"

She reached into her jacket pocket. "They gave me this." She pulled out the business card she'd given Wilton and handed it to Randall. "They thought I'd want to have it."

He turned the card over. On the back was a single word, scrawled in feeble pencil:

Krypto.

Robert Gebhardt did not want to go to the party. He could think of a dozen ways he'd rather spend an evening than attending another schmooze-fest with members of the financial community. He'd already put in a full day at the office, after an equally full week of analyzing portfolios and evaluating stock offerings. Surely he had earned some time off.

But the party was being hosted by Michael Gower of Gower Electronics, who had entrusted the care of his millions to Western Pacific Bank's trust department under Gebhardt's watchful eye. If Michael Gower wanted him at the soiree, Gebhardt would be there, and he would listen with great interest to exaggerated claims about performance, liquidity, and return on investment, all the while wishing he were at the San Francisco Opera with his wife.

At precisely 9 o'clock, Gebhardt entered the lobby of the Sheraton Palace Hotel. The invitation had instructed him to wait in the lobby by the event sign, which read "Gower Electronics - Stansfield Room." A young woman with auburn hair and a startlingly strapless red gown stood beside it.

"Are you here for the Gower party?" she beamed.

"Yes." He handed her his invitation. "Robert Gebhardt."

"If you'll come with me, Mr. Gebhardt, I'll escort you to the party. My name is Terri."

"Terri," he said, a faint smile creasing the corners of his mouth. Perhaps this evening would not be so painful after all.

The Stansfield Room had been designed in the English-club style, with a high wooden ceiling that sported a gold-embossed heraldic shield. A chandelier hung from the center of the shield, casting jewels of light around the room. A fireplace blazed with a small bonfire of logs, flanked on either side by bookcases with row upon row of volumes that had been color-coordinated to the decor of the room.

The guests—several dozen of them, each with a suitably congenial escort—moved among buffet tables laden with hors d'oeuvres and two well-stocked bars. The attendees were all pillars of the financial community.

Terri placed a solicitous hand on Gebhardt's arm. "What can I get you to drink?"

He ordered Glen Livet—if he was going to listen to the typical overblown financial chatter, he would need something stiff—and watched intently as her backside swiveled beneath the gown.

A hand landed on his shoulder. "Well, Bob, I see you got sucked into this too."

Gebhardt turned. The thick mustache and wide grin of Stanley Weinstein met him. Gebhardt and Weinstein had worked together at Western Pacific before Weinstein left to manage his own portfolio. They had never been close.

"Al. It's good to see you."

"Great to see you, Bob." A young woman stood next to Weinstein, straight blonde hair falling to her bare shoulders. "This is Kristin," he said, his nostrils flaring slightly. "She's taking care of me."

"I'm sure she is."

"Quite the affair," Weinstein said, gesturing around the room with a half-empty martini glass.

Indeed, most of the major financial players in the Bay Area were either present or represented: both directors of Pinnacle Management, principals from the Emerald Bay Equities and the Jared Foundation Trust. On the far side of the room was Helen Zettman, who was on the board of trustees for half a dozen major employee pension funds and stock ownership plans. Zettman was talking to Michael Gower and another man that Gebhardt didn't recognize: blade-thin, with metallic hair swept back over his head. His dark eyes scanned the room, appearing to take in everything and everyone there.

"Who's that Gower's talking to?" Gebhardt asked.

Weinstein glanced over. "Ronald Eden. Cortez Fund."

"Ah." The Cortez Fund was a new growth vehicle that specialized in high-technology stocks. Eden's position next to Gower, the party's host, indicated something about the purpose for the party. "I take it there are a number of computer people here."

"Gower's buddies," Weinstein said, tossing down the remainder of his drink. He pointed out the president of Future Technologies, the CEO of Advantage Software, and several other high-tech executives. Gebhardt recalled that Stanley's portfolio was built around companies like that: high risk, quick growth stocks for investors with nerves of steel and money to burn.

Bob Gebhardt was not one of those. He didn't know the high-tech companies well and he didn't care for them. He took an attitude of amused tolerance toward the entrepreneurs who had burst upon the financial scene on a tide of cash and computer chips. They were brash, incautious, and ignorant of the unwritten rules of social and fiscal etiquette. They represented the new money, which, if possible, one would have liked to ignore. Unfortunately, one couldn't. There was too much of it.

"Have you seen Advantage's new release?" Weinstein

asked. "Very impressive."

"I'm afraid not." Gebhardt was of the generation of businessmen who associated computers with office equipment, and office equipment with secretaries. Managers had more important things to do than write their own letters, or whatever else one did with a personal computer.

Weinstein tut-tutted. "Bob, we've got to get you up to speed on this computer stuff. These days, if you're not on the Internet..."

Gebhardt smiled benignly. Stanley was beginning to sound like Gebhardt's niece, Shelley. A few months ago, Shelley—an intense young woman to begin with—had joined some kind of computer group. Now, everything was computers with her. Computers were going to solve all the world's problems, computers were going to bring mankind together. She had even tried to convert her uncle Bob to the wonders of computers, unsuccessfully. He couldn't be bothered.

The one exception to Gebhardt's antipathy to high tech companies was Gower Electronics, and that was only because Michael Gower's father had been his close friend. And the presence of Gower Electronics on his client list was a symbol that, regardless of the ebb and flow of technology, Bob Gebhardt was still in the game. He had all the bases covered.

Gower was walking toward them, Ronald Eden at his side.

"Michael," Sam Weinstein called, a shade too loudly, and nodded towards Gebhardt. "Maybe you can talk this old dog into learning some new tricks."

"I doubt it," Gower said, grinning, and introduced Eden to them.

"Good to meet you," Weinstein said. "Michael tells me good things about your little fund."

"He has to," Eden said. "He knows I'll dump his stock if he doesn't."

Weinstein pointed a knobby finger at him. "So that's where Michael's stock is parked."

Gebhardt looked away briefly, embarrassed for Gower. Parking stock—the practice of placing stock in a mutual fund to conceal its true ownership—was illegal. If Michael really was hiding stock in the Cortez fund, it was nothing to joke about.

The comment made Gebhardt nervous for another reason. Michael had alerted him that Gower Electronics was about to license its core technology to CompuSys International, a deal that would net millions of dollars for Gower and probably double the value of the company's stock. Gebhardt had been investing Western Pacific's trust funds in Gower Electronics all along, and if he increased that investment just before the value of the stock doubled, that was a fortunate coincidence, and no one could prove otherwise.

But the Cortez Fund didn't have the same kind of cover. If the SEC heard rumors of stock parking, they might start sniffing around all of Gower's investors. Given that a number of investment managers were now occupying cells in federal institutions for insider trading, Weinstein's comment was, at the very least, in damned poor taste.

Gower grabbed Weinstein by the elbow. "Al, your glass is empty."

Weinstein looked at his glass in mock surprise. "Jeez, you're right."

"Come on, let me fill you up again."

As he steered Weinstein toward the bar, Ronald Eden said to Gebhardt, "I see Western Pacific has been having a very good year."

Gebhardt bowed modestly. "We've been doing well."

"I'd call 176 million in growth better than 'doing well.'"

Gebhardt smiled, surprised that Eden could call the exact figure to mind so readily. Did he know that kind of detail about every company at the party? "It has been a busy year."

"I imagine so, especially with the Golden Gate acquisition."

"Yes." Western Pacific's purchase of Golden Gate Savings had resulted in a pile of new trust accounts landing on Gebhardt's desk. He'd spent weeks going over the Golden Gate investments, deciding which to keep and which to dump, weeding out the blue chips from the cow chips. It was the kind of activity that made investors nervous, and Gebhardt's days had been filled with placating old and new clients, mollifying the bank's board of directors, and trying to plan for growth, all the while keeping his head above the tide of paperwork and bullshit. "The acquisition has increased our burden," he said simply.

Eden leaned toward Gebhardt. "I'm sure you're going to want to reposition some of those assets."

Gebhardt glanced into Eden's coal-dark eyes. "That is a possibility."

"If I were you, I'd start generating liquidity as soon as possible." It was advice Gebhardt didn't need, certainly not from an upstart like Eden. "Thank you for your advice," he said dryly.

"I'm aware of an opportunity about to come up," Eden said, quietly enough for no one else to hear. "One that could be highly beneficial for a discreet investor."

Gebhardt was beginning to be annoyed by Eden's boldness. "I beg your pardon?"

"I think we can work together on something that will be mutually advantageous." He raised his eyebrows.

"Very advantageous."

Gebhardt's mental alarms clanged loudly. He stared at Eden, the corners of his eyes narrowing. "I'm certain that whatever the opportunity, you will find investors for whom integrity is not an impediment to financial success. Western Pacific is not one of those." He began to turn away.

Eden put a hand on his arm. "Wait. Before you solidify your position on this, let me share some additional information with you."

Gebhardt glared at him. The idiot didn't get it. Bob Gebhardt had been around a long time. He was not about to be strong-armed by some high-tech hustler with a harebrained—and probably illegal—scheme.

Eden pulled a document from the suit jacket and handed it to Gebhardt. "I think this will change your feelings about working with us."

Gebhardt took the document reluctantly and unfolded it, frowning. His eyes fixed on the first page.

FROM: Donald Witmer, Witmer Detective Agency
SUBJECT: Robert Gebhardt

Gebhardt frowned at Eden, who looked away casually, sipping his drink. Gebhardt scanned the document. For the most part, it seemed to be a fairly dry recitation of his job history. A paragraph at the bottom of the page, however, had been marked with a pen.

In 1982, while he was loan officer for the Fidelity Savings Banks, Gebhardt approved a multi-million dollar loan to the San Francisco Development Corporation.

Gebhardt flinched. The loan to SFDC had been undercollateralized and unsecured, a fact no one else knew. It was one of the few such loans he'd ever made.

The loan was to be used to build a high-tech industrial park on land owned by Fidelity Savings in San Mateo. That loan seems questionable, since it appears that the SFDC had never before built anything of that magnitude. The development was begun, but when the market for high-tech office space plummeted in the 1980s, the project went belly-up.

Granted, Gebhardt thought, it had been a risky investment. But everyone took risks. That was how one made money.

Unfortunately, the money had already been spent, resulting in a loss of several million dollars on the part of Fidelity's depositors

It was true, the bank had lost money on the deal. But no depositors had been harmed; the FDIC had reimbursed them during the settlement of the bank's failure. It had all been part of the S&L "bailout," as it had been unfortunately labeled. But it was all perfectly legal.

Also, because of the way the contract was written, it seems that the bank owed the SFDC for work already done on the project—even though the deal fell through and the project was never completed. To settle that debt, the bank signed over the real estate to the SFDC, which subsequently subdivided and resold the land, netting nearly 250 million dollars in profit.

Gebhardt's heart pounded. He knew what was coming next.

The ownership of the San Francisco Development Corporation is clouded by layers of holding companies and intertwining corporations. However, it appears that the chief beneficiary of the SFDC deal is a gentleman named Edward Ulrich. Interestingly, Ulrich is married to Rachel Gebhardt Ulrich, the daughter of Robert Gebhardt by his first wife, Eleanor Harris Rockwell. Ulrich is Gebhardt's son-in-law. Thanks to his father-in-law's assistance, Ulrich cleared a quarter-billion dollars on the SFDC deal.

No charges have even been filed with regard to the SFDC deal. Gebhardt is currently the trust officer for Western Pacific Bank, where he is responsible for nearly a billion dollars in trust funds.

Gebhardt stared at the final paragraph, his mouth dry, his hands trembling. Eden retrieved the document from him, folded it, and tucked it back into his jacket. "I haven't shared this with anyone else yet. But I'm certain the folks at Banking Weekly would take an interest in it."

Gebhardt placed a hand on the back of a leather chair, steadying himself. If the press got word of this, his career would be over. He might even be sent to jail. Of course, he had a reasonable explanation for everything that had taken place. But an army of government investigators with subpoena powers might not see it that way.

What did Eden want? If he meant to ruin him, he could have simply given the information to the press. He searched Eden's face for a trace of empathy, of esprit de corps.

There was none. Behind Eden's calm, reasonable smile was a look that said he would sell his mother to the devil if a deal depended on it.

Gebhardt tried to keep his voice steady. "What would you suggest I do?"

Eden placed a hand on Gebhardt's shoulder. "I wouldn't do a thing right now. I'd simply liquidate as many assets as possible and keep my eyes open for new opportunities. I'm sure something will be coming along soon. And you won't be sorry."

He pulled a gold business card holder from his suit coat and handed a card to Gebhardt. "I'll be in touch. Let me know if anything comes up that affects your situation."

"Yes. Yes, of course," Gebhardt said, staring at the card. "I'll do that."

26

Livvy Giordano stopped stirring the spaghetti and stared at her husband, her eyebrows knotted together. "You what?"

Phil glanced up from his computer, which they kept in an alcove off the kitchen. "I put the money into the Family fund."

She frowned. "Don't you think we should have talked about it first?"

"There wasn't any time. This stuff is about to explode. We've got to get in while we can."

"But Phil—"

"Check this out," he said, pointing to the screen. "Now that we're Guides, we've got our own personal finance area."

She stood behind him, still frowning. "So?"

"So watch." He clicked on a button labeled "Check Your Investments." A ticker tape began scrolling across the screen.

YOUR INITIAL INVESTMENT...$25,000

"I can't believe you put it all in the Family," she said. Phil hushed her and pointed to the screen.

THE CURRENT VALUE OF YOUR ASSETS

IS...$25,074.15.

"Look at that. We've already made money, and we've only been in for a day."

"Seventy four dollars? Is that good?"

"That's incredible," Phil said. "At this rate, we'll be rich. Of course, the returns may not always be this good. But what a start."

BREAKDOWN OF YOUR INVESTMENT IS AS FOLLOWS...CRTZ FUND...100%...

"What's that mean?" Livvy asked.

"I don't know," he shrugged. "It may be the name of the mutual fund. At any rate, you can't argue with their choice of investments."

Livvy leaned against the door frame, tapping the wooden spoon against her pursed lips. "Hmm. Maybe we should consider getting that Saab now instead of next year."

Phil put an arm around her, drew her to himself, and kissed her belly. "Let's wait till we get a positive test on one of those little strips."

She feigned disappointment. "Ooh-kay."

The computer beeped, alerting them to the arrival of mail. It was a message from their FamilyHealth representative.

Dear Phil and Livvy,

Congratulations on your upgrade to Guide level. As part of the upgrade process, we have undertaken a complete analysis of your financial, medical and personal status in order to assist you in making plans for your future well-being.

"Our future," Livvy said wistfully, running her fingers through Phil's hair as they continued reading the message.

In the course of our analysis, it has come to our attention that the payments made to providers of infertility diagnosis and treatment on your behalf have temporarily exceeded the limits for this type of care. I'm sure you will understand that, to provide the optimum level of health care for all Family members, some financial and time limits must be placed on certain categories of nonessential treatments.

"What's this about?" Livvy asked.
Phil shook his head. "I'm not sure."

Note that this is only a temporary suspension of benefits. We anticipate that changes in your financial status and shifting costs of health care will allow us to restore this type of treatment in the near future.

Livvy squeezed onto the chair next to Phil. "They've cut off the treatments?"
"It looks like it."

Our analysis of your current financial status reveals that this would probably not be the best time for you to start a family. For background, you may want to examine the following information:

The figures were all there, and they were frightening. The amount of money necessary to raise a child according to their standard of living was staggering.

The good news is that with your recent investment in the Family's investment program, we project that you should be able to begin your family at some time in the not too distant future.

Livvy leaned her head against Phil's shoulder, her eyes filling with tears. "Oh, Phil..."

He drew her closer. "It's OK, honey. You saw what they said. We wouldn't want to start having kids without adequate planning, would we?"

She shrugged feebly, sniffing. "I guess not."

"And the way our investment is going, we should be able to go ahead in no time."

She looked into his eyes. "You think so?"

"I know so." He kissed her. "Come on, let's check our investment again. Maybe we've made some more money."

Alan Reingold completed his report on the Giordanos.

Formatting has begun. Subjects have been successfully upgraded and enrolled in investment program. Augmentation of initial investment is proceeding according to standard schedule.

"Augmentation" involved giving first-time investors an extra return. In a word, the initial returns were padded. This cost the Family a bit of money on the front end, but it inspired confidence in the investment program, and confidence was crucial to the success of the program.

Alan checked his mail before logging off. There was a message from HomeWatch, the section assigned to assist members with household management.

Just a reminder that we are currently boycotting American Foods for its sponsorship of the television program "Eyewitness" which recently broadcast inaccuracies and fallacies related to the Family. Bright 'n' Bold laundry detergent is an American Foods product. Your continued cooperation with the boycott is requested and appreciated.

He placed the computer in standby mode and went to the kitchen, where Margaret stood pouring sauce over a casserole dish of spaghetti. "Did you buy some soap called Bright 'n Bold?"

She placed the casserole dish on the table and eyed him cautiously. "Yes. Why?"

"It's an American Foods product," he said, pulling his chair out sharply.

"Oh." She turned back to the stove.

"Didn't you get a list of products you weren't supposed to buy?"

"Yes, but I was in a hurry, and I didn't have the list with me."

Scott entered the room and took his place at the table, studiously ignoring his parents' conversation.

"I don't see what's so hard about carrying a list—"

Margaret dropped a bowl of salad on the table with a thud. "Would you like me to throw the soap away?"

"Of course not. It's just that we need to be careful. Especially now."

They ate dinner in silence. When they had finished, Alan stood and headed back to his study. "Don't forget, we have a special session at seven."

Margaret said nothing and began running the dirty dishes under the faucet.

The session began exactly at seven. Margaret took the chair Alan had pulled up for her. She sat, hands folded on her lap, as Alan logged on and entered the special password Overseer Blackburn had given him.

Welcome. I am Administrator Mansfield. I will be the supervisor for the division of Overseers to which you belong.

Alan and Margaret glanced at each other. Neither had ever heard the term "Administrator" before.

First, let me congratulate you. You have advanced to a level beyond that of most members of the Family. Only those who are spiritually advanced, like yourselves, can hear and accept the message you are about to receive.

As Overseers, you will play a vital role in the ongoing mission of the Family. That mission is to unite all the peoples of the world, to use the power of computers to eliminate poverty, injustice, and racial unrest, to cure the problems that have plagued the earth for generations. For the first time, we possess the technology to address those issues, to bring about an era of peace and harmony.

The literature of the world contains many prophecies referring to our day, a time when all people will be able to live together in peace. In some religions, this has been called the time of enlightenment, the golden age. In Christian prophecy, it is said that this time would be brought on by the second coming of the Messiah, a coming that is described as lightning.

The word 'lightning' was highlighted, an indication that clicking on it would bring up more detailed information. Alan positioned the cursor over the word and clicked. A box appeared with a verse from the Bible.

"For as the lightning cometh out of the east, and shineth even unto the west; so shall also the coming of the Son of man be." - Matthew 24:27

He clicked on the box, closing it.

In times past, various individuals have claimed to be the Messiah. None of those individuals, however, flashed from east to west like lightning. What does flash like lightning? A computer network, based on electrical impulses—the very stuff of which lightning is made.

Thus, the Bible contains an amazing prophecy of a time when a computer network would encircle the globe. It is clear that the Family is the fulfillment of that prophecy, and our Father is the Messiah.

This is knowledge that must not be divulged to anyone outside of the Family or at a lower level within the Family. Most people did not recognize the Messiah at his first appearance. The so-called "Christians" of today will not recognize the Messiah this time, either. They are the modern Pharisees, blind to His coming again, just as they were blind to His first coming. Only those who have been privileged to receive this secret knowledge will take part in the preparation for the coming kingdom.

Alan and Margaret's disagreement was all but forgotten.

As Overseers, you may be required to undergo testing and verification to ensure that your commitment to the Father is complete. But do not fear. The Father will be with you when the time comes, and great will be your reward.

The eye of the Father is upon you.

27

R andall pressed buttons wildly, trying to make the computer work. No matter which keys he pushed, the screen merely flashed cryptic messages:

Unable to recover Wilton. Try another?
Please enter correct password:

He tried to remember the password, but could not, and began guessing frantically.

HANDHELD
Incorrect password. Please try again.
FATHER
Incorrect password. Please try again.
COMPUSYS
Incorrect password.
KRYPTO
Incorrect password.
Incorrect password.
Incorrect password.
Incorrect password.

He pounded the keyboard with both fists. An alarm sounded, a ringing that drilled through the fog in his brain. The sound stopped, then started again. But it wasn't right.

It wasn't an alarm.

It was a telephone.

His eyes creaked open. He had fallen asleep on the sofa, his head next to the telephone on the end table. He pulled the phone from its cradle clumsily.

"Hello?"

"May I speak to Peter Jacobson, please?"

It was a woman's voice, one that sounded familiar. But the question irked him. Whoever it was, didn't she know Peter was dead? He rubbed his eyes with his free hand, waking up now. "I'm afraid that won't be possible."

"Well, could I leave a message for him?"

He pondered a response, still searching for the woman's voice. Then it came to him. "Linda?"

She paused. "Yes?"

Linda. The receptionist from the Peabody Herald. "Linda, it's Randall," he said, propping himself up on one elbow.

"Randall? What are you doing there?"

He tried to collect his thoughts. Why was she calling Peter? "This is my friend's apartment. The one who...passed away."

There was silence on the line. "Oh, my God."

"What?"

"Randall..." She hesitated. "There's a message here for you. It came just before you left. I'm sorry, I didn't know who it was." She began speaking rapidly, not making much sense. "I was saving it till you got back, but then Dodge told me you weren't coming back. He wanted me to call everyone who left messages for you and see if I could take care of them."

He still didn't understand how she had tracked him down, or what was so important for him to know. "What's the message?"

"Hold on."

There was a pause, then a click and the familiar sound of the voicemail system. "Friday...May 19," it said. "Eight...twenty...two...p.m."

"Randall?" the message began. "This is Peter."

He sat up, breathing hard, fully awake now.

"I need your help with something," Peter said. The message was muffled—it sounded as if he'd called from his car—and there was an odd whirring sound in the background. "There's a guy named Alexander Smith who teaches computer science at St. Regis College up in San Rafael. He went to Dartmouth. Can you go up to Hanover and see what you can find out about him? Tell them you're working on a piece about alumni in the computer field or something. But don't say anything about this to anyone, OK? I mean anyone." He paused, as if wanting to say more. "Call me as soon as you can."

Randall asked Linda to play the message again and scribbled the details on a pad. As he hung up, he heard a car door slam in the street. He looked out the front window just in time to see the rental car pulling away, a van from the rental agency following close behind it.

"Damn."

Erica pulled up in front of the apartment as Randall emerged carrying the cellular laptop. "Are you going to take notes this time?" she asked.

He slapped the laptop as he squeezed into the car. "Just call me Randall McLagan, alumni reporter."

St. Regis College was an upper-middle-class enclave of brick classroom buildings, tall trees and neat houses that belonged to the faculty and staff. The students of St. Regis came from California's better private schools and comprised an eclectic mix of races and religions, with only one characteristic in common: they were all brilliant.

One of these, a young man with dark dreadlocks and a

wispy goatee, approached Erica's car as Randall rolled down the window.

"Can you tell us where Professor Alexander Smith lives?" Randall asked.

The student directed them to Del Monico Drive, a broad avenue that ran from the back of the campus, past houses with wide manicured lawns and flowering trees. They traveled on a long stretch with no houses, to where the street ended in a cul-de-sac surrounded by tall juniper shrubs. A wrought-iron gate framed by stone pillars filled the only break in the shrubbery.

They pulled up to the gate. A bronze plaque on the left-hand pillar read, "Smith." Below it was an intercom button. Erica leaned out and pushed the button.

A deep male voice said, "May I help you?"

Randall leaned across her to the window. "Is Dr. Smith at home? We'd like to speak to him."

"Whom shall I say is calling?"

"My name is Randall McLagan. I'm a fellow Dartmouth alumnus. I spoke to him about doing an interview for the alumni magazine."

There was no response. A moment later, the gate swung open.

They drove through and the gate swung silently shut behind them. Erica glanced into the rearview mirror. "I sure hope we don't have to leave in a hurry."

The driveway was a smooth curving sweep bordered by more junipers. As they rounded a bend, a magnificent three-story brick house rose into sight.

Randall whistled. "This guy's doing all right for a college professor."

"Amazing what tenure will do."

They parked in front of the house and knocked at the door. The man who opened it was tall, in his forties, with sandy brown hair, a mustache and a full beard that bore light traces of gray. His eyes were well-ridged by lines, and he wore a dark, heavy-knit fisherman's sweater over a flannel shirt. Not at all what Randall had expected from the voice on the intercom.

"Hello," the man said. It was not at all the voice on the intercom. "I'm Alexander Smith."

He brought them to a study off the entryway. "You said you were from Dartmouth?"

"Yes, I work for the alumni magazine," Randall said, holding up a copy of the magazine he'd found at Peter's apartment.

They engaged in small talk about Dartmouth, how it had changed since Smith had been there, how it hadn't changed. Smith answered Randall's questions concisely, conversing only enough to satisfy the requirements of courtesy. Long pauses punctuated the spaces between his comments, during which it seemed as if he might be talking to himself, or listening to something in the distance that only he could hear.

Finally, as if aware that he wasn't being sufficiently cordial, Smith asked "Do you live around here?"

"No," Randall said. "I was just...visiting. When I travel, I often look for alumni who might make good subjects for interviews."

Smith nodded, seeming neither flattered nor surprised by the idea. Randall cleared his throat. "So, uh...I was wondering if you could explain a little bit about your work?"

"My work," Smith said, crossing his legs at the knee and resting his folded hands on them.

"Yes. The, uh...scope of it. How it fits into the...academic setting." He was bluffing, speaking in vague generalities, since he had no idea what Smith's work was, aside from having something to do with computers.

Smith stared away for a moment. "Well, there's the teaching, of course." He shrugged. "The usual slate of uninspired undergraduates and angst-ridden graduate students. Fortunately, my graduate students take up enough of the slack to let me get some research done."

"What is your research about?"

"I've been exploring human-computer intelligence," he said.

There was a pause, and it became clear he wasn't going to elucidate further on his own. "I'm afraid I'm not very computer literate. Can you explain that to me?"

Smith crossed his arms and stroked his mustache. "The human brain is the most powerful computer in existence. It dwarfs anything that man has been able to create. And the computer is the most powerful tool created by man. The problem is—has always been—the connection between the two, how to make them communicate."

For the first time since they had arrived, a spark of life and enthusiasm seemed to enter Smith's voice. "In addressing that problem, biologists, neurobiologists, and physiologists all focus on the brain, which is incredibly complex. Those of us who come from a computer background start with switches and relays. The problem is bringing the two disciplines together."

He leaned forward, gesturing with his hands. "Human interaction with computers began with punch cards. Then came the keyboard, the mouse. Today, we can talk to computers, interact in three dimensions—now we're getting somewhere. But all of this is still outside of the brain." He tapped his temple with two fingers. "We still have this massive barrier between the power in our heads and the power in our computers. We need to find ways to connect human and computer intelligence more directly."

"How did your interest in this area come about?"

Smith examined Randall's face for a moment, then

seemed to come to a decision. He rose from the chair and said, "Come with me."

Randall and Erica followed him out of the study and down a wide, mahogany-lined hallway to a closed door. The door was large, and inordinately wide. To one side was a panel bearing several buttons. Smith knocked, and a muffled voice responded. "Just...a minute."

A moment later, the door opened with a smooth, silent sweep, as if not by human hands. Smith motioned them through.

The room they entered was large, with a high, dark ceiling that gave way at the far end to glass panels, through which sunlight flooded down onto a small swimming pool. In the center was a living area, consisting of furniture that seemed oddly arranged, with far more space between the pieces than would normally have been provided.

As Randall's eyes adjusted to the light, he saw the explanation for the room's eccentric design: beyond the living area was a young man in a wheelchair, seated before a complex arrangement of computers, monitors, keyboards, and other equipment whose function Randall could only guess. The boy's thin arms lay lifeless, hands folded on his lap. Behind a pair of thick glasses, his face was bent into an expression that was either pain or intense concentration. His eyes flickered, seeming to follow the action on a computer screen, where words appeared through no apparent action of the boy's. The sound of clicking came from somewhere, though the boy's hands were nowhere near a keyboard.

The clicking stopped, and the wheelchair turned to face them, apparently of its own volition. The boy looked up at them, his jaw twisted slightly, his eyebrows performing a slow, random dance. In spite of those anomalies, the resemblance to Smith was obvious.

"This is my son, Jonathan," Smith said.

With an almost imperceptible electronic whine, a mechanical arm unfolded smoothly from the right side of the wheelchair, picked up the boy's arm as if it were a kitten in its mother's mouth, and held it out to Randall.

"How do...you do?" Jonathan said, his face contorting, the words coming from his mouth and—almost simultaneously, in perfect, unslurred speech—from a tiny speaker in the wheelchair's headrest. A thin microphone hung suspended in front of the boy's mouth, jutting out from his left ear and connected by a wire that ran down his neck to the wheelchair. The blending of the synthesized speech with Jonathan's tortured slur produced an odd, buzzing echo, but one that was perfectly understandable.

"Hello," Randall said, shaking Jonathan's hand; the mechanical arm responded with a perfect simulation of the human gesture.

"My son has cerebral palsy," Smith said. "The result of an accident at the time of his birth. One aspect of my work has involved developing adaptive technologies that allow him to live a normal life."

As if on cue, Jonathan's wheelchair turned back to the workstation and the computer screen.

"There's a special eye-tracking apparatus built into his glasses," Smith explained. "A low-powered beam tracks the movement of his pupils and translates them into computer commands."

They could see lights flickering across the inner surface of the glasses.

"It's menu-operated," Smith said. "The menus, sub-menus, and so on are projected on the inside of his glasses by a series of ultra-miniature LEDs. He can flip through the menus by glancing at key words and blinking. This allows him to operate all of his computer equipment, as well as the mechanized devices that let him feed himself, move about on his own–"

"I can also...control the devices...in the room," Jonathan said. "The lights..." As if by magic, the overhead lights dimmed, then came back up to normal level.

"The doors..."

The door to the hallway opened again, then closed.

"The windows..."

At the far end of the room, the glass panels beyond the pool dimmed, as if converted into giant sunglasses.

"The panels are giant liquid crystal displays," Smith said.

"I can control...the light level...passing through them," Jonathan added. "I can also control the television...radio...CD player..."

"I've networked everything in the house to Jonathan's system," Smith said. "And the connection between his wheelchair and the computer is a radio link, so he can control everything without being physically connected to the workstation. The goal is to provide him with the same flexibility that everyone else has."

"Incredible," Randall said, still wondering what this had to do with Peter and why he had wanted information on Smith.

"How does the voice synthesis work?" Erica asked. "It seems very smooth."

"The system...has been tuned...to my voice patterns," Jonathan said. "After much use...it has learned to understand...my somewhat strange accent." His mouth twisted into a grin.

Randall couldn't help but admire the kid. With all his difficulties, he could still poke fun at himself.

"The system matches my words...with a large library of...words and phrases...created in a synthetic voice...one that is easier to understand...than my normal voice...The system then...constructs sentences using...those words and phrases...It smooths them...and matches them to my speech."

Erica shook her head in amazement. "Like changing the font in a word processor document."

"Yes," the elder Smith said. "If he's tired, Jonathan can also communicate through the synthesizer using the eye-tracker. And he can also adjust the vocal quality of the synthetic voice. It doesn't make sense to have the voice of an old man coming from a seventeen year old."

"Almost...eighteen."

"Right. Of course, much of his communication takes place electronically, where the sound of his voice isn't even an issue.

"I received my...high school diploma...online," Jonathan said. "And am currently...working on my...bachelor's degree...in computer science..."

"He's already completed programming projects for clients that he met online," his father said.

"They are often surprised...to learn that I am...physically challenged."

"We'll let you get back to your work," the elder Smith said, and led Randall and Erica back to the study. As they were seated, the monitor on Smith's desk flickered on. It showed Jonathan, looking up from his wheelchair.

"Dad," he said, his voice sounding unnaturally clear as it came through the computer's speakers, undistorted by his own deformed words. "I forgot...to tell you...I had another message from...Uncle Gerry...he asked me to say...hello."

Smith nodded, his face darkening. "All right. Thank you."

"Uncle Gerry?" Randall asked as Smith turned away from the darkening monitor.

Smith sighed. "Gerald Barr."

Randall glanced at Erica. "He's your brother?"

"No. We used to work together."

Erica stared at Smith, her eyes widening. "Wait a minute. You're Sandy Smith."

A slight frown furrowed his brow. "Yes."

"Sandy?" Randall asked.

"I thought the name sounded familiar," Erica said. "It was the Alexander that threw me. I didn't make the connection."

"Have you two met before?" Randall asked, perplexed.

"No," Erica said. "But I've certainly heard of him. He and Barr founded CompuSys."

28

Smith looked at Randall with combined amusement and disbelief. "You didn't know that I was one of the founders of CompuSys?"

Randall flushed. "Well–"

"I assumed that was your real reason for wanting to interview me. I wondered when you were going to get around to asking about it."

Randall decided to come clean. "I'm afraid I'm not really from the alumni magazine."

"I see," Smith said, frowning. "Who are you?"

"I'm a newspaper reporter. But that's not why I'm here. I'm trying to find out what happened to a friend of mine named Peter Jacobson."

Smith frowned. "What do you mean, what happened to him?"

There was something in the way he asked the question. "Does the name mean anything to you?"

"It does. He contacted me about a week ago and said he wanted to talk to me. He made an appointment to meet me at my office on Monday. But he never showed up."

Randall paused. There was no easy way to say it. "That's because he's dead."

Smith fell back against his chair. "My God."

Randall explained what he knew about Peter's death. "Did Peter say what he wanted to talk to you about?"

"No. He was rather mysterious about the whole thing."

Randall paused, considering how much he could trust Smith. He decided not to beat around the bush. "Do you know anything about an organization called the Family?"

Smith ran his fingers through his beard. "It's an online service of some sort. Why?"

Randall glanced at Erica, who shrugged. "I believe Peter was murdered. I think it had something to do with the Family. And every time we look at the Family, we keep tripping over CompuSys."

"I don't understand the connection."

"Neither do we," Erica said. "We were hoping you could tell us that."

Smith shook his head. "I'm afraid not. Of course, I've been out of the picture for some time now. There could be something going on that I don't know about."

Smith explained how he'd first met Gerald Barr, just after he got out of Dartmouth. They had formed a company originally called Genius Computing. "But Gerry decided we needed a name that would sound professional when the company went public."

"He was thinking that far ahead?"

"He was always thinking ahead—planning strategies, building the company. I was happier just writing programs, coming up with new ideas." He stared away for a moment. "I think that was what drove us apart, in the end."

"How so?"

"When the personal computer revolution came along, Gerry decided we needed to move the company to the west coast. So we did, and we started putting in 16 hour days, sleeping in the office. The company was growing like a weed. But we had less and less time to do the stuff we really enjoyed doing—programming, playing games, driving the fancy new cars we could suddenly afford. On top of that, I had just gotten married, and my wife and I wanted to have a family."

Randall made a mental note; he hadn't seen signs of a Mrs. Smith anywhere. Had the marriage not survived that time?

"I wanted to relax," Smith said. "Do some different things. But Gerry wanted to take over the world. He had this vision of CompuSys as a major international corporation. And he was driven—staying up all night, living on pizza and Coke. That stuff is OK when you're just out of college. But after a while, I got tired of it."

"I imagine that put a strain on your family life," Randall said.

A trace of sadness seemed to pass over Smith's face. "My wife began to resent all the time I was spending at the office. Meanwhile, Gerry was insisting on a hundred and ten percent dedication to the company. We began to argue a lot, about the direction of the company, how much time I was putting in, even what to call new products." He paused, and took a deep breath. "One night, after a particularly bad argument, my wife came to pick me up. She asked me to drive. I shouldn't have." He looked away, blinking. "I was still angry and I was driving too fast. The road was wet. We came around a corner..."

Smith fell silent. Randall looked at Erica, who nodded. Apparently she knew the story.

"We skidded off the road," Smith said. "My wife was seven months pregnant with our son. She gave birth to him in the emergency room and died shortly after. Jonathan's disability was caused by the accident."

For a time, there was nothing to say. Clearly, Smith's pain was still very present. "After the accident, I didn't have much heart left for the business," he said. "I'd go to work and stare at my computer without even turning it on. Eventually, I lost any influence I'd had in the company.

Gerry lined up everybody and everything in the company to support him."

"And that's when you left?" Erica asked.

"There wasn't much else for me to do. We split the company down the middle. I handed responsibility over to Gerry, put half my stock in a trust for Jonathan and reinvested the other half in bonds for the college here. That, along with my experience at CompuSys, got me a teaching position. I threw myself into teaching, and began doing my research. That's kept me pretty busy, what with taking care of my son."

"It must have been a hard time for you," Randall said.

"It was hell," Smith said succinctly. "I'm afraid I neglected my son during that time. I wasn't in the mood to be a very supportive father. He was largely raised by nannies. I immersed myself in my research. It was a kind of escape."

Randall felt the need to steer the conversation back to CompuSys. "Did you keep in touch with Barr?"

"No I hadn't heard from him in years, other than a company Christmas card every year. Not that I particularly cared. Then, a few months ago, he and Jonathan began corresponding by e-mail."

"Really," Erica asked. "How did that come about?"

Smith shrugged. "Jonathan sent him an e-mail message. For a kid who's into computers, I suppose Gerry is some kind of hero. So he wrote to him. You know, fan mail, the way kids do. Gerry wrote back, and since then, they've been corresponding fairly regularly. He even came by here a few weeks ago." His face wore a look that was hard to interpret. Was it doubt? Sadness? The animation that had enlivened him when talking about his work or his son's achievements was gone now. He seemed to have retreated back into a darker place.

"Did it surprise you to hear from Barr again?"

"A little. It's not like Gerry. He isn't the type to cultivate personal relationships without some good reason." He shrugged and shook his head. "Maybe I'm being paranoid. I may be too sensitive about that kind of thing when it comes to Jonathan."

"Why is that?"

Smith looked out a window at the large pine trees that shaded the lawn, as if framing his response. "I did a lot of spiritual searching after my wife died—reading books, listening to tapes. There were a lot of odd people coming and going around here." He smiled ironically. "Tragedy seems to bring the missionaries out of the woodwork."

He rubbed a hand across his forehead. "One of the groups that came calling was a faith-healing movement. For them, everything boiled down to faith. If you have enough faith, God will take care of everything for you. Pay the bills, fix the car. Heal your diseases."

He sighed, regret written large across his face now. "Jonathan picked up on this, and became convinced that God was going to heal him. He fasted. He prayed. When he wasn't praying, he was reading the Bible. These folks told him that God had a great plan for his life and that if he only had enough faith, God would cure him."

He was silent for a time, then continued. "Needless to say, it didn't happen. And Jonathan was crushed. He thought something was wrong with him. God didn't love him. He didn't have enough faith." He thumped his fist on the arm of the chair. "That's when I decided that I didn't want anyone to take advantage of my son ever again. I didn't want him to be gullible. So I taught him to think logically, to ask questions. I taught him to keep an eye out for people who might try to take advantage of him, to use him."

"Do you think Gerry Barr is using him?" Randall asked.

Smith hesitated. "I don't know. Maybe he just feels guilty. About the company, the accident. He's not married and doesn't have any children of his own. Maybe he's having twinges of fatherliness."

"Has Jonathan told you what they talk about?"

He shook his head. "My son is almost eighteen. I try not to treat him like a person who needs constant monitoring."

"Did you talk to Barr yourself?"

"Only briefly. When he came here, he mentioned that some big things were going to be happening with the company."

Randall's journalistic instincts smelled something. He tried not to sound too anxious. "What kind of things?"

"He wouldn't say. But he told me I should consider converting Jonathan's stock. He said the returns would be sizable."

"What does that mean?" Erica asked.

"Jonathan's stock—the stock I put in trust for him—is preferred stock," Smith explained. "It pays a fixed nine percent interest, which is how we set it up. But now Gerry wants us to convert it to regular stock."

"Why would you do that?"

"Apparently there's some advantage at this point. I don't know. I don't have time to follow all that financial stuff." He sighed, and his shoulders seemed to sag. "Besides, it's really not my decision. The stock is Jonathan's, and I won't argue with whatever he decides to do."

"Even if it helps Barr?"

"I gave up fighting Gerry Barr a long time ago," he said, resignation darkening his eyes.

Whatever Barr was up to, Smith no longer had any desire to do battle with him. Clearly, he was content to live the quiet life of a university professor, tending his grief like a dark, barren garden.

Erica eased the car down the driveway. "If Barr stole the company out from under Smith, why would he suddenly be so friendly?"

"Just what I was wondering."

"And what's the business about his stock?"

"I don't know. But I know who might." He pulled out the laptop, booted it up, and called Tom Landulfson.

"Landulfson."

"Tom, it's Randall." He introduced Erica and said, "We just paid a visit to the founder of CompuSys."

"You're kidding."

"Not the founder you're thinking of." He explained about the relationship between Sandy Smith and Gerald Barr, including Barr's recent visits to his old partner.

"Fascinating. So what does Barr want with him?"

"Good question. He told Smith that big things were happening at CompuSys, but didn't say much more."

"He couldn't say much more. The SEC takes a very dim view of that kind of thing. It's called insider trading."

"But Smith's not an insider anymore," Erica said.

"Doesn't matter. If it involves information the general public doesn't have, it's insider trading. The question is, why would Barr care what he does with his stock?"

"It's actually his son's stock," Randall said. "But Barr told him he should trade it in, said there'd be good money in it."

"Ah. Light dawns. It must be convertible preferred stock."

"He said something like that. What's it mean?"

"There are two kinds of stock, common and preferred. Preferred stock is generally only issued to founders and management. It pays a guaranteed interest rate, which means those folks get their money even if the regular stock is suffering. The 'convertible' part means they can trade it in for common stock if they want."

"Why would they do that?"

"A couple of reasons. Even though preferred stock pays a higher interest rate, it's not voting stock, while common stock is. So let's say Barr wants to free up his cash flow while building support for himself within the company. He goes around to the people who hold preferred stock and tells them if they convert their shares, he'll issue them a more lucrative stock later on, maybe a two-for-one deal. That way, the company doesn't have to pay out the high interest rates, and the new votes will be in Barr's pocket because he's promising to make those folks rich later on."

Erica shook her head. "Sandy Smith didn't seem to care much about CompuSys or getting rich."

Landulfson was quiet for a moment. "How old is the son?"

"Seventeen, going on eighteen."

"That may explain Barr's sudden interest in him. When the kid turns eighteen, he can do whatever he wants with the stock, without his father's permission. All this may dovetail with some things I've been finding out about the Cortez Fund. Turns out it's actually a group of mutual funds. Legally, each one of the funds is a separate entity, and every one of them has CompuSys stock in it. But none of them owns more than five percent of the company."

"Which means they don't have to report the purchases to the SEC," Randall said, recalling their earlier conversation.

"You got it. Right now, Cortez holds a pretty big block of CompuSys stock. That made me suspicious. So I looked into the individual funds and the stocks in them. And I noticed an interesting pattern."

There was a dramatic pause, and Randall remembered that Tom loved telling a good story. "Every one of the companies represented in the Cortez fund has done business with CompuSys in the recent past: partnerships, licensing arrangements, that kind of thing. And the Cortez Fund managed to buy into them just before the stock started climbing."

"You said the fund manager was a lucky guy."

"Well, this was beginning to look a little too lucky. On a hunch, I compared the upper management of those companies with the folks who have invested in the Cortez Fund. Guess what? Just about every Cortez investor is also a major player in one of the companies the Cortez Fund holds stock in."

"So the investors are tipping off the fund when their companies are about to make a deal?" Randall asked.

"Looks that way to me," Landulfson said. "How else would Eden know exactly when to get into those companies?"

"So much for brilliant investment strategy," Erica said.

"No brilliance required," Landulfson said. "And here's the capper. According to the prospectus for the Cortez Fund, Ronald Eden was recently appointed to the board of directors of a certain large software company."

"CompuSys?" Randall said.

"Bingo. He was put on the board at about the same time as the Cortez Fund started accumulating stock in the company."

"What a coincidence."

Landulfson laughed. "It's about the cleverest stock parking scheme I've ever heard of."

"Come again?" Erica said.

"Stock parking. That's when you get someone else to buy stock for you, as a way of controlling the stock indirectly. It's an old strategy, used to circumvent the SEC rules on disclosure. Also highly illegal. The beauty of this particular scheme is that Barr is parking the stock non-voting hands—mutual fund stocks are non-voting. Which makes it easier for him to control things."

"I don't get it," Randall said. "How does parking stock in non-voting hands help him?"

"Ah, there's the genius in the plan. How much stock do you think you need to control a company?"

"I don't know. Fifty-one percent?"

"No. You only need fifty-one percent of the voting stock. If ninety percent of a company's stock is in non-voting hands—like mutual funds—you could control as little as six percent of the stock and you'd still be calling the shots for the company."

Randall sighed, exasperated. This business seemed like a giant jigsaw puzzle, and he had no idea what the picture was supposed to be—nor whether it had anything to do with Peter. "All right," he said slowly. "Let me piece this together. The Cortez Fund, which has several CompuSys connections, is buying up CompuSys stock. This makes the other stock, the voting stock, more powerful."

"Right. That's the stock owned by Barr or his old friends, the Smiths. And the funny thing is, all the negative publicity CompuSys has been getting has driven the price of the stock down, making it easier for Barr and his cronies to buy it up."

"Seems like a funny time to be buying up stock, when the company's in trouble," Erica said.

"Maybe he thinks the stock is going up sometime soon. Or maybe he knows it will."

"So the people talking CompuSys down are actually helping Barr buy up the stock," Randall said.

"At bargain prices," Landulfson said. "But this gets even more interesting. I did some digging on the Senate investigation into CompuSys. The head of the committee is a senator named Tomaccio from New York. He's been preaching hellfire and regulation against CompuSys for some time now. But the funny thing is, despite all his posturing and blustering, the committee hasn't actually done anything."

"Sounds like typical government red tape," Erica said.

"No, I mean anything. They haven't subpoenaed any witnesses, they're not interviewing experts. The committee hardly even meets, except to deal with procedural matters. It's as if the whole thing was designed to be drawn out forever. And it's all spurred on by this one fire-breathing congressman."

"...who is actually helping Barr by driving down the cost of the stock," Randall said.

"So when the Family attacks CompuSys, they're actually helping Barr, too?" Erica asked.

"Yeah, isn't that a kick in the pants? Barr is probably laughing all the way to the bank."

She shook her head. "Knowing Barr, he's probably behind it all."

There was a pause. "Now that's an interesting thought," Landulfson said. "Maybe he is behind it all."

Randall stared out the window. They were still driving, approaching the Bay Bridge, where multiple lanes of cars came together, picking up speed as they funneled onto the bridge. A picture formed in Randall's mind, something he'd been staring at so hard that he couldn't see it, like one of those damned 3-D images. The pieces had all been there: the mentions of CompuSys in Peter's notes. Laurie Donoway, trying to steer him away from the story. The ads in PC Monthly that stopped when Peter wrote about the Family. The strange stock market stuff. And somewhere in all that was information Peter had found out, information that someone didn't want him to know. Information that had killed him.

259

He turned to Erica. "Maybe he is behind it all."

In 1861, the Western Union Company strung a telegraph line from New York to San Francisco, terminating on a knobby promontory that came to be known as Telegraph Hill. The new technology made previous attempts at rapid communication—like the pony express—obsolete. Telegraph Hill became the symbol for the proliferation of electronic communications that took place between the 19th and 20th centuries.

Willie DeSalvo didn't know a thing about the history of Telegraph Hill, and he didn't care. All he knew was that it was a good high place for him to conduct business. Willie had his own name for it: Goldmine Hill.

Like most other small businessmen, Willie wrestled with government regulations that hampered his work. There was, for example, the twenty minute parking limit atop the hill, instituted to control the tourists, people who had nothing better to do but wait in line just so they could drive up the curving road to the top, park their cars for a few minutes and walk around to look at the city.

If Willie wanted to, he could have ignored the time-limit. He could easily write off the parking tickets as cost-of-business. But given his line of work, the last thing he wanted to do was attract attention from nosy meter readers. So he had developed a routine.

Every day for the past few months, Willie parked his car at the foot of Telegraph Hill on Montgomery Street, where there was always plenty of parking until early evening. He hiked up the ivy-bordered footpaths to the top of the hill carrying a lunch box, a portable stereo with earphones hanging around his neck, and a small black leather case containing a laptop computer.

At the top, Willie found his favorite location, next to a large blue spruce on the south-east side of the hill, looking out over the financial district. The tourists generally preferred the other side of the hill, with its views of the Golden Gate Bridge, Lombard Street and the wharf. But for Willie's purposes, the south-east side was better.

He leaned against the tree, plunked his lunchbox down, and opened the portable computer on his lap. Passers-by, if they noticed Willie at all, paid little attention to him. They weren't likely to notice that Willie spent most of his day there. Regular hikers and joggers assumed he was a writer; San Francisco was besieged with those. And no one ever noticed that the headphones Willie wore did not go to the stereo, but into the lunchbox, which was also connected to the portable computer through an adapter in its side.

Inside the lunchbox was a mobile cellular scanner. Willie was trawling—listening for cellular telephone traffic—which was abundant in the financial district of San Francisco. His radio had been specially adapted to pick up signals in the 800 megahertz region of the UHF band, the area assigned to cellular telephone traffic. Although the calls he intercepted were sometimes interesting—horny young stock brokers talking to their girlfriends, drug dealers arguing with their suppliers— Willie's real interest was in the periodic short bursts of static, which meant nothing to him, but were electronic gold to the computer. They were the sound of cellular phones communicating with their base stations. Once every minute, every cellular telephone had to report in to the nearest cellular tower, sending a signal that included the telephone number and the electronic serial number of the phone itself. That was how the cellular phone companies kept track of where the phones were, to keep them connected to the traditional telephone service.

Generally, Willie's job was simple. The receiver in the lunchbox picked up the signals and passed them to the laptop computer, which translated them into human-readable data. Later, Willie would sell the numbers to a broker, who would program them into another phone and sell it. The legitimate owners of the telephone numbers never realized that their numbers had been stolen until they started getting charges for calls to places like Paraguay.

Willie had considered getting into the programming and sales aspect himself, but had decided against it. Selling stolen phone numbers was a federal offense. So Willie merely acted as a clearinghouse, providing the serial numbers and phone numbers to third parties. What they did with the numbers was up to them. It was easy work, the pay was good, and there were occasional freelance jobs that paid very well–like the job he'd been on for the past several days. His contact had given him a single phone number to scan for. If there was any activity on that phone, he was to record it and pass it on. Willie was being paid by the hour, and had already made a pile of money simply sitting, listening to the squawk of the receiver as it scanned the crowded airwaves for the mystery number.

True, after two days of this, he had begun to get bored. There was no challenge to simply sitting there. He wasn't stealing anything, he wasn't tracing anyone. He was simply sitting.

A bird flitted in and out of the branches of a nearby tree. Willie watched as a chipmunk ran up the trunk of the tree.

Suddenly, the crackle of stray signals coalesced into a normal phone conversation. Willie sat up quickly and switched on the recorder in the lunchbox.

"...big things were happening at CompuSys, but didn't say much more."

"He couldn't say much more...

Willie tried to follow the conversation, but it was all gibberish to him, something about the stock market, mutual funds, and computers. He leaned back against the tree. Whatever it was about, the conversation was interesting to someone, someone who was interested enough to pay him top dollar for it.

The conversation ended a few minutes later. Willie switched off the recorder, flipped up the top of the lunchbox, and pulled out a cellular phone.

"Yeah, it's Willie," he said. "I've got some stuff for you."

29

Harry leaned back in his chair and his eyebrows peaked over the top of his glasses. "You want to what?"

"I want to get on the CompuSys computer system," Randall said.

"I don't know about that."

"Why? We got onto PC Monthly's system easily enough. It's not as if it's a government system."

"We'd be better off if it was. That I know I could get into."

Erica sat, her arms crossed, listening to the conversation in disbelief. "I can't believe you're even talking about this."

"Why?" Randall asked.

She threw her hands up. "Because it's impossible. It's like breaking into the Wicked Witch's castle."

Harry shrugged. "I didn't say it was impossible. CompuSys has an incredible system. But nothing's impossible."

"I can't believe this," Erica said. "You realize if they catch you, they'll kill you."

"Then we wouldn't be the first, would we?" Randall said. "Or the second."

Harry frowned. "The second?"

Randall told him about James Wilton. "Another

computer error, apparently."

"Bastards," Harry said, and Randall knew what he was thinking: if he'd found Wilton sooner, he might still be alive.

"He may have tried to leave us a message," Erica said. She showed Harry the card with Wilton's scribbling on the back.

"Krypto," Harry said, musing. "Superboy's dog."

"What?"

"Never mind." He took off his glasses and massaged the bridge of his nose. "All right," he said, as if coming to a resolution. "We'll do it. But she's right, it won't be easy."

"Personally, I think it's impossible," Erica said. "And stupid. But if you're determined to do it, count me in."

Randall hadn't counted on Erica being involved in the break-in. He looked at Harry, who raised his hands slightly, refusing to take sides. "I don't think so," Randall said.

Erica's eyes flashed. "Why?"

"Because you've got too much to lose. And he was my friend."

Her gray eyes became lasers: highly focused, charged, and ready to fire. "He was my friend, too."

"I just don't think–"

"What?" She leaned into his face. "And don't give me that 'this is no place for a woman' line. It's a little late in the century for that."

He sighed. Half of him agreed with her. The other half wanted to protect her from what could be a dangerous situation.

She didn't wait for him to make up his mind. "Don't bother coming up with a rationalization." She turned and left, slamming the door behind her. They listened to the sound of her car peeling away.

"There goes my ride," Randall said.

"Doesn't matter," Harry said, picking up the phone. "We've got a lot to do."

"What are you doing?"

"Planning an attack on the witch's castle."

30

The Mar Vista Apartment complex was located 1.2 miles from the headquarters of CompuSys International. A warren of tightly-clustered townhouses, the development was popular with CompuSys employees who didn't want to commute and for whom the lack of any social or cultural life in the area was not a problem. They didn't have a life outside CompuSys anyway.

Ferret pulled his smoke-windowed van to the curb a block away from the Mar Vista, switched off the headlights, and killed the engine. Flipping on the inside light, he pulled out a printout of the Mar Vista grounds and showed it to Randall and Harry. "Here we are," he said, and gestured across the street to a pair of brick pillars bordering a wrought-iron gate. "Once you're inside, cross the courtyard to building G," he said, tracing the route on the map. "You'll find apartment G-3 on the ground floor."

"Who's apartment?" Harry asked.

Randall was surprised he had asked, but Ferret seemed amused. "Terry Cook."

Harry winced. "Oh, my god. Terry Cook?"

"Who's that?" Randall asked.

"One of the top programmers in the country," Harry said. "Worked for Apple, IBM, all the big companies. But I thought he lived on the east coast."

"He did," Ferret said. "Or does. He's been doing freelance programming for CompuSys for about a year, but he's got an ex-wife and two kids back in New York. He works out of his apartment here three weeks out of every month, and then flies back to see the kids for a week."

"And this is his week away?"

"Not quite. I ran a check on his airline records. This week he's down in Scottsdale, Arizona. He's been making a lot of trips down there lately," he added significantly.

"Scottsdale," Harry said. "Home of Microm."

"What's Microm?" Randall asked.

"One of the largest manufacturers of microprocessors in the country."

"Why's he going down there?"

Ferret shrugged. "Who knows? But there must be something big going down if Terry Cook's involved."

"Let's just hope he doesn't come back early," Harry said, gazing across the street.

"He won't. His flight comes in next Friday."

"You're sure we can get into the CompuSys system from here?" Randall asked.

Ferret frowned, as if he wasn't in a mood to be second-guessed. "Nothing's sure. Their system is so tightly guarded that the only way to get on is from one of their own nodes. Most of those are on the company grounds, or in the off-site offices, which are also heavily guarded. Terry Cook has one of the few direct connections from a private apartment." He pulled a piece of paper from his shirt pocket and handed it to Harry. "This is a list of the passwords he uses on other systems. If none of them works, you're on your own."

He pulled out a small black box with a wire attached to it. The other end of the wire was connected to a printed circuit board the size and shape of a credit card. "The doors use magnetic key cards. This will get you in the door. It'll take a minute or two to figure out the correct code, so make sure no one's watching when you start."

Harry pocketed the device and said to McLagan, "Ready?"

Randall hesitated. "Should we have disguises?"

Ferret looked amused. "Disguises?"

"In case someone sees us. Maybe we should look like painters or electricians."

"You've been watching too many spy movies. Think about it. The resident manager sees a couple of workmen walking around in the middle of the night. He knows he didn't call them. What do you think he's going to do?" It was a rhetorical question. "He's not going to question two ordinary guys. So look ordinary. If anyone sees you, they'll figure you're visitors. Unless of course you look suspicious. Just act as if you belong there." He held up his cell phone. "You got this number memorized?"

"Got it."

"All right." He gestured to the laptop Erica had lent Randall. "When you're done, call me from that thing and I'll pick you up. Don't use Cook's phone. I'll be around the block, out of sight." He paused, then added, "If anything goes wrong, you're on your own."

On the sidewalk outside, a young woman approached the gate to the complex. "There's your ticket," Ferret said. "Get going."

Randall opened the door to the van and stepped out. Harry handed him two shopping bags, grabbed two bags for himself, and nudged the door closed behind him.

The street was empty. They crossed quickly, reaching the gate just as the woman pulled her ID card from the security slot and the door buzzed opened.

"Could you hold that gate?" Randall said.

"Sure." she said, noting the grocery bags. "You guys

having a party?"

Randall glanced at Harry. "No, not really." They didn't need anyone stopping by. "Just stocking up."

"Too bad," she said, and strolled off in the opposite direction, looking back over her shoulder with an inviting smile.

They crossed the courtyard and Harry muttered, "How come that only happens when you're committing an illegal act?"

Randall shook his head, repeating Ferret's instructions as if they were a mantra: Act as if you belong there. Act as if you belong there.

Short shrubs lined the walkways between the buildings, providing far less cover than Randall would have liked. They came to building G at the far end of the complex and followed a path around the side to a dimly-lit alcove. Randall sighed with relief; the door to apartment 3 was out of site of the courtyard, blocked by shoulder-high shrubs.

Harry stuck the card end of the black box into the key-lock and switched it on. Instantly, it began entering 4-digit codes.

0001
0002
0003
0004

A door opened on the other side of the courtyard. They listened as footsteps emerged and crossed the yard to main entrance. The gate opened and closed, and the footsteps walked away.

The unit flew through possible combinations.

7146

7147
7148
7148

"This better be a 4-digit code," Harry whispered.

"Why?"

"Because there are a hundred thousand possible five-digit combinations. I don't feel like standing out here that long."

The unit beeped, and the lock clunked. The unit had stopped on a number.

9578

Harry exhaled heavily. "Doesn't get much closer than that."

The door opened into a living room, obviously the abode of a single male. Light from outside filtered past heavy drapes and fell on a coffee table piled high with computer magazines, catalogs and old TV Guides. Beneath the picture window was a futon sofa. A large-screen television dominated the wall opposite the futon.

Harry closed the door quietly and switched on a dim, pen-sized flashlight. The narrow beam guided them through the living room, past a small kitchen, and around a corner to two other rooms. One was a bedroom, the bed unmade, with a barren institutional dresser and the stale smell of dirty clothes.

They turned to the other room and a telephone rang in the living room. They halted, listening as the phone rang, as if it were an accusation, an indictment that they should not be there. Harry held a finger to his lips. The answering machine clicked on.

"Hi, this is Terry Cook," the machine said. "You know what to do."

The machine beeped, then came a dial tone. Whoever it was didn't leave a message.

They entered the second bedroom, which had been made into an office, with two computers, miscellaneous hardware, shelves loaded with books, manuals and software. High up on the wall, a single window cast dim light into the room.

"Good," Harry said, peering out the window on tip-toe. "It's an alley. No one's likely to see any light from here. Close the door."

He switched on a lamp above the desk, then found the power strip for the computer and switched it on.

"Hold it right there," a male voice said. "Who do you think you are?"

They spun around to the door. It was still closed.

A box had appeared in the middle of the monitor.

This system is protected by AudioGuard.
Click here and speak your name.

"Damn," Harry said. "Voice analysis software."

"Can't you just say his name?"

"No. It uses the actual sound of your voice to control access to the system."

"Is there any way around it?"

"Maybe. Most of these systems let you enter a password from the keyboard in case you have a problem." He pulled out the list of passwords Ferret had given him and entered each of them. None of them worked.

"Now what?"

Harry shook his head. "I don't know." He scanned the desk for clues until his eyes fell on a telephone next to the computer. "Wait a minute."

He left the office and returned a moment later carrying the answering machine.

"What's that for?"

"Watch." He plugged the machine in and held it next to the microphone atop the monitor, then clicked the mouse in the box on the screen.

"Hi, this is Terry Cook," the machine said. Harry hit a button, cutting off the rest of the message.

The message on the screen changed.

AudioGuard access granted.

The computer whirred and the screen became a wild assortment of colorful icons.

"This guy's not exactly a neatnik," Randall said.

"This guy's a genius," Harry said. "He doesn't have to be neat."

He found an icon with the CompuSys logo. Beneath it were the words 'Net access.'

"Here we go." He clicked on the icon. Almost instantaneously, a box appeared requesting a password. Before he could find the password list, a series of asterisks appeared in the password box, and they were on.

CompuSys International

Use of this system is restricted to employees of CompuSys International. Unauthorized use is a federal crime and is punishable by law.

Harry raised his eyebrows. "Well, that was easy."

"What happened?"

"He uses an automatic log-in program. It filled in the password for us. I'll bet CompuSys doesn't know he's doing that." He entered a series of commands, then signed off.

Randall looked concerned. "What did you do that for?"

"Even Terry Cook doesn't have unlimited access to the system. If we stayed on under his ID, we'd be running up against brick walls all over the place. So now I'm going to log on as superuser."

Randall wondered if he was kidding. "Superuser?"

"Right. It basically gives me unlimited privileges on the system, which I'll need. This is a complicated system. It's a little like walking into New York City on foot, without a map. So I just gave myself the key to the city."

"That should help."

"Yeah. Now we just have to find our way to city hall."

31

The headquarters of CompuSys International looked like the campus of a well-endowed liberal arts college. Neat roadways curved gracefully between a dozen granite buildings, past brick walkways, manicured lawns and perfectly-trimmed shrubs, all unencumbered by telephone poles, wires, or cables. Those had been hidden, buried in underground pipes. "Don't clutter up the interface with components," Barr had told the designers.

At the edge of the grounds, a tight row of evergreens blocked the campus from the highway. The early-morning sun tipped over the trees, casting long shadows across the grounds and falling on Building One, the main building of the campus, where it passed through an enormous picture window in the office of Gerald Barr.

Barr stood at the window staring at the trees. "Norman," he said, "you have the soul of a CPA."

Norman Benchley sat alone at the huge conference table. He was overweight, with dark-rimmed glasses and prematurely thinning hair combed awkwardly to one side. He wore a long-sleeved white shirt and a conservative blue tie. He did not look comfortable. "You see–"

"The soul of a CPA, you know that?"

Benchley sighed and entered the remark into his personal journal of Barr's offenses. He had worked for Gerald Barr for six years, and had despised him for five and a half.

Benchley had come to CompuSys from General Foods, where his financial wizardry and obsessive attention to detail had made him the chief financial officer. At the peak of his career, the company had been swallowed by Phillip Morris, and Benchley became a minion to the Morris executives. Shortly after the takeover, his girlfriend had broken up with him, citing his almost complete lack of spontaneity. "You need to take more risks in life," she'd told him.

In response, Benchley had done two things, neither of which restored the affections of his girlfriend. He had purchased a bright red Corvette, and he had signed on with CompuSys as its chief financial officer.

Within two months, Benchley had regretted both decisions. The Corvette was uncomfortable, impractical, and demanded constant attention. And the job at CompuSys was a personal nightmare. That realization had dawned on him during a staff meeting in which Barr had dressed him down—in front of his own people—over a minor bookkeeping blunder. Barr had finished his tirade and stormed out of the room, leaving a red-face Benchley to pick up the pieces with his staff. They were not unsympathetic. "Welcome to CompuSys," one of them had said.

Gerald Barr had forgotten the incident within the hour, but Benchley had not. For the next five and a half years, he had maintained a meticulous, running account of Barr's offenses—his insults about Norman's style, his criticism of Norman's technological ignorance, his jokes about Norman's dating life, or lack of one. He kept track of them all. And he planned his escape.

Just now, though, he had to explain legal intricacies he knew Barr didn't want to hear about. "According to the Employee Retirement Income Security Act–"

Barr raised his hands. "I don't see what's so complicated about this. You write a check from the pension fund and invest it in a mutual fund. What's the problem?"

Benchley adjusted his glasses. "My concern is that this particular investment might not appear..." He hesitated, searching for the best word. "...appropriate."

"To who?"

"To the Securities and Exchange Commission. Or the Pension Benefit Guaranty Corporation." The PBGC was the government organization that policed company pension funds. "I'm afraid this is the kind of thing that might seem improper."

"Why? For God's sake, the employee stock fund already owns shares in the company."

"Yes, but that fund is controlled by the individual employees. Pension funds maintained by the company are another matter." He clasped his hands, as if pleading with Barr to understand him. "If the government suspects this investment is being made for the benefit of CompuSys rather than its employees–"

"What's good for CompuSys is good for the employees."

Benchley forged on. "...especially given that the new trustee you've appointed for the pension fund is...associated with CompuSys in other ways."

"What's that supposed to mean? So what if Ronald Eden is on our board of directors. Is that against the law?"

"No." In fact, Benchley had been the one to nominate Eden for the company's board of directors. "But appointing a board member to be trustee of the pension fund when that same person just happens to manage an outside mutual fund that happens to invest..."

Barr shook his head to stop him. "All I know is the Cortez Fund is a highly successful mutual fund. That's all

I need to know."

Benchley nodded, swallowing. It was true. The Cortez Fund was a highly—some might say spectacularly—successful fund. That was thanks, in no small part, to Norman Benchley.

CompuSys stock had been sliding. With Barr's every movement under observation by the SEC, he had instructed Benchley to shore up support in the investment community. He had left the choice of means to Benchley. "Don't bother me with the details," he had said.

So, Benchley had concocted the scheme with Eden, arranging for his appointment to the CompuSys board and then suggesting to the company's key financial and technological partners—in a dozen subtle and totally untraceable ways—that the Cortez Fund was "worthy of their consideration." The price of membership in their little club—apart from the purely financial investment, of course—was a willingness to provide other members with advance notice of impending news, and a tacit loyalty to the founder of the club.

Getting the other players on board had been easy. Because of its contacts with hundreds of other high-tech companies, CompuSys held inside information about new products, mergers, delays—a hundred events that could—and did—affect the stock market. Benchley had simply salted the mine with a few well-timed and absolutely accurate "rumors," which had netted the members of the club millions of dollars. By now, they were ready to follow him wherever he led.

The results had been prompt and rewarding. The Cortez Fund had used its large infusions of cash to invest in CompuSys stock, ceasing its downhill slide. The company's partners were happy, the shareholders were happy, and Barr was happy, since a large portion of stock had been shifted into obliging hands.

It was, of course, a convenient arrangement for Barr. If the SEC ever decided that CompuSys had committed illegal actions, Barr could simply point to Benchley. "Gosh, I simply told him to reassure the investors. I had no idea he was going to do anything illegal."

And although Barr wasn't supposed to know how the arrangement had come about or what it involved, Benchley was sure he knew it involved Ronald Eden and the Cortez Fund. Barr was far too smart not to know that. So when Barr announced he planned to make Eden the trustee of the employee pension fund—with the tacit understanding that the pension funds would be invested in Eden's Cortez Fund—Benchley was less than thrilled. Given his illicit relationship with the Cortez Fund, anything that drew attention to it could put him in legal jeopardy. "My concern is the appearance of impropriety..."

"What's improper about investing the employees' pension fund in a highly successful mutual fund?" Barr demanded. "It's a 5 billion-dollar fund."

Theoretically, Barr was right. The company's pension fund would only be a small portion of the Cortez Fund's holdings. And the fund held stock in many other companies. But if the CompuSys pension plan invested fifty million dollars in the Cortez Fund and Cortez turned around and purchased fifty million dollars' worth of CompuSys stock, an unsympathetic observer might smell a skunk, even if it didn't trigger the usual reporting and disclosure requirements.

Benchley sighed and closed his briefcase, a tacit admission that Barr had won. "All right."

"Good boy, Norman," Barr said. Without another word, he walked to his desk, sat down, and began checking his e-mail. The gesture told Benchley he was dismissed.

Benchley left, closing the large oak door behind him. Good boy, Norman. Another deposit in the ongoing account of Garr's abuses.

Norman Benchley was a patient man. For a long time, he had been content to merely catalog Barr's offenses against him. Soon, however, he would settle with Gerald Barr. He was looking forward to closing the account.

32

An hour had passed, then two—more time than Randall was comfortable with—and they still hadn't found anything on the CompSys system that connected the company to the Family. The sky outside the small window had begun to lighten.

Finally, Harry said, "Well, that's interesting."

Randall glanced at the screen.

N:\DALLAS
N:\DAYTONA
N:\DENVER

"What are those?"

"Probably code names for new projects. Barr always chooses cities for the code names." He sighed. "Sure wish I had time to peek in there."

He kept scrolling, came to a directory called GRNDZRO, and scanned its contents. "All right. Here we are."

"Really?"

Harry pointed to the screen. "Ground Zero," he said. "Dead center of a nuclear blast. Welcome to City Hall."

He continued scanning the files in the directory. "Well, what do you know." He pointed to screen.

HDFIX.DAT

It took Randall a moment to recall where he'd seen that before. "Wasn't that on PC Monthly's system?"

"Right. And every other system that was infected by the Houdini virus."

"You're saying the CompuSys computer was infected?"

"Looks that way," Harry said. "Odd. Very odd."

He kept scanning. "I don't see anything about the Family, though. Let's see if they've erased anything that might be helpful."

A minute later, a list of erased files appeared on the screen. "Son of a gun."

?OGIN.EXE 5-29-90 5-29-90 -3

"That's the same login program that was on PC Monthly's system," he said. "Whoever did that installed a trap door here, too."

"When?"

"Yesterday."

Randall frowned, trying to put the pieces together. The Family had broken into PC Monthly's system. Now it looked as if they'd broken into the CompuSys system. But if Gilbert Barr was behind the Family...

"Why would Barr install a trap door in his own system?"

"I don't know," Harry said. "But that reminds me..."

He entered a command, but the system did not respond. He tried again, with no success. "Huh."

"What's up?" Randall asked.

"Trying to delete my login program to cover our tracks. But something's wrong. It's ignoring me."

"I thought you could do whatever you wanted."

"I should be able to." He stared at the computer for a moment. "Damn."

"What?"

Harry said nothing, but entered another command, one that would delete all the files in the system directory.

The system sat, unresponsive.

"Damn," he said, slamming a fist on the desk. "I should have known."

"What?"

He turned off the computer. "That delete command should have worked," he whispered fiercely. "The only reason it wouldn't was if someone was intercepting the commands, making sure we didn't do anything to harm the system."

"You mean someone's watching us?"

Harry cracked open the office door. "This whole thing was too damn easy. The hang-up phone call—how else would we have guessed that Cook's name was on the answering machine? The automatic log-in that didn't even need a password? It was all too easy." He peered out the door. "Come on, let's get out of here."

They moved quickly down the darkened hallway to the living room. As they crossed the room, a sound came from the sidewalk outside the apartment: a scraping, then a quiet squawk, like the sound of a walkie-talkie or radio.

The door to the apartment flew open. A brilliant light outside the door exploded on, silhouetting the shapes of a half dozen uniformed men as they burst through the door. The light reflected off weapons, all of which were pointed at Randall and Harry.

"Freeze," a voice shouted. "Don't move."

33

In the morning shadows outside Terry Cook's apartment, a van waited, its rear doors flung open. Randall and Harry were tossed inside and shoved onto benches facing each other, a massive guard on either side. Dim light shone from the front of the van, highlighting patches on the gray uniforms: the letters C and W with a lightning bolt across them.

"I can't wait to tell the police that CompuSys is abducting people from private property," Randall said.

The driver glanced in the rear-view mirror. "The property belongs to CompuSys," he said, his voice flat. "I don't think the police will mind."

Randall sat back against the wall. No wonder why it had been so easy to break in. He wondered: was Ferret in on the sting?

He glanced at Harry, who seemed to read his mind. "Ferret didn't know," he said. "I can promise you that."

"Shut up," the driver barked.

The van roared out of the apartment complex. They rode for only a few minutes, down broad highways that turned to industrial park side roads. The van turned onto a long lane lined with well-groomed trees and passed a mammoth concrete and steel sign bearing the CompuSys logo. It pulled up in front of a large building, where the guards yanked their prisoners from the van and ushered them through the glass doors of the front entrance.

They entered a plush lobby, lit only by morning light filtering in through the front windows and low-intensity track lighting along the walls. Quiet muzak sounded from hidden speakers. A middle aged woman looked up quizzically from the receptionist's desk as the group passed.

Harry said to her, "Tell Auntie Em I'll be a little late getting home."

A guard shoved them roughly into the nearest elevator.

They rode in silence, the doors opening to an office suite that, despite the early hour, seemed to be in full swing. If anyone was curious about two men being hustled along by a squadron of security guards, they were too busy to acknowledge it.

At the end of a carpeted hallway they passed through a large, unmarked door. As they entered, a stout man in a white shirt and blue tie stood aside to let them pass, a look of cold resignation on his face.

A secretary looked up from her desk, saw them, and nodded to the guards. She lifted a telephone, waited a moment, and said, "They're here."

With another nod from the secretary, the guards shoved Randall and Harry into an inner office.

Gerald Barr stood yelling into a telephone. "Bullshit. This company has never been stronger."

Barr saw them and gestured to the guards to deposit Randall and Harry on a sofa next to the door. The guards pressed them into the sofa and took up positions on either side of it. One guard placed on Barr's desk the belongings they had earlier confiscated: wallets, Harry's pass-code device, and Randall's laptop computer.

Light streamed in through the window behind Barr's desk, silhouetting him as he argued with the caller. "I don't care what he says," Barr insisted. "Anyone with half a brain can see the trend."

The argument continued briefly and ended with Barr slamming the phone down. "Idiot," he said. He turned and frowned at Randall and Harry. The phone rang again.

Barr grabbed it and yelled, "What?" He heard the response and sighed. "All right. But after this, hold my calls."

His tone changed abruptly as the caller came on line. "Arthur, how are you?" He was a different person now, one who had been having a thoroughly delightful morning. "Fine, Arthur, fine. Look, I just wanted to make sure you're on board with us here." He listened patiently, smiling broadly as if the caller were his best friend in the world. "Well, I know you do. And I think it's in the best fiduciary interest of your clients to stick with CompuSys." His smiled dimmed just slightly. "No, I can't give you a guarantee, you know that. But I'm sure you'll be sorry if you transfer those funds."

Randall glanced at Harry. It looked as if Landulfson was right. Barr was involved in a battle to line up support among investors.

The phone conversation ended and Barr's smile evaporated. He glanced at Randall and Harry impassively, picked up their wallets and pulled out the licenses. He laid the licenses on the smooth surface of his desk like a croupier dealing 21, then crossed his arms. "Well. Randall McLagan and Harold Arnofsky." He glared at them. "What were you doing on my system?"

Harry shrugged. "Hacking. Seeing what we could see."

Barr slammed an open palm on the desk. "Bullshit! You think I don't know people are out to get me? Who are you with? Megasoft? Dulterra?"

Randall shook his head. "We were there on our own."

Barr looked at the security guards for sympathy, as if he couldn't believe what he was hearing. "More bullshit.

There's no way you could have gotten on the system without help."

"That's what I thought," Harry said. "Pretty convenient—the girl at the gate at just the right time. The auto-login."

Barr looked at the guards. "What the hell is he talking about?" The guards shook their heads and Barr continued, "You've got about 5 seconds to tell me what you were doing, then I'm calling the police."

Harry shrugged. "I told you, we were hacking."

"We'll see about that."

Barr punched an extension on the telephone. "I want a complete run-down on a couple of people." He read Randall and Harry's names, social security numbers, and birth dates off their driver's licenses, then slammed the phone down. "Believe me, if I turn you over to the police, you'll go to jail for so long your relatives won't be able to identify your bones. And whoever you're working for won't be able to help you, I promise you that."

"Fine," Randall said. "I'm sure the police will be interested in some of the things we can tell them about Peter Jacobson's death."

If he expected Barr to be shocked, he was wrong. "Who?"

Randall studied Barr's face. He was either a good actor, or he honestly didn't recognize the name—a thought that troubled him even more. If you were going to kill someone, you should remember their name. "Peter Jacobson," he said sourly. "He was a columnist for PC Monthly."

"So?" A look of comprehension crossed his face. "Wait a minute. Is that the guy who jumped off the bridge?" He didn't wait for a response. "What does this have to do with me?"

"That's what we'd like to know," Harry said.

"Maybe it has something to do with CompuSys canceling its contract with PC Monthly just before Peter died," Randall said. "And renewing the contract immediately after he died."

Barr looked incredulous. "I've heard some weird conspiracy theories before, but that takes the cake. This is a billion-dollar company. I don't even know what magazines we advertise in."

"Then you don't deny it's true?" Randall asked.

"Oh, for God's sake." Barr grabbed the telephone and yelled into it. "Get me Clifford in marketing." A moment later, he barked, "Did we cancel our contract with PC Monthly recently?" The answer, judging from the frown on his face, was affirmative. "Why?" A moment later, he yelled, "Don't give me that bullshit. I want to know who did it and why."

He listened to the answer, his face turning red, the veins in his neck throbbing. "Fire them. Fire the whole damned outfit."

Barr slammed the phone down and stared at Randall. "That action was taken without our knowledge by an account rep at our outside marketing firm. Our former marketing firm."

Laurie Donoway, Randall thought.

Barr splayed his hands on his desk. "All right, let me get this straight. You're telling me this guy was so upset about our canceling the contract that he killed himself?"

"No," Randall said. "He was pushed."

Again, Barr was not fazed. "Pushed? By who?"

Randall took a deep breath. "The Family...or someone connected with it."

For the first time, Barr seemed attentive. "What?"

"The Family. It's an online–"

"I know what the Family is." Now Barr looked like a mechanic who has heard a familiar, troubling sound in the engine. "What did they have against this friend of yours?"

"He was writing about them. I think he found out something he wasn't supposed to know."

"And what does this have to do with me?"

"You tell me," Randall said. "There are a lot of threads in this mess that point to you and CompuSys."

A look of disgust passed over Barr's face. Before he could speak, there was a knock at the door. A sheepish young woman entered, handed Barr a sheaf of papers, and hurried out.

Barr scanned the pages. "Randall McLagan," he read. "Reporter for the Peabody Herald in Peabody, New Hampshire." He snickered. "You're a long way from home." Flipping through the rest of the pages, he added, "And your finances are a mess."

"Tell me about it."

Barr took longer reading Harry's papers. "Harold George Arnofsky. Independent computer consultant." His eyebrows went up slightly. "Impressive credentials. How come you've never worked for us?"

"I don't work for fascists."

Barr smiled slightly, put the papers on the desk, and moved toward the sofa. "Harry? Can I call you Harry?" He didn't wait for an answer. "I don't know what you've heard about me, but let me give you some advice." He leaned closer to Harry and hissed, "Don't screw with me. I guarantee that you will be very, very sorry."

"Is that what you told James Wilton?" Harry asked icily.

Barr recoiled slightly. "What about James Wilton?"

"Aside from the fact that he's dead?"

The color drained from Barr's face. He straightened, looked away for a moment, and appeared to come to a decision. He looked at the security guards. "Take off."

The guards left and Barr returned to his desk. Built into

the top of the desk was a flat panel display of some kind. He punched several buttons on the panel and said, "This is going to be a very private conversation. Now, what happened to James?"

Randall told him about the attack and the medication error. As he did, Barr closed his eyes, as if pained. He pondered a moment, then said, "James was one of the best programmers I ever knew."

A realization dawned on Randall, and he felt like an imbecile for not coming to it sooner. Harry saw it too. "Wilton worked for you?"

"Yes," Barr said. "He was a genius. Out of school only two years and we had him working on some of our biggest projects. Then he went off the deep end and joined that damn group."

"The Family."

"The Family," Barr said, a knife edge to his voice. "I didn't want to let him go, but eventually I had to. I kept an eye on him for a while, just to make sure he didn't sign on with any of our competitors. Then he dropped out of sight. I couldn't locate him."

"Well, someone found him," Harry murmured.

"The Family," Barr said, his mouth forming a thin line. "Those lunatics have been a pain in the ass ever since..." He left the sentence hanging.

"Ever since you bought out Fordham Graves?" Randall asked.

Barr shook his head. "That son of a bitch. I could have gone into competition with him and put him out of business. Instead, I bought his worthless company and made him a millionaire. So what does he do? Turns around and joins that miserable bunch of psychos. I've got a Senate committee breathing down my neck, the press on my back, and I'm losing good people. And now I've got fanatics demonstrating against me in front of computer shows."

"Bad timing, huh?" Harry asked.

Barr's tirade halted abruptly. "What do you mean?"

"When you've got a big project in the works."

"Who told you that?"

"Your ex-partner," Randall said. "I paid him a visit."

"Sandy? He doesn't talk to anyone. What did he tell you?"

"Not much. Just that there was something big happening."

"Who else have you talked to?"

Randall side-stepped the question. "I'll tell you who we haven't talked to. So far, we haven't met anyone who can tell us what happened to Peter Jacobson."

"Look," Barr said, shaking his head. "I'm sorry about your friend, but I have no idea what happened to him. I've got enough problems of my own without trying to keep track of every harebrained journalist who jumps off the Golden Gate Bridge."

Randall clenched his teeth. "How about a journalist who was pushed by someone who worked for you?"

"That does it." Barr picked up the phone and punched out a number. "I'll let the authorities take care of you."

"Fine," Randall said. "Given your present difficulties, I'm sure there are people who would be interested in the story I'm writing about Peter's death and how it relates to CompuSys."

Barr pointed a finger at Randall. "I told you–"

"Not to mention the mysterious death of a man who was formerly your top programmer," Harry said.

"That had nothing to do with me."

Randall drove it home. "Or the mutual fund that's managed by someone on the CompuSys board of directors, a fund that's been buying an awful lot of CompuSys stock lately. Of course, there's probably nothing illegal about it. But I'm sure the SEC would be interested anyway."

Barr looked like a chess player who'd been caught off guard by an unexpected move from an underrated opponent. He paced for a minute, then faced them. "What exactly do you want?"

"All I want is to find out what happened to Peter Jacobson."

"That's it?"

Randall thought about his job, his credit cards, his personal records. But all that would have to wait. "That's it."

Barr seemed to consider for a moment. "All right. I'll make a deal with you." He pointed a finger at Randall. "You want to find out what happened to your friend, right?"

"Right."

He looked at Harry. "Meanwhile, I've got leaks in my system somewhere. What I need is an outsider, someone who's not connected to the company, someone with the know-how to track those leaks."

"You want me to bug-proof your system?" Harry asked.

"You were good enough to get on by yourself."

Harry snorted. "You made it easy for us. A third-grader could have gotten in that way."

Barr shook his head. "I have no idea what you're talking about."

"You set us up," Harry said angrily. "You said yourself we couldn't have gotten into the system without help."

"You didn't get any help from me."

"Then how did you know we were there?"

He shrugged. "We knew you were coming. Someone tipped us off."

"Who?"

"No idea. We just got a message to be on the alert. We were watching for you and started tracking you the moment you came in."

"And you didn't set up an automatic log-in from Terry Cook's place?"

Now Barr looked alarmed. "What?"

Harry told him about the trap door in Cook's machine. "Someone wanted us to get on to your system. So they made it look like an automatic log-in program."

"I can promise you that wasn't anyone from my company," Barr insisted.

"Why would someone else want to make it easy for us to get onto your system?" Randall asked.

"I don't know," Barr said, his eyes hardening. "But it had to be someone who knew a lot about the system. No one gets into our system unless they belong on it or are invited."

"I see," Harry said. "And did you invite the Houdini virus on to your system?"

Barr's face reddened. "Our system is scanned for viruses constantly. We eliminated Houdini shortly after it was introduced to the system."

"I know," Harry said. "I saw HoudiniFix on the system."

"We didn't use HoudiniFix," Barr said, looking offended. "We have our own software for removing viruses."

"Well someone used HoudiniFix. I saw the data file."

Barr wasn't having any of it. "Why would they do that? I told you, we eliminated the virus right after it was planted."

Harry was silent for a moment. Slowly, a look of realization spread across his face. "Maybe the real purpose of HoudiniFix wasn't to get rid of the virus."

"What?"

"I can't believe I didn't see it earlier," Harry said, turning to Randall. "Remember the PC Monthly system? Someone planted a trap door there, right?"

"Right?"

"And that system had been infected by Houdini, right? How much you want to bet there's a trap door on every system that was ever infected with Houdini?"

Randall was confused. "Houdini planted a trap door in the systems it infected?"

"No," Harry said excitedly. "Houdini was just a decoy, a way to get people to run HoudiniFix. That's what planted the trap door."

"And then erased the evidence," Randall added.

"Right." The pieces were coming together now. "Mark Roberts wrote HoudiniFix."

"So what?" Barr asked.

"He's a member of the Family."

"Who told you that?"

"It was in a column Peter Jacobson was working on when he died," Randall said.

The telephone buzzed. Barr picked it up angrily. "I thought I said..." He frowned. "All right, put him through."

In an instant, Barr was jovial again. "Senator, thank you for calling...Yes, sir, everything is going fine...We're right on schedule..." He glanced at his watch. "Yes, sir, we'll be making the announcement at noon today..." He listened patiently for a few moments. "Well, we're hanging in there, despite the efforts of some of your colleagues." The senator made some witticism and Barr laughed. "Yes, well that could explain his problem...No, no problem whatsoever, Senator. Please call any time."

He hung up the phone. "That bastard would stab his grandmother in the back if he thought it would get him re-elected."

He was interrupted by three quick beeps and turned to his desk, puzzled. The noise was coming from Randall's laptop computer.

He flipped it open and glanced at the screen. "You've got a message," he said, and turned the screen toward Randall.

Mail has arrived.

Randall frowned. "I haven't used this for e-mail. What do I do?"

Barr shook his head. "They give these things to anybody these days." He pressed the Enter key.

CompuMail
From: Erica Steiner
To: Randall McLagan
RE: Important
I need to talk to you. Meet me at Peter's apartment ASAP.

"Who's that?" Barr demanded.

"Erica Steiner. She used to work with Peter. She's been helping me out."

Barr considered for a moment. "All right. I'll have security take you there." He made a call and two of the thugs returned. Barr instructed them to take Randall to the apartment.

Harry stood to leave also, but Barr said, "Not you. You stay here with me."

"Great," Harry said. "I always wanted to get my hostage badge."

Barr shook his head. "You're going to help me find the leak in my system."

"What's the matter, don't you have any decent

programmers here?"

"I don't want whoever planted that trap door to know I've found it."

"You haven't found it yet."

"You'd better hope we do." There was menace in his voice.

34

S enator Richard Hornsby wasn't fooled by Gerry Barr. He had been around long enough to know when he was being patronized. After two decades in politics, he had been schmoozed by the masters.

Hornsby's political career had begun in the California state legislature, where he had established a record of strong support for business and industry. He'd ridden that horse all the way to Washington. True, he had sometimes been accused of catering to businesses like CompuSys too much, caving in to pressure from his major contributors. But CompuSys was one of the largest and most important employers in California. It was his duty to make sure CompuSys remained a strong, financially viable institution.

During his first few years in the Senate, Hornsby had simply paid attention, followed the rules, and learned the ropes. Two terms later, by dint of patience and careful deal-making, he had become chairman of the Senate subcommittee overseeing appropriations for the Treasury Department, the IRS, and a less well-known but equally powerful agency known as the General Services Administration.

The GSA was, in essence, the country's purchasing

agent, controlling every purchase made by the U.S. government. It was also in charge of property management, building construction, and a host of other activities. The GSA had an annual budget in the billions of dollars and a staff of thousands of employees.

As chairman of the appropriations subcommittees that oversaw the GSA, Richard Hornsby had not used his influence excessively. He'd been saving his chips for a project that had suggested itself in his early years, when he'd served on the agriculture committee.

During a routine hearing on soil erosion, a clerk complained that the computers in the offices of the Soil Conservation Commission and those in the Farmer's Home Administration—both divisions of the Department of Agriculture—couldn't communicate with each other.

With a little research, Hornsby discovered that a similar situation existed throughout the government: workers at the Treasury Department couldn't access data from the Office of Management and Budget. The army's computers couldn't talk to the navy's. And no one knew how the IRS computers worked, not even the IRS.

Richard Hornsby was about to fix all that.

The plan was simple: within a year, every computer operated by an agency of the federal government would have to conform to a standard known as the Uniform Federal Computer Code. The UFCC would ensure that every computer in every government office would be compatible with every other government computer.

The standard had been set forth as a policy rather than as legislation, so as to avoid the scrutiny of other lawmakers. As a policy, it would not be subject to the kind of long, drawn-out public debates in which politicians ground their private axes against a piece of legislation.

Information about the UFCC standard had been tightly

controlled. And although Hornsby had refrained from providing any direct input to the standard itself, the administrator of the GSA—who had been nominated under Hornsby's watch—was well aware that one of the software companies in contention to provide software for the standard, one of the largest software companies in the world, was located in Hornsby's home state.

Other agencies had provided input to the standard. Any system that was to be adopted by all the offices of the U.S. government would need to be absolutely secure, and the armed services, law enforcement and intelligence communities had all made their needs known in that regard. Those aspects of the standard were, by necessity, secret even from Hornsby. But he had been assured that the CompuSys proposal met all the requirements of the standard.

The UFCC would anchor Gerald Barr's support for Hornsby in cement. Hornsby was counting on that support when it came time to make a run for the presidency. There was only one possible hitch in Hornsby's plan: Albert Tomaccio.

Albert Tomaccio had been a thorn in Hornsby's side ever since he arrived in the Senate. A scrappy fighter who seemed more at home in a west-side bar than in congressional chambers, Tomaccio had emerged onto the national scene from political obscurity. Before coming to the Senate, the only political office he'd held was as a state representative from the Bronx, a position that he juggled with his full time business as a meat wholesaler. When Edwin Skillings, the revered senior senator from New York, passed away, Tomaccio had announced his intention to run for office and complete his term. Most people had laughed. No one took him seriously.

Lacking the support of the New York political machinery, Tomaccio's campaign had looked, at first, as if it were doomed to failure. But when the dust settled, Albert Tomaccio had been elected to the U.S. Senate. And because he was completing Skillings' term, he'd inherited the elder statesman's committee assignments, which included a seat on the powerful Judiciary committee.

Tomaccio's personal trademarks included cheap cigars, an outsider's attitude, and hostility towards one company that bordered on hatred: CompuSys International. When Tomaccio became chairman of the Judiciary committee, he was in a position to do something about that hostility.

Soon after taking charge of the committee, Tomaccio had initiated a special investigative subcommittee to look into allegations of unfair trade practices on the part of CompuSys. He was joined in this crusade by another committee member, Howard Covering of Oregon.

Hornsby could understand Covering's antagonism toward CompuSys, given that the WordRight Corporation—a major competitor of CompuSys—was located in Oregon. Despite Covering's complaints that CompuSys was monopolistic and anti-competitive, the real problem was the company's astounding success, for which Covering could find only one explanation: CompuSys must not be playing by the rules.

But Hornsby was mystified by Tomaccio's animosity. As far as he could determine, none of the big computer companies in New York—like IBM—had ever contributed to Tomaccio's campaign fund. So what was he up to?

Hornsby had followed the progress of the investigation closely, fearing that unfavorable revelations would sabotage CompuSys' contribution to the UFCC standard. But as far as he could tell, Tomaccio's committee hadn't uncovered any smoking guns. He suspected—and hoped—that Tomaccio's charges were simply sound and fury signifying nothing.

He pressed a button on the phone. "Evelyn, get Raymond Williams at GSA for me, would you?"

He drummed his fingers. He could have called Williams himself. But senators didn't make their own calls, and it wouldn't do to let anyone know that he was not absolutely swamped with work.

"Good afternoon, Ray. I just spoke to Gerry Barr." It pleased him to refer to Barr so casually. "He tells me they're ready to make their announcement at noon today. I just wanted to make sure you folks are in synch with that."

"Yes, sir, we are. We'll post our press release to the wire services at 1 o'clock their time, 4 o'clock our time."

Hornsby chuckled. "I guess the west coast is always ahead of the east, isn't it, Ray?" Williams was a native of Georgia, and the senator enjoyed tweaking him about the superiority of California over the peach tree state.

"Yes, sir, I guess it is."

"Well, I just wanted to check in. You take care, now."

"Thank you sir."

Ray Williams smiled thinly as he put the phone down. The west coast is always ahead of the east.

We'll see about that, he thought, spinning around in his chair. He slid up to a computer that was already on and typed a simple message.

U.S.S. Cosmos will launch at 15:00 EST. We are preparing to raise the standard at 16:00 hours EST as scheduled.

The message was delivered, and within minutes it had been passed along to the executive director of the fastest growing online service in the world.

Fordham Graves leaned back in his leather chair and read the message again, savoring it. He had been planning this day for a long time.

He remembered the day he'd received his first e-mail message about the Family. It was an odd message, one that had come anonymously, asking if he would be interested in discussing an executive position with a rapidly growing online organization.

He'd almost dismissed it as a prank. At the time, he'd never heard of the Family. And the more he learned, the people involved with the group seemed to be a bit quirky, to say the least.

To begin with, there was the interview, conducted electronically, by a group of eight people—the Administrators, they called themselves. The Administrators had grilled him for three hours about his previous employment experiences, his attitudes, his personal life. Despite their questions, it soon became apparent to Graves that his interrogators had already known everything about him before asking.

Meanwhile, his questions about the organization elicited strange responses, or were simply ignored. It appeared that the day-to-day operations of the group were overseen by the Administrators. As far as he was concerned, "leadership by committee" was a sure-fire recipe for disaster.

Nevertheless, it appeared that the Family was already a profitable operation. The group would, he was told, have no trouble meeting the large six-figure salary he required. In fact, the Administrators implied that the salary would probably double within a year, which it had.

Despite some concerns about the organization, Graves' instincts had told him that the time was ripe for an explosion in online services. And the timing of the offer had been propitious, coming as it had on the heels of his battle with CompuSys. He had been "examining new opportunities"—a thin cover for "still out of work"—for a shade too long. So he had accepted their offer, expecting it to be only a temporary position, something to keep him occupied and prevent the kind of embarrassing gap in one's résumé that bespeaks career problems.

It was only after Graves had signed on as the Executive Director that he learned about the Father.

The Father, he was told, was the founder of the Family, the inspiration behind it, and the object of veneration on the part of its members. From the beginning, Graves' questions about the Father had been met with silence. Who was he? What was his relationship to the Administrators?

For security reasons, he was told, the Father had little contact with members of the group. The Father's time was far too valuable to waste on the day-to-day operations of the organization. He rarely sent e-mail, and when he did, it was a special occasion.

In time, Graves realized something that astounded him: even the Administrators did not know the identity of the Father. And then he understood the brilliance behind the elusive persona. All followers need an authority figure to believe in—a politician, a rock and roll idol, a guru—and the more mysterious, the better. The Father, whoever he was, merely provided Family members with what they secretly desired. Graves recalled the words of Voltaire: "If there were no God, it would be necessary to invent him."

Graves' chief assignment was to see to the expansion of the Family. The Father made his wishes and opinions known, and Graves and the Administrators carried them out. The actual mechanics of operating the organization— including the technical aspects—fell to the Administrators. Fortunately, they seemed to know what they were doing in that regard, which was a good thing. Graves' forte had never been technical issues. His strength was in running a business. He knew what pieces of equipment were necessary and he knew where to find them. Among the first pieces of equipment he'd gone shopping for when he took over the reins of the Family was a good senator.

He used the word "good" in the utilitarian, not the moral sense. He had picked up Albert Tomaccio for what he considered to be a bargain price, like distressed merchandise at a fire sale. Tomaccio was a man with flexible principles, a checkered past, and a campaign that was in trouble.

After the deal had been struck with Tomaccio, his campaign problems were remedied in short order. With a single message to the Administrator for New York—dutifully passed along to the local Shepherds and then to the general membership—Tomaccio's campaign had undergone a "dramatic turnaround" as the media called it. The exuberant meat salesman had been elected to Congress in a landslide that even the most prescient pollsters had not foreseen.

As a senator, Tomaccio had already proven to be a useful asset to the Family. His influence with the Judiciary committee had been instrumental in the release of Mark Roberts from Danbury prison. And while Fordham Graves held no personal fondness for the juvenile virus-maker, he didn't want the lad sitting in a prison cell where he might someday decide to unburden his guilty soul to a representative of the federal government. Those career representatives were, ultimately, more important to Graves than elected officials like Tomaccio. Senators came and senators went, but government agencies last forever.

That was why Graves had instructed the Administrators to place as many members as they could inside government agencies. Those members—in contrast to the average member—had been instructed not to proselytize or in any other way draw attention to themselves as members of the Family. Their effectiveness depended on their true allegiance remaining hidden. To their coworkers and supervisors, the members employed by government agencies were merely aides, clerks, and secretaries, performing their jobs diligently, gaining the confidence of their supervisors and coworkers.

To infiltrate, emulate. It was a principle that had proven highly effective, whether one was trying to exert influence within the government, the New Age movement, or a Baptist church. The true usefulness of the hidden members would be proven after a majority of Americans had joined the Family—a process that Graves anticipated would take a few more years.

Of course, the Family didn't really need a majority of citizens to be members. Given that only a small percentage of the general populace actually voted, the near-complete turnout of Family members invariably gave them influence beyond their numbers. Soon, the Family would no longer have to exert influence through indirect campaign contributions and political action committees. Family members would—at their Administrators' direction, of course—elect officials who were sympathetic to the cause, many of whom would themselves be members of the Family.

Eventually, the Family would be able to select who would be president. Perhaps that person would be Albert Tomaccio. Or perhaps not. Graves would have to see how things went. Maybe, he thought with amusement, he would run for president himself.

And of course, some day the influence of the Family would encompass the whole world. Even now, that thought took Graves' breath away. He'd had no idea when he signed on with the Family just how powerful an idea could be.

There were others, Graves knew, who held similar

goals of reforming government, and even rebuilding society to meet their particular agenda: the Mormons, the Christian reconstructionists. But they were going about it all wrong. They didn't understand that computers had fundamentally changed the face of democracy. In the near future, voting would be unnecessary. Why bother to ask people what they thought, when the information could easily be surmised through a computerized evaluation of their lifestyle, their educational history, the kind of car they drove?

Of course, before the new order could be realized, the groundwork had to be laid. The Family needed a foundation upon which to build. And the cornerstone of that foundation was Krypto.

There was something poetic about the technology behind Krypto, Graves thought. Thanks to Krypto, the Family would soon have the "keys to the kingdom" in its hands.

"And the gates of CompuSys will not prevail against it," Graves chuckled.

Graves' personal secretary appeared in the doorway. "This just came in," she said, depositing a sheaf of papers on his desk.

Papers often arrived on his desk unannounced and unexpected. He had learned not to question their origins.

The papers appeared to be a transcript of a telephone conversation. The Family had paid listeners located in key areas around the country. As he read through the transcript, his jaw set, creasing the lines that ran from the corners of his mouth and framed his chin.

He turned to his computer and sent three messages. The first was to a young member who worked in the office of Senator Albert Tomaccio. The second was to the Chief Financial Officer of CompuSys International.

The third was to the Father.

35

Detective Latimer threw his pager on the coffee table, settled into the lounger and clicked the play button on the remote. He had recorded the basketball game the night before. By carefully avoiding radio and television since then, he had managed to avoid finding out who had won. Thanks to the miracle of videotape, he was going to ignore the fact that it was Monday morning and that the rest of the world already knew the outcome of the game. He reached for the bag of taco chips as the phone rang.

Latimer sighed and hit the mute button on the remote. "Bill Latimer."

It was the switchboard. "We just got a call from San Francisco Medical. Possible wrongful death. They need a visit."

The NCAA logo flashed on the muted 24-inch screen. "Right away?"

"Afraid so. The body's already been in the cooler a couple of days."

Latimer sighed and hung up, wondering what was up at San Francisco Medical. It was probably some old bird who thought her husband had been done in by the doctors.

The administrator of the Medical Center welcomed Latimer into his office and closed the door. "Arthur Korning," he said. "I appreciate your coming by so quickly."

"No problem," Latimer said. Just don't tell me who won the game.

Korning lowered himself into a massive leather chair and folded his hands on the mahogany desk that sat between them. "A patient...passed away in our intensive care unit on Friday night." He seemed to be choosing his words carefully. "Upon examination, the...circumstances of his passing give us some cause for...concern."

"What circumstances would those be?"

Korning glanced into Latimer's eyes uneasily. "It appears that the patient was a diabetic. He...inadvertently received an intravenous infusion of D5W...which sent him into a diabetic coma."

"Dee-what?"

"I'm sorry. D5W. A solution of 5% dextrose in water."

Latimer tried to remember his high-school chemistry. Dextrose. "That's...sugar?"

Korning sighed. "Yes. I'm afraid so."

"Not a great thing to give a diabetic."

"No." Korning cleared his throat. "The nature of the patient's injuries were so severe that the...challenge presented to his system by the introduction of the dextrose was sufficient to..." He stopped, searching for a word.

"Kill him."

Korning cleared his throat again, his face crimson. "The patient expired at 4:05 PM on Friday afternoon."

Latimer pulled out a notepad and noted the time.

"We have conducted a thorough review of the patient's records," Korning said, his tone hopeful and apologetic. "And we've conducted interviews of all the personnel involved with his care."

I'm sure you did, Latimer thought.

"In the course of that investigation, we discovered that the patient's computerized records had been...changed just after his admission to the hospital."

"Changed in what way?"

Korning pulled a thick manila folder from the side drawer of his desk. "It appears that someone broke into our computer system and deleted the fact that the patient was a diabetic. If that fact had been in the records, this incident would never have occurred."

"I see." Latimer began writing again. His note-taking was largely a screen to give him time to think. He was thinking this: the last thing San Francisco Medical needed was a multi-million dollar malpractice suit and the resulting bad publicity. What better way to pass the buck than to blame the incident on computer hackers? It was a ploy Latimer had seen less-sophisticated criminals use all the time: find a likely suspect, someone who is probably guilty of other crimes anyway, and pin the blame on them.

"Here are the documents related to the patient," Korning said, handing him the folder. "You'll find a computer audit of his records on top."

The audit consisted of several pages of computer print-out, single-spaced, in a typeface not designed for easy reading. He skimmed it quickly, jumping to the last page, where several lines of arcane terminology indicated that the words "diabetes mellitus" had been deleted from the record.

That didn't necessarily mean anything. He knew that a clever programmer on the hospital staff could probably have rigged the audit to make it look as if an outsider had broken in and changed the records.

He flipped through the rest of the chart. On a page labeled "Visitor Log" were two names. One of them was Randall McLagan.

It took Latimer only a moment to place the name. Maybe it was just a coincidence. Maybe anyone could happen to know two people who passed away mysteriously within a week.

Or maybe not.

Norman Benchley had two computers in his office. One, on top of his desk, was connected to the CompuSys network. The other, hidden in the recesses of the desk, was not. It had been installed by one of the company's own technicians—Benchley told him he needed to isolate the company's high-level budget projections from the main system for security reasons. The technician had agreed not to tell anyone else about the setup, and was later transferred to a high-paying new position in the company's east-coast office.

The hidden computer used the same monitor as the computer on top of Benchley's desk—a button underneath the desk switched the monitor from one system to the other.

An electronic chirp alerted Benchley that he had e-mail. He pressed the button, and his Family account appeared on the monitor, the mailbox icon blinking.

The message, no more than three words, was from Fordham Graves.

Initiate Operation Jujitsu.

Benchley took a deep breath, like a man about to leap from the top of a bungee-jump platform. He deleted Graves' message and composed a new one. There was no salutation to the message. The recipients would know who it was from.

Well-placed sources indicate that the Senate investigation into CS's business practices will take a new direction in the immediate future. Potential ramifications include investigation by federal agencies into possible violations of insider trading regulations.

He knew the last phrase would send a chill down every recipient's spine. No one wanted the SEC nosing around their recent trades, or finding out exactly how much money they'd made.

It has been strongly recommended that the fund divest itself of all CS stock immediately. Such preemptive action will forestall allegations of impropriety while allowing the fund to achieve respectable returns on its investment in CS.

In the interest of speed, and to avoid drawing attention to the divesting of our interest in CS, the shares will be placed privately, in a lump offering to a large financial institution. An appropriate buyer has been located.

Of course, the other reason for not placing the shares on the open market was to keep the price from going into the basement. Dropping a large block of stock into the market was like dropping a boulder into a pond; everyone involved took a bath. By selling the stock to an institution that could afford to swallow the entire lump, the stock price—with any luck—would not be affected much.

Needless to say, this information must not be shared outside this forum, as it would adversely affect share price and result in capital losses, as well as being an actual violation of SEC regulations. As time is of the essence, the sale has been undertaken without obtaining your feedback. Failure to act quickly could have the direst consequences.

He added the last line to drive home the point. No one was going to argue with him about the wisdom of dumping a hot potato that was about to come under the scrutiny of the federal government.

Benchley addressed the message to a select list of recipients. The list included investment advisors, state pension trustees, bankers, and other well-endowed and highly placed individuals, each one a major investor in the Cortez Fund. The first name on the list was that of Ronald Eden, the trustee of the fund, whom Benchley had so easily manipulated Gerald Barr into appointing as trustee for the CompuSys pension fund.

Officer Sherry Brown pulled the fax from the tray. It was a typical alert, with a grainy black-and-white photograph and a paragraph about the suspect.

Individual is believed to be in the San Francisco bay area at present. In addition to numerous felonies, the suspect is known to be highly computer-literate and has recently been implicated in computer-related crimes including but not limited to theft, illegal access, and falsification of records. Subject has been classified as a violent felon and personnel are instructed to exercise due caution when apprehending.

Brown copied the suspect's name and social security number into the department's computer. It was standard procedure to check all bulletins against the department's records, looking for any prior contact. More than one career criminal had been nabbed simply because a parking ticket tipped the police off to his whereabouts.

The computer beeped, indicating a hit, a match between the information on the bulletin and the data in the system.

"Hah. Gotcha."

The dispatcher's log—which listed every individual to come into the police headquarters—showed that the suspect had been sitting in the office of a department detective just a few days earlier.

She printed a copy of the log, stapled it to the alert bulletin, and tossed it into a basket for immediate delivery to Bill Latimer.

Whoever he was, Randall McLagan's luck was about to run out.

This time, Randall rode in the passenger seat of the CompuSys van, though neither the driver nor the guard in the back spoke to him the entire time.

The driver double-parked in front of Peter's apartment, just behind a Pacific Telephone van. Erica's car was nowhere in sight.

"This shouldn't take long," he said. The driver nodded noncommittally.

The front door to the apartment had been propped open, as if someone had been carrying things in. He climbed the stairs and saw that the door to the apartment was also open.

"Hello?"

A voice came from the living room. "Hello?"

A young man stuck his head around the corner. He was on his knees, wearing a brown uniform and holding a wire in one hand and some kind of test box in the other.

"Something wrong with the telephone?" Randall asked.

The repairman shrugged. "They told me there was some problem here. I'm just checking to make sure it's not a mechanical problem."

"Oh. OK." He decided not to tell the guy the problem wasn't in the equipment. "Have you seen anyone else around?"

"Nope. Just the landlady. She let me in and then took off to go shopping. Said she'd be back in a while."

"How about a young woman? Red hair?"

The repairman grinned. "No. I'd remember her."

Randall returned to the kitchen. A clock over the refrigerator ticked loudly.

Minutes passed. He waited, pacing the kitchen, then sitting, staring at the clock. Still no sign of Erica.

It was getting late. He didn't want to keep his CompuSys escorts waiting any longer than he had to.

He picked up the phone to call Erica, then remembered the repairman. Walking back to the living room he asked, "Are you going to be much longer?"

The repairman seemed to be concentrating on his work. "No. Just another minute."

The laptop computer sat on the kitchen table where Randall had left it when he came in. Of course. He could use that to call her.

Erica answered on the first ring. "Steiner."

"Where are you?"

She didn't have to ask who it was. "At the office."

"What are you doing there?"

"Working," she said sourly.

"I thought you wanted me to meet you at Peter's."

"Who told you that?"

"You did. By e-mail."

"I didn't send you any message."

"What?"

The repairman passed through the kitchen and waved to Randall. "You should be all set."

"OK," Randall said distractedly. "Thanks."

"Who was that?" Erica asked.

"Someone from the phone company," he said, steering the conversation back. "What do you mean you didn't send me any message? It had your name on it."

"Well, I'm telling you, I didn't send you any mail."

"Could someone have forged your name?"

"Probably."

"Why would they do that?"

She pondered a moment. "Maybe they just wanted to get you there."

"Why—

"Randall, you've got to get out of there."

He thought about it, and made a decision. "No."

"Randall, they may be on their way there right now."

"Fine. If they're looking for a fight, they're going to get it."

"Are you crazy? You have no idea who you're dealing with. These people are dangerous."

"I'm not that crazy. There are a couple of well-armed mesomorphs waiting for me in a van outside."

"What?"

He picked up the laptop and wandered into the living room as he told her about his unplanned visit to the CompuSys headquarters. "I don't think Barr's gorillas are going to let anyone touch me before they take me back to him."

He glanced out the window to the street. The telephone repairman emerged from the building and passed the CompuSys van. As he did, he nodded to the driver of the van, a quick gesture that a casual observer would have missed.

The CompuSys van began to drive away.

"Hey," Randall yelled, as much in surprise as anger.

"What is it?" Erica asked.

"They're leaving."

"Who?"

"The CompuSys people."

Now the telephone van pulled out, and Randall saw its

driver pull out a cell phone and dial a number with his thumb.

"I don't get it." He walked back to the kitchen. "Why would they just–"

The telephone in the living room rang.

He turned and stared at the phone. With sickening clarity, he knew what was happening.

"Randall," Erica yelled. "Get out of there. Now!"

He slammed the laptop shut and bolted out the door.

The phone rang again, echoing in the empty apartment.

He leaped down the stairs, three at a time, bracing himself against the side walls as he hurdled down.

The phone rang a third time.

He fumbled with the outside door, opened it, and cleared the front steps in a single leap.

He heard the faint sound of the phone as it began to ring the fourth time. Then came the blast, a deafening roar accompanied by a rush of wind that threw him to the ground next to a parked car. The front of the building disappeared in a hailstorm of bricks and mortar that flew up and into the street, showering him with red dust and fragments.

He hugged the laptop to his chest. Footsteps came running towards him. He looked up through red-dusted eyelids at two figures blocking the sun. Four strong arms grabbed him, two on either side, and lifted him to his feet. The arms were attached to bulky men in dark business suits. Moments later, the men had hustled him down the street and into the back seat of an unmarked car.

They did not speak to him during the drive. The car wound through the business district and ended up at a nondescript parking garage with a post, where the driver pressed his thumb to a tiny glass window with a flashing LED that caused the gate to rise and allowed the car to enter.

His hosts led him into an elevator, up several floors, and deposited him in a room with the barest of furnishings: a table and three chairs, a stand in the corner with a television set and VCR. A remote control device sat in the middle of the table.

The taller of his captors pointed to a door in the opposite corner. "There's a bathroom in there if you need it." He placed the laptop on the table and left.

Randall examined himself in the bathroom mirror. There was a small cut over his left eye, but it had stopped bleeding. He was sore and covered with dust, but otherwise unhurt.

He exited the bathroom and sat at the table. The door opened and agents Karin Baker and Bill Polk walked through.

"Mr. McLagan," she said. "Are you all right?"

Randall closed his eyes, a wave of relief followed by anger. He was at the Secret Service headquarters. "Would you mind telling me what the hell is going on?"

Baker sat down, eyebrows raised. "We were going to ask you that."

"Why am I here?"

Polk crossed his arms over his chest and leaned against the wall. "You were seen running out of a building as it was being blown up. That's just a bit suspicious."

"Why would I blow up a building that I was in?"

Polk shrugged. "Explosives sometimes go off before they're supposed to."

"Well, it wasn't me. There was a telephone worker in the apartment when I got there. I think he rigged something to the phone."

Baker pulled out a notepad. "We'll check with the phone company to see if they had anyone in the neighborhood at the time of the blast."

"Don't bother. I doubt he really worked for the phone company."

"Then who did he work for?"

Randall hesitated. Who was he supposed to trust?

The door opened and the driver of the car entered, carrying a cardboard holder with three styrofoam cups, sugar packages and creamer. He placed the coffees on the table and left. "Coffee?" Baker asked.

He took the cup without thanking her, his hands trembling.

Polk emptied three packages of sugar into his coffee and stirred it aggressively. "What were you doing at the apartment?"

"What were you doing there?" he asked. "The last time I talked to you, you didn't seem all that interested in anything I had to say."

"We received additional information that led us to believe there might be more to your story than we'd suspected," Baker said.

"What kind of information?"

She didn't answer, but picked up the remote control from the table and pointed it at the VCR. The television flickered on and showed a woman in a hospital bed.

It was Allison.

Randall started up out of the chair. "Where is she? What did you do to her?"

Polk moved to restrain him, but Baker put a hand on his arm. "Relax. Your friend is fine. She came to us."

Randall scowled at her. "What?"

She nodded to the television. The camera zoomed in on Allison's face. Although she wore a look of pain and despair, she did not appear to be hurt. A female voice outside the camera's range said, "How long have you been a member of the Family?"

Allison spoke slowly. "About a year and a half."

Randall stared at the screen.

"How did you become involved with the group?" the interviewer asked.

"I was lonely. I didn't have any friends. They were nice to me." Her eyes were only half open, as if she'd been medicated.

The interviewer paused, as if waiting for Allison to say more. "How did you meet Peter Jacobson?"

Allison's eyebrows came together in pain. "They arranged it. They told me to delay some airline tickets so he'd have to come to our office to pick them up. That's when we met."

"Why did they want you to meet?"

"They said they wanted me to keep an eye on him." She bit her lip and looked in the direction of the interviewer, her eyes pleading. "I didn't think they were going to hurt him."

"But they did?"

She closed her eyes and nodded, crying.

"Were you involved in that?"

"No," she said quickly. "I loved him."

"That wasn't part of the plan, was it?"

Allison shook her head, sobbing.

The tape jumped, as if it had been stopped and restarted. Allison was calmer now, her eyes still red. Randall sat down.

The interviewer asked. "Why did the Family feel the need to eliminate Peter Jacobson?"

She answered slowly. "I don't know. It might have had something to do with a story he was writing. About the group."

"Had he found out something they didn't want him to know?"

"I don't know. He wouldn't tell me." Her eyes began to fill again. "I think he was trying to protect me."

"What was the group's interest in Randall McLagan ?"
Randall's heart pounded.

"He began asking questions. He found out things."

"What kind of things?"

"Someone broke into Peter's system at work. They made up a police record that said he was a drug dealer." She looked up at the interviewer. "Peter didn't have anything to do with drugs."

"Who broke into Peter's system? The Family?" Allison said nothing, and the interviewer tried a different tack. "Did Randall McLagan think it was the Family?"

She nodded. "I was mad at him. But he was right." She rubbed her hand across her eyes. "I'm tired."

Static filled the screen. Baker turned it off.

Randall leaned back in the chair, silent. He had been a damned fool. Allison was a member of the Family. She had spied on Peter. She had lied to both of them. He sighed, shaking his head at his own blindness. "I didn't think she even liked computers."

Baker flipped open a manila folder. "Allison Hughes. Graduated from Scottsdale High School in Arizona, where she showed a strong aptitude for computer science. Attended Arizona State University, but dropped out after 2 semesters. Her psychological profile is that of a highly intelligent, if somewhat unstable young woman. Her family background was...dysfunctional, to say the least. Apparently, the Family provided a stability she'd never known in her life."

Polk picked up the narrative. "Hughes came to the Bay area six months ago. She took a position with the Worldwide Travel Agency. The job gave her easy access to flight information, travel plans–"

"And Peter Jacobson," Randall said.

"And Peter Jacobson."

Baker closed the folder. "Her involvement with

Jacobson presented her with a dilemma. On the one hand, she was committed to the group and intensely loyal to it. On the other hand, she was in love with Peter Jacobson. The more Jacobson found out about the Family, the more doubts were raised in her own mind, creating a grave psychological crisis for her."

"Until he died," Randall said blankly.

"Exactly. In a strange way, his death resolved the crisis for her. Despite the intense grief she was experiencing, she no longer had to confront issues about the group. She could go back to looking the other way, avoiding difficult questions." She hesitated. "Until you came along."

Baker was right. If he hadn't gotten involved, the whole thing would probably have been swept under the rug. No one would ever have known what happened to Peter, and Allison could have gone on ignoring the warning signs about the group. The last thing she wanted was for him to dig into the circumstances of Peter's death.

Baker sipped her coffee. "Miss Hughes expressed some concern about your safety."

Randall glanced at her warily. "She did?"

"In part, that's why she came to us. She was afraid you might find something that would put you in danger, as it had Peter Jacobson."

"What was I supposed to find? I haven't exactly been Sherlock Holmes so far."

Baker glanced at Polk and nodded. Polk left the room and returned a moment later carrying a briefcase.

Randall recognized it instantly. It was Peter's.

Now he knew. "Allison had it all along."

Baker nodded. "She took it from Jacobson's car after his death."

Randall shook his head. Something still didn't make sense. "Why didn't she give it to the Family?"

"I'm not sure. She says she couldn't deal with it

because of the connection to Mr. Jacobson. But I suspect that she had begun to distrust the Family, and was unconsciously holding it back from them."

"What's in it?" Randall asked, trying not to sound anxious.

Polk opened the case, using the lid to conceal its contents from Randall. "Some press releases. Business cards. And this." He held up a small, hand-held computer. "Does this look familiar?"

It was, Randall was certain, the evaluation unit from PC Monthly. "I think it was Peter's. Can I see it?"

"I'm afraid not," Baker said. "In light of the explosion, this is now considered evidence."

"So why are you showing it to me?"

Polk placed the hand-held back in the briefcase and closed the lid. "Does the word 'Krypto' mean anything to you?"

Randall's mind raced. It had become a poker game. He knew some things, and they knew some things. And if they weren't going to show him their cards, he wasn't going to show them his.

"Krypto? Sure. That's Superboy's dog. Escaped from the planet Krypton in one of the dozens of experimental ships that barely made it into space before the planet blew up."

Neither Baker nor Polk smiled. "Is that all it means to you?" she asked.

"I'm afraid so."

She glanced at her notepad. "How about 're-op'?"

"Ree-op? As in bee-bop?"

"Ree-op," Polk said, scowling. "R, e, o, p."

"Not a clue." Which was true. The word meant nothing to him. But they had tipped their hand, if ever so slightly, and he filed the word away for future use.

"Do you have any travel plans in the near future?"

Baker asked.

"How do you mean?"

"Will you be going to any major cities other than San Francisco?"

He shrugged. "You never know."

"How about Detroit?" Polk asked.

"Detroit?" He pretended to search his memory. "I don't think so. Why?"

"Did Peter Jacobson have plans to go to Detroit?"

"I don't know. What's in Detroit?"

They ignored him. Angry, he crossed his arms over his chest. "I've told you everything I know. Can I go now?"

"I'm not sure that would be wise," Baker said. "For your own sake. Whoever blew up that building probably knows that you're still alive."

"Does that mean I'm under arrest?"

"No," Polk said. "But we could arrange that. I'm sure the police would be interested in talking to you about that building."

Baker shot Polk an annoyed glance and said to Randall, "You're not under arrest. We just think it would be better for you to stay here for the time being."

"I think I'll take my chances with the police."

Baker looked at Polk and gestured towards the door. "Excuse us for a moment."

They stepped outside and closed the door. "He's bluffing," Polk said. "And he knows a lot more than he's telling us."

"Maybe," Baker said.

A young woman came down the hall and handed a fax to Baker. "This just came for you. Urgent."

Baker scanned the fax. It was the response to an RBI— a request for background information—that she had filed with the central office.

Request for Background Information
Subject: Krypto
Information is attached.
Information is classified as follows:

No information is available.

At the bottom of the form was a handwritten note:

Where did you hear about this? Forward complete details immediately.

The word 'immediately' had been underlined twice. The signature was an anonymous section number.

Polk read over her shoulder. "They sound pretty anxious to know how we came up with this, considering there's no information available."

"Just what I was thinking."

From inside the room, McLagan called, "Is it all right if I use the bathroom?" There was a trace of sarcasm in the request.

"Of course," Baker said through the closed door.

The young woman appeared again, holding a portable phone. "It's Washington."

Baker took the phone. "Agent Baker here."

"This is Hutchison at section 11." The name meant nothing to her. "I've got a copy of your RBI on something called Krypto."

"Yes sir?"

"Where'd you hear about this?"

She raised her eyebrows in Polk's direction. "We're in possession of a hand-held computer that mentions it in connection with some kind of government project."

"Where did you get the computer from?"

"It was brought to us by the girlfriend of the man who

owns it."

"And where is he?"

"He's dead, sir."

"Dead?" There was a pause. "Hold on to that computer. And don't let the girl go anywhere. Don't let anyone who knows anything about this go anywhere. I'll have someone there to check this out ASAP."

The line went dead.

They returned to the interview room. Water was running in the bathroom sink. They sat and waited for McLagan to come out.

The water continued to run. It ran steadily for two minutes. Baker looked at Polk. His eyes narrowed.

He pounded on the door. "You all right in there?" There was no answer.

Baker looked at the tabletop. The laptop was gone. "Damn."

Polk forced the door open. The room was empty, water splashing unattended into the sink. On the wall high above the toilet was an open window, just large enough for a man to squeeze through.

36

Richard Hornsby made his way through the Senate cloakroom. He stepped into the hallway that led back to his office. There was Albert Tomaccio, headed in his direction, an aide plastered to his side.

Tomaccio had seen him. It was too late to step back into the cloakroom. So Hornsby stuck out his hand. "Senator," he said noncommittally.

Tomaccio grabbed Hornsby's hand and pumped it as if it were a meat-tenderizing mallet. "Dick," he said cheerfully. "How you doing?"

Hornsby nodded gravely. "I'm well, thank you." He had little else to say to Tomaccio, but decided he might as well get a word in for CompuSys. "I would be better if I could understand why the Judiciary committee finds it necessary to invent mythical charges against major American corporations."

Tomaccio grinned. "Just doing our job, Dick."

"Of course," Hornsby said. That wasn't what he'd wanted to say, but the unwritten rules of senatorial courtesy forbade him from calling Tomaccio a damn liar.

As they parted, Tomaccio chuckled to himself. Poor Hornsby. He took all this stuff so seriously. You'd think he'd been here long enough to know how the game was played.

Take the CompuSys business. Despite his public

pronouncements, Al Tomaccio didn't really have anything against CompuSys. In fact, he didn't even know that much about the company. All of his speeches on CompuSys had been scripted by one of his aides, a smart young kid who'd just graduated from Cornell. The kid—he had a real name, but Tomaccio always called him the kid—knew his way around a computer like Tomaccio knew his way around the back streets of New York.

The kid not only knew computer technology, he knew the players in the computer community, and he knew how to pull together their support. He was the one who had gotten Tomaccio's campaign going when it was stalled in the starting gate. Tomaccio had been ready to call it quits when the kid walked in off the street and offered to help computerize the campaign, get him online, and develop a web site.

He was persuasive, and with nothing to lose, Tomaccio had taken him on. Within days, the campaign had begun turning around. If it weren't for the kid, Al Tomaccio would still be arguing with Empire Beef about how much horse meat they were putting in the hamburger.

So Tomaccio owed a debt to the computer folks who had been largely responsible for his election. If those people thought CompuSys needed to be taken down a peg or two, then so be it. That's what democracy was all about. Elected officials were supposed to listen to the voice of the people. And Al Tomaccio was a man of the people.

He had barely settled behind his desk when the kid appeared in his doorway.

"Senator, do you have a minute?"

Tomaccio raised his eyebrows. "Sure. What's up?"

The kid cleared his throat. "You remember I told you we might want to shift our position on CompuSys at some point?"

"Yeah?"

He held up a folder. "Well, I've been working on that. I think it's time to make our next move."

"You do, huh?"

"Yes sir. Now's the time to do this if we want to be properly positioned for future races."

Tomaccio looked at him with a mixture of respect and amusement. They both knew what he meant by "future races." Although Tomaccio hadn't originally known all that much about computers or politics, he had learned a couple of important things. First, if you wanted to be ready for the next generation of technology, you had to have people around you who knew what was coming down the pike. And if you wanted to make progress in politics, you needed the same kind of people, people who knew what was up with whom. You didn't need to understand all that stuff yourself, you just needed someone who did, someone you could trust.

For Tomaccio, that person was the kid. Someday, Al Tomaccio would be occupying the Oval Office in the White House. And the kid was his secret weapon for getting there.

He took the folder from the kid and opened it. There was a short speech on top, followed by an in-depth position paper. He glanced over the paper. "You sure about this?"

"Absolutely, Senator."

Tomaccio paused a moment longer—just long enough to seem thoughtful, but not so long as to appear indecisive. "All right. This is how we'll go, then."

"Very good, Senator."

The kid left, and Tomaccio went over the speech, noting the key points, planning the dramatic gestures he would use at the press conference. As usual, the kid had highlighted the words and phrases that would push the right buttons with the press and the public. And the kid was always right. It was as if he had a program that generated perfect sound bites, guaranteed to make the evening news.

Tomaccio chuckled. This new position would surprise a few folks, maybe even piss a few of them off. But at least Dick Hornsby would be happy.

The phone rang in the plush office of the Western Pacific Bank's vice president for trust funds. Gebhardt pressed the speakerphone. "Yes?"

"I've got a Mr. Ronald Eden for you. He says it's urgent and personal."

Gebhardt took a deep breath. "All right. Put him through."

Eden was smooth, unruffled, as if this were nothing more than a social call. "Bob," he said. "I've got good news."

"Yes?"

"That opportunity I mentioned to you has come through."

Gebhardt's heart rate notched up, faster than was safe for a man his age. "I see."

"Let me give you the details." Eden spelled out the terms of the transaction, which would effectively tie up every dollar of liquid funds in the trust department of the Western Pacific Bank.

"When did you envision this transaction taking place?" Gebhardt asked.

"Oh, right away." He paused. "Is that a problem, Bob?"

"No, no," Gebhardt said quickly. "Not at all."

They completed the details of the transaction and Gebhardt hung up. He stared down at his desk, his heart still pounding. In less than a minute, he had completed the largest transaction of his career, involving more money than some countries spent in a year. In the process, his bank—and to all intents and purposes, he—had become a major shareholder in the largest computer software company in the world. And unlike the Cortez Fund, the Western Pacific Bank could vote its shares.

37

A wall-length bookcase ran down the far side of Gerald Barr's office. In the central section of the bookcase was an oak panel that folded down to reveal a complete computer workstation. For over an hour, Harry had been using the station to explore the CompuSys network, with Barr watching over his shoulder.

"Well?" Barr asked.

Harry shot him an annoyed look. "You're asking me to find a quarter-inch hole in a mile-long dike. It's going to take some time."

"I don't have time," Barr said. "Not today."

Harry shook his head. His chances of quickly finding the leak in the CompuSys system were not good. There were too many places where the intruders could have drilled the hole.

He ran a hand through his wild black hair, and an idea came to him. Maybe he'd been going about this the wrong way. Instead of looking for the hole in the CompuSys dike, he would examine the drill that had made the hole. "I need a copy of HoudiniFix," he told Barr.

"Why?"

"If I can figure out how it works, I may be able to find where it planted the trap door in your system."

"All right," Barr said grudgingly. He logged on to the net and handed the keyboard back to Harry, who located the file in seconds, downloaded it, and began tearing it apart.

Someone knocked at the door. A young man with tousled hair appeared, a clipboard held against his flowered shirt. "Can we set up now, Gerry?"

Barr frowned and glanced at his watch. "I guess we'll have to." He saw Harry's quizzical look. "We're doing a product announcement in here. A big one."

Harry nodded, recalling Barr's comment to the senator. This must be big. He went back to work.

The door opened wide and people streamed into the office carrying lights, monitors, and cameras. Within minutes, the room had been transformed into a broadcast studio, with Barr's desk as the focus of the set. Surrounding the desk were signs and banners, each of which bore a Saturn-like globe with the word "Cosmos" emblazoned across it.

Barr oversaw the set-up, then turned back to Harry. "Well?"

"Whoever wrote this thing knew what he was doing," Harry said. "It's got some kind of protective shell around it."

A short woman with frizzy hair approached Barr. "Gerry, can we do your clothes and makeup now?"

He sighed. "All right. But let's make it quick."

She led Barr to his desk and began powdering his face, while technicians aimed lights around him. Monitors blared with bursts of video and upbeat music as the technicians ran through the production. There were shouts of, "Can I get a level on that?" and "Let's do something about that shadow."

At the workstation, seemingly oblivious to the chaos, Harry continued dissecting HoudiniFix. He ran the program slowly, tracing every move it made to see how it worked. Behind him, Gerald Barr had been transformed from a pasty-skinned hacker into an executive yuppie with a healthy glow, his faded T-shirt exchanged for a designer polo shirt. The young man with the clipboard, who seemed to be directing the operation, appeared at Barr's elbow and coaxed him into position behind his desk. "OK, that's great," he said. "We should be ready to go in a couple of minutes."

Harry continued typing. The director looked over at him. "You're going to have to stop that."

Harry glanced at Barr. "But I've almost—"

Barr nodded. "It'll have to wait."

The director raised his hand. "Let's have it quiet, everyone." He put a hand to the headset in his ear, apparently listening to instructions from elsewhere, then pointed to Barr.

Barr's face broke into a cheerful smile. "Hello, I'm Gerald Barr," he said, reading from a teleprompter. "Thank you for joining us at our live press conference. Today, members of the media are joining us from locations around the world via private satellite, telephone, and online connection. It's appropriate that we should have a worldwide audience for this announcement. Today, we are announcing the most significant advance in computer technology since the introduction of the keyboard," he said. "We call it Cosmos."

Barr went on to explain how Cosmos would affect every aspect of computing in the years to come. The speech was peppered with words like "revolutionary" and "interactive." Multimedia clips demonstrated how Cosmos would open up the world of computing to even the least computer-savvy user. Cartoon characters assured viewers that they too would now have access to the world of computers, thanks to Cosmos. Cosmos had it all, from the computerized home to the wide world of Internet access.

Harry listened closely, wondering whether Barr had

written the script himself. It was a masterpiece of PR puffery, highlighting all the positive aspects of Cosmos while avoiding substantive information and steering clear of issues that might cause anyone alarm.

The presentation lasted for several minutes. Barr finished on an upbeat note. "Thanks for joining us. We look forward to telling you more in the days to come about the exciting new world of cosmic computing...with Cosmos."

The music came up, the director raised a hand and then dropped it. "OK. That's it."

The crew burst into applause. Bottles of champagne appeared and began popping. Someone offered a glass to Barr, who waved it off and returned to Harry, who had already gone back to work. "Any luck?"

"I've managed to take the program apart," Harry said. He pointed to a screen-full of complex instructions. "That's the part that creates the trap door."

"So where's the trap door in my system?" Barr asked.

Harry shook his head. "I don't know. As far as I can tell, HoudiniFix just chooses a random location to plant the trap door. That makes it harder to find."

"Keep working," Barr said, frowning. "I want that leak plugged."

The director hollered to Barr. "Gerry, we've got the feed from the GSA up on the big monitor."

Barr returned to the group. They had gathered around the largest of the monitors. On the screen was an empty podium, with a United States government symbol on the curtain behind it. Technicians crossed in front of the camera, adjusting microphones. It was a live satellite feed, including all the preparatory activity that home viewers never got to see.

A man with thin, graying hair appeared behind the podium, cleared his throat, and at some unseen signal, began reading from a script.

"Good afternoon. My name is Raymond Williams, administrator of the General Services Administration. Today, I have the pleasure of announcing a new policy that will improve the efficiency of our government's vast network of computer systems. Let me begin by explaining the background for this new policy."

Williams detailed the spaghetti-like state of the government's computer systems, consisting of thousands upon thousands of computers that used a hodgepodge of hardware, software, and interconnections. It was, he said, a situation that often led to mistakes, inefficiency, and countless other problems. "To resolve this situation, we have developed the Uniform Federal Computer Code, a new standard that will guarantee the compatibility of all government computers."

The CompuSys staffers greeted the announcement with cheers. Harry listened in amazement. In a single, seemingly mundane announcement, the government had established a standard that would dictate the type of computer that would be used by millions of people. He was fairly sure why the CompuSys folks were so enthusiastic about the new policy.

Williams continued, "Working in conjunction with major manufacturers of computer hardware and software, we have developed a standard that will incorporate the best technologies currently available."

"Like Cosmos," a CompuSys staffer shouted, and his coworkers echoed his enthusiasm.

Of course, Harry thought. Now it made sense. The new standard would mandate that all government computers be Cosmos-compatible. Once the federal government standardized on Cosmos, state and local governments would have little choice but to sign on to the standard. And any private company that wanted to do business with the government would come on board. Eventually, the entire computer industry would be forced to adopt the standard—which would be based on the new technology from CompuSys. Of course, no one would be forced to use Cosmos. But anyone who didn't would eventually be out of business. Including Cosmos in the new federal standard would provide, in essence, a monopoly contract to CompuSys.

Williams went on to describe the standard, but by now the CompuSys staff was hardly listening. Apparently, they'd already known most of the contents of the speech. The mood was jubilant.

"Cosmos, Cosmos!" they cheered, as if they were in a football stadium and not an executive office. Champagne flowed, and even Barr seemed to be caught up in the party atmosphere.

The announcement ended and the scene on the monitor shifted to a news room. A man in an open shirt sat at a desk. Digital numbers flashed in the lower right hand corner of the screen, signals to which the local television and cable affiliates could synchronize their systems.

"All right, we have another live feed coming up in five," the man on the screen said. The counter marked down and the scene changed. It was another press conference, this time against the backdrop of a mahogany paneled room. A short, beefy man in an expensive suit appeared behind the rostrum. It was Senator Albert Tomaccio.

Someone booed and Barr said, "Quiet."

"After months of investigation," Tomaccio said, "the special Senate committee has determined that the charges against CompuSys of unfair and anti-competitive business practices are without merit or foundation."

Harry stopped typing and listened. Tomaccio sounded as if he were reading from a script; phrases like "without merit or foundation" tumbled out of his mouth like polished stones that someone else had put it there.

"I am therefore announcing the conclusion of the investigation and the adjournment of the Senate committee. In part, this decision is based on an agreement that the government has reached with CompuSys regarding the licensing of new technology that will prove crucial to the future of America's predominance in the computer industry."

If the mood in Barr's office had been jubilant before, now it became euphoric. Apparently, Harry thought, they hadn't expected this announcement. Someone turned up the monitor so that Tomaccio's speech could be heard above the noise. "The agreement on the part of CompuSys to provide inexpensive licenses for its new Cosmos technology will be a fundamental part of the new UFCC standard."

Harry pondered all this. It had turned into a red-letter day for CompuSys. A new technology, a new government standard that incorporated the technology, and a clear path to take over the industry without government interference. Even the government's dropping of its investigation against CompuSys could be played to the company's advantage. To the average person, it would look as if CompuSys had agreed to a bargain, offering the government and industry a low licensing fee for Cosmos technology in exchange for judicial leniency.

In fact, Harry knew, it made sense for CompuSys to charge a low fee. Now, competitors who wanted to comply with the UFCC would probably adopt Cosmos rather than spending money to develop their own compatible technology. A low licensing fee essentially guaranteed universal adoption of Cosmos.

The phone on Barr's desk rang. At first, there was too much back-slapping and high-fiving for anyone to notice.

Finally, after several rings, someone picked it up.

"Gerry, it's for you. Outside call."

Barr took the phone. "Gerald Barr here."

"It's Randall McLagan," he said sourly. "Thanks for taking my call."

Barr blinked and frowned. He'd clearly forgotten all about McLagan. "Where the hell are you?"

"You mean, why aren't I in a morgue?"

"What?"

"It was a great plan, Barr. I'm sure the police would never have figured out how I got back to the apartment."

"What the hell are you talking about?"

"I'm talking about almost being blown up, you son of a bitch."

"What?" Barr said. "Where are my guards?"

"You tell me."

Barr hesitated, then let the phone drop for a second. "Shit." He handed the phone to Harry. "It's your friend."

Randall filled Harry in as Barr got rid of his staff. When the office was empty, Barr switched the phone to a speaker.

"...the Secret Service," Randall was saying. "They didn't seem anxious to let me go. So I left on my own."

"The Secret Service?" Barr said. "Wonderful. That's exactly what I don't need today. I want you back here immediately."

"Right," Randall said. "Given the welcome you had waiting for me at Peter's apartment, I'm not inclined to accept your invitation."

"I didn't have anything to do with that," Barr said.

Harry raised his eyebrows. "Then you've got a real problem in your organization."

Barr hesitated for only a moment. "I'll deal with that after your friend gets back."

"How do you propose I do that?" Randall asked. "Your

goons left me, remember? And now I'm being chased by the Secret Service."

"Can you get back to Peter's apartment?" Harry asked.

"Maybe."

"Is Peter's car still outside the apartment?"

"Yes, I think so."

"Good. He used to keep a spare key under the left front bumper, in one of those magnetic boxes."

Barr interrupted. "What did the Secret Service want?"

They heard a sound like air brakes squealing, followed by the opening and closing of doors. It was clear Randall was on a bus.

"Well, for starters, they wanted to know if I'd ever heard of Krypto," Randall said, more quietly now. "Then they asked about something called re-op."

"Re-op?" Harry asked.

"Right. And they wanted to know if I was planning any trips to Detroit."

Barr looked at Harry. "Detroit is the code name for Cosmos."

"What?" Randall asked.

Barr explained about the Cosmos announcement. "So what's re-op?" Randall asked.

"It's an old command, left over from the first operating system we ever developed. It's been in every piece of software we've sold."

"What does it do?" Harry asked.

"Nothing. It's like your appendix—a vestige left over from the early days of development."

"So why leave it in?"

"I developed that piece of code myself," Barr said, sounding almost embarrassed. "It's like my signature. But no one else knew about it."

"So how did the Secret Service find out about it?" Harry asked.

"Probably from Peter," Randall said. "They've got his briefcase. I'm not sure, but I think his hand-held computer was in it, along with the notes from his last meeting with James Wilton."

"I still don't understand why the Secret Service would be so interested in all this," Harry said.

Barr hesitated. "I can't tell you."

"Listen, you bastard," Randall said, his voice hissing from the speakerphone. "Someone just tried to kill me. It's pretty clear your own organization is riddled with spies. So unless you want me to take this bus to the nearest newspaper office and start spilling my guts, you'd better start explaining what's going on, now."

Barr sat down, pondering his options. He decided he had none. "All right. It has to do with Krypto."

"Which is...?" Harry said.

"A new technology for encrypting files—converting them into a form that can't be read until you decrypt them. It operates at a level the user never sees. And it prevents anyone from having access to the user's files except the user or someone else the user gives a special key to."

"Or the government," Harry said sourly.

Barr shrugged.

"I don't get it," Randall said.

"The feds have been getting uptight because everyone is using computers to communicate," Harry said. "In the old days, if they thought someone was doing something illegal, they could just get a court order to tap your phone. Now, if they tap the phone, they may get just computer data, and even that's likely to be encrypted. So they want to force everyone to use a system they know how to decrypt. The government would hold the keys that would let them unlock anyone's communications. It's like giving them a master key to everyone's home."

"What's this got to do with CompuSys?" Randall

asked.

Barr sighed. "Krypto will be built-in to Cosmos. Every time you save a file, or send it, it will be automatically encrypted. And no one will be able to decrypt that file or message except you and people you give a key to."

"And the government," Harry repeated.

"Yes, the government," Barr said, annoyed. "That was an important component of the UFCC standard. The feds wanted a system that would provide them with access in case of emergencies."

"Right," Harry said. "Emergencies like spying on dissidents."

To Harry, the pieces were beginning to fall into place. What the government couldn't do on its own, the marketing power of CompuSys could. By mandating that all its computers be Cosmos-compatible, the government would also be establishing Krypto as the encryption standard. Soon, everyone would be using Cosmos computers, and all of those would use Krypto. The government would have a set of universal keys that let them read the files and e-mail of every Cosmos computer. And the Secret Service, the FBI, the National Security Agency—all the agencies involved in surveillance—wouldn't have to do a thing to bring this to pass. CompuSys would do it for them. Market forces would take care of the rest.

"What if someone doesn't want to use Krypto?" Randall asked.

"They don't have to buy a Cosmos system," Barr said.

"If there aren't any other systems available, they won't have much choice, will they?" Harry said.

"I suppose," Barr conceded. "Within a few years, every computer in the country—and most of them outside of the country—will be using our system."

"And the government will have access to all of them,"

Harry said. "Not to mention CompuSys."

"That's the kind of paranoid bullshit I'd expect from the Family," Barr said. "All Krypto does is ensure that the government will be able read a person's files if they need to. No one will be able to get at the files without a court order."

"But CompuSys will have the keys," Harry said.

"We developed the technology," Barr said. "We have to have the keys."

"And we're supposed to trust CompuSys and the entire government not to use the keys indiscriminately?"

"Only selected government agencies will have keys to Krypto," Barr said.

"Which ones?" Randall asked.

"The FBI, the NSA, the Department of the Treasury—"

"Oh, great," Harry said. "The folks who brought you the Waco conflagration. This is like hiring Jimmy Valentine to install your security system."

"The government has to have access," Barr insisted. "Do you want people like the Oklahoma bombers running around without being watched?"

"That doesn't make sense," Harry said. "If you were a terrorist, would you encrypt your messages with a system that you knew the government could break?"

"Hold it," Randall said. "Back up. Where does this re-op thing come in?"

"That's the part of Cosmos that Krypto connects to," Barr said. "Since re-op wasn't being used for anything else, it made a convenient place to hook Krypto in."

"Why would Peter have mentioned it in his notes?"

"That's a good question," Barr said. He looked at Harry questioningly.

Harry shook his head. "You've got me." Then, a light seemed to go on. He turned back to the workstation and began typing.

"What are you doing?" Barr asked.

"Where do you keep the source code for Cosmos?"

"Forget it," Barr said.

"Look, do you want to find your bug, or not?"

Barr hesitated, then took the keyboard and directed the system to the area where the source code for Cosmos was stored.

As Harry scanned the source code, Barr said, "What are you looking for?"

"Drill holes," Harry said. A moment later, he stopped. "Son of a bitch."

Barr looked over his shoulder. "What?"

Harry pointed to the screen. "Does that look familiar?"

Barr stared at the jumble of computer instructions on the screen and frowned. "No. Where'd it come from?"

"That's part of re-op. In Cosmos."

"It can't be," Barr said. "I wrote re-op. I never saw that stuff before."

"Yes you did," Harry said. He entered a command that split the display screen into two windows. In the second window, he called up another section of programming. He scrolled through it till he came to the section he was looking for.

Barr pointed to the new window. "What's that?"

"That's the part of HoudiniFix that plants a trap door in the systems it's run on."

Barr looked back and forth between the two windows, one showing the re-op section of Cosmos and the other displaying HoudiniFix. They were identical.

Barr looked pale. "You're saying HoudiniFix planted a trap door in Cosmos?"

"Worse," Harry said. "Cosmos contains the same instructions as HoudiniFix. Any system that runs Cosmos will have a trap door planted it."

"What?"

"Someone took the part of HoudiniFix that generates a trap door and incorporated it into Cosmos. That will give them access to any system that runs Cosmos."

"That's impossible," Barr sputtered. "No one knew..." He stopped.

"Who wrote the Krypto section of Cosmos?" Harry asked.

Barr looked away, hesitating. Finally, he said, "James Wilton."

"So he knew about re-op?"

"No," Barr said firmly. "He just wrote the encryption software. I made the final connection to Cosmos myself. I told you, no one else even knew about re-op."

"Well, Wilton found out about it somehow. And he managed to add a little something of his own to it."

"This is impossible," Barr yelled, storming back to his desk. "We're already in production. There are a million copies of this software. It's being hardwired into new computers."

A burst of static came from the speakerphone. Harry and Barr looked over at it. They'd forgotten all about Randall.

Barr pressed a button. "Are you still there?"

The line was dead.

Emma Bouchard banged the top of the scanner with a wrinkled hand. "Oh, come on, you silly thing. Don't stop now."

The obstinate scanner ignored her, hissing like a nearly-dry teakettle. She banged it again. Nothing. And just when they'd begun talking about something interesting.

She hoisted herself from the rocker and shuffled in the direction of the bathroom. The scanner was still tuned to the frequency she'd been listening to before it was interrupted. Maybe the signal would return by the time she came back from the bathroom.

Emma Bouchard was a contest nut. Over the years, she had tried them all. She especially liked the contests that made you do something to win—figure out a secret message or collect all the pieces of a puzzle—rather than simply sending in a sweepstakes form. So of course she'd been interested when her friend Vera told her about the scanner game.

"It's easy," Vera told her. "They give you the scanner, and some numbers to listen for. All you have to do is listen in for a conversation. When you hear something on one of the channels, you write it down and call a special phone number. Depending on what you hear, you could win prizes. Sometimes even cash."

Emma had tried the game, and within days she was devoting all her free time to it. And Vera was right, it was easy. She could do it while knitting or watching television. And she'd already won prizes: a case of cat food for Abby, a supply of her favorite dusting powder. It was amazing how appropriate the prizes were, as if they had been chosen just for her. The contest people seemed to know exactly what kind of cat food Abby ate and the powder she liked.

Occasionally, she had qualms about the game, wondering if it was quite legal, listening in on people's conversations this way. But then, it was really no different from gossiping over the fence or listening in on a party line, and she'd been doing that for years. Gradually, she'd become an expert at piecing together conversations, figuring out what people were talking about. After all her years as an amateur eavesdropper, she had simply become a paid professional.

Periodically, the people who ran the contest would give her new numbers to listen for. She was especially excited today, because she had received a fresh number just that morning. A new number always excited her. After a while, the old numbers grew stale. A new number was more likely to have some action on it.

And the number had paid out already. Of course, she hadn't understood most of what they'd been talking about, but she had managed to take a few notes before the signal went away. It wasn't much—but that didn't seem to matter to the folks who ran the contest. They always congratulated her on her entries, regardless of how insignificant a clue might seem. Still, she wanted to win a big prize—a new TV set perhaps, or one of those microwave ovens. So she continued listening, hoping for more information to come over the channel.

The scanner was still hissing with static when Emma returned from the bathroom. In the interim, the cat had taken up residence in the warmth of the seat. "Shoo, kitty" she said, swatting the cat out of the chair. Abby jumped down, complaining quietly.

Emma settled herself in the chair and fiddled with the receiver, but it was no use. For some reason, the signal had been lost, and she couldn't recapture it. The competitive spirit in her rankled, but the signal did not return, and Emma was getting anxious. What if someone else had overheard the conversation and called in the clues first? It was first come, first served, and she didn't want anyone else cutting in on her.

She picked up the phone and dialed the special number. As always, a young woman answered without identifying herself. "Hello?"

"Yes, this is..." Emma hesitated. She could never remember her code name, and they insisted that no one ever use their real name. "Oh, just a minute," she said. She pulled the card out from under the scanner. "This is Verity Rocket," she said, giggling. Verity Rocket, indeed. The name sounded like a pop singer her granddaughter would listen to.

The sound of typing came over the line. "Yes, ma'am. And the number you're reporting on?"

"All right, just a minute." She adjusted her glasses and read the number on her worksheet to the girl.

"Go ahead, ma'am. Did you get a message?"

"Yes," she said excitedly. "There were three people on the line. One of them said something about being chased. Then he said he was going back to someone's apartment. Let's see, it was..." She read from her notes. "Peter's apartment. And it sounded like he was going to borrow Peter's car."

"Was there anything else, Ma'am?"

"Oh, heavens, then they started talking some gobbledygook that I couldn't understand. Something about Krypton and bee-bop and I don't know what all else. Then I lost the connection."

"Are you able to pick it up now, Ma'am?"

"No. I waited before calling you because I wanted to see if I could pick it up again, but it hasn't come back."

"All right. I'll record your entry."

"Did I give you enough to win a prize?" Emma asked hopefully.

"Well see, Ma'am. You never can tell."

Margaret Reingold answered the phone. It was for Alan. She handed the phone to him with a concerned look. "It's Administrator Mansfield."

Alan reached for the phone slowly. He had never received a call from an Administrator before.

"This is Alan Reingold."

"Overseer Reingold, the time has come for your testing." The voice was deep, cold. "You are to sign on and read the encoded message. Follow the instructions exactly. You must do this immediately. And you are to tell no one what the message says, including your wife. Do you understand?"

"Yes," he said. "All right."

He hung up the phone without speaking, went to the computer and signed on. He read the message quickly, his color draining.

Margaret stood in the doorway. "What is it?"

He hesitated. "I have to go out."

"Why?"

He turned in his chair, trembling slightly. "I can't tell you."

"Alan, what is it?" she asked, fear in her eyes.

"It's all right," he said, though his tone contradicted him. "I just have to go out for a while. I want you to go down to the den and stay there till I come back."

"Alan–"

"Go," he insisted. "Now."

She covered her mouth with her hand and left.

Alan closed the door behind her and went back to the desk. He read the message on the screen one more time. At the bottom of the screen was a small square.

Click here to print image.

He clicked on the square. Seconds later, a grainy photograph slid from the laser printer. He folded the paper in quarters and put it aside.

Removing a key from the desk, he reached down to the lowest drawer and unlocked it. From beneath a pile of papers he removed a pistol and cartridges. His hands trembled as he loaded the gun.

He checked to make sure everything had been put away, then stepped into the hallway. He put on a long overcoat. The photograph went into the left pocket, the pistol in the right.

As he left the house, a trolley passed, descending the steep angle of Hyde Street toward the bay, its bell ringing loudly. The sound unnerved him somehow, as if it were attracting attention to him. He was glad when the trolley had passed on. Head down, he walked down the street in the direction of the pier and the Marina.

38

The door to Gerald Barr's office opened and his secretary stood there, her brow wrinkled. "What?" Barr shot at her.

"I've been trying to get through to you. There's someone from the Wall Street Journal on the line."

"I don't want to talk to him. I don't want to talk to anyone about Cosmos right now."

She looked apologetic. "It's not about Cosmos."

"Then what does he want?"

"Maybe you'd better talk to him."

Barr picked up the phone. "Gerald Barr."

"Hello. Andrew Peckham here, from the Wall Street Journal. I wonder if you have a comment in regard to the Western Pacific transaction?"

"The what?"

"You're aware that Western Pacific Bank has filed a Schedule 13-D with the Office of Tender Offers?" That was the form a buyer filed with the SEC when acquiring more than 5% of the shares in any company. Barr said nothing. "Mr. Barr?"

He blinked, as if awakening from a trance. "Of course, of course." He hesitated. "I've got someone else on the line. Can I get back to you?"

"Well, sure–"

"Fine. Give your number to my secretary." He punched

a button. "Take this guy's number. And get Benchley up here now."

"Something wrong?" Harry asked as Barr replaced the phone.

"I'm not sure. Someone may be taking a run at us."

"Trying to buy the company?"

Barr nodded. "It's bullshit, of course. They could never muster the votes to pull off something like that." He grabbed a remote and clicked the big-screen monitor on. "They may just be trying to run up the price."

He flipped channels till he found the financial news. A square-jawed reporter sat behind a desk, the daily financials ticking by at the bottom of the screen. In a small window beside him was an image of a round seal with the letters "UFCC" embossed on it.

"On the heels of the government's announcement comes some surprising news related to CompuSys. It appears that Western Pacific Bank has purchased a large block of stock in the company..."

The office door opened and Norman Benchley entered.

"Norman," Barr barked. "What the hell is this about?"

Benchley shrugged. "They're buying CompuSys stock. I thought that was what you wanted."

"Where did they buy it from?"

Before he could respond, an image flashed on the screen—a conquistador's helmet. A voice-over said, "The purchase was made in a block transaction from the Cortez Fund, which had previously acquired a large stake in CompuSys..."

Barr turned on Benchley. "Why the hell is Eden selling our stock?"

Benchley shrugged. "Maybe he thought it no longer represented a wise investment."

Barr blinked, his fury rising. "Eden is working against me." He pointed a finger at Benchley. "This is all your fault."

"I didn't appoint him to the board of directors," Benchley said. "Or make him trustee for the employee pension fund."

"It's my money in that fund," Barr said, pounding the desk. "I want it invested in my own company."

"It's the employees' money, remember?"

"Don't get smart with me, Norman. This is not the time."

On the news, a woman had joined the newscaster. The scroll at the bottom of the screen identified her as a financial analyst. "That's right," she said. "The transfer of these shares from a mutual fund to an institution with voting status means that Western Pacific now holds the majority of outstanding shares in CompuSys."

"Bullshit!" Barr exploded. "This is my company, and I've got the votes to make sure it stays that way."

Benchley shook his head. "She's right," he said calmly. "I've run the numbers. Since your attempts to convert our preferred stockholders to voting stock have failed, Western Pacific has the majority now."

Barr stared as if Benchley had just slapped him. Eden had gained control of Barr's own assets, as well as the employee pension fund, and used them to take over the company. It was like a martial arts move in which you use your opponent's own weight against him.

On the screen, the reporter said, "Don't institutions like banks usually vote with management?"

"That's true," the analyst said. "But Western Pacific's allegiance to the current CompuSys management is uncertain. Depending on the mood of Western Pacific's client base, it's possible that Gerald Barr could lose control of the company."

"Well, it's great timing for Western Pacific," the reporter said. "Today's news about the new Cosmos technology from CompuSys makes this acquisition good news for Western Pacific's clients."

"Absolutely. Western Pacific manages the assets of a number of big-ticket investors, including a fast-growing online service known as the Family. The Family may have its own reasons for wanting to own a piece of CompuSys."

"The Family," Barr said, turning to Benchley with fire in his eyes.

The edges of Benchley's mouth curled slightly. "Well, what do you know?"

Barr's phone rang, but he ignored it. "They knew about Cosmos," he said, spitting the words. "And the standard."

"Good boy," Benchley said, his voice like acid etching metal. "You finally figured it out."

Another line lit up on Barr's phone, then another. The door opened and his secretary stood in the gap, a room full of worried staff members behind her. "The phone's ringing off the hook," she said. "What do I do?"

Barr wheeled on Benchley. "You son of a bitch. You're fired."

"Maybe," Benchley said, smiling and heading for the door. "But I doubt it."

Randall tried the CompuSys number again. Still busy. He'd been knocked off line by a passing tractor-trailer, its driver hollering into a cellular phone. For some reason, the line to CompuSys had been jammed ever since. "Answer the damn phone," Randall muttered.

The bus came to a stop and the driver hollered to his mirror. "End of the line."

Randall looked up and realized he was the only one left on the bus. The signs on the street outside indicated the corner of Jefferson and Broderick, in the Marina.

He stashed the laptop away and strode to the front of

the bus. "Can you point me to Mallorca from here?"

The driver gave him directions and Randall left, the laptop slung over his shoulder. He tried to jog, but grew short of breath quickly. The explosion had taken more out of him than he'd thought.

He came to Mallorca and stopped. The area in front of the apartment had been cordoned off by a police barrier. A crowd stood outside the barrier, gawking, examining the rubble, pointing up to what remained of the building. Police cars lined the street.

Peter's car was parked just outside the police barrier, heading away from the apartment. If he could find the key without attracting too much attention, he might be able to get away before anyone stopped him. He'd have to be careful. Anyone with a car parked near the scene of the blast would certainly be asked if they had seen anything, and that was the last thing he wanted.

He headed down the sidewalk opposite the apartment, feigning nonchalance. A police car pulled out from in front of the gutted apartment and cruised slowly in his direction. He determined not to look at the squad car as it drifted by him, though he could almost feel the cop's eyes passing over him.

Opposite the apartment, a man in an overcoat stood surveying the scene, a worried expression on his face. He looked up as Randall approached, then looked down, as if embarrassed, and glanced at a piece of paper in his hand.

Randall gazed at the apartment and shook his head. "Some mess, huh?"

The man's eyes darted in Randall's direction. He nodded quickly, but said nothing.

Out of the corner of his eye, Randall saw the police car that had passed him. It was turning around.

Instinct told him there was no time to lose. He crossed the street toward Peter's car, his pulse quickening. By now, the police car was heading back in his direction. His eyes fixed on the left front bumper of Peter's car, where Harry had told him the extra key was hidden.

He reached the car, walked to the front, and stuck his hand up under the bumper. Nothing there.

Blood pounded in his ears. He slid his hand to one side, and his fingers touched a small rectangular box. Prying it loose, he stood and walked quickly to the driver's door, allowing himself a glance in the direction of the police car. It had stopped on the opposite side of the street, lights flashing. The door opened.

He fumbled with the key, inserting it into the lock and twisting it. The lock opened with a clunk.

The officer emerged from the car and shouted, "Hold it right there."

Pretending not to hear him, Randall opened the door and slid into the seat. As he closed the door and leaned forward to insert the key, he heard a pop, and a loud crack echoed through the car, like an egg breaking. He turned and saw a hole the size of a dime in the driver's side window, spiderlike lines rippling out from it. Behind the cracked glass stood the man in the overcoat, a gun aimed directly at him.

Before the gunman could fire again, there was another pop, like a firecracker going off. The man's left leg buckled underneath him and he fell to his knees, looking with dismay at the officer who had fired at him.

"I said hold it!" the cop yelled. He ran to the gunman's side and pressed his face to the pavement as Peter Jacobson's car roared to life and took off down the street. The car's draft caught a piece of paper that lay beside the gunman's hand. As it blew away, the cop caught a glimpse of what looked like a mug shot.

Randall's only thought was to get out of the

neighborhood as quickly as possible. The cop had seen him, he was sure of that, and the police would be looking for the car soon. He figured he had at least a few minutes before the word got out.

As he turned the car onto Cervantes, a voice said, "Friday, May 19."

Randall grabbed the steering wheel hard and looked around. There was no one else in the car.

He heard a hissing sound, and glanced at the dashboard. The light on the car's tape player was on.

The voice spoke again. This time, he recognized it instantly. "Meeting with James Wilton."

It was Peter.

Then he remembered—the odd whirring sound in the background of the message Peter had left on his voice-mail. It was the sound of a tape player rewinding. Peter must have rewound the tape and turned the car off without stopping the tape deck. If he hadn't turned the car on, he'd never have realized there was a tape in the player—nor would anyone else who had searched the car.

He wanted to pull over, to listen to the tape closely, but he couldn't take a chance on stopping. He turned on Marina Boulevard in the direction of the Golden Gate Bridge. He would turn before the bridge, heading south on Route 1, out of the city and back to CompuSys headquarters. At this point, he didn't know where else to go.

The tape clicked, and the sound changed. He heard voices, muffled as if by cloth. Peter had probably put the recorder inside a pocket.

He turned the sound up, but could only make out occasional words above the static and rubbing cloth.

"...Krypto...CompuSys," Peter said.

Another voice, flat-sounding, male, responded. He heard the words "government standard," and "in control."

He was fairly certain it was James Wilton.

"How?" Peter said clearly.

The response was garbled, but he heard "re-op" in it.

Peter asked a question that seemed to end in "...behind it all?"

Wilton paused, and then said something that ended with "Smith."

Peter asked something that was unintelligible, and Wilton responded, "Alexander..."

"...Gerry Barr...CompuSys?" Peter asked.

"Harvard," Wilton said, then appeared to correct himself. "No...Dartmouth...after college."

Randall listened, transfixed. The car had become a time machine, transporting him by the sound of Peter's voice. Wilton was telling Peter about Alexander Smith, the Dartmouth alumnus.

There were muffled sounds, then the tape clicked and fell silent. He pressed the fast forward button, but the rest of the tape was blank.

He wanted to hear more. He wanted to hear Peter's strong, confident voice. He wanted Peter to tell him what to do.

And then, as clearly as if the words had been on the tape, he heard Peter say, "Ask the next question."

He took a deep breath. All right, ask the next question.

What does re-op have to do with all this?

Re-op is the part of Cosmos that Krypto connects to.

Who knew about re-op?

Gerald Barr, the one who wrote the code for it. And James Wilton.

Ask the next question.

Barr said he was the only one who knew about re-op. So how did Wilton find out about it?

Someone else must have told him.

Ask the next question.

357

Who could have told him? No one else was around when Barr wrote...

He hit the rewind button on the tape player.

"...might...alk to... Smith," he heard Wilton say.

He rewound the tape again.

"You might...talk to...andy Smith."

Now he was certain. Wilton had said, "You might want to talk to Sandy Smith."

The turnoff for Route 1 appeared. In an instant, Randall made up his mind. He bore to the right, a route that would take him over the Golden Gate Bridge, in the direction of San Rafael and the home of Alexander Smith.

The TrafficMaster 1000 was a programmable traffic light manufactured by National Traffic Systems. The heart of the unit was a small, dedicated microprocessor capable of operating the unit's lights individually or in concert, in a wide variety of flash patterns, timings, and illumination levels.

There were two ways to program the TM-1000. One involved the use of a custom keypad connected to an input jack in the base of the unit. That meant traveling to the site of each individual traffic light, a time-consuming task.

The alternate method of programming the unit—and the reason it had been chosen by the California highway department for installation throughout the city of San Francisco—was its remote access feature. While earlier programmable traffic lights required special lines to control them remotely, the TM-1000 used ordinary telephone lines, each of which communicated with the central computer at the San Francisco office of the highway department. The computer polled each traffic light regularly to determine its status. Any problem occurring between polling times—say, a mechanical failure or programming conflict—caused the affected light to send an error message to the computer. Often, the problem could be corrected from the main office.

San Francisco was the perfect test-bed for the TM-1000. In the aftermath of the 1989 earthquake, several of the city's major arteries had been shut down, and rebuilding them had become a tangle of regulation and dwindling resources. Traffic had become a nightmare. The entire city could be sent into gridlock by a single mishap—an accident at a crucial off-ramp, or someone deciding to jump off a bridge at rush hour.

The TM-1000 promised to alleviate those problems. From the control center, traffic technicians could oversee the operation of the lights in the entire city. The system's software used principles of statistical analysis, flow patterns, and chaos theory to coordinate the activity at the city's lights, lengthening the stop at some, shortening others, turning other lights off completely, like a conductor orchestrating a complex musical composition. The software was more effective than any human could ever be at resolving problems, and the technicians had taken to relying on it even for ordinary, daily maintenance of the system. While the technicians had been fully trained to run the system manually, they rarely had to do so. As a result, most of them had forgotten all but the most basic commands.

Irene Watson sipped her coffee, watching the display flicker over a map of San Francisco as the system polled the lights. It was mid-afternoon, and all was well.

She picked up the day's paper and scanned it. As she did, she failed to notice a string of commands appear across the bottom of the screen. The commands had not been entered by anyone at the highway department, nor had the computer originated them.

Watson glanced up at the screen. Every light in the city of San Francisco had turned red.

She put her coffee down. "Hey..."

She waited a moment for the system to notice the problem and correct itself. It did not.

Watson thought quickly. If she were to put the system back into manual command mode, she would have to reset all the lights herself. Fortunately, there was a command to restore the lights to their default configuration.

She pressed a button marked "Manual."

The system did not respond.

She pressed the button again. "Come on, damn it."

Still no response. Her supervisor, a middle-aged man named Reynolds, approached. "What's going on?"

She waved at the screen. "The system put all the lights on red, and I can't get it into manual mode."

Reynolds pushed her aside and entered a series of commands. The system refused to acknowledge them. "Damn."

He sat down and tried again. Still nothing. "We're going to have to reboot," he said, and hit the Reset button on the computer.

The screen went blank, the computer beeped and began to run through its startup routine. When it came back up, they would have to work through the lights manually, resetting each one to its default settings. The process could take hours.

Randall glanced nervously at the light at the intersection of Route 1 and the Golden Gate Parkway. It had been red for over a minute. Horns began to blare, as if those at the front of the line could do anything about it. Randall looked into his rear-view mirror.

In the line behind him, several cars back, was a white van. The passenger door to the van opened, and a tall, blonde man in a dark jacket emerged. He jogged between the cars, headed for the front of the line, his right hand in his jacket pocket as if trying to keep something heavy from bouncing out.

Randall studied the face. It was the man from Peter's apartment who had called himself Agent Rose.

He looked up at the light. It was still red. None of the cars going the opposite way were moving either—the lights were red in both directions. Something was wrong with the lights.

There was only one car ahead of him, a beat-up Chevy Malibu in the right-hand lane. If not for the Chevy, he could turn right, giving him a straight shot to the bridge with no traffic lights to slow him down.

He pressed the horn and gestured to the driver of the Chevy to move ahead. The man glanced into his mirror and gave Randall the finger.

Randall looked back. Rose was approaching at a rapid clip. He looked to the right. There was a narrow space between the Chevy and a telephone pole on the sidewalk. He needed to enlarge that space.

He put the car into reverse and backed up several feet, colliding with the bumper of the car behind him. The driver beeped angrily as Randall put the car into drive and floored it, ramming the rear of the Chevy and shoving it several feet into the intersection. He turned sharply and gunned the car over the curb, onto the sidewalk, and back down onto the road on the other side of the intersection.

Glancing into the rearview mirror, he saw the driver of the Chevy shouting hysterically in his direction. Rose was running back to the van.

39

Randall headed to San Rafael, driving as quickly as he could without drawing attention to himself. If he was stopped now, it was all over.

At the pillared entrance to 14 Del Monica Drive, he pressed the button below the nameplate.

"May I help you?" came the programmed recording.

"I want to talk to you, Smith," Randall said fiercely. "Now."

"I'm afraid Dr. Smith is not available," the voice said.

"Then he'd damn well better get available, fast."

There was no response.

"Open the gate, you son of a bitch!"

The gate did not move.

Randall contemplated his next move for about three seconds. Shifting into reverse, he backed up twenty feet, threw the car into gear, and pressed the accelerator to the floor.

The car met the wrought-iron gates with a bone-jarring crash, but achieved the desired effect. The gates parted, swinging helplessly open, banging back against the sides of the car as he drove through.

The car stalled just inside the gate, its front end crumpled. He restarted the car, but it stalled again. On the third try, he got no more than a dull click from the starter.

He jumped from the car and jogged up the driveway in

the direction of the house.

It had begun as a joke. He had posted the message—with its talk of the light dawning and the culmination of the ages—as a parody of the pathetic, self-aggrandizing prophecies that always seemed to accompany the birth of a new religion. The only difficult part about the prank had been creating an online identity that could not be traced. He had done that merely to add an air of authenticity to the posting.

To his amazement, he had received dozens of replies to the message. The senders begged him to reveal the secrets of the universe, calm their existential anxieties, save their marriages. He had responded in kind, maintaining the farce as a kind of online tableau: he was merely the principal actor in an ongoing, cooperative theater piece.

Gradually, a realization had dawned on him: to the others, this was not a game. They actually believed that he was who he said he was. So he had decided to humor them. Who was he to disabuse them of their fantasies? If they needed a Father, he would be their Father.

At first, he had allowed himself the luxury of making pronouncements willy-nilly, simply for the pleasure of seeing their effect. When Pizza World refused to deliver a large double-cheese pizza to Del Monica Drive, he instructed his followers not to patronize Pizza World restaurants for a month. The result was a dip in the chain's national sales figures—a minor dip, to be sure, but a very real one nevertheless. He had realized then the power that was his to command. He had, at first, felt a responsibility to exercise that power for the good of mankind.

But his first attempts at effecting meaningful change had been disappointing. He did not have enough followers, and they were poorly organized. If he were to accomplish anything substantive, he would need a structure, a set of goals, and a marketing plan. So he set about to study the world's great religious and political movements, and to construct his own movement, a movement for the 21st century and beyond.

Thus, the Family was born.

The plan had succeeded beyond his wildest expectations. New members were being added at a phenomenal rate. The influence of the organization grew daily. And over time, the realization dawned upon him that even he had not truly understood the importance of what he was doing. He was not merely pretending to be the Messiah.

He was the Messiah.

There had been opposition, of course, as there had been to all great leaders. One couldn't expect to bring the kingdom to earth without meeting resistance. He had been forced to deal with such opposition severely. The cause was too important for any individual or group to stand in its way.

For the most part, those who opposed the Family had been easy to check. History and technology were on his side. With the tools available to him, hunting them down was almost too easy, like hunting rabbits with laser-guided missiles. He had actually welcomed the adversaries who eluded him for a time. They made the hunt more interesting. Rarely had an adversary actually challenged him in any real way.

But now, for the first time, a foe had fought back. For the first time, the prey had come to him. This made the hunt all the more interesting.

Randall approached the front door and raised his fist to pound on it. This time, he would not ring the bell.

The door opened before he had a chance to strike it.

He stepped into the entryway and the door closed

silently behind him. Classical music drifted down from the ceiling, and in the darkness of the corners, where the walls met the ceiling, he made out video cameras, panning the entryway like birds of prey seeking game.

Now, in the darkness, he realized what he had not before. This was the entryway to the Family, the one users saw every time they entered the Family's home.

Then came the voice.

"Welcome."

The voice was deep, bass-laden, like the sound of thunder rolling across the hills. It did not sound human.

Randall looked up, trying to identify the source of the voice, reorienting himself to the house—the doors on either side of him, the wide stairway leading to a second floor, the hallway leading to the rest of the house. "Where are you, Smith?"

In response, every door in the house seemed to open, slowly and in unison, as if the house were a huge, gilled creature opening its vents to take in a breath. Then they closed, with a bang like a lightning strike, rattling the floorboards and shaking the chandelier overhead. The room turned pitch black, and the music stopped.

"Level one," the voice said.

Randall reached for the wall behind him, trying to get his bearings in the dark. "What the hell is going on?"

There was a pause, as if the voice was thinking. "Have you never played an adventure game, Mr. McLagan? This is a puzzle, and you must solve it."

"No thanks. I'm not in the mood for any more games."

"Oh, but you must. You have come so far. You cannot quit now."

Randall groped along the wall behind him till he bumped into a piece of furniture. He reached down. It was a table with a smooth, polished top. His hands came upon a thin cord and followed it to a telephone.

It took him a moment to recall the layout of the numbers on the typical pad. He picked up the handset and dialed 911.

The phone rang twice and was answered. "A nice attempt," the voice said over the line. "However, I don't think I'll allow you to call any friends, Mr. McLagan. This is a two-player game."

Randall slammed the phone down and continued creeping along the circumference of the entryway. He came to the study, but the door was locked.

"Would you like a clue, Mr. McLagan?"

"Go to hell, Smith."

"Very well, then. You are on your own."

He found the stairway, and cautiously made his way up. At the top of the stairs, dim lights along the floorboards indicated a hallway that led to a number of doors, like emergency lighting strips on an airplane.

He moved quickly down the hallway, trying the doors, and came to one that was unlocked.

It was a bathroom. As he opened the door, a door on the other side of the room closed.

He raced across the tile floor and tried the door. It was locked. He turned, and the door he'd entered through slammed shut.

"Level two," the voice said.

In a blinding flash, every light in the room came on: the makeup lights around the mirror, the overhead lights, lights in the shower, and a series of high-intensity heat lamps overhead. The glare blinded him, and he closed his eyes tightly. The temperature in the room rose, and sweat began to pour off of him.

As his eyes adjusted to the brightness, he found the control panel for the lights. None of the buttons or dials worked.

"Too obvious," the voice said. "One must use one's

imagination in these games."

The temperature continued to rise. In a short time, he was going to be baked to death.

He looked up. Thick, protective covers shielded the heat lights. There was no way he could break them.

He scanned the room. A series of drawers lined the cabinets below the countertop. He rifled through the drawers and a glint flashed off a small round hand mirror. With the mirror in hand, he climbed onto the countertop. He held the mirror up against one of the lamps, reflecting its rays back upon itself. The mirror grew hot, and he wasn't sure he could hold it there for long.

With a pop, the lamp exploded. He switched hands and held the mirror to the next lamp. In short order, he had burned them all out.

"Very good, Mr. McLagan. You may move on."

With a clunk, the door unlocked and swung open.

He stepped quickly back into the hallway. The voice came instantly, from somewhere above him.

"After that effort, you will undoubtedly want to cool off."

The fire sprinkler over his head burst on. As he ran down the hallway, each successive sprinkler was activated, drenching him. Somehow, Smith knew every footstep he was taking.

He tried every door in the hallway. They were all locked. At the end of the hall, he came to another set of stairs, heading down. He went down one flight to a landing with a locked door. Another level down and the stairs ended at a metal door. This one was unlocked.

The door opened into a basement maintenance room. He looked around for something to hold the door open—he didn't want to get locked in again. Beside the door was a shelf full of paint and repair supplies. Keeping his hand on the door, he grabbed a tube of silicone caulk and wedged the door open.

Dim light filtered in through basement windows as he crossed the concrete floor. From somewhere above him came the sound of movement. He came to a door on the other side of the room and tried the knob. It was locked.

There was a click behind him. He turned in to see the door he had entered through swing open wide, dislodging the tube of caulk. Before he could race back, the door slammed shut.

40

As Randall pressed against the door the voice said, "Level three. Out of the frying pan, into the freezer."

A low rumble vibrated across the floor, like the sound of a large engine starting.

"The temperature in every room of the house is separately controlled," the voice said. "It may be lowered to as much as ten degrees below zero for extended periods of time."

Randall nodded to his invisible host. "I bet that's a big plus when it comes to resale."

The response was a rush of cold air, like an arctic wind. Still soaking wet, the blast cut through him like a knife. He would not be able to stand this for long. Within minutes, he would freeze to death.

He scanned the room, taking inventory. Along one side were workbenches and storage shelves. In the middle of the room was the heating and cooling unit. Frigid air blew out of the side vents, while the large ducts leading from the top were barely cool to the touch. Those must be the ducts leading to the other rooms of the house. He shook the ductwork, testing its strength. The ducts were riveted firmly at the seams.

On the tool rack, he found a hand ax, the kind used for making kindling. With short, swift strokes, he hacked at the largest duct, slicing it open in a jagged line as if he were using an old-fashioned can opener. Soon the duct hung gaping open like a mechanical maw. He looked around for something to stand on so he could climb into the vent.

The cooling unit stopped.

"Not an elegant solution," the voice said. "But effective nevertheless. I won't make you actually climb through the duct. That would merely prolong the game."

The door on the far side of the room swung open.

He threw down the ax and passed through the door. There was a stairwell, with a door opposite and stairs that led up. He tried the door, not particularly wanting to go back up into the house. The door was locked, but a small window above the knob revealed that it opened into a garage.

He took the stairs slowly, up one level, through a door and into the kitchen. The kitchen was empty, the lights out. From a hallway on the other side of the kitchen came the sound of footsteps.

Chasing the sound, he came back to the entryway. As he did, the door to Smith's study on the other side of the foyer closed.

He ran to the door and pulled it open. It was empty.

"Smith, you bastard. Where are you?"

With a force he could not resist, the door slammed shut, pushing him into the room. He fell to the floor as the monitor on the desk flickered on. The screen coalesced into the image of Jonathan Smith, sitting in his wheelchair.

Randall stood and moved toward the screen. A camera atop the monitor whirred quietly, tracking his movements. "Jonathan, where's your father?"

A twisted grin distorted the face on the screen. "I'm afraid...he is out," the boy said in his painful slur. "But...no matter...he is not...a fan of games."

The realization came to Randall in an instant, and he felt foolish, idiotic that he hadn't seen it before. The voice of Jonathan Smith was the same voice that had taunted him throughout the house, without pre-programmed phrases and ominous overtones. It was not the elder Smith that he'd been fighting. It was Jonathan. He was the Father.

"You have...done well," the boy said in his broken, staccato manner. "You have reached...the final level..." He made a noise like a quiet hiccup. "However...I'm afraid...this is where...the game ends."

Randall turned, surveying the room. There were two large windows, but the only door was the one he'd come through.

"Do not...bother...there is no way out...of the room."

Randall knew he needed time. "Jonathan, does your father know about all this?"

"My father is...unable to appreciate...the significance of...my work. His own work...keeps him busy."

"Where is your father?"

Something like a smile appeared on Jonathan's face. "My father...will be of...no assistance...to you...By a...convenient coincidence...he is away...from the house...just now...thanks to...a friend of yours."

The screen flickered and the image of Jonathan was replaced by that of the driveway in front of the house. Jagged lines raced across the screen, as if a videotape were being rewound. The image cleared, and Randall saw a car parked outside the door, one that hadn't been there when he arrived—a bright red Nissan Sentra. Erica's car.

Randall fought to keep the fury out of his voice. "Where is she?"

Jonathan's image returned to the screen. "Your troublesome friend...arrived about...an hour ago...a short time later...she left...with my father...Apparently, they...found it necessary...to conduct their discussion...away from...my presence...One can...only imagine...the reason why."

Randall knew. Erica had figured it out. Somehow, she had put the pieces together, and taken it upon herself to talk to the senior Smith.

"She is...an intelligent woman..." Jonathan said. His tone darkened. "I will have...to deal with...her later."

"What's that supposed to mean?"

"People are expendable...Mr. McLagan...just as in...programming...the code is...more important than...any individual module...you should have...learned that from...your visit...with Gerald Barr."

At least he was still talking. If Randall could keep him talking, there was a chance Erica and Sandy Smith would return. "What's Barr got to do with this?"

A look came over Jonathan's face that, despite its contortions, could be mistaken for nothing other than pure, unadulterated hatred. "Gerald Barr...killed my mother...he stole...my father's company...he...consigned me...to life...in a wheelchair."

Randall considered arguing that his father's temper and bad driving had more to do with those events than anything Gerald Barr had done, but he decided against it. "Is that what this is all about? Getting back at Barr?"

Jonathan's head whipped from side to side spasmodically. "No...Gerald Barr...does not matter...any more...This is...more important than...Gerald Barr...He merely holds...the key to the puzzle...a key...that will shortly...become mine..."

"CompuSys," Randall said blankly.

Something that passed for a nod whipped Jonathan's head up and then down. "When I am...in possession...of my...rightful inheritance...Gerald Barr...will be...swept aside...as a minor...footnote...to the story...of the Family."

"Just like Peter Jacobson," Randall said, his jaw tightening.

"Your friend was...a worthy opponent...It was a shame...to have to...delete him...But he...got too close...and may have...disrupted...my plans...I could not...allow that...to happen."

Randall looked away, fighting to hold back his anger. If he was going to reason with Jonathan, he would have to stay calm.

"Your friend... made a... fatal mistake. One must always... be careful of... the people... with whom... one... makes alliances..."

Randall knew he was talking about Allison. He wanted to put his fist through the monitor.

The mechanical arms on Jonathan's wheelchair unfolded and began making adjustments outside the view of the camera.

"It is time...for the...final level," Jonathan said. "Armageddon...the day of wrath."

Randall said nothing.

"A fire...is about to...break out...in the kitchen," Jonathan said. "Ironically...a computer error...will cause...the automatic sprinkler system...to malfunction...The police...will find that...the fire...was begun...by an intruder...who had hoped...to take advantage...of a poor cripple...while his father...was away...but was...accidentally killed...in the blaze."

Randall moved close to the screen. "Jonathan, you don't want to do this. You don't want to die."

Jonathan's head rocked backward, his mouth open, as if he'd been on a bucking horse. It took Randall a moment to realize he was laughing.

"Don't worry...about me...I will not...be here...during the conflagration...although the world...will not...know that...My disappearance...will be the...prologue to...the next step...in the evolution of...the Family..."

As he spoke, the mechanical arms began to lift his lifeless limbs. "Every...religious movement...needs a martyr..." His arms were held out now, in a mechanically-assisted gesture of sanctification. "In lieu of an...actual resurrection...an electronic one...will have to do...I am certain...my followers...will be sufficiently...impressed."

Randall's mind raced, searching for ways to stall him. "What about your equipment? You don't want to destroy all that."

"The equipment...while useful...is outmoded...And this location...is no longer...sufficient...for my...needs...The plans have...already been drawn...for modifications...to the CompuSys headquarters...which will make it...the center of operations...for the...worldwide ministry...of the Family."

Randall glanced at his watch, wondering how long Erica and Sandy Smith had been away. "What about your father? What will he think?"

"My father's...opinions...are no longer...of any...consequence...I have...progressed...beyond his level...My mission...is more important...than any...personal connections."

"Your mission?"

"Yes...the reason...I was sent...the reason...I arrived at...this particular...time in history..."

"I don't get it," Randall said.

A frown wrinkled Jonathan's twitching brow. "Do you...really...not know? Are you so...dull...that you...cannot recognize...your lord and master?"

Randall stared at him, finally understanding. This was not merely about revenge, about retaliation for the imagined wrongs Gerald Barr had committed against the Smith family. It had gone beyond than that. The years of isolation, cut off from normal social interaction, the intense concentration on computers and electronics, combined with his anger and physical challenges, had all taken their toll.

Jonathan Smith was insane.

"Final round," he said, and the monitor went dark.

The room lights dimmed. A dark cloud passed over the house, obscuring the sunlight that had shone in through the windows.

Randall tried the windows and found them, as he expected, locked. He pressed against them, testing their strength, wondering whether he could break them.

An acrid smell rose from floor vents along the walls. Smoke. The fire had begun.

He heard barking and looked out the windows. Three Dobermans stood below them, growling ferociously up at him.

So much for the windows. He didn't remember seeing dogs before, but it was clear they would tear him to pieces if he tried to get out the windows.

The smoke grew thicker, the temperature in the room rising. He considered breaking a window to get some fresh air, but remembered that would probably just cause a draft and draw the fire into the study even faster.

He stared at the windows and a glint of light flashed across them, like a television screen flickering. He blinked—the dogs still barked.

To one side was a fireplace with a set of brass tools. He picked up the heaviest one—a poker with a pointed head—and swung it at the window with all his might.

The impact rattled his arms and cracked the window in a lacy pattern. The light outside brightened instantly, and the barking stopped.

He looked out. It was the same sunny day it had been when he arrived, and the dogs were gone. His hunch had been right. There had never been any dogs, merely a projected image on giant LCD screens built into the windows.

He attacked the windows again, but the reinforced glass refused to budge even as it crackled under the blows. What good was it to get rid of the dogs if he couldn't get out?

The walls of the study were warm to the touch. The fire was spreading and he had no idea what to do.

Ask the next question.

He tried to calm himself. All right. What are the options? Doors, windows, and vents.

The vents are too small. The doors and windows are locked.

Ask the next question.

How are the doors locked?

Not mechanically. No one touched them when they were locked.

Ask the next question.

Then how are they locked?

The answer seemed obvious. By computer.

A power strip sat next to the computer on Sandy Smith's desk. He flipped it on and the system booted. Scanning the icons, he found one labeled "HOME" and clicked it.

A diagram of the house appeared, with glowing lights above each of the entryways. The lights were all red, except for one. A single green light shone on a small square with the label ELEV on it.

An elevator. That was how Jonathan planned to escape.

The smoke grew thicker, etching his throat with each breath. He wouldn't have much time.

He searched until he found the program's section on unlocking doors.

To unlock a door or window, click on that object. If this

action is in conflict with previously programmed actions, the door or window will revert to the previous setting in three seconds.

A long section followed on changing the programming. He didn't have time for that. He would have to open the study door and get out in the three seconds before it locked again. But how?

Ask the next question.

He tried to think slowly, logically.

How do the door and windows operate?

They're electronic.

What do electronics require?

Electricity.

He looked around the desk. The power strip ran down to a socket on the wall behind the desk. He opened the desk drawer and pawed through its contents— elastic bands, erasers, a letter opener.

And a pen.

An ordinary, inexpensive pen. Not a mouse, or a keyboard, or even a pen-input device. A good old-fashioned pen.

He unscrewed the pen and pulled the spring from the barrel. Using the letter opener, he straightened the wire and stuck one end into the outlet. The other end went into the other side of the outlet, just enough to hold it there.

The smoke was thick now, barely breathable. Grabbing the mouse, he clicked on the screen image of the study door. The light above the door turned green, and a soft clunk came from the actual door.

With a swift movement of his foot, he pressed the wire fully into the socket. There was a spark, and the computer died.

As he ran for the door, he passed the fireplace and grabbed the fire iron—with the computer down, he might need it to open another door or window.

He stepped into the entryway, where a blast of intense heat struck him. Smoke filled the room, lit by the flames that consumed the rooms beyond it.

He tried the front door, expecting it to be locked. The lock turned easily. But he hadn't unlocked that door from the computer—a safely mechanism must have unlocked all the doors when the power failed.

He hesitated before the door, his eyes stinging. Once he opened it, a powerful draft would suck the fire into the entryway and through the rest of the house. Anyone stuck inside would be fried to a crisp.

He made the decision quickly, before he had time to change his mind. Running to the end of the hall, he pulled on the door to Jonathan's room. It opened easily.

The room was hot and smoky, but the fire hadn't spread to it yet. Jonathan was nowhere to be seen.

Randall crossed the room, trying to remember the diagram on the computer and the location of the elevator. He opened what appeared to be a closet next to the workstation. Behind it was an elevator door with a small glass panel. Through it, he could see the car stuck, several feet below the level of the floor. A sound came from within the car, like the moan of a wounded animal.

"Hang on," Randall yelled. "I'm going to get you out."

He searched for a safety switch, a crank, anything to move the car without power, but there was nothing.

A voice asked why he was doing this. The bastard killed your best friend. He killed James Wilton. And he just tried to kill you.

But he was a human being. He was not in his right mind. And he was trapped.

Using the fire iron, Randall tried to pry the door open. It wouldn't budge. Another safety precaution, he presumed, designed to prevent people from falling into the shaft when the car wasn't there.

He beat at the glass with the fire iron. It cracked, then shattered. Clearing the pieces away with the iron, he reached in.

On the right, his hand found a small box with a contact switch facing the shaft. It was a magnetic switch. When the car arrived at a floor, a magnet mounted on the car touched the switch and opened the elevator door.

He needed a magnet.

He thought for a moment and remembered Peter's key case. His hand dove into his pocket. The case was still there.

Thrusting his arm through the window again, he held the back of the case to the switch. It grabbed on, and he heard a click.

The door opened easily.

He jumped down the few feet to the car and opened the safety hatch.

Jonathan Smith looked up at him through thick glasses. There was fury in his eyes. "Ah...wiw...kiw...you..." he said, his speech garbled now.

"Not too likely, you little bastard." He held out a hand. "Give me your hand."

The wheelchair backed into the corner, its battery power unaffected by the outage. "Ah...dohn need...yaw...hep."

"You're going to burn up in here if you don't get out," Randall shouted. "Now give me your hand."

Jonathan eyed him. Slowly, the wheelchair's left appendage picked up Jonathan's arm and lifted it toward Randall. Randall gripped Jonathan's hand, and the mechanical arm released.

He began to pull Jonathan up. As he did, mechanical arm swung up, grabbed him, and began pulling him down into the car.

"Let go, damn you!"

He grabbed the mechanical arm with his free hand and shook. But the arm was stronger than he, and he felt himself being pulled into the car. He shook harder, rocking the wheelchair from side to side. Then, with one violent shake, the wheelchair tipped, and Jonathan's glasses flew off. Without them, Jonathan had no control. The mechanical arm stopped dead.

Randall shook the mechanical arm off like a dried branch and lifted Jonathan out of the cab. Without his wheelchair and his workstation, he was helpless, like a puppet whose strings led nowhere.

He shook his head violently. "Ah...nnn-need...mah...chay-ah..." he bawled.

"You're lucky you've still got your ass. We're getting out of here."

He carried the twisted body to the far end of the room, beyond the swimming pool. Setting Jonathan down, he picked up a chair and tossed it through the plate glass window. The window shattered, and he kicked the shards out of the way.

Hoisting Jonathan over his shoulder, he ran into the side garden and away from the house. He set Jonathan down and looked back. By now, the flames had engulfed the front of the house and reached the roof. The cedar shingles went up like a torch. In a minute, the entire house was in flames.

Tires squealed up the driveway. Randall looked over a low hedge that bordered the garden. The white van that had been chasing him roared up to the front of the house.

Jonathan leered up at him. "Mah...rahd...hah...arrahved."

"Great," Randall said, ducking below the hedge and hoping they hadn't seen him. The doors to the van opened and he heard footsteps jump out.

Jonathan taunted him. "Introodah...shawt bah... securtie...gahds... whahl... runnin' from... burnin'...home."

"Shut up," Randall hissed.

A series of loud pops came from the direction of the van. Jonathan jerked, and a grunt escaped his twisted lips. "Unh..."

Randall looked down. A red stain appeared on Jonathan's chest. The men in the van had fired in his direction, not knowing Jonathan was there as well.

They fired again. It was time to leave. Jonathan's own people would have to take care of him now.

He bolted toward the back of the house. With luck, Jonathan's wounds would slow them down. If he could make it around the house, maybe he could get down the driveway without them seeing him.

The house was a fireball now, throwing burning embers into the air, searing the side of his face as he raced around it. He emerged on the other side of the house and stopped. The van was there, the occupants gone.

He took a deep breath and made a run for the driveway. Out of the corner of his eye he saw someone standing behind the hedge where he'd been moments earlier.

He heard a yell, then the familiar popping sound. Chips of bark flew from a tree as he passed it. He rounded the first bend in the drive and felt a searing pain in his right shoulder. He staggered, but kept running.

As he turned the next corner, a police car was headed right at him.

He dove to the side of the road. The car passed him without stopping. It was followed by two more cars carrying police. Then came a bright red Nissan Sentra with two people in it. The car pulled up next to him, and Erica Steiner jumped out.

He fell to his knees as she ran to him. "Are you all

right?" she asked, kneeling beside him.

Randall nodded numbly, and lost consciousness.

Epilogue

Erica Steiner's kitchen window looked out on a tiny garden bordered by a graying wooden fence. Randall sat at the kitchen table, staring out the window, then went back to pushing a pen across the surface of a spiral-bound notebook. Next to the notebook was an open Bible.

Erica walked into the kitchen and glanced at the books. "You turning into a Bible student?"

"Not quite. It's Peter's. I finally figured out who Matt is—the one in his notes." He pointed to the open page. "The gospel of Matthew, chapter twenty-seven, the twenty-eighth verse."

She read, "For as the lightning cometh out of the east, and shineth even unto the west, so shall also the coming of the Son of man be." She looked bemused. "What's that's about?"

"The second coming," Randall said. "Now read the next verse."

"Wherever there is a carcass, there the vultures will gather." Her brow wrinkled. "OK, now I'm really lost. What's that supposed to mean?"

He shrugged, an action that sent a twinge of pain

through his shoulder. "I don't know, but I'm pretty sure it means Jonathan wasn't the messiah."

"Shoulder still bothering you?"

"It's OK." He held up the pen with his good arm. "Amazing what you can do with one hand."

"Yeah. Makes you grateful for analog input devices."

She handed him several pages still warm from the laser printer. "Let me know what you think of this when you have a chance."

Below her name and the word count was the title:

TrendWatch: The Real Reason Cosmos is Delayed

He scanned it quickly. "Sounds like a great first column."

She shrugged, deflecting the praise. "Your friend Landulfson gave me some good background on the stock angle. It seems Western Pacific bowed out of the CompuSys deal as soon as it found out the SEC was stepping in. I bet some heads will roll there."

Randall flipped to the last page of the column. "And Barr gets to keep control of CompuSys."

"Right. The rich get rich..."

"And the poor write books," he said.

"Your time will come. Needless to say, the Family isn't going away."

A beeping sound came from the study.

"Mail call," she said, and returned a moment later with a printed e-mail message. "It's from Harry."

Randall,

Here's something for the epilogue to your book. The Family is playing Jonathan's death as martyrdom, and the guys who killed him as infiltrators out to destroy the movement. They're telling insiders that the Father has ascended to the highest level of the Family. Kind of an electronic nirvana, I guess.

Meanwhile, they're cranking up their web-based access. People won't need a sign-on disk, they'll download the installation software—complete with all the "special features," I guess.

And they're already coaching people about how to respond to your book. (Wonder how they found out about it?) According to them, the Family is an innocent organization that only wants to help people and you're a self-serving journalist printing vicious lies about them just to advance your own career. Pretty typical.

I'll keep you posted. As always, YDGTFM.

Harry

Erica pointed to the string of letters at the end. "What's that?"

Randall smiled faintly. "You didn't get this from me."

"Ah. You worried about what they'll do?"

"Not really. The Family will have to be pretty careful about anything they do to me now. Besides, they may be entering a different stage. Ed Truman calls it the post-prophet stage. At this point, they're poised to become a billion-dollar empire. They'll be careful about doing anything that might jeopardize that. He says they're more likely to use subtle pressure—squelching the book by taking over any publisher that agrees to print it. That kind of thing."

"You think the members actually buy this stuff about

the Father ascending to another level?" she asked.

"Who knows? People will believe anything if you put the right pressure on them."

She grabbed a jacket from one of the chairs and picked up her briefcase. "I've got to go hand in the column. I'll be back around supper time." She hesitated briefly. "Will you be here?"

He sensed there was more to the question than whether she should thaw out one or two pork chops for dinner. After his brief stay in the hospital, she had offered to let him stay at her apartment as long as he needed to. Now, on a Monday morning, he was well enough to be off, if he wanted. But he had no plans, other than writing the book and—with help from Harry and Ferret—putting his financial life back together. There was no particular reason to return to the East Coast, and Erica assured him there were plenty of newspapers and magazines in the area that could use a good reporter.

And there was Erica. Now, with the dazzling glare of Allison dimmed by the cold light of truth, he had come to see Erica more clearly. And he liked what he saw.

"Yes," he said, with a smile that answered more than one question. "I'll be here."

Cindy Conners stood at the center of the San Francisco State campus, where the major routes to classes, dorms, and study halls intersected. It was only ten o'clock in the morning, but she was bone-tired. The all-night on-line sessions were exhausting, though she knew they were necessary. At least she was no longer hungry. The special diet her Shepherd had put her on was hard at first, but now, after following it for three weeks, she didn't feel as if she needed much food any more.

In spite of her fatigue, Cindy Conners was happy. For the first time in her life, she had a purpose. She was part of a movement, the most important movement in the history of the world. And she was doing her part to advance the cause.

Her parents didn't understand it, of course. They'd told her she was crazy to leave her job at the law office. But how important was being a secretary, compared to the task of spreading the word about the Family?

A young man in blue-jeans and a polo shirt headed past her. He glanced at Cindy, his eyes flickering over the short skirt and bra-less T-shirt. She'd been instructed to dress that way when recruiting on campus. She'd also been told to look for people who were alone, or seemed lonely. She held out a colorful pamphlet.

"Hi," she said brightly. "Would you like to try out a new on-line service? It's free."

The End

Acknowledgments

Tom Landulfson is a fictional character, though based on a real individual to whom I'm extremely grateful for sharing his knowledge of the stock market and the intricacies of corporate strategy. Thanks also the San Francisco police department for background on the investigative procedures surrounding homicide. The Gordon-Conwell Theological Seminary library provided many insights on the inner workings of religious cults. Finally, my thanks to the early readers who provided feedback and encouragement.

Cover design by David Nelson
dnelsondesign@gmail.com

The Family was previously published as *The Code*.

About the Author

Michael Manley is the pen name of journalist and author Ken Sheldon, former West Coast Bureau Chief for Byte Magazine, where he reported on the beginnings of the computer revolution.

Connect with Michael Manley online at

michaelmanleybooks.com

Facebook: www.facebook.com/michaelmanleybooks

Email: michaelmanleybooks@gmail.com

Continue reading for a preview of Michael Manley's

PROBABILITY OF DETECTION.

PROBABILITY OF DETECTION

Prologue

The missionary had been to the farm before, a cluster of decrepit buildings on the outskirts of the village, where an elderly man named Ishmael had recited his daily prayers, cared for his orphaned grandson and tended a few sheep. She had brought medicine, drunk tea, and purchased vegetables she did not need, simply to supplement the old man's meager income.

But all that was before the grandson had grown and gone off to join the militia, before the old man had passed away. After that, the farm had fallen into ruin, the surrounding fields overgrown with weeds, the barns and outbuildings leaning like old men themselves.

She had been brought back to the farm, she and the other four, bound and blindfolded. But even blindfolded, she had been there often enough to recognize the smells, the sounds of other farms in the distance. Then she recognized the grandson's voice. Later, she became sure it was him, despite the traditional keffiyeh covering his face, the gun belt, and the swagger.

Why had they been kidnapped? Probably because they were easy targets. These were not professional criminals, they were barely more than boys, who only a few years before had been chasing a soccer ball around a dirt playground. The fact that she and the others were missionaries was probably of no real importance to them, though the hard-core among them doubtless used that fact to justify the abduction.

She had lived in the valley long enough to feel certain the kidnappers did not intend to harm them. She and the others were merely pawns, chess pieces in the complex battleground that Lebanon had become. That did not guarantee they would come to no harm, of course. But if both sides were patient, if no one did anything foolish, she believed they would be OK.

She lay back on the cot, watching a sliver of moonlight that shone in through the single window, repeating the words of a Psalm that had been her theme ever since coming to the valley, words that had become her lifeline in the past weeks.

Blessed are those whose strength is in you,
   whose hearts are set on pilgrimage.
As they pass through the Valley of Baka,
   they make it a place of springs.

Early Aramaic versions of the scriptures translated the second line as "the valley of tears" or "weeping," a translation that made sense given the parallel image of springs. It also spoke to her own experience.

"Blessed are those whose strength is in you," she whispered. "Blessed are those whose strength is in you."

From beyond the outbuildings came gunshots, and then shouting. An explosion of gunfire followed, and more shouting. Doors slammed in the house, cries of pain and anger. In the midst of the chaos, she heard a sound that confused, then dismayed her. Some of the shouting was in English.

1

The conditions for finding a missing person were bad and getting worse. The day had dawned humid, the sun filtering through layers of mountain haze. The forecast called for temperatures in the 90s, unseasonably hot for spring in Vermont. The air was a sponge and thunderstorms were likely.

Darcy Cameron's hiking boot came down on a dew-soaked rock and slipped. The next moment, she was down, draped over a fallen tree, a broken branch sticking up like a dagger inches away. If she had fallen on it, the branch would have impaled her.

She picked herself up and whistled softly. Pepper, a four-year-old black Lab wearing an orange search vest, leaped a fallen tree and bounded to her side.

"I'm OK, girl," Darcy said. She squirted her water bottle into the dog's open mouth and took a drink herself. "OK, let's go."

The dog moved off, zigzagging through an area that looked like the aftermath of an apocalyptic battle. Recently logged, it was covered with gnarled trees, stubs and broken branches, the leftover rubble of the timber harvest. Last winter's ice storms had added to the devastation, bringing down countless branches and smaller trees. The forest floor was thick with wild blueberries, bittersweet and honeysuckle, pioneer species that always appeared after logging.

The ground began to slope uphill, and the tangle of wood became even denser, a larger-than-life game of pick-up-sticks. Several hundred feet further, they came to a level area and Pepper's behavior changed. She stopped and put her nose high into the air, her whole body tense. Ahead of her lay a massive pile of fallen trees and branches, thrown together by the elements. Roughly round and at least a hundred feet in diameter, it looked like a primeval fortress.

Pepper's behavior became more frantic now. She darted around the pile, looking for a way in. She spotted a narrow opening, climbed up, and crawled into the mass of debris, disappearing from sight.

Darcy headed for the spot where Pepper had entered the pile, hindered by the slash and branches. Before she got there, Pepper crawled out, leaped to the forest floor and ran to her, barking furiously. There was no mistaking this behavior. She had made a find.

"Show me, girl. Show me."

Pepper ran back to the pile and crawled in. Darcy grabbed her radio. "Base, this is Unit 14. I have K-9 alert and find behavior. Going is difficult. It'll take me a couple minutes to work to the site. Stand by."

She studied the massive heap before her. She would never be able to get into the tiny space through which Pepper had crawled. She circled the pile in search of another entry point, still struggling over the debris, till she found a space that looked big enough for a human to squeeze through.

A low rumbling in the distance had resolved into sharper booms and cracks. It was getting dark fast. The storm was close. She mumbled a short prayer that it wouldn't track directly over their location.

Working her way through the opening took several minutes. She wished she'd brought her leather gloves. Broken branches scratched her hands, and she didn't even want to think about what kind of wildlife might be lurking in the pile.

She inched forward carefully, not wanting to dislodge anything that might bring the whole structure down on her head. A moment later she emerged into an open space and saw that the pile was actually a huge donut-shaped structure, like an open-air theater. Inside was a large flat area, surprisingly clear of forest rubble. In the middle sat Pepper, her tail wagging wildly. She'd found what she was looking for.

Darcy stared, her breath coming back to her in harsh gulps, her heartbeat steadying. She'd seen suicides before, but this was bad. There was blood everywhere. The woman sat on a stump, slumped over against a branch. The gun was on the ground below her outstretched hand, blood dripping from her fingertips.

The only way to deal with a horrific situation like this was to follow procedures. Darcy analyzed the situation. The subject was obviously beyond help. She'd decided to kill herself, and she'd made a mess of it. Instead of a quick shot through the head, which seldom left much blood, the victim had aimed for her chest. And it had obviously taken more than one shot to finish the job.

Darcy reached for her radio and took several more deep breaths before pushing the transmit button.

"Base, this is Unit 14. I have a confirmed black tag."

Dan, their base operator, was cool and professional. "Message received, 14. Confirming your black tag at 1:27 PM. Secure the area."

Darcy shook her head wearily. Her blond hair, plastered to her head with sweat, felt like a damp helmet. She gazed at the limp body and sighed. "You know, you could have found a more convenient place to kill yourself."

The woman opened one eye. "Yes, but what fun would that have been?"

She sat up, wiping away a glob of stage blood that had dripped in her eye. "Besides, a real suicide isn't going to make it easy for you."

The "victim" was Ellen Westheimer, a member of the Vermont K-9 Search and Rescue team, and a master at hiding herself. The word was that if you could find Ellen, you could find anyone.

She looked at her watch. "Damn, forty-three minutes. You are hard core."

"High heels slowed me down," Darcy said. "I'll do better next time."

The first fat raindrops began to fall as Pepper circled Darcy, gazing expectantly at her. Darcy grabbed a tennis ball from her pack and threw it a few feet. To search dogs it was always a game, whether training or a real search, and the reward at the end was a chance to play with their favorite toys. Even dogs that specialized in cadaver work wanted their reward after a job well done. It was not unusual to see them cavorting playfully around human remains, completely indifferent to the horror nearby.

Darcy had joined the K-9 search and rescue team a year earlier, shortly after moving to Vermont. Before the move, she'd had a husband, a job at the same prestigious Boston law firm where her husband worked, and an equally prestigious mortgage in the suburbs. Three years into the marriage she discovered her husband's secretary was providing him with services that weren't exactly covered in the job description.

They were divorced a short time later, after which the atmosphere at Lessard, Sterling and Jacobs cooled glacially. She was passed over for promotion, while her ex was made a partner. The whispers among the senior partners—whispers that were not-so-subtly allowed to leak out to the staff—suggested that Darcy might want to consider what her next career move would be. She had beaten them to the punch, announcing that she was moving to Vermont to open a private practice.

"Vermont?" her colleagues had said. "What the hell is in Vermont?"

To begin with, she had told them, her father. Upon his retirement, he had moved to The Village, an exclusive retirement community in Eastham. Not long after moving in, he'd been diagnosed with Alzheimer's. Then came Darcy's divorce. All in all, it hadn't been a great year.

She had moved to Eastham because it was as good a place as any to escape to, and because she was damned if she was going to let her father slip into the twilight of dementia without getting to know him better.

But Eastham, Vermont was a world away from Boston and the adjustment hadn't been easy. The night life in town consisted of pool at the Rusty Gate Grill, the ladies' book group at the library, and the occasional concert at the church. The locals were friendly once you got to know them—it just took twenty years to know them.

Then, out for a run with Pepper one day, she'd met Janis Levine, who headed up the area's canine search and rescue team. Janis invited her and Pepper to join them for a training session.

It had been one of the most physically demanding days of Darcy's life, and she loved every minute of it. For eight hours, she and Pepper—who seemed born for search and rescue work—climbed hills, forded streams, and tramped through dense thickets of underbrush. She did not think about her father, her struggling law practice, or her ex-husband.

Within months, Darcy had become a full-fledged

member of the team, and search and rescue work became an antidote to her struggling law practice, which increasingly felt like an exercise in drudgery-filing papers, placating clients, and arguing with opposing lawyers about whose fence was over which line. Rescue work, on the other hand, was straightforward and elemental: Find a missing person before they died.

Ellen removed her stained shirt, stuffed it in a plastic bag and pulled a fresh one from her pack. "Nice day, huh?"

"Lovely," Darcy said, mopping the back of her neck.

"Make you wish you were back in that air-conditioned high-rise?"

"And miss all this? No way."

Ellen took a long tug from her water bottle. "How's Marshall?"

Darcy snickered. Not many people called her father by his first name—another thing she appreciated about the people on the search and rescue team. Unlike other folks in town, they didn't seem impressed that her father was famous, nor exhibit a morbid curiosity about his condition.

"The same. Sharp enough to come up with a lame excuse for blowing me off."

"Bingo?"

"Bridge. Which he doesn't even play." Although The Village offered a full schedule of social events and activities for residents, her father rarely took advantage of them except, she suspected, as a reason to avoid seeing her. "Sometimes I wonder why I even moved here."

Ellen gazed at her levelly. "You moved here to be close to him, even if he doesn't appreciate it."

"Thanks," Darcy said, forcing a smile.

The rain began to fall in earnest now. The women found waterproof ponchos and pulled them on. As they did, Darcy's radio crackled. "Unit 14, this is base. Return to base immediately."

She hit the call button. "It'll take us a while. The going's rough and we're about a quarter mile from the trail. We need to take a break first."

"Just return to base, Darcy."

Darcy glanced at Ellen. There was genuine tension in Dan's voice, and he'd used her name instead of her unit number—a breach of protocol that was unlike him. She pressed the transmit button again. "What's the story?"

"Darcy, this is not a drill. This is a code 2." Code 2 meant a real search.

"We're on our way."

By the time Darcy and Ellen returned to base—a clearing just off a dirt road at the foot of Mount Connell—they were soaked to the bone, but at least the rain had begun to let up. Most of the other team members had already arrived and were packing up, throwing equipment into vehicles, putting dogs in their Crates. There was no time for the usual banter that came after a successful training session.

Darcy called to Dan as she headed for her truck. "Where are we going?"

Dan acted as if he hadn't heard her, slamming the door of his ancient Subaru and tearing off down the road, spattering mud as he did.

She shook her head, wondering what that was about, and pulled down the truck's gate. "Pepper," she called. "Come on, girl."

Pepper hopped up into her mobile crate. Janis Levine trotted over as Darcy pulled off her backpack and tossed it into the truck. "Where's the search?" she asked. "Apparently Dan couldn't be bothered to tell me."

Janis put a hand on her shoulder. "Darcy."

Darcy turned to face her. Janis was normally all business on a search, the last person to waste time with small-talk.

"What?"

"We're going to The Village." Darcy's heart sank. "Oh, God."

Janis nodded. "It's your father."

Continue reading Probability of Detection at your local independent bookstore or ebook retailer.

Made in the USA
Lexington, KY
18 February 2015